STEALTH DRAGON SERVICES

Lucinda Hare

Book Four of the Dragonsdome Chronicles

lucinda@dragonsdome.co.uk
http://www.dragonsdome.co.uk/
http://thedragonwhispererdiaries.blogspot.co.uk/

Published by Thistleburr Publishing

Stealth Dragon Services
Thistleburr Publishing, ISBN: 978-0-9574718-1-8

Women in the Royal Air Force

In 1995 Joanna Mary Salter became Britain's first woman fast jet pilot, flying the Panavia Tornado ground attack aircraft with 617 Squadron.

Flt Lt Kirsty Moore became the first woman to join the RAF Red Arrows display team in 2009 as Red Three. Her arrival triggered more interest in the RAF by young women.

o-o-o-o

Book Five of The Dragonsdome Chronicles

Dark Dragon Dreams

Main Characters

Quenelda DeWinter: is growing from a girl into a young woman but her inner dragon whisperer is also emerging. How can she learn to control her unique magic without hurting those about her? Will she ever achieve her dream of becoming the first girl to be a Dragon Lord?

Root Oakley: is not only the first of his people to become an esquire, but has navigated an Imperial across the frozen Ice Isles The young gnome is struggling to find a way to protect Quenelda without breaking his people's tradition of never bearing arms. Using a mundane frying pan he single handedly captured the hobgoblin warlord Galtekerion.

Tangnost Bearhugger: has achieved the impossible! He has flown an injured battledragon, Quenelda, Root, Quester and an overweight fledgling dragon into the frozen wastes of the north and brought them all back alive along with the missing Earl. Tangnost is the anchor in all these young adventurers' lives. He has watched over Quenelda since the day of her birth and with her powers unfolding he has a lot of work ahead.

Drumondir: the BoneCaster of the Ice Bear Clan is a skilled teacher and healer who is tough enough to take the Earl's daughter's tuition in hand.

The Earl Rufus: crippled and blind, he initially refused to come home to become a burden to those who love him. But Quenelda and his battledragon Stormcracker have taught him how to see through his dragon's eyes so that he can still command a battlefield true to the soldier he is at heart. But has he returned in time to prevent the marriage of the treacherous Lord Protector to the Queen?

The Lord Protector, Hugo Mandrake: Handsome, darkly charming, the most gifted sorcerer of his generation has it all in the palm of his hand: his son, the Queen, the Guild and the Court, and yet he craves more. Seduced by the power of chaos, his ambition knows no bounds. His marriage to the Queen is only days away and then the Seven Kingdoms will be his to command.

The Earl Darcy: Finally Dragonsdome is his and the young Earl Darcy sheds no tears for his missing father; he has a beautiful wife and a fortune to spend. Darcy has no intention of joining the fight against the hobgoblins. He now commands the Queen's Household Cavalry. His true father Hugo Mandrake has promised him a kingdom.

The Countess Armelia DeWinter: sugar and spice and all things nice, Armelia is now married to Darcy and is the Queen's dearest friend and lady-in-waiting. She has achieved everything she dreamt of and more. And yet...and yet she has begun to admire Quenelda for following her dream.

Sir Gharad Mowbray: a renowned Dragon Lord, now Constable to the Queen and mentor to the Earl Rufus.

Jakart de Bessart: Arch BattleMage and Commander of the SDS following the disappearance of the Earl. **Guy DeBessart** is his only son who lost a hand because of Darcy's reckless behaviour.

Dragons

Stormcracker Thundercloud: the Earl's injured Imperial Black battledragon

Two Gulps Too Many: Quenelda's overweight juvenile sabretooth battledragon

Phoenix Firestorm: Guy DeBessart's Imperial. The name was chosen by *Phoenix Wilson* from Yorkshire aged 8 years.

In memory of Dumpling, a Romanian
street cat who shared my life for a year.
He crossed the rainbow bridge on 21ˢᵗ
December 2013.
He was one and a half years young.
He died of FIP.

He danced through the snow
and whispered up trees
as light as a feather
as swift as the breeze.
Through winter and spring
the summer and fall
he danced just the once
and then he was gone
taking my heart
and ending the song.

PROLOGUE

Exhausted, wounded, cradled in the arms of Tangnost Bearhugger on the back of an Imperial battledragon heading for the safety of Dragon Isle, Quenelda DeWinter was thinking of her recent adventures.

All her young life, Quenelda had wanted to fly Imperial Black stealth battledragons, the greatest dragons on the One Earth at the side of her father, the Earl Rufus, Commander of the Stealth Dragon Services, the SDS. But young ladies did not fly dragons. And young ladies did not study at the SDS Battle Academy either, that was strictly for young men, unless you were a dwarf. In fact girls generally had nothing to do with dragons whatsoever. Nor did they wear a scruffy jerkin, patched breeches and heavy buckled flying boots, crowned by a hairstyle which looked like she had fallen through a hedge backwards. Quenelda was also so hopeless at magic and courtly romance that one by one her tutors had all given up on her, save for the dwarf Drumondir, BoneCaster of the Ice Bear Clan. So when it came down to being an accomplished young lady, Quenelda failed on all counts. Which was rather embarrassing, given she was the daughter of the greatest Earl in the Seven Sea Kingdoms and now heir to Dragonsdome.

Perhaps it had something to do with the fact that Quenelda was no ordinary girl that kept getting her into trouble. Quenelda was a lone dragon whisperer in a world at war, a world where dragons have characters and voices of their own; and the Seven Kingdoms were threatened by the hobgoblins who had united under a single warlord – Galtekerion.

If that were not dangerous enough the SDS were betrayed by Sir Hugo Mandrake, then Grand Master of the Sorcerers Guild, and were annihilated by the hobgoblins at the battle of the Westering Isles. No one returned from that dreadful battle to betray the Lord Mandrake's treason or to reveal that he was a WarLock who commanded chaotic magic.

But that was when Quenelda's unique bond with dragons changed everything. Finding her father's injured and starving battledragon bound with baleful chains in a brimstone mine, she and Root had returned him to Dragon Isle. The only survivor, Stormcracker Thundercloud became a symbol of hope to the SDS that the defeated Dragon Lords would rise again. Learning from Storm that her father had survived the battle, Quenelda set out along with Tangnost Bearhugger, Root, Quester and Two Gulps Too Many to search for the missing SDS Commander and return him home. Only her father, the greatest soldier of his generation and the Queen's Champion, could unite the Seven Kingdoms in the face of the Lord Protector's growing power, and prevent him from raising the Maelstrom and unleashing chaos.

Against the odds this unlikely group had found her father, but were they in time to prevent the Lord Protector's marriage to the Queen? Only once they reached the sanctuary of Dragon Isle would they learn any answers.

CHAPTER ONE

New Dawn

The crowded flight hanger cavern of Dragon Isle was gradually clearing as the SDS Commander Jakart DeBessart and his escort finally landed, bearing the last of the badly injured and dying from the Smoking Fort. Imperials newly returned from the battle were swarming with scalesmiths, surgeons and roost hands. Those uninjured were back in their roosts being fed and cared for; others were being tended on the pads and armour pits for their injuries first. Wounded troopers and commandos were getting stretchered onto the huge porting stone directly to the hospital in the Academy far above. Flight crew were heading for debriefing, swapping stories and rumours as they went. Had their missing Commander truly been found? Despite losses taken at the Wall there was a growing sense of hope and excitement.

'We're home, lass,' Tangnost said softly to the girl wrapped in his cloak. 'We're finally home.'

Home? Quenelda stirred groggily in the dwarf's arms; she was so tired and she ached all over! She knuckled her bleary eyes and her hands came away black and sticky. *Dragonfire! It wasn't a daydream! It was true!* 'We did it...' she smiled up at Tangnost. 'We did it! Papa is safe?'

'Yes, we did,' the dwarf hugged her gently to him before getting stiffly to his feet, sucking in a breath as his broken ribs grated. 'Can you stand? Let me help you.' He lifted her effortlessly to her feet.

'Ahh!' Leg buckling, Quenelda cried out as a stab of white hot pain lanced through her injured thigh. Despite her cry Two Gulps continued to snore loudly on his back, plump tummy rising and falling.

'Let him sleep, he earned it! Here,' the dwarf offered an arm. 'Lean on me.'

The pair hobbled down the Imperial's wing, one in no better state than the other: filthy, stinking, looking like scarecrows. 'You need proper rest, hot food and a bath! We all do!'

'But what about Root and Papa and Quester?'

'They will be with the healers,' Tangnost said firmly. 'Let them do their work. They will send news when they can. I promise.'

Quenelda nodded reluctantly, but she was beginning to learn patience, even if it was difficult! 'More haste less speed,' Drumondir had cautioned her, a wise lesson slowly learnt.

The pair slowly dismounted onto the gantry. Tangnost waved the healers away. 'There are badly injured on board, tend them first.'

But their landing had not gone altogether unnoticed. Already heads were turning at the sight, for the second time that day, of the DeWinter standard flying behind the SDS Commander's, an honour ordinarily only given to Dragon Lords. The Earl was already with the surgeons and physicians which meant only one thing; his missing daughter had been found!

A barrel-chested dwarf waded through the dismounting soldiers towards them. 'Bearhugger!' he bellowed. 'You're back, man! And in one piece!'

Tangnost accepted Odin's arm before the dwarf realised who it was at his friend's side.

'Lady!' Odin said with relief. 'I didn't recognise you. They said you were missing on the battlefield, cut off from your father!'

Taking her hand, giving Quenelda no time to protest, Odin raised her arm. 'DeWinter!' he bellowed. 'DeWinter!'

'DeWinter,' the cry was taken up. 'DeWinter!'

And suddenly Quenelda was surrounded by a sea of smiling faces, murmured words of thanks and approval, tears and joy flowing freely. And then next thing, they had hoisted her and Tangnost up on their shoulders and the pair were carried above the crowd, oblivious to their pain, caught up in the joy of the moment. 'De Winter! DeWinter!' Cheers rang out and grew like a wave of sound that filled the cavern and washed back again. Everyone wanted to greet them, to thank them. Everyone: save Root and Quester and her father.

Exhausted, Quenelda stumbled as they finally put her down, quickly righted by a dozen hands, and then the crowd parted to form two ranks, clearing a way to the porting stone. As she hobbled along, fists were placed on hearts in the age old SDS salute for a Dragon Lord. Biting back tears, head held high, ignoring the dreadful ache of her muscles, Quenelda walked proudly forwards, not seeing Tangnost's nod of pride and approval behind her. She was heir to Dragonsdome, had seen only thirteen summers, yet had already earned her spurs in battle!

CHAPTER TWO

Home again

As they were stepping up to the Commander's porting stone, his son Guy DeBessart materialised and stepped off, almost tripping over them in his haste.

'Lady!' Seeming able to recognise the black faced scarecrows in front of him, Guy's relief was palpable. 'Dragon Master! We are all so relieved to find you safe.' He was boyishly grinning from ear to ear. 'And Lady, you found your father where everyone else failed!' Stepping back smartly in an echo of what had just gone before he saluted them both, frank admiration in his eyes. 'My father asks you both attend him in the Situation Room once your wounds are tended to.'

'Tsssk' Drumondir tutted as she cut away Quenelda's filthy leggings and the crude clotted bandage, to reveal the wound below that was a finger width and deep. 'Lie still, this will hurt a little. I have to put in some stiches.'

'Oww!' Quenelda squirmed as the Bone Caster probed the wound as gently as possible. 'Ho-**ow**!' the needle went swiftly in and out. 'How are Root and Quester?' she asked anxiously, trying to ignore the pain. The hospital beyond this alcove was packed with the injured on pallets and stretchers, but she could spot neither of her friends. 'And Papa? How is he?'

'Your brave young friend, Root is also injured,' the Bonecaster replied. 'He has a broken arm which I have splinted, and I prepared an infusion of black nettle and starwart for the pain and to fight infection. He discharged himself from the healers' care many bells ago.'

'A-and Quester?' Quenelda hardly dared to ask as Drumondir swabbed the wound with a cleansing decoction before bandaging it. 'Tangnost said he was badly injured?'

Drumondir sighed. There was no hiding from it. In war people died. 'Drink this,' she ordered, handing Quenelda a bone mug with a sweet smelling herbal tea. 'He is badly injured and fighting for his life...the surgeons and healers have been working since dawn to save him and many others. They are not finished. There is nothing to be done for now. I suggest you rest.'

'I have to go to the Situation Room at the CAC.'

'CAC?'

'The Command and Control is the SeaDragon Tower.'

'Then go to your friend, Root, first. He needs your comfort, and to know you are safe.'

Quenelda nodded. She knew where she'd find him.

Unlike the battleroosts, the domestic roosts on Dragon Isle were almost silent, the paddocks all but empty of people.

Roost hands, ostlers, scalesmiths and surgeons; they had all been summoned to cope with the incoming injured. Only stable boys and apprentices remained and they were cleaning tack or mucking out. Not recognising the dirty dishevelled boy, they continued with their work as Quenelda limped by to where chameleon and dale dragons were stabled. The Earl's daughter hobbled awkwardly up the steps trying to favour her sore leg. It was dim inside, the smell of hay musty and warm. Only a single lantern was lit. She stood a moment to let her eyes adjust.

Root was on his knees, arms about Chasing the Stars, who was lipping and blowing on the youth's face as he clung to her for comfort, their joyous reunion tinged by grief. Quenelda hesitated, knowing how much her friend had missed his own dragon whilst they were away searching for her father; but sensing her arrival, Chasing the Stars bugled in welcome. *He is home....*her joy was complete. *You have brought him home to me...*

The gnome spun about. His splinted left arm was in a sling and he had two black eyes. At any other time it might have been funny. They stared at each other seeing strangers. They had both changed, both grown, both unrecognisable after four moons of adventure.

'You look awful!' Quenelda said truthfully.

'You look worse!'

They limped towards each other and hugged.

'Ow!'

'Ahh!'

'You're injured!'

'You too! Tangnost told me! Root, you captured *Galtekerion*! You took him prisoner! The hobgoblin warlord himself!'

But Root wasn't listening. 'Quenelda?' he blinked back tears. He had bravely held back his fears until the effort was unbearable. 'I - we – Oh, Quenelda! We thought you were dead! When the dragonfire was lit we couldn't see you...and then Galtekerion attacked us and there was no time to think...' the words poured out of him. 'Quester saved your father. The hobgoblins had overrun the Guard, everyone was dead or fighting. He stood between them with the Earl's sword doing everything Tangnost had taught him.'

Root's eyes brimmed and tears finally tracked down his face. 'H-he's - he's dying! The surgeons have been with him since Stormcracker returned.' He wiped away the tears angrily. 'What if he dies? I couldn't bear to lose anyone else.'

And remembering that Root had lost his father, his family and entire warren to the hobgoblins already, giving him an underlying fear of loneliness, Quenelda hugged him as Chasing the Stars gathered them both under her wing. 'You will never lose us, Root. We're your family too now, Tangnost, Papa, Drumondir, Two Gulps and Chasing the Stars. You'll never be alone again. I swear it!'

'Eugh! Chasing the Stars, stop it!' Root protested, not really meaning it as his dragon's hot rough tongue wiped away the tears.

'Come on,' Quenelda gently took his hand. 'We're needed in the Situation Room.'

'The Situation Room?   Me?' Root wiped away tears with a dirty hand. 'Why would they want to see me?'

'Root!   You helped find my father and bring him home. And you captured Galtekerion. *Everyone* is going to want to see you!!'

CHAPTER THREE

Situation Room

'We have no time to waste,' Jakart DeBessart spoke even as his esquires stripped away his scored and bloody armour. The SDS Commander reached hungrily for the platters of bread, cheese, cold mutton and fruit that were being laid out on the table and took ravenous mouthfuls. 'Once the Lord Protector becomes King there will be war if we challenge him. The Black Isle is full of his men and the Army of the North will fight for him; they are all his creatures and the Guild were fools not to see it. He has the Guild and most of the Court under his thrall. Who knows how many others his gold has bought? We have to capture him now, quietly and quickly, and remove him to Dragon Isle.'

'How will you explain his arrest, my Lord?' his son Guy asked tentatively. 'Will they not say the Earl has lost his wits? How can we prove it? What if none will believe us until it is too late?'

'I have a plan in mind,' said a voice from the opening doors. 'One that will flush our friend from cover and reveal Hugo's true colours.' At the sound of that once familiar voice, before even they saw him, chairs grated as all the soldiers and technicians tending the banks of high magic displays stood to attention.

'My Lord!'

'Rufus!'

SDS officers stepped forwards to surround the Earl, delight mingling with dismay at his blind eyes, the ruined flesh.

'Rufus! Gods, man!' Jakart protested. 'You should be abed! You've just been in a battle!'

'So Drumondir said,' a smile tugged the Earl's mouth as Quenelda, followed by a reluctant Root, helped him forwards. 'But I feel stronger....something strange is happening to me.... My daughter tells me the Hand Fast Wedding Ceremony begins on the morrow?'

Jakart nodded. 'But first take a seat, Rufus, before you fall!' He pulled out his High Chair from the round table.

'He will expect news of the battle soon,' the SDS Commander resumed, once the Earl, Quenelda and Root were seated. 'We think none of Galtekerion's Chosen escaped the battlefield, and if Hugo had spies at the Wall, none have passed through our guard into the glen.'

'Then let us give him the news he expects and more.'

'What are you thinking, Rufus?'

'Send news of the battle and my rescue both...give him no time to think. Good and bad news are more likely to be believed. Force him to betray his hand before witnesses, those whose word will be believed. Use bait Hugo cannot refuse: me. He weds on the morrow. He has everything to lose.'

'And so do we,' Jakart pointed out dryly.

'How, Papa?' Quenelda asked.

And so the Earl laid out his plan.

Jakart nodded. 'It is fraught with risk...we must choose our messenger carefully.'

'Franyard Rogran,' the Earl determined. 'He is brave but honest and has no head for politics and the Court. If Hugo is looking for, or can touch minds as my daughter has described to me, then he will find no deception.'

'Is anyone to be given warning?' Guy asked. 'The Queen? The Constable?'

'Sir Gharad,' the SDS Commander suggested. 'He is not in his dotage as some would think. Frail, yes, he acts the part well, but a keen mind lies behind those grey eyes, that vague demeanour.'

'And the Queen?' Quenelda intervened anxiously. 'What if he hurts her...or-or kidnaps her...should she not be warned?'

'No...' her father replied thoughtfully. 'Caitlin ever wears her heart on her sleeve...he would not even have to touch her mind to know something was amiss.'

'But how do we protect her?' Quenelda persisted.

'We have an unexpected ally deep in the heart of the enemy's council,' Jakart DeBessart revealed. 'And she can protect the Queen better than any. None would question her place at the Queen's side.'

Eager faces turned towards him as he told them.

'Armelia?' Quenelda scoffed. '*Armelia*?' She could hardly believe her ears. 'But she's an empty headed - '

'I think,' the SDS Commander smoothly intervened, 'you will find her much changed. You had more of an impact upon her than you know, and she is fiercely loyal to the Queen. The Countess Armelia has passed many messages for us. And she has certain potions provided by our alchemists against such times as we needed it. She can drug the guards if needs be.'

There was movement as the guards at the door admitted a newcomer. With a nod Tangnost grimly took his place at the table. He had been talking to Odin to discover what had befallen Dragonsdome in their absence. None of the news was good.

'The Lord Protector and Darcy hoped to use the Countess to spy upon the Queen,' the SDS Commander further explained. 'And in particular, to report the Queen's dealings with myself; whether we still looked for the Earl, troop losses and deployments; some of which were true, enough to dupe them, but others not. To the Court and her husband, the Countess Armelia appears the same frivolous young lady whose head is turned by the Lord Protector's extravagant gifts, who spends her time dancing and shopping and organising great banquets at Dragonsdome. But she listens, very carefully, to all that is said around her. She will do all she can to protect the Queen.'

'It is a very dangerous game she plays,' the Earl judged. 'Hugo is a master at deception. He would not hesitate to kill her and pass it off as an accident.'

'She is very brave,' Jakart agreed. 'She knows what he is and the risks, yet she would not give up hope that you and Quenelda would return. And she is not altogether alone. Hugo has made one mistake. He has ignored the palace servants and the common people who love their Queen. Sir Gharad and I planned against this day. If we are to take the palace, word needs to be taken to the undercook Agnes Dingleweed who will drug the Lord Protector's men. The code word is oat beer.'

'Oat beer?' The Earl smiled. 'Such a mild word for rebellion!'

'But spiced and perfect for doctoring!' Jakart's smile did not reach his eyes.

'How do you intend to send word to the Constable? Who can we trust to get past Hugo's honour guard? It cannot be anyone either Hugo or my son would recognise, yet someone Gharad would trust on sight. He can then pass word to the Countess.'

'I'll go,' Root piped up. 'He knows me.'

Tangnost nodded. 'That he does, lad, and that will count for more than any token.'

'Dressed in servant's garb,' the Earl agreed. 'They won't see the boy beneath. Servants are invisible.'

'Will this work?' Quenelda was anxious and afraid for Root. 'His arm is already broken. Won't that attract attention?'

'No. Accidents happen every day,' Tangnost reassured her. 'An overturned cart, a slip on the ice, a dozen different things.'

Quenelda's father nodded. 'Hugo would never make the connection between Root and Galtekerion's capture and my return. Sky above! How many would? I can scarce believe myself one so young has captured the most feared WarLord in the Seven Kingdoms!'

Root coloured with pleasure and embarrassment as he was asked to tell how Galtekerion was captured. 'But it was Quester,' he ended sadly, voice husky with emotion, 'who fought Galtekerion, who saved the Earl, not me! And he is dying!'

'You have both been exceptionally brave, young Root,' Jakart DeBessart praised the youth. 'But you are not a warrior nor trained to fight, yet overcame your fear. That is true bravery.'

'And the rest of us? Me?' Quenelda asked with a twinge of jealousy once Root had been congratulated for the dozenth time by all the officers present. 'What shall I do?'

'Rest. Get some sleep,' her father smiled. 'You've earned it!'

'But I - ' Quenelda protested.

'Will remain here, Goose, for your own safety. It would not do for Hugo to capture you as well as me, and you have had more than enough adventures to last a lifetime! Rest as best you may. It will soon be over.'

'But, Papa! How will you fool him?'

'We put on an act,' her father answered bitterly. 'Just like our dear Lord Protector. If Hugo can do it, so can we; the stakes cannot be higher. We gamble with the very future of the Seven Kingdoms.'

'No pressure then...' Root muttered under his breath as he headed for the servants' quarter.

CHAPTER FOUR

The Rumours Are True

'Commander,' Franyard Rogran saluted. The old knight was tired and cold and far too old to still be in the saddle with barely a rest since the battle. But with so many lost to the hobgoblins, almost a generation had died on the Westering Isles, the Queen needed every loyal man she could muster. And the battle at the Smoking Fort had been a hard one; the SDS had lost twelve precious dragons pushing the hobgoblins back over the cliffs.

'Franyard, here, sit,' Jakart DeBessart pulled a leather camp seat closer to the fire and beckoned servants forward with hot food and drink. Ice dripped from the knight's armoured feet onto the hearth, smoking on the hot tiles. Jakart let the old man rest and take his fill before he began to speak.

'Franyard, you know the Earl has been discovered?'

The old man started, almost spilling his drink. 'The rumours are true, then?' A tired smile lit his eyes. 'There have been so many false rumours that I dared not hope. This is a glad day indeed!'

18

DeBessart nodded but didn't smile. *Forgive the lie!* 'The battle surgeons are fighting to stabilise him as we speak. I - '

'He is dying?'

'I fear so. It's the Black Death. How he survived this long after the battle...?' DeBessart shrugged and shook his head in genuine amazement, thinking on the hurried tale of the lost SeaDragon Citadel....*legends spring to life.* 'He may die at any moment and I know her Majesty will wish to see him, even if only to say goodbye.'

Franyard sagged in dismay. He closed his eyes. 'I pray to the Gods it is not so, that I am not to be the bearer of bad news.'

'Now, fly swift and true to Her Majesty. Ask that the Queen's Surgeon and the Gentlemen of the Physicians and Apothecaries Guild await Rufus's arrival. We will follow as soon as we may with the Earl.'

'Make sure,' Jakart said casually on parting, as if it were an afterthought. 'That the news also reaches his dear friend, the Lord Protector.' *Who will not be able to turn down one last opportunity to kill the Earl, to finish the job himself.*

CHAPTER FIVE

Through the Back Door

The twilight deepened from lavender to blue. The dark blanket of night rolled out swiftly, stealing winter's light in a breath. But tonight, packed from gutter to garret, the Black Isle was not asleep, for the Queen was to wed the Lord Protector on the morrow, and for many, celebrations had already begun in earnest in the streets and taverns.

Goblets and glasses were raised from the great tree-lined boulevards and sprawling palaces of the wealthy, through corkscrewed cobbled streets down to the overcrowded gutters of the poor, and the harbours. Buskers drummed and juggled and played with fire to earn a farthing or two, while vendors sold hot sausages of dubious repute for a groat. Others were hanging coloured lanterns from every lamp and street corner, every turret and tower, so that the city shone in the darkness.

Vampire dragons flitted around the royal palace towers and turrets, frost crackling on their wings. Stamping to keep warm, the guards huddled about the braziers and envied their fellows off duty, already drinking in the taverns. Streamers of music curled out from the great hall below, and marigold light splashed out of the mullioned windows beneath steep gabled roofs. Smoke from four score chimneys hung thickly in the still air. And down below stairs, an army of thousands prepared for the three days of festivities.

There was a steady stream of latecomers still climbing the steep Castle Wynd to the palace, carting provisions to the castle kitchens. In the midst of all this activity, no one noticed the youth swathed in cloak and cowl who joined a mess of scullions tramping across the inner pentangle yard to the kitchens with water from the wells.

Sir Gharad Mowbray, the Queen's elderly Constable, made his way laboriously along a corridor to his chambers, leaning heavily on his staff. His very bones ached in the cold, but the heavy limp and quavering step were feigned. However the despair in his thoughtful grey eyes was not. A WarLock was about to take command of the Queen and Kingdom both, and he was powerless to prevent it. No word had reached them from Bearhugger and Quenelda since they had left the land of the Ice Bears, although a message that the SDS had been scrambled following a major attack on the Wall had arrived by courier many hours ago, and nothing since.

The kitchen was full of enticing aromas and glorious warmth. Root's mouth watered, you could get fed up to the back teeth with a diet of cold porridge, smoked fish and oat bannocks; their staple diet for many moons when he, Tangnost, Quenelda and Quester flew north on Stormcracker. Snatching up a small truckle of hard cheese to look like he was doing something useful, Root wove his way through the milling throng of maids, cooks and butlers towards a large lady dusted in flour who was kneading bread with muscled arms that would have done a dragon handler proud. She was the only one in the kitchen who fitted the description he had been given.

She caught his eye. 'What'yer staring at, boy? 'aven't you a job to do? 'ere, who are you?' The lad had two cracking black eyes. 'Ain't seen you before.'

Root gulped. 'Oat beer,' he blurted, louder than he had intended. 'For my Lord Constable.'

Agnes Dingleweed blinked, her mouth dropping open in surprise. She closed it just as hurriedly as she almost choked on the cloud of flour that caught the back of her throat. The young Countess had discussed this eventuality as they planned menus. *This must mean… could it possibly mean? The Earl had returned?*

A wide smile spread from ear to ear. Agnes winked meaningfully, wiping an eye with a floury hand. Her eyes shone as she squared her jaw determinedly. The undercook loathed these uncouth, bragging, bullying soldiers that the Lord Protector had garrisoned the palace with, who had banished the Queen's men to the streets in search of work without a penny to care for their families. Agnes turned, searching the kitchens for one of the pantry maids who could turn a head with her long auburn hair and winning smile.

'Millie,' she shouted. 'Let's warm up that special vat of

oat beer for the brave lads on patrol. It's getting cold out there! And lad,' the cook said softly. 'Let's see what we can do to hide those black eyes of yours, shall we? Don't want to draw attention to yourself.'

The Queen's Guards in bright polished ceremonial armour were posted at every stair and corridor of the royal chambers as Root carried the small cask of Mucklemore oat beer, one of the Constable's few tipples. His broken arm was throbbing despite the bitter brew Drumondir had made him swallow to dull the pain. He had only sipped, anxious that it might dull his mind also. The sharp eyed Captain outside the Constable's chambers stopped him. They were all SDS veterans.

'Who are you then, lad?'

'Helping Agnes out in the kitchens.'

The guard nodded and opened the door without further question. He was one of Agnes's very large extended family. You didn't want to get on the wrong side of Granny Agnes...she'd put the fear of god into the hobgoblins themselves!

The old man inside was seated by the fire. Only a few candles were lit. Head in hands, Gharad Mowbray did not even look up as Root placed the cask on the table and bent to draw the beer, waiting for the inner chamber door to be closed by a curious servant.

'My Lord?'

The Queen's Constable frowned at the youth in front of him. He was thin and pale as the moons, with two shadowed eyes. 'What's this?' It only took him a moment or two. 'Root?' He trailed off as the grinning gnome gathered him into a awkward hug. Amazed, delighted, Gharad found himself hugging the boy back, planting a kiss on his head.

'Root? He-you-he's alive?' the Constable whispered, suddenly alert, suddenly hopeful. 'You've found him? Haven-haven't you?' He closed his hands about the youth's and clutched it to his wildly hammering heart. 'He-' the old man swallowed, throat suddenly dry, eyes brimming.

'Yes! Yes! My Lord.' Root nodded, delighted to bring such good news. 'Yes, he's alive. At Dragon Isle…'

'Ah, thank you! Thank you, boy. You have made an old man happy….Is he-how - '

'My Lord,' Root interrupted urgently, 'there is a plan. They are coming…to take back the palace and the Queen.'

'When?'

'Tonight.'

'Tell me then….'

CHAPTER SIX

Tomorrow and Tomorrow

Feeling faint, Sir Gharad Mowbray stopped on the stairs to take a breath, waving away a soldier who stepped up to take his elbow. He pressed a finger to his temple and tried to slow his pulse which was galloping out of control. So much might go wrong and Rufus was blind! Blind! Although Root had insisted the Earl could now see through Stormcracker's eyes and was able to fight, that wouldn't help inside the palace.

Despite supervising scores of tasks in preparation for the wedding, the hours dragged and the Constable fretted and his temper became frayed with the endless stream of people who came with news, or for orders, or to resolve quarrels. Sir Gharad did not worry that anyone should see his agitation; as Master of Ceremony the responsibility for following three days of festivities was his. It was natural that he should be anxious.

'At dark fall, before the sickle moons rise,' Root had told him, and darkness was now falling. Returning to his chambers, unable to rest, Gharad Mowbray paced up and down like a caged bear. The trap was set, they had done all they could and yet...and yet... 'Should I tell her?' the old man was talking to himself. 'No, no, she could not hide it, could not keep it secret from him...all had better proceed as normal...'

'My Lord Constable?' The Queen's equerry had arrived in person. 'Her Majesty asks if you are well and will attend the festivities in the hall below?' He hesitated. 'She needs you by her side, my Lord,' he added meaningfully. He too was fiercely loyal to his mistress, afraid for tomorrow.

'Yes,' the old man nodded in agreement. 'I will be down shortly.'

Donning his bright ceremonial robes, Sir Gharad looked out towards the barracks. Snow was softly falling, filling the crisscrossed tracks of the commons. A group of darkly clad soldiers were gathered about a brazier. He frowned and squinted through the thick glass. Firelight glinted off the chain mail and plate armour beneath their heavy cloaks. They weren't wearing the royal livery. He summoned the Captain of his guard.

'Whose men are those? In the Royal Quadrangle? They are not the Queen's Guard!'

'The Lord Protector's, my Lord Constable. His own men now guard much of the palace, allowing the Palace Guard to join the festivities. On the Queen's orders, his Lordship said. Since he is to marry the Queen on the morrow we did not bar them. They are also flying patrol. Did we do wrong?'

Gharad Mowbray cast about him. 'A quill and ink,' he

barked at a servant. 'Now, Captain...' he hastily scrawled a message and poured sand on it. 'Take this to the SDS Commander with all haste. Lives may depend on this. Speak to no one else, least of all the Lord Protector. Give no clue anything is amiss. Now go!'

CHAPTER SEVEN

The Sabretoothed Squirrel

The Banquet had been underway for several hours in the opulent Red Squirrel Hall of the Sorcerers Guild on the Black Isle. High above the intricately carved stone pillars the great onion shaped bronze and enamel domes were buried beneath three strides of snow, and the thick panes of glass that opened onto a balcony with views of the entire city were frosted. But none of winter's chilly touch penetrated these thick walls. The hardships of the common people were out of sight, and hence out of mind.

Polished mirrors reflected the candlelight a hundred-fold, their flickering warmth winking off golden plates. It was oppressively hot. Despite the three dozen candelabras that lit the hall and the four great hearths, the Guildsmen were extravagantly dressed, each attired in a dozen gauzy layers to outdo the other and proclaim their guild or league the greatest in all the kingdoms. Sorcerers' hats, too, in a wealth of colours and wonderful shapes proclaimed their badge of office, just as knights' helmets did. Glorious tapestries depicted the rise of the Guilds and the acquisition of great wealth. Indeed the rise of the merchant classes to a wealth greater than many noble houses caused endless friction at Court. But politics was the last thing on these Guildsmen's minds. The Ceremony of the Sabretoothed Squirrel dated back thousands of years and took place only on the eve of a royal wedding.

A hundred servants bore in great platters of roast swan, boar with tayberry sauce, marzipan sweets, pastries, spiced meat pies, eel stew, egg custards... If the peasants and general populace were starving, the Guild most certainly were not. Delicately cut crystal goblets were filled with deep red wines from the Fifth Kingdom, or cool, clear fruit juices from the Sixth. So it came as no surprise that the muffled thuds that suddenly reverberated through the building, rattling a few casements, were barely noticed.

'More wine!' Rumpole Spellskin hitched his stomachs over his belt. An ineffectual mouse of a man raised to Grand Master of the Guild when the Lord Hugo Mandrake took on the mantle of Lord Protector, he beckoned a servant forwards, stifling a belch of appreciation. He could still barely believe his unanimous elevation to Grand Master; naively unaware that he was Hugo Mandrake's puppet in all things, as were those who voted for him. Instead his mind, what little there was left in his later years, was awash with the superlative wines being served and the promise of things to come. As Grand Master he would participate in the Hand Fast wedding procession tomorrow, and then be a guest of honour at the high table for the wedding banquet. It had all quite gone to his head!

Sipping a fourth glass of mellow Elvish champagne, Winifred Needlespin, Matron of the Nimble Fingered Seamstresses Guild also felt a bit giddy and not just from the alcohol. Her seamstresses had been working night and day for two moons to finish Queen Caitlin's wedding dress in time, a feather light confection of moon pearls and black dragon diamonds on dove pale silk. It was an exclusive Esme Titchmouse creation, the best kept secret at Foresight & Hindsights, leaving the Court awash with rumour as to which designer had been chosen.

And yet...and yet...in private the Queen was clearly still bowed by grief at the death of the Earl Rufus, and had none of the joy one would expect from a young bride about to marry the people's Champion. *The Lord Protector!* Winifred thought wistfully, fanning herself, wishing she were younger. *Such a handsome man! How could any woman not wish to marry such a noble Lord? Such...*

Her musing was abruptly cut off when there was the clatter of feet and armour and brusque voices. Protests were cut short. The doors were thrown open with a crash, knocking footmen on the inside to the ground. A silver tureen of soup sloshed across the flagged floor as a servant screamed. Spellskin had such a fright himself that he swallowed the wrong way, wine coming out of his nose in a fine red mist.

'W-what is the meaning of this intrusion?' he blustered, covering his fright by dabbing his nose with his napkin as ranks of BoneCrackers fanned out around the table. They were armoured, bandaged and bloodied, and smelt of magic and murder. The Grand Master reached for the citrus pomander at his waist.

A grizzled dwarf sergeant from the III Firstborn came to his side and to attention.

'Orders, Grand Master,' she barked, 'from the Commander. He requires these gentlemen and ladies to come with us immediately!' She thrust out a parchment with the wax seal of the triple-headed dragon, forcing Spellskin to sit down hard in his seat or get hit on the chin. Then the sergeant took a step backwards, eyes staring straight ahead.

A flurry of consternation swept round the table as the Grand Master broke the blue wax seal and read the message.

'What?' The aged League Master Tumbleweed of the Seafaring Ship Wrights frowned, putting a hearing horn to his ear. 'C-come with you? Who? Where?'

'When?' Spellskin added eyes still glued to the parchment.

'Now, Sir. If you please.'

'*Now?*' The Grand Master was horrified. 'But...but ...the banquet has barely begun. The Ancient Ceremony of the Sabretoothed Squirrel has yet to be....we-'

'*Now*, sir,' the sergeant said firmly. 'We have a cloaked Imperial waiting on the lower pads.'

'*What?* An Imperial?' Spellskin's voice rose to a squeak. 'Us! An Imperial? Cloaked? Why? What has happened?'

31

'Couldn't say, Sir. Just ordered to bring you to the palace *with all haste.*' At her signal the escort closed in.

Rumpole read out the list in a quavering voice. 'Masters Stogepuddle, Moreteeth, Underwell, Longshanks, Sardlacke, Twiddlethwaite, Matron Winifred, Ma-'

'What,' Matron Winifred tucked in her many chins and, sucking in a deep breath, stuck out her formidable chest as if it were a wall to be scaled. 'If we refuse?'

This declaration of war was met calmly. 'Then we have orders to bring everyone in this room.'

That had the desired effect as those nominated were shoved forward unceremoniously by their fellows. League or Guild masters and Matrons, one and all...they were herded out the door, leaving a stunned silence behind.

CHAPTER EIGHT

We Have Found Him

Winter Festivities were drawing to a close but the Royal Wedding would begin on the morrow to herald in the Year of the Inquisitive Two-tailed Wood Mouse. The sounds of flute and bodkin rattled out a jig as a whirling kaleidoscope of satin and silk broke and reformed and broke away again.

Armelia proudly watched her Queen take to the dance floor. Dressed simply in an embroidered kirtle of blue threaded with silver, and an unadorned band of silver about her head, Caitlin was a dove amidst gaudy peacocks. The Queen's heart and her thoughts lay elsewhere, with a man she thought dead. Armelia now knew the Queen loved the missing Earl with all her heart and soul, and had done so since her childhood, but Caitlin moved graciously through the Court as a Queen should, that inner heart hidden from hostile gaze.

Just as she must hide her thoughts, so I must! Armelia's mouth was dry despite the wine, and her hands were shaking. She hastily put down the goblet least it betray her, and bent to her companion to discuss the wedding dress design, aware of a familiar strange stillness behind her as the Lord Protector passed. *Am I the only one to feel it, like a kiss of frost?*

Watching lazily, the Lord Protector's eyes narrowed as a courier approached the Constable further along the table. The old man visibly started. Eyes sweeping the room, searching for the Queen, he stood with difficulty, helped to his feet by his body servant, a young gnome boy.

So... the news of the battle has arrived. But what news did they bring? That the Smoking Fort had been attacked and overrun? Incursions had died back as winter set in and the hobgoblins returned to the spawning pools to hibernate. *This attack was fully out of character; what would they make of it? And the Earl? Buried in a pit! Unrecognisable amongst the scores of corpses on a frozen battlefield...*

At the same moment there was a flurry of activity at the far entrance. A fully armoured knight stepped into the candlelight, he too searching the crowded room and the raised dais at the far end. Only his was black battle armour. There were murmurs of consternation and pain as the knight elbowed his way through the press, elbows and delicately stockinged ankles meeting cold steel.

'Who is that officer? His armour is filthy...'

'He is ruining the dance...'

But Armelia knew who he was, for Sir Franyard had served with her uncle at the Howling Glen. She slipped out onto the dance floor. *Could she play her part in the deception to come?*

Hands linked, the Queen and her ladies were coming forwards towards their partners when Amelia bent urgently to her ear.

'Caitlin, Majesty, there is a knight come from the battlefield.'

Searching the crowd, the young Queen caught the eye of the advancing soldier and held it as the measure advanced and fell back around them. The music dragged, Caitlin moved as if through treacle...time stood still as the knight advanced slowly towards her, holding her gaze with intent brown eyes. Her heart was fluttering in her throat like a captured bird. Around them dancers were in disarray, falling back to give the Queen space, whilst others, carried away by the music had yet to notice, and careened into them. Courtiers tripped and fell.

The old soldier did not stand on duty. In fact it looked like Sir Franyard could barely stand at all. He was trembling from head to toe, his face grey with fatigue, his armour rusty, although Armelia had a horrible feeling it was dried blood.

'Madam, Majesty,' the old man went down on one knee with a fearful clang, but his face was alight with joy. 'We have found him!' Ignoring protocol, he grasped at her hand, holding it in his blunt frozen fingers. 'The Smoking Fort was attacked last night and overrun, but we have taken it back.' He took a deep breath. 'I am just returned to Dragon Isle where I heard the most wondrous news. The Earl,' his voice broke. 'Was airlifted out of the battlefield!'

'*The Earl?*' The Queen gasped hand to heart, it was more than she could have hoped for. Armelia firmly held her elbow as Caitlin almost collapsed, shielding her from the Lord Protector's dark gaze. '*Alive?*' A wealth of hope and joy was invested in that one whispered word as the Queen raised the old man to his feet, the pair holding each other up.

The old knight nodded, his joy mirroring hers, tears unashamedly running down his face. 'Alive, Madam!' Franyard confirmed. 'He is blind and badly injured, yet he survived....He-' Franyard blinked. Where *had* the Lord Protector come from?

'Why, my dear, you are trembling...good news I trust?' Hugo's pale piercing eyes came to rest on the old knight.

'My- My Lord Mandrake...' which title should he use? *King?* No, he was confused, the marriage was tomorrow. 'Yes! The Earl, he has been found!'

'Where? Where is he,' the Lord Protector demanded eagerly. 'How is he? You come from battle?' The Lord Protector spoke to the old knight but his eyes were on the Queen, searching for any sign she had known. He paid Armelia no interest.

'The Smoking Fort was almost overrun by the time we arrived, but somehow,' the elderly knight looked bewildered. 'They found the Earl on his old battledragon at the heart of the fight, returned from the abyss. I fear he is gravely ill, but safe on Dragon Isle with our battle surgeons...'

Dragon Isle! I cannot touch him there! Possibilities raced through the Lord Protector's head. He reached out to grip the old man's shoulder in pretence of keeping him on his feet. *Tell me the truth...*a black thread coiled through the soldier's mind, searching...*he is dying...* finding no deception the cold predatory thoughts withdrew and the old man staggered.

'Franyard! Are you unwell? Are you injured? Summon my surgeons!'

'No-no, your Majesty. Weary perhaps.... over excited, that must be it!' Franyard passed a hand through his thinning hair. 'Majesty, once they are sure he is stable, Lord Jakart will bring him here to your physicians. They know you would wish it so.'

'Then he is dying?' the Queen whispered.

The old man shook his head regretfully. 'Majesty, I do not know, only that he is gravely ill and that Commander Jakart and the healers from the Academy are with him, and they are the greatest in all the kingdoms. Jakart will bring the Earl here with all haste as soon as the surgeons allow it; he may have more answers for you. He asks for royal physicians and apothecaries to attend the Earl.'

Swallowing her fear, her hope, Caitlin laid a hand on the old man's arm. 'Rest here for the night.. Chambers will be prepared for you next to mine. Your news is... overwhelming. After all this time....'

And then Caitlin's head whipped up when she felt the familiar *thump* running through the stone as far above three Imperials put down on the Winter Tower pads, their combined weight driving it down to where the landing gantries were crowded with soldiers.

'Go... go... go!'

BoneCrackers from the Earl's own FirstBorn regiment stretchered the dying man in through the private King's Gate entrance and into the royal apartments: the missing SDS Commander was finally home.

CHAPTER NINE

Unhappy Landings

The flight had been cold and uncomfortable for pampered guildsmen, used to luxurious appointed carriages with glass windows and padded warmth. Their old bones needed cossetting, and sitting on their rumps atop a battledragon in winter was freezing and uncomfortable, and the sheer speed downright frighten-ing. It was the first time they had experienced cloaking and it left a slight sense of dislocation, of nausea. Expectations that they were attending the Queen's evening festivities for some surprise were rapidly dispelled as they put down near the deserted parade ground to the south of the palace grounds.

Instead of a lavish welcome befitting their rank they were herded by grimly silent commandos into the empty Guard barracks. There on the second floor of the massive Red Gate House, they found the SDS Commander and four of his BattleMages in conference. Plans of the palace spread over the mess table were being studied by shielded candle light.

Perplexed, rudely ignored, the Guildsmen began muttering into their beards, with the exception of Matron Winifred who only had a moustache. What on the One Earth was going on? All this cloak and dagger nonsense! How the SDS loved their little dramas!

'What – what is the meaning of this?' the Grand Master demanded feebly in response to his colleagues' meaningful looks.

'Outrageous...' another muttered, eyeing the SDS Commander warily. It was well known Jakart DeBessart did not suffer fools lightly.

'Forgive me,' DeBessart finally said, in a tone implying that he did not give a fig whether they did or not. 'But this meeting is vital to the wellbeing of the Queen and the Seven Kingdoms. A great evil stirs within these very walls...the Lord Protector is a WarLock; and it is he who betrayed the SDS to the hobgoblins on the Westering Isles. Now he will try and complete the work he began by killing the Earl DeWinter tonight.'

There was a breathless pause as they all stared at him in open mouthed disbelief.

'A WarLock?' Someone scoffed.

'A traitor?'

''Why would he kill the Earl Darcy?'

They shook their heads in denial, setting bells tinkling...jewels glinting in the candle light.

'What manner of jest is this?'

'No jest, Masters, Mistress. The Lord Protector conjured a maelstrom that wiped out the entire battlegroup save a handful of survivors. The Earl Rufus lives yet. At this very moment he lies in the royal chambers attended by the Queen's physicians. He is both blind and was badly injured. Somehow his daughter has saved him; that tale is for telling another time.'

'The Earl *Rufus*!?'

'Was?'

'He's alive? Rufus is alive?'

'It is a long story, a fairy story some might say; now he is on the road to recovery...but word that he is critically ill has spread to reach the ears of those who would wish to believe it. Thus the trap is baited and set.'

'My Lord Commander!' Grand Master Spellskin shivered. 'These are-are *outrageous* allegations you make. You must- you must prove them true; else he has played us all for fools. Else,' he hiccupped, becoming rapidly sober. 'Else we have a...warlock in our very heart.'

'That, Masters,' DeBessart smiled grimly. 'Is what we are about to do and why you are here. Hugo cannot risk the Earl's return for many reasons; not least, his marriage to the Queen tomorrow will spur him into action. We believe he will allow nothing to jeopardise his hold on power. The Lord Protector will betray himself. You are here to bear witness to that betrayal, to see a WarLock revealed.'

Now he had their undivided attention. They were horrified, a dozen protests forming on their lips. They huffed and fluffed and shook their braided beards in denial.

'The Queen, -' Spellskin began hopefully.

'Knows nothing of this,' the SDS Commander said

bluntly. 'This Warlock can touch minds...can read what lies in another man's thoughts and the Queen could not resist his dark arts. Her surprise and fear for the Earl will make Hugo confident that he is not yet discovered. You alone on the Black Isle are the only ones who know what will happen here tonight. The Warlock has men everywhere; the risk of betrayal is high. Gold buys many, ambition or fear, others. As you all know, Master Blackburr of the Wool Merchants Guild 'slipped' off his dragon pad when he opposed the law granting Hugo the right to breed Imperials. Others too...' Jakart left them to ponder the demise of their colleagues in a fresh light, and reach their own conclusions, while he returned to his men.

Shedding his ceremonial Court robes, the SDS Commander revealed the same dark tunic of mottled black and grey as his companions. Motionless, Spellskin realised, they were hard to see in the candlelight, merely shadows on darker shadows. The only armour each wore was a vambrace that protected the lower arm and was inlaid with sophisticated battle runes. Each then retrieved their short battle staffs.

'My Lord, I do not understand why *we* are here,' the old man repeated querulously. 'We are none of us soldiers.' There was an enthusiastic nodding of heads. 'We cannot fight him. We would only hinder you.'

'You are all Guild Masters or Elders. All know you are to be trusted. You must bear witness.'

'But,' Spellskin coughed, still searching for a flaw in the plan. 'Do you not risk the Earl's life?'

'We do, else the bait might not be taken. It was

Rufus's own idea. And as to your safety, that is why you are to be escorted by four battlemages and myself. We will protect the Earl, and you, with our lives.'

'M-my Lord Commander,' Spellskin could not keep the tremble from his voice. 'I-' he sighed in resignation. 'If you insist.' He had no wish to go anywhere near a warlock, a figure of fear out of distant history books. But now that he thought about it, there was something about the Lord Protector that was unsettling. *An aura almost... ...cold....* He shivered as goose bumps ran up his back.

'How can you hide us all? Not behind a curtain or tapestry surely?' Matron Winifred asked doubtfully. 'Will we not be discovered?'

'Ah,' Jakart DeBessart bit back a fleeting smile. There was no tapestry in the palace large enough to hide Winifred Needlespin behind! 'The palace has many hidden passages. It is through them that I will lead you till we come to the royal chambers. Like many others it is hung with a hunting tapestry, woven of many woodland creatures and birds. Their eyes are peepholes.' He turned back to his men.

'Grimbold and Harken, your sole task is to protect our guests.' He was turning to go, when a soldier was admitted by the guards posted outside.

'My Lord...Lord Commander, it is urgent from Sir Gharad...' the Constable's Captain pressed a crumpled paper into Jakart DeBessart's hand.

'Abyss below!' the SDS Commander swore softly, as he read it beneath the gutting candle light. 'He *is* stacking the odds in his favour. The man is cunning; he has replaced the Queen's Guard on the battlements and on patrol with his own men. But we, too, planned for just such a turn of events.' DeBessart pressed a rune set in his arm vambrace and spoke softly. 'Scramble... scramble... scramble... Dark Nights, take the castle. Guards are hostile.'

'Masters, no sound,' Jakart warned a final time. 'No sound at all or it may be the death of you, of us, and all we hold dear. Her Majesty is depending upon us to reveal the truth of the matter. I will shed just enough light for you to see your path. Once close all light must be extinguished. When I signal, take your place behind the eye holes.'

He pressed the wooden wainscoting. With a soft click, a door swung open.

CHAPTER TEN

The Long Wait

'What is happening? Why have they not come out?' Caitlin was pacing up and down in her ante-chamber, followed by a nervous gaggle of ladies-in-waiting who nearly collided with her as she turned.

'Back!' Armelia hissed protectively. 'The Queen needs space to breathe!' *How am I going to keep her safe if they storm the castle? What if Lord Hugo forces her with him?* She glanced to where the Earl supposedly lay at death's door. *How do you stop a warlock?*

'I *must* go to him!' Caitlin whispered. 'I could not bear him to die without me by his side.'

How Armelia longed to tell her Queen that he would not die, that it was all a ruse, a horribly dangerous ruse; one that might go wrong in so many ways. *I wish I were like Quenelda, strong, I can only cast silly dream spells and charms...how can I possibly protect Caitlin?* Sudden realisation came to her. *I must learn! I must be like Quenelda! Be brave.*

'Come,' the Queen beckoned Armelia. The pair swept

through the royal apartments to where the Earl was being tended. As she approached the outer door, two of the SDS knights posted by Jakart DeBessart barred her path.

'Majesty', Guy DeBessart went down on one knee but kept the door blocked with his good hand. 'My father's orders; we cannot admit you on fear of banishment. It is too dangerous for you until a nexus is cast.'

Sighing, Caitlin laid a hand gently on the young man's head. 'Thank you for your loyal service.' 'Surely,' she whispered to Armelia. 'They will let me in soon?' She turned away biting back tears.

But the festivities below had finally finished before the Queen's own surgeon came out. He looked grave. 'Majesty,' he said gently, softly for her ears only, ignoring the Lord Protector. 'Caitlin. It is indeed the Black Death. Rufus is blind and weak, and his power has gone....we have cocooned him in a healing nexus so that you may safely see him now. But I fear the worst...'

His power is broken! The Lord Protector's thought was full of glee.

The Queen went pale, nearly collapsing. Swiftly, in a heartbeat, the Lord Protector was there stopping her fall, shoving Armelia roughly out of the way. *Why, you are trembling, my dear...what a pity it is too late for him...and you...* 'Come, my dear, a short time only and then you must rest. Tomorrow is our wedding day.'

They stood looking down at the man who had once been the greatest soldier in the Kingdom and wept at the ruin of his face and arm, the hesitant rise and fall of his chest. Overcome, the Queen fainted.

'Take her to her chambers!' the Lord Protector snapped, as Armelia struggled to bring Caitlin to her feet. 'Her Majesty needs rest,' he added more gently to his son's wife. It would not do to betray himself now! 'I do not want her upset so.'

He spoke softly to his wife to be. 'Caitlin, I shall watch over the Earl tonight, my dear.' He spoke to her as his eyes roved over those surrounding the Queen - none shifted their gaze. 'He is my oldest and dearest friend. I will call upon you the moment he regains consciousness.'

Amelia kept her head down, hiding the flush of fury that suffused her checks and would betray her, and the Queen with her.

'Wait,' the Queen pleaded, as her surgeon turned back to the sick man's chamber. 'Kieran, is there no chance?'

Her surgeon took a deep breath, but nodded slowly. 'Yes, Majesty. There is a chance. Few survive the Black Death, and if they do their wits have fled. And yet somehow the Earl has, for nigh on a year. The BoneCaster Mage who tended him has described a herb to us, a weed, with healing powers....with which they treated him; those who nursed him also took it and did not fall ill. We are searching the archives to see if some may be found.'

'Has he spoken?' the Queen asked.

'Majesty, yes,' the physician paused and frowned. 'But nothing that makes sense...'

The Lord Protector raised his eyebrows in query.

'He is delirious, my Lord, speaking of treachery...'

'Treachery?' The Lord Protector's heart slammed

against his chest.　He had to move swiftly.　*He must not regain consciousness.* 'It sounds,' he suggested sadly. 'As if Rufus's mind is also damaged by his injuries...'

CHAPTER ELEVEN

Crossed Legs and Chamber Pots

It was dark and musty in these old stone passageways. Spiders over the centuries had held sway here, and the ground was thick with dust and tiny brittle bodies. It was cool but not cold as the Guildsmen scuffed forwards through the stone heart of the castle, hand on the shoulder of the one in front, the faint light from the SDS Commander's staff barely visible up ahead. Occasionally chinks of light crept through crumbling masonry, lighting their way.

Finally the murmur of many voices was heard growing clearer and louder, as they crept forwards towards the royal apartments. They had passed by three outer chambers when what little light shone from the Commander's staff was extinguished and they passed into a fourth, far quieter, with only the murmur of the Queen's surgeon and the unmistakable imperious voice of the Lord Protector to be heard. As their eyes adjusted, the reluctant spies found themselves in a small chamber, dimly lit by dozens of tiny twin shafts of light from the chamber beyond. The SDS Commander turned, finger to lips, although only those next to him could see the gesture in the gloom. Now was the hard part: waiting; waiting to see if the Lord Protector would finally betray himself.

It was silent now; after all the noise and excitement, the royal apartments were strangely hushed and deserted as if the very castle held its breath. News of the deathly ill Earl's return had raged like dragonfire throughout the palace and already into the city beyond, passing from mouth to mouth, from tavern to tavern, exciting celebration and speculation in equal measure.

In the great hall below, and in the palace's countless chambers and corridors, crowded towers and turrets, nobles and lords, guests and guards, soldiers and servants had gathered in muted groups to wonder and gossip at this amazing twist of events. Many simply did not believe it.

'How can the Earl be alive after an entire year? Where has he been?'

'Where was he found?'

'I heard he is on his deathbed...'

'Will the wedding take place with the Earl so ill?'

'Will it take place at all? Rufus was Caitlin's Champion before the Lord Protector stepped up.'

No one had any answers, only more questions. But many fervent prayers for the Earl's recovery were whispered as they headed for bed. The Lord Protector was feared as much as he was revered.

Digby Wrinkleworth, elderly Master of the Tanners and Saddlers Guild fidgeted with his robes and tried not to think of chamber pots. Time ticked by. The surgeon had long since departed. The remaining apothecaries argued over whether to steep or infuse a herb. The Earl tossed and turned restlessly.

'The Queen has retired, you may do so also.' It wasn't an invitation. 'I will watch over my friend tonight. I will call you if needs be.'

'My Lord Protector,' the apothecaries and healers bowed and withdrew.

'Lads,' the plump serving girl fluttered her eyelids, 'some spiced beer. It's a cold night...Cook said this would warm your cockles....' This drew a laugh.

'But the boss said no drinking, he - '

'To hell with the boss, he ain't here is he?'

Having chased the Earl's daughter half way round the Seven Kingdoms, Knuckle Quarnack's men were exhausted, saddle sore and rebellious.

'Everyone else is drinking, why not us?'

' 'ere, Maisie, we'll help you with that,' another of the guards lifted the small cauldron and hung it over the brazier beneath the tower gate. It was going to be a long cold night filled with resentment.

'Cook said, t'aint fair everyone celebrating 'cept you. Here,' Maise called. 'Gaff, Fathrin, Dornoch, come on lads, no one will notice. 'elp yerselves, there's plenty more.'

Unhooking leather mugs from their belts the soldiers

gratefully dipped in.

'Brrr,' one of them shivered. 'This is good…warms me up!'

'That will be the cinnamon,' Maisie suggested. *Sweet dreams, boys!*

CHAPTER TWELVE

Operation WarLock

The cloaked Imperials glided in softly over the Black Isle, banking as they spiralled down. Ten thousand lights and lanterns flickering below reflected the winking stars in the clear night sky. You could see the vampires with the naked eye as they patrolled about the brightly lit palace. If they were fortunate there would be no other cloaked Imperials nearby, or the risk of collision was real, but then the Lord Protector was not expecting trouble; so no one was looking skywards.

The lead navigator checked his instruments, the image of hot reds dots on a dark background merging with the outline of the palace on his helmet mounted monocular display. 'Forty guards, thirty on perimeter, two on each tower. Ten vampires on patrol; altitude five hundred strides.'

'Take them down,' the calm voice ordered over helmet coms. 'Lethal force sanctioned.'

The pilot leading the attack arrow of three Imperials flipped down his heads-up display and a defensive nexus flared into view. The glowing green net shifted and reformed into a never ending pattern of energy: both subtle and skilled. It was the pilot's first experience of chaotic magic.

'Complex...this is going to be tricky...' The pilot depressed several runes on his arm vambrace, then quickly pressed a combination cartouche on his witchwood chair. 'Level four and it's good, but there is a weak point. Softly, softly, does it.'

Black filaments fell through the air. Where they made contact with the defensive net the green vanished; the black sizzled along the threads, eating them up. Battle runes flared and then the net winked out.

'Archers ready,' the second Imperial came in low and slow. The elven archers of the Queen's Own Silver Arrows on its flanks took out all ten vampire guards in the first pass. Swiftly corralling the riderless dragons and leading them away, those of the vampire Highland Black Watch took their place. Then the second wave of Imperials glided down over key targets all over the Black Isle: the palace, the Guild, the Observatory, the Watch and the harbours.

'Get ready...' Sergeant Major Badgerlock strode down the lines of BoneCrackers, checking the cleats of their abseiling lines held fast. A rune embedded in the Imperial's spinal plates winked green.

'Right lads, go... go... go!' Badgerlock urged them down. Forty BoneCrackers and four battlemages from the ShadowWraiths Regiment rappelled down onto the palace roof. They had barely touched the steep gabled crenellations than their Imperial was past, only a faint whisper to mark its passing. The guards on the castle battlements fell without a sound. Eased to the ground by their silent assailants, their cloaks and helmets were removed and exchanged. The perimeter guard resumed its watch.

'Dark knight one ~ check'

'Dark knight two ~ check'

'Palace roof top secure.'

Moving swiftly, the four battlemages supported by commandos penetrated the castle. Securing stairs and corridors they moved inwards towards the Queen's apartments, leaving teams at key tactical positions. Unfriendly guards were overcome; those who tried to fight were despatched with ruthless efficiency. The four battlemages met again about the Royal Chambers to cast a subtle complex nexus, the most powerful they could conjure without alerting the Lord Protector in the adjoining chamber. The Queen was now protected.

All over the Black Isle, the same thing was happening; the City Watch, the crenellated City walls, the Guild, the barracks and stables, the harbours; one by one they all fell to the SDS and were secured.

CHAPTER THIRTEEN

A Truckle of Cheese

'Right, lads, extra vigilant tonight. Just in case there's trouble. ' Knuckle Quarnack was doing the rounds of his men guarding the drawbridge and outer perimeter. For over four moons he'd been pursuing the Earl's daughter and Dragon Master with only one aim in mind: to let them find the Earl and then kill them all. He had failed – miserably. After the battle at the Smoking Fort it had taken two days for him and what remained of his men to slip through the SDS cordon around the Sorcerers Glen, and only then by splitting up and joining the entourages of latecomers for the royal wedding. He had arrived to learn that the Earl was safe on Dragon Isle, ending his fervent hopes that the Dragon Lord had been killed during Galtekerion's attack.

Unfortunately, the Lord Hugo Mandrake was not a forgiving man. Knuckle's orders were clear: the Earl would die tonight on the eve of the wedding. That had meant hastily switching the Queen's Guard on watch about the castle with the Lord Protector's own chosen men, on the Queen's orders of course. No one, least of all the Queen knew, and the royal household had far too many tasks to prepare for the wedding to pay attention to who walked the battlements. But with a number of his men missing or injured, and some who had not made it through the cordon, Knuckle was overstretched and his men not at all happy. He glanced up to where the Lord Protector's escort of vampire dragons were circling overhead, and he could see his master's men pacing the battlements. One of them waved in answer to his call. He shook his head. His men would have little to do before they were relieved on the morrow to finally join the celebrations. Perhaps the wedding would soften his master's displeasure.

' 'Ow about the Cork 'n Cask?' Gaff protested, trying to stifle a tell-tale burp. 'It's so cold and we was going to join in the celebrations!'

'Well you're not now, unless you want to tell 'is Lordship why not?'

'But why? Why's the Queen's Guard allowed and we're not?'

'Haven't you heard?' Knuckle scratched irritably at a rash of scale-mite bites. 'The Earl's been found! He's here in the palace.'

'The Earl's been found?' Gaff was baffled. 'Didn't know he'd been lost! Ow! What was that for?'

'You dunderhead!' Knuckle swore. 'Not the Earl Darcy! The *lost* Earl; the one we've been chasing these past four moons!! The Earl Rufus! And it could mean trouble, big trouble. H-'

Eyes crossing, Gaff suddenly keeled over with an alcoholic burp.

'You're reeking!' Knuckle accused him, grabbing him by the collar. 'I said **no** drink tonight! Where'd you get drink?'

'Jussomespicedbeer, Cap'in,' Gaff slurred, eyes crossed. 'Kitchen gave us, cause sooooooo cold t – '

Two more men folded.

'Something don't feel right!' Knuckle ran about the moat to the parade ground and barracks. More of his men were slumped on the ground. Rounding up all who were still capable of standing, he headed for the kitchens.

Agnes was considering the smoked joints of ham on a trestle table when hobnailed boots clattered on the flagstones and cries of alarm grew closer. Dishes crashed to the floor in the outer pantries. The doors were flung open and the Lord Protector's tall thin Dragon Master entered, sword in hand, eyes menacing as they swept the scene in front of him. The kitchen was as hot as the weather outside was cold. Steam rose in billows from the sinks. Nothing looked untoward but something felt wrong. You didn't survive in the Gutters without an instinct for survival.

'Come on, lads.' Knuckle barged through, laying about him with the hilt of his sword to clear his path. 'Let's get to 'is Lordship. Four of you wait here and keep an eye on this lot.'

Agnes stepped to block his way as the Dragon Master roughly knocked a young maid to the floor who began crying; one of Agnes's multitudinous daughters-in-law.

'Hungry are we, boys, who wants some food?' Agnes balanced a ham in her large hands.

'Out of the way, you old baggage!'

'Old baggage, is it? You need taught some manners.' With that Agnes swung the smoked ham.

'Ufffh!!' The impact carried the Dragon Master full across the trestle table and onto the ovens. With a scream and a hiss he rolled off, where he was finished off with a smoked sausage by one of the spit boys. His men fared little better,

Clang! Ding!

Rolling pins dented helmets. A soldier was knocked clean out by a ten pound salmon, leaving a fishy red welt on his face and a mouthful of scales.

'Oww, get it off!' another cried as an angry lobster took its revenge for being stuck in a pan. Well aimed cheddar truckles felled three more, and a sauce pan finished off the last two. Two late arrivals screamed as a pot of boiling soup doused them as they barrelled into the kitchen. Weapons discarded, turning on their heels, they barrelled out even faster to the frozen water pump.

'There we go!' Agnes dusted off her hands with satisfaction. 'Truss 'em up like chickens and hang them in the larder where they can do no more mischief!'

CHAPTER FOURTEEN

A WarLock Unmasked

The bell struck the hour of the howling wolf. Still the Lord Protector made no move, save to stoke the dying fire. The dwindling moons fell below the mountains and a cold breeze began to blow.

How much did Rufus remember? He must learn that before the Earl died; learn if there were others who knew. Curse Bearhugger and his troop of children!

Doubt also began to gnaw at Jarkart DeBessart. *What if they were all wrong? What if the Earl's wits had deserted him and the Lord Protector was no more than he seemed? And Quenelda...? A gifted but troubled young girl with a vivid imagination? But no, no ordinary child could do what she had done...could enter the HeartRock...command battledragons...it was just so hard to believe in ancient legends...*

The Lord Protector barely moved his fingers, words silently forming on his tongue. Power, delicately cast, rippled out to encompass the west wing of the palace. Outside in the corridor, the Queen's guards became still as if carved of stone. Eyes gazed unseeingly, their chests barely rising and falling, they stood as rigid as their spears. Only the SDS battlemages and those under their protection remained free to move. DeBessart tensed, his soldier's instinct warning him something elusive had changed. Perhaps the Earl had also felt it because he groaned and shifted restlessly. Then his eyes opened.

So it is true, the Lord Protector exalted. *He is blind!*

'So, you survived, Rufus. How did you manage that?'

'Hugo?' The voice was feeble and slurred. His left hand on the cover moved weakly, searching blindly. 'Hugo, old friend? It is good to be home at long last...'

'Sadly not for long...old friend...'

Jakart DeBessart raised his staff and signalled his coterie to ready themselves. The guildsmen and women moved reluctantly to the spy holes inset into the thick stone, looking out through the eyes of deer and wolves and unicorns.

'But first,' the Lord Protector continued softly. 'Let me see what you know and what you have done...' Slowly, silently, the Lord Protector rose to his feet. In the near dark his eyes flared green before dying back to embers, making Spellskin draw back in horror with a stifled gasp.

'What a pity that you died of your wounds and did not live to see me crowned King.' The Lord Protector bent over the Earl who suddenly lashed out with the pummel of his sword hidden beneath the blankets, causing the Lord Protector to stumble back against the wall in surprise, raising a hand to bloodied lips and a broken cheek bone.

Without pausing to open the hidden door Jakart DeBessart unleashed a lance of light that streamed hotly from his staff. No stunning spell this, but powerful battlemagic, a bolt designed to kill. It annihilated the heavy wooden panelling behind the tapestry, striking the Lord Protector full in the chest and spinning him about. As he slammed into the wall, a stream of virulent magic arced from the WarLock's fingers to where DeBessart was leaping into the room through the burning remnants of the tapestry, two battlemages at his heels. Raising his staff, the SDS Commander deflected the attack which slammed into the damaged wall. Guildsmen ducked and screamed as burning splinters and broken stone peppered them, and then the percussion of the spell rebounded in the chamber to blow the door and windows out. Down the corridor, the BoneCrackers held in readiness raced forwards behind their battlemages.

The Lord Protector raised his hand and a green latticework of crackling power streamed from his fingertips striking the chamber at random. The battlemage still guarding the Guildsmen swiftly cast a shield which took the brunt of the spell; but Spellskin screamed as a stray fiery kiss struck him in the face, shattering tooth and bone. Those Guildsmen still standing behind the now dubious protection of the wall tried to flee through the secret passageways in all directions as death erupted about them.

'To the Earl!' Jakart shouted as commandos now poured into the chamber over the rubble of the collapsed wall. 'Protect the Earl!' he repeated as he ducked beneath the Lord Protector's guard to strike him with a sword sheathed in sorcery. It buckled as if the WarLock were made from stone.

Behind the SDS Commander, the Earl, protected by battlemages and a knot of soldiers with interlocked raised shields was moving towards the corridor. Enraged at seeing his prey escaping, the WarLlock struck. The corridor collapsed, crushing several soldiers and trapping one. Explosions continued to bracket them as they fled, and five BoneCrackers died. Then the Earl was passed into the care of three more battlemages who cast a nexus about him. He vanished from the WarLock's awareness.

The air stank of burnt tin and scorched stone as the remaining Guildsmen struggled to their feet. Stumbling over the rubble, Spellskin felt as if wool plugged his ears as he hastened after the Earl to where a battlemage cast a protective net about the old man. Tapestries had caught fire, the flame runneling up to the wooden beams which were rapidly blackening. Silhouetted against the flames, the SDS Commander and Lord Protector's staffs struck and pulsed with light, raising coruscating showers of magic.

As two battlemages converged on him, the Lord Protector raised his hand and the torches gutted and went out. An aura of dark power bloomed about him. Then the air was alive with icy winds. A roiling darkness churned in the small chamber and bone chilling ferns of frost climbed the walls.

'Fools!' the WarLock stood his ground. Ducking

DeBessart's strike, he counter attacked, and one of the battlemages died. Power rippled about the WarLock spreading through the stone bones of the palace. 'Do you truly think your petty magicks can stop me?' His voice changed, became harsh, grating on the ears of everyone in the chamber, setting teeth on edge. The chandelier shattered. 'I have the power of chaos at my fingertips… you cannot kill me. I am death itself!' His voice rose, uttering words not heard in a thousand years….the fabric of the world ripped, and a black hole began to form.

Struggling to his feet, blood pouring from ears and nose, the SDS Commander's staff glowed brightly in the darkness as he fired bolt after bolt at the Lord Protector, but they were simply swallowed by the growing darkness. The Lord Protector vanished into the black hole. There was a clap like thunder as the hole collapsed, punching those still standing to the floor. The concussion thundered through the castle wing. Stone rippled and shifted. The castle rocked as its stone bones fractured and split. It sounded like the very earth was groaning, and then there was silence.

CHAPTER FIFTEEN

Today I Marry a Man

The clatter of shod unicorn hooves on the cobbles was unnaturally loud in the frigid air of early morning. But thankfully, Darcy thought, as he nudged his pedigree mare, Magic of the Moon, forwards, the overnight storm had abated. He didn't want this wonderful pageant and his prominent role in it obscured by inclement weather! Thunder had struck the city last night with such deafening clarity dozens of windows had shattered, and dust still hung where part of the castle had been tumbled by forks of green lightning.

Although the sun had yet to breast the mountains the crystal blue of the sky gleamed off the polished serpent of silver and steel as the Gold and Royals and the 1st Dragoons of the Household Cavalry wound their way from the Unicorn Guard Stables through the wide boulevards to the palace. The coats of the golden unicorns shone, their dappled hides rippling as they walked, tails and manes combed out; both ivory horns, the long and the short, polished and perfect. The cavalrymen themselves wore soft cream breeches, braided jackets of white fashionably worn over one shoulder and heavily embroidered, silver breastplates and high helmets topped with golden unicorn hair that swayed as their mounts walked. Every thirty paces a unicorn peeled off to take up position along the route.

'Fooorm Lines!' At Darcy's command the unicorns swung neatly round in ranks of four to line up on either side of the drawbridge. And then Darcy's eyes caught movement on the Winter Tower as a breeze lifted the standard that hung there: the silver on black wolf's paw sigil of the DeWinters. It had not flown since the Earl Rufus' death, on the orders of the Queen. Darcy smiled. She had finally relented and acknowledged him as Earl!

The great oak doors across the moat were opened to admit him as he clattered over the drawbridge. Only then did he realise that there was no sight of his father the Lord Protector's men; instead, BoneCrackers and Mountain Rangers wearing battle and not parade armour were posted everywhere. Angrily, he wondered who had permitted this to happen. As he climbed up the great staircase, his unicorn tossing her head, his sense of disquiet grew. Where were his father's men?

But the hall ahead was packed just as it should be. Courtiers and Guildsmen, high ranking SDS officers, Dragon Lords, dwarf Chieftains and Bone Casters, elven Princes and lords, troll Thanes, and great lords were assembled in their ceremonial finery. As Darcy entered the great hall with its soaring pillars, statues and ancient flags, silence fell. Uneasily he nudged his unicorn forwards. Scented candles could not quite mask the strange smell of scorched stone and...spent magic?

The Queen sat on her throne. Dressed in cream brocade stitched with gold thread and dragon pearls, a simple gold circlet about her hair, she was beautiful and pale, her eyes afire. Black armoured SDS Dragon Lords, including Jakart DeBessart and his son Guy, Darcy's one time companion stood about her, along with her ladies-in-waiting. Armelia sat on the steps to the throne; she looked tired but smiled at him. She was very lovely. Guy's gaze was hostile and hard.

'Majesty.'

'My Lord Darcy,' the Queen acknowledged his salute as the young Earl brought the pommel of his sword up to his face before dropping his guard.

'Will you wed today?' Darcy asked the traditional words.

'I will wed the man who will keep my kingdoms safe; who will lead my armies and command the SDS; who will defend us from all threats, both within and without the Seven Kingdoms.'

'My Queen,' Darcy smiled as he dismounted and knelt as tradition demanded. It was as his father Hugo Mandrake had promised; for now, one day, the Seven Sea Kingdoms would also be his.

'It is his hand that I take you to.' He stepped forwards to take her hand and help her mount. As the Kingdom's greatest Earl, the honour was his.

'No, my Lord,' Queen Caitlin did not offer her hand. 'It is not the Lord Protector of whom I speak.'

'Not? Wh-?' *Did she say Lord? Not Earl?* Darcy felt a frisson of fear. Heard the confusion ripple out behind him.

A Dragon Lord stepped forwards. He was armoured in black from head to toe, SDS armour but different...it seemed... oddly familiar. As did the stance of the man who wore it, once tall but hunched as if in pain. Quieting his prancing unicorn, Darcy stared in confusion. *From Dragonsdome! That's where he had seen such ceremonial armour! In the ancient dome where the bones of Earls of old lay entombed with their mounts.* And that mask, it was said to belong to the first Dragon Lords of old who bonded with the mighty sea dragons, long since dead. His frowned deepened. *Why would his father don SDS armour? Unless he intended to command the SDS himself?*

The man reached up to remove the mask. A sigh swept round the packed hall as ladies and lords, soldiers and courtiers knelt. So the rumours *were* true! A lady near the throne fainted. Others cried the Earl Rufus's name out with wonder. But Darcy did not share their delight.

'N-no!' The Earl's son staggered backwards. 'It cannot be you! You died!'

Blind milky eyes turned towards the sound of his voice. It was his father! Scarred and burnt, and yet... and there behind the Earl, his sister moved forwards! Taller, pale, she had changed since he last saw her a year ago, before Bearhugger spirited her to Dragon Isle, no longer a child but on the cusp of becoming a young woman, but it was undeniably Quenelda. Her intent eyes were cold.

'No!' Darcy still denied it. '*I* am Earl, not you. You are

a cripple and blind! You were defeated!'

'No!' The voice was cold and flat. 'I was betrayed! *We* were betrayed...'

'Betrayed?'

'By the Lord Protector.'

Again a collective gasp ran round the hall followed by a babble of voices expressing incredulity, disbelief and anger, matched by denial and fear among those who owed Hugo Mandrake their allegiance.

'Lies,' Darcy shouted, his voice hungry with hatred. 'It's all lies. Your wits have fled you, old man! He rescued your precious dragons at the Howling Glen! How could he have betrayed you?'

'He betrayed Operation Crucible to the hobgoblins. He brought us down by wielding the Maelstrom. He is a WarLock and a traitor; his life, lands and titles are forfeit to the Crown.'

'That's a lie!'

'You say that again, and be you my son or no, I will have you clapped in irons. This is no game we play, Darcy. The future of our kingdom hangs by a thread! The Maelstrom is rising.'

But even as a shockwave of fear rippled out and rebounded amongst those watching, inside Darcy suddenly knew it to be true. Now all the turmoil of his childhood made sense and he didn't care! His father, his *true* father Hugo Mandrake, had given him the Earldom that was rightfully his! Hugo always cared for him, as this man had never done. Hugo understood him as this man had never done.

'He will deny your falsehoods,' the words choked in Darcy's throat. *Was everything lost? Dragonsdome was no longer his? All he wanted was suddenly ashes and dust.* The young man felt like weeping. *But where was his father, his true father, Hugo Mandrake?*

'The Lord Protector has fled,' Sir Gharad Mowbray stepped forwards towards the young man, pity in his eyes and voice. 'He's gone, Darcy,' the Constable reaffirmed softly for the young man's ears only. 'He fled! But not before he killed dozens and injured as many again who were trying to protect your father. There are many witnesses.' He gestured to where an elderly man swathed in bandages sat.

'I-I-I,' The Grand Master was in great pain and a childhood stutter had returned to plague him, as if a broken cheek and jaw were not enough. 'I b-bore witness to this truth.'

Darcy vaulted onto his mount which reared up. '**No!**' His face twisted in bitterness and grief as he tore the cavalry helmet from his head. Courtiers danced aside as it was flung down to tumble amongst them. 'No! I'm not your son!' He was determined to wound as he gathered up the reins, to inflict the pain he felt on all of them. 'I'm going to my *true* father! You'll pay for this!' His scornful glance swept over the Court. 'You'll *all* pay for this!' Wrenching the unicorn about he cruelly spurred it forwards and galloped from the hall as courtiers dived to get out of his way.

There was stunned silence as the sound of hoof beats faded. Helped by those about him, the Earl sat down in utter defeat. Once again his son had forsaken him instead of taking his rightful place by his father's side. Taking her father's trembling hand in her own, Quenelda was bewildered by the strength of her step-brother's hatred. *Why?*

Beside the Queen, Armelia was rooted to the spot. Deathly pale, she stared after her husband.

'Go to him,' the Queen urged softly. 'Go! My dear. He will need you now, more than ever before.'

Kicking off her ridiculous shoes and lifting her skirts, ignoring the curious and pitying glances that followed her from the hall, Armelia ran to find her husband.

Hurtling along a corridor, ignoring the stich in her side, Armelia followed the sounds of her husband's fury. Darcy had smashed things as he ran, their wreckage littering the floor as bewildered guards stared wide eyed as she ran past. Furniture and fittings were thrown about their chambers. Her husband was flinging doublets onto the four poster bed and shouting at his servants. Trying to unbuckle the breast plate, he cursed and swore and ripped it off. His cheeks were hot points of fury.

'Darcy, I - ' Armelia had no idea what she was going to say but she never had the chance.

'We're leaving...'

'Leaving? I don't understand. Where? Why?'

'North...to Roarkinch.'

Armelia had never heard of it. 'But why?'

'I'm no longer Earl,' he stared at her incredulously.

'But you will be...' she had about to say, still heir to

Dragonsdome...only...only he wasn't any more. Dragonsdome would once again fall to Quenelda.

'But – but I am the Queen's dear friend now!' she pleaded. 'We will keep our apartments here, and you are still Lord of Kinross, Atholl and the Orkney Isles. We still have Dragonsdome as our home! I am sure your father will want you to stay. He - '

'My father?' Darcy repeated softly.

She nodded, alarmed by the fury in his green eyes, by the strange tone of his voice.

'My father? That broken old man is not my father!'

'Darcy? You're not making sense. He is your father, yes he's injured, bu - '

'No! He's not my father! He never loved me. And he never loved my mother. He sent her away. He killed her!'

'Not?' Armelia was frightened now... 'I don't understand.'

'The Lord Protector...*He's* my father! My *true* father!'

'No!' Armelia clamped her hand over her open mouth in horror before she could stop herself. 'Hugo Mandrake is your *father*?'

Darcy's lip curled. 'Why? Don't you like him?'

'No! Yes, I - ' Armelia tried to cover her mistake. 'I'm – I had no idea. But where would we go?'

'To my father's lands. Beyond the Wall.'

'Beyond the – Darcy, I can't...my parents, the Queen...'

'Your husband?'

'Darcy, I *can't*. What could I do beyond the Wall?' She held her hands palm up in supplication, in appeal. 'The

Court and the Sorcerers Glen are my home!'

'Then stay!' He flung her away from him with a snarl. 'I don't need you. My dragon,' he shouted at a guard. 'Summon my Dragon Master! We fly to Dragonsdome then the north. Go!' He spat at her. 'I don't need you.'

CHAPTER SIXTEEN

For Whom the Bell Tolls

The bell was the first warning. Although distant, its urgency carried clearly over the uproar caused by the return of the Earl and the equally mysterious departure of his son.

Danger...danger...danger... the bells rang out. Fire was a threat to the whole city which was mostly made of wood; a city which was packed to its wooden rafters with refugees, and visitors for the royal wedding.

Heads were turning when the Earl suddenly stood. 'Dragonsdome! That's our belfry!' For a man used to command his voice carried clearly.

'Papa?' Quenelda began. 'Wh - ?'

There were shouts and cries as a dragon clattered to a barely controlled halt in the hall, flanks heaving, mouth foaming, sending courtiers and lords and ladies scattering in alarm for the second time in barely one bell. For a hopeful moment, Quenelda thought it might be her brother, but it was Chasing the Stars!

'Fire!' the fear in Root's voice cut through their cries.

'Fire!'

'Root!?' Quenelda was stunned as her esquire all but fell off Chasing the Stars screaming with pain as he knocked his broken arm. She ran to help him up. Like his beloved dragon the young gnome was gasping for breath..

'Q-Quenelda!' he looked stricken. 'Dragonsdome's on fire! We-we were in the roosts, and then we smelt the-e,' he gulped a breath. 'Smoke. Tangnost has roused everyone he could find, but it's already out of control. We flew here as fast as we could...'

'On fire?' Quenelda's heart stopped. .

'Quenelda!' the Earl commanded. 'To Stormcracker! Fly! Quenelda, go! I will follow!'

'The dragon pads!' Quenelda turned to her esquire and his exhausted mount. 'Root, bring her as swiftly as you can, you can fly back with us on Storm!" She turned, almost colliding with Armelia.

'Quenelda!' The Queen's lady-in-waiting timidly snagged her arm as the Earl's daughter tried to pass.

'Let me come with you,' Armelia begged. 'Let me come! It's my home too now. I must try and stop him leaving!'

Quenelda looked at her doubtfully, finally noticing the blotchy tear-stained face and the bare feet. Against her will, it tugged her heart: whatever had just passed between her step-brother and his wife, being married to Darcy could not be all she had dreamed of, and now those dreams were surely shattered. She nodded. 'I'm taking Stormcracker?' she warned.

Armelia nodded resolutely. Quenelda nodded her consent. 'Follow me, then!'

For the second time that morning, Armelia picked up her skirts and ran.

CHAPTER SEVENTEEN

These Boots are Made for Walking

As they stepped off the porting stone and out onto the frost rhymed gantries, Armelia quailed inside, her brave words choking in her throat. The dragon in front of them was...was the size of a mountain! As vast and black as the night. How could anyone control such a creature? How could Quenelda fly this huge dragon? As if the leviathan could hear her panicked thoughts, the massive head swung about and a huge golden eye, shot through with strands of red and copper, considered Armelia closely. The dragon's pungent breath enveloped her in a steaming crystal fog. She froze, barely daring to breathe. It lipped curiously at her, the surprisingly soft muzzle giving her a nudge. Armelia opened her mouth to scream but only a pitiful squeak emerged.

'Lift off! Lift off, Lift off!' Quenelda screamed at soldiers running up the pad steps. Turning back to grab Armelia, Quenelda hauled the petrified girl onto the flight pad, ignoring the squeals of pain as Armelia stubbed her toe.

'Home! Dragondome's on fire, Storm! You!' The Earl's daughter grabbed at a passing trooper. 'Give Lady Armelia your cloak and boots!' And then Quenelda was off, running up her dragon's wing. Armelia remained frozen to the spot as the trooper unquestioningly removed his boots and cloak.

'Lady?' The dwarf waved a hand in front of Armelia's eyes to no effect. Smothering a smile he kindly placed the cloak about her shaking shoulders, then placed the boots at her feet. Nodding gruffly, bare footed, he joined the other troopers streaming onto the pad. The metal grating beneath Armelia bounced as the last of them thundered up onto the huge dragon's back, but she barely noticed. Surely this was all a horrible dream? Darcy leaving her... *The battledragon... The boots...The fire...* her eyes fluttered....

Then she heard a familiar voice, and turning, saw a familiar face; Root, pulling a reluctant Chasing the Stars onto the flight deck by her reins. The mare was resisting stubbornly. So she wasn't the only one who was scared, somehow that made Armelia feel braver.

Hopping from foot to foot in her silk stockings on the freezing decking, Armelia still couldn't resist sniffing the offered boots. Wrinkling her nose she tried to lift one. It was so heavy she almost dropped it on her toes. Realising she was being watched with great amusement by the troopers, she sat and resolutely pulled on the buckled, steel toe- capped boots. They were four times too large, but warm. Holding her skirts so she didn't trip on them, Armelia clumped clumsily across the decking to join Root.

'Push, will you, Lady?' he asked desperately. 'I can't manage very well with one arm. She's petrified.'

'She's not the only one,' Armelia muttered. She warily contemplated the tail end of the dragon and the powerful tail switching back and forwards in agitation.

'Erm...how?' She peered about the mare's girth. 'Which bit?'

'Which bit what?'

'Which bit...do I, err, push?'

'Her rump. Heave! Come on, girl.'

Nothing happened. Root stepped to one side to see what Armelia was doing. She was flapping her hands about, her face a mask of incomprehension.

'Her bottom!' Root rolled his eyes in exasperation.

'Oh, right!' Derrière was the word young ladies used if they used it at all. Armelia considered the mare's 'bottom', then, putting her back into it, studded dwarf boots firmly gripping the mesh decking, she shoved with all her strength. The mare suddenly leapt forwards, but barely a moment too soon. With a clank and groan the anchor chains fell away and they began to rise slowly up until they could see dark roiling smoke rolling over the Black Isle like night.

'W-why don't we just take off from here?' Armelia asked, clutching the cloak about her. Her teeth were chattering from stress and cold.

'Because Storm's too big,' Root explained as he tethered Chasing the Stars, soothing her, blowing softly on her muzzle. 'The downdraft alone would destroy the nearby houses and lanes, would kill folk. Have you ever seen a swan taking off from a loch? The way they tread water before they take flight? Well, heavy dragons are the same. Storm would destroy everything in his path with his claws and tail until he got airborne!

Also,' he added as the pad rotated, 'they are only supposed to follow certain flight paths over the city.'

'Oh! Why?' Armelia asked, anything to keep talking. She wasn't remotely interested in the answer, but her jangled mind was desperately refusing to believe that Darcy had left without her, that her dream marriage was over. Half of her hoped to find him fighting the fire at Dragonsdome, the other half petrified of further rejection. Panic had her in its grip and her tongue was racing away with her.

Root looked at her sideways as he stroked his trembling dragon. 'Um, well, the bigger the dragon the bigger the...'

'The?' Armelia shook her head baffled

'Well, you know...'

'No,' Armelia frowned... 'No, I don't,' she insisted.

'Em,' Root remembered the unfortunate incident the first time he had met Armelia. 'Dung. The bigger the dragon the bigger the droppings, and well, Stormcracker could bury a house!'

'Oh! I never thought of that, I – ahhh!' Armelia clutched her hand to her chest as Stormcracker launched from the pad, leaving her stomach behind. Her knees buckled and she sat down with a cry. Concerned at her deathly pallor, unaware of what had happened at Court before his arrival, Root made her comfortable in the straw beside Chasing the Stars.

'Look after her?' he asked his dragon, 'Look after each other!' He gave the astounded Armelia a hug to demonstrate his point. 'I must go to Quenelda.'

The placid dragon turned slowly to consider the shaking girl struggling to hide her tears, and carefully, gently, invitingly, opened a wing.

CHAPTER EIGHTEEN

Dragonsdome

Quenelda wasted no time in gaining more height. They swept down, barely clearing towers and chimney pots, and flew straight as an arrow for Dragonsdome, slowly picking up speed and gathering scores of bunting strands and flags as they went, joining a stream of lesser dragons which were answering Dragonsdome's call for aid.

Ding dong… ding dong… the Guild bells were peeling out joyously. Hearing Dragonsdome's bells, thinking the wedding ceremony complete, the bell ringers were putting their backs into it. They had been practicing for a full moon and weren't going to put that to waste. Families spilled out of their houses, revellers out of the taverns to join the crowds surging forwards for a better view of the royal couple, blocking the narrow streets.

Down the dark Ink Grinders Alley in the old Quarter, in deserted Plum Lane near the Guild, behind the packed bonded Guild warehouses at the eastern docks, and at windmills all over the city, figures in dark cloaks that concealed their lord's badge of a striking adder merged into the holiday crowds. The Lord Protector would be well pleased with their work. He was a man who thought of every possibility. The bells of Dragonsdome were their cue to fire the city, a signal that their Lord was gone. Ampules of dragonfire had been stored in cellars, taverns and mills disguised as beer kegs and barrels of flour. Once ablaze nothing on earth could quench dragonfire. The WarLock's men slipped down steep wynds and alleys to the rowing boats tethered at the harbour piers, ready to row out to where their ship waited to take them to the Isle of Midges, to await their master's word.

Stormcracker plunged into the roiling oily smoke. Visibility was reduced to scant strides. Emerging briefly into clear air over Dragonsdome's outer bailey walls and paddocks, where people were streaming towards the fire and dragons were milling in fear, they were swallowed again as they flew over the great hall. Suddenly there were flames all about the huge dragon, below them, beating hotly against Stormcracker's belly and sucking up the air.

A bonded warehouse of whisky in the east docks was the first to explode. Ribbons of fire arced out, landing in the crowded harbour and setting sails and rigging on fire. Flame spread swiftly to tarred planking and masts as crews abandoned their ships. Flaming comets rained down on surrounding warehouses of grain, as well as several windmills. The wind shifted, fanning the flames uphill. Beneath winter's freezing mantle the city was a tinderbox. Thinking this was all part of the spectacular fireworks displays to come, children chased the beautiful blue sparks that were floating like thistledown in springtime.

Reining Stormcracker in, Quenelda put the big dragon down in one of the paddocks closest to where Tangnost was, further panicking a dozen dale dragons that smashed through a fence and fled.

'It's already out of control,' Tangnost's voice was thick and rough from smoke. He knuckled his streaming eye. 'I've rounded up everyone still here and sent runners to fetch the rest back,' he pointed to where chains of leather buckets were being passed hand over hand from the huge courtyard well to the lower landing pads over the east wing. 'The other wells are all frozen.'

'Where did it start?'

'The Earl's chambers in the east wing, and also the library. The fire has climbed the oak panelling and the rafters are alight. It's too dangerous to go in any more. The roof will collapse soon.'

'What?' Quenelda frowned as Root and Armelia joined them. 'How can that be? A fire can't start in two places!'

'Not,' Tangnost coughed and spat. 'Not unless it was set.'

There was a look of utter horror on everyone's face.

'Set?' Quenelda asked.

'What do you mean?' Armelia asked. 'Do you mean

that this fire was started deliberately? Who would do such a thing?' But a horrible suspicion took root in her mind. *No! Darcy couldn't have! Could he? But where is he?*

Fire leapt from house to house. In the already crowded, narrow winding streets people were pouring out of smoking buildings, or leaning out of windows crying for help. Panic was building rapidly. Finally, too late, the City Watch bells were tolling out a warning. Fire! Fire! Fire! But by now there were so many they didn't know where to begin and the wells were frozen anyway.

'Fire! Fire! Fire!' The cry was taken up by the crowds, sowing panic, those behind shoving those in front. The old and young collapsed and were trampled. Away from the blue flames, the islanders were running and colliding and cursing in the confusion, desperate to put distance between themselves and the onrushing wall of dragonfire. Women rushed to gather their children, whilst soldiers cut a path to the safety of the loch. Those with dragons got away. Those without were left within the burning city walls.

Frost dragons scrambled from the palace Winter Guard were already skimming low over the dome that gave Dragonsdome palace its name, their breath riming everything in frost in an attempt to stop the fire spreading to the oldest parts of the castle. But it was too little, too late.

'Run,' the Dragon Master screamed. 'Run!' as part of a wall crumbled in a cloud of dust and debris. They stood there helpless as Dragonsdome fell into ruin.

'Root! Root!' It was Drumondir, anxiety and pity plain on her face as she dismounted a vampire. 'Root!' she called again, her voice drowned beneath the fire and the soldiers and servants gathered with buckets.

'Boy,' one of the men-at-arms pointed to where the BoneCaster was negotiating her way through the human chain of buckets. The youth turned from the crowded paddock wall with sudden dread. Drumondir had stayed on Dragon Isle to tend the wounded. Fear fluttered in his chest like a trapped moth.

'Q-Quester?'

'He is out of surgery but very ill. I think it best you go to him. They gave me a dragon to fetch you.'

Quenelda, seeing Root's sudden stillness ran over. 'Go,' she said. 'There's nothing more you can do here!' but already her friend was running towards the waiting dragon, stifling the sobs that welled up.

The entire east wing had collapsed and flames poured from scores of gaps in the roof. Somewhere the sun was setting but the choking black cloud made it impossible to know it.

'Where's Darcy?' Quenelda finally realised her step-brother was nowhere to be seen. She frowned. 'Where's Darcy?' she asked Armelia. 'Why isn't he helping?'

'He's gone,' Armelia said in a small voice, hating the fact that everyone was witness to her misery. 'He said if I wanted to stay, he would leave without me. I wouldn't go…I couldn't,' her voice broke as humiliation and misery overwhelmed her. 'He's gone!' Her shoulders shook. Looking helplessly at Tangnost for guidance Quenelda gathered the girl in an awkward hug, and tried to find the right words for Darcy's betrayal, but the worst had yet to come.

'Where?' Tangnost frowned and shook his head. 'Where would he go? Urquhart, Boarzall?'

'No,' Armelia's voice sank even lower, so that the Dragon Master had to strain to hear her reply against the hungry roar of the fire consuming the city. 'He said he was going north to his father. His true father.'

'What?' Tangnost and Quenelda said in unison.

CHAPTER NINETEEN

In the Name of the Father

By nightfall the fire lit the sky a lurid red glow and the glen was shrouded in fog. Countless fires still raged out of control. The heat given off was a tangible living thing so voracious that it had devoured half the city, the wind now driving the flames westward. By nightfall the City Watch and royal soldiers were pulling homes and shops down in a desperate attempt to create a break the flames could not leap.

The causeways were jammed with the carts of fleeing islanders, and Imperials were trying to airlift the trapped from the stricken city. The loch itself was crowded with rowing boats and Guild merchant galleons as the citizens fled the flames and chaos. The shores were crowded with the dispossessed and those killed by the freezing water.

The Earl closed his eyes. *Where is my son? I've not seen him in a year.*

'Papa?'

The Earl turned, sensitive to the hesitation in his daughter's voice, the reluctance in her footsteps.

'Goose?' Warmth and a great weariness tinged his welcome.

'Papa, Armelia...' she looked at the distraught girl... 'She has some...news. Darcy...' Quenelda bit her lip, wishing with all her heart she was not going to add to his grief.

'Come,' the Earl beckoned them both forwards to a settle by the fire.

'Oh, Papa...Tell him, Armelia.'

'Darcy,' Armelia took a deep breath and lifted her head defiantly; she had barely stopped weeping and her eyes were puffy and raw. 'H-he said - he said when he left, he was going t-to his real father...the...' she could hardly bear to say it. 'He says his true father is the Lord Pro...the WarLock.'

There was a silence. The two girls looked fearful.

'There's more,' Quenelda swallowed as Armelia shook her head, unable to speak. 'Armelia thinks it was Darcy,' she took a deep breath. 'Who ordered Dragonsdome to be burnt down. He said he was going there before flying for Roarkinch.'

'Thank you, Goose, Armelia,' the Earl said, his voice flat, drained of emotion. 'The pieces of the puzzle finally fall into place. What I fool I was.' He turned away, resting his head against the cold windowpane.

'Come on,' Quenelda said softy, steering Armelia out so they could not see her father's tears.

Chapter Twenty

The WarLock King

A storm was bearing down from the north, blotting out the hills. Soon it would be dark. One snow-clad valley looked much like any other in this weather and Darcy no longer knew if they were even flying in the right direction. Not used to being in the saddle for this long, or at this punishing pace, he was trembling with tension and exhaustion. Darcy's mount was also beginning to flag despite the spurs and whip he used so recklessly. The heat of his earlier anger had died into bewilderment at the sudden change in his fortunes, his onetime father's accusations ringing in his ears.

WarLock... a word sheathed in dread...*Hugo is a warlock...a warlock...a warlock... L*ike a beating heart the word kept thumping through his head. In his heart of hearts, Darcy had had suspicions, had sometimes felt a dark nimbus that hung about Hugo like a shadow on a bright day. *But to betray the SDS and destroy three regiments? To command the hobgoblins?* That he had never imagined even in his wildest dreams. But there was no going back. Feeling sick with fear, Darcy spurred his mount forwards.

The wind gusted and dark was beginning to fall. The snow was falling so fat and thickly it was all the young man could do to keep his exhausted dragon from crashing into the trees that appeared out of nowhere. Now visibility was down to a few strides and they would be forced to put down soon for their own safety, as they had the day before, when they were lucky to land near a peasant's croft. There they had found a fire and food. Poor fare, but food nonetheless. The farmer had tried to stop them eating any of the meagre provisions that would see his family through the winter, and had paid dearly for it. Unless they could find refuge, his bereaved family would starve. Three of his escort and his scout were missing or fled when Darcy put down on a slope and called his Dragon Master forwards.

'My Lord?' Felix DeLancy, one time Dragon Master at Dragonsdome had no idea where they were, or why he had been summoned on this headlong flight from the Sorcerers Glen. He had risked Darcy's wrath when he first refused to fire Dragonsdome before they fled, but threatened with being left behind, he had done it.

There would be no place for him at Dragonsdome now the Earl Rufus and his Shield, Tangnost Bearhugger, had returned. His inexperience and downright ineptitude had shown through; he had been wholly unable to control sabretooths let alone Imperials, and had earned the hatred of all those who were unfortunate to serve under him. His bravado was wafer thin. Now, finally, he thought he understood why Dragonsdome was fired. The SDS would have no time to follow; they would surely be too busy trying to rescue the palace?

'Find Dunsinain!' Darcy ordered his Dragon Master into the wilderness. 'Find the castle.'

As Felix turned to go, the ground shuddered and trees about them cracked and were crushed. Three Imperials materialised about the small group, giving Darcy a moment of raw fear until he realised they were strangely armoured and flew the striking adder standard of his father. On the Imperials' backs the small group made rapid headway despite the weather. In under a bell the huge castle appeared.

Dunsinain castle was ancient, built as the First Alliance moved north. It clung to the high crags of a long extinct volcano, once an eyrie of golden dragons. From its high perch, the castle looked down on the great flat flood plain of the river Forth. There were no military dragon pads here; they had to land where they could, so Darcy and his escort took off whilst the Imperials put down at the base of the crags.

Choosing the small outer bailey, cursing the treacherous cross winds that whistled about the walls, Darcy swung his hippogriff about and into the headwind, cursing as they were buffeted dangerously from side to side. With a vindictive jerk of the reins, Darcy forced the reluctant beast down. They landed badly; the hippogriff went down with a scream throwing him. Face flaming hotly, Darcy pushed away the offer of help from his Dragon Master as he struggled to his feet, furious that everyone had seen the mess he'd made. 'Unhand me, damn you!' he snapped. Pride, already battered, was in tatters, like the ragged cloak that whipped about him. 'Stay here,' he barked at Felix. 'Tend to the mounts.'

Sodden, frozen, relegated one more to esquire, Felix turned bitterly from his Lord.

A tall grizzled man, dressed in black bordered with fur, and with a heavy black chain of office inset with emeralds about his bony shoulders, introduced himself as Erskin, Dunsinain Castle's Constable. He wore armour beneath his robes and an old sword in a battered sheath.

'My Lord Prince,' Erskin bowed low. 'We have been expecting you.'

The hail was battering off his helmet. Darcy removed it so he could hear better. Servants ran to take it for him as the Constable guided him forwards into shelter. 'This way, please.'

Unadorned except for an infestation of gargoyles, the castle looked stark and unwelcoming from outside, but Darcy was agreeably surprised at the obvious wealth in the furnishings, the great fires that warmed the hall as they entered.

'This way, my Lord Prince. Your Lord father the King has been expecting you.'

'King?' Darcy checked in his stride, but the Constable continued, although he slowed until Darcy was at his side once again. 'The WarLock King, my Prince.'

The WarLock King? Darcy was stunned. It was the first time anyone had openly named his father either a

WarLock or a King! Hugo Mandrake was easily picked out by his height and a large group congregated about him at the far reaches of the huge hammerbeam hall. Soldiers and men-at-arms were everywhere, as were servants bearing hot mulled wine and bowls of steaming beef stew.

'So many?' Darcy wondered out loud. It was as large a gathering as the royal Court, and as Darcy passed they doffed caps and knelt. *They don't seem surprised to see me?* 'Who are all these people?'

'Lords and Thanes of Alba, Caledonia, Athol, Kyle, Stramash and Moray; loyal to your Lord father for many years... and to you.'

There were other lesser lords Darcy recognised from Court, and many Guildsmen in their opulent robes; mostly the woody hues of the Worshipful Company of Shipwrights, the white of the Carders and Canvas, the knotted, gold-tasselled robes of the Guild of Knot Tyers and many more. Darcy frowned. *All this needed to wage war by sea...? That makes no sense...*

They all bowed low as Darcy passed, just as artisans should, the haughty young man thought contemptuously. Too many merchants had got above their station in the Sorcerers Glen, marrying into nobility, lending money to noble houses impoverished by the war while they grew wealthy and fat.

'Darcy!' Hugo Mandrake, now the WarLock King, clasped his son warmly. 'Come, let's eat, you must be famished!'

Two bells later, Darcy sat back and closed his eyes. The hot food had filled him, the great fire behind had warmed him, the mellow wine relaxed him. He felt a hand on his arm. His father was standing over him.

'Go and rest, my son. I will come to you later.'

'What are you doing?' Darcy looked at the great table, now cleared of trenchers and food and covered in maps. Hard scarred men and nobles and war captains were bent over them. 'What's happening?'

'I am calling all my lords and captains of the Army of the North to war. We are mustering our troops. I intend to hit the SDS now while they are in disarray. You can join us once you are rested.'

'My fa-' Darcy shook his head to banish the cobwebs. 'The Earl and the SDS, they will be hot on my heels. They'll track us here! There are not enough men at arms. Not enough Imperials.'

'No, they won't,' the WarLock said calmly. 'You fired Dragonsdome as I instructed?' *If I could not find the Chronicles, neither will they now....and they will think it revenge...that I seek to delay them, which is true also...*

Darcy nodded mutely, the magnitude of what he had done finally catching up with him. He felt confused, elated, frightened, all at once.

'That was the signal for my men on the Black Isle to fire the city.'

'What?' Darcy was shocked, stunned by his father's ruthlessness. 'But it's packed for the weddi-.' Too late he remembered whose wedding it was. And was firing the city any worse than firing Dragonsdome?

'Exactly,' the Warlock King calmly agreed. 'The Glen and City are crowded. They will have more than enough to do to bring the fire and the populace under control – if they can. Dragonfire will not stop until it has devoured their city; there will be chaos and food riots. The warehouses and mills were fired first; now they'll starve. They are weak, ready to fall.'

'You'll be shown to your chambers. Rest. I will come later.' He turned back to his lords and captains.

It was nearly the witching hour before the WarLock finally sought out his son. He found Darcy brooding before the fire in the upper chamber of the keep. Empty wine flasks littered the rushes, and broken glass littered the hearth. The boy was hopelessly drunk.

'I see you have been celebrating.'

'Celebrating? It's all gone,' Darcy raged, angry at the tears that streamed down his face. 'It's all gone!'

'What? You miss Dragonsdome?'

'Of course!' Darcy rounded on him. 'Everything! Dragonsdome was finally mine!' He thumped his chest. 'The Court...the Black Isle, my friends... Armelia...' his voice cracked with bitterness and rage. 'She wouldn't come with me. She said the Queen needed her! She stayed! My own wife!'

'Take another wife! We are building a new kingdom here in the north.....a new dynasty! Here you are a prince...you are my son and heir. Is that not enough? There will be plenty willing brides to choose from at court. Nobles are flocking to join us.

As to friends, we have many who have been waiting for this moment, who have secretly been loyal to me, and they have been summoned here. Indeed one has just arrived. Come.'

Descending into the great hall, the WarLock motioned to where men were removing sodden travelling cloaks and helmets. With a rush of hope Darcy recognised the tall thin faced, dark haired man with an eye patch who turned to stride across the hall before kneeling.

'Lord Grimson,' the Chamberlain announced. 'And the Lord Rupert, his son.'

'Rupert!' Darcy embraced one of his childhood friends with relief and delight as more young men entered the hall on Rupert's heels, including Gwyhelm and Euan, two of Quester's five older brothers and Cameron Woodville, son of one of the oldest noble houses whose lands lay far to the south, on the border of the Old Kingdom.

'The kernel of your Household Guard,' Darcy's father told him.

Rupert stood back, holding Darcy at arm's length. 'My father chose to fight for yours long ago. He is loyal to the WarLock King, as I am to you. There are many others gathering their men at arms to come north. A few are staying behind who will continue to hide their true allegiance to your father.'

'W-when you left, Dragonsdome. Was-was it-?'

'Up in flames,' Rupert confirmed. 'And half the city too.'

'And Guy? Will he be coming?'

'No, he fights for the SDS like his father; he's already

flying Imperials out of Dragon Isle – I haven't seen him in moons. But Aubrey and Dickon are coming!'

'My father fights for Dragon Isle, too,' Cameron admitted reluctantly. 'He's disowned me. I have nothing. I'm penniless.'

'Don't worry,' Darcy grinned, life was beginning to return to normal with his friends about him. *Damn Dragonsdome and the Earl and Quenelda; let them rise from the smoking ruins!* 'There are castles out there for the taking and wealthy estates ripe for the picking.'

They clasped hands. 'Darcy's Devils will ride again!'

CHAPTER TWENTY-ONE

Up in Smoke

Dragonsdome was gone.

Only the ancient Elder-built Keep and Dome, both bound with sorcery, still stood. Room after room was a hollow shell open to the sky. In many places masonry was still too hot to touch. A dense choking yellow fog hung over the entire city making it impossible to see more than a few strides, and difficult to breathe.

'How *could* he?' Finally Quenelda's tears came. They had gone through so much to bring her father home, to rebuild their family, and now home was in ruins because of Darcy.

'He killed Two Gulps and You're Gone and now he's destroyed Dragonsdome. I hate him!' she clenched her fist in fury.

There was a rumble and the ground shook. All about her everyone staggered or fell, save for Stormcracker with the Earl on his back, who lifted his wings and sprang into the air. The north wall of the library shook then wobbled and came crashing down, raising a fresh cloud of debris and soot.

Tangnost climbed to his feet white faced, 'What was that?'

'Quenelda,' Drumondir began. 'Y-'

*You do not control your anger...*Stormcracker admonished, beating Drumondir's protestation. *That is dangerous...you could kill those you love around you...you must shed your juvenile skin and become strong and wise...*

But I don't know how! I -

Then you must learn, Goose. You are no longer a child and this is no game you play. You are my heir, and if you are to become a Dragon Lord you must leave childish emotions behind...Drumondir will be your tutor, will teach you control...

Papa! Quenelda turned wide eyed to her father in wonder, wiping her nose with the back of her hand. *You can hear me! Oh, Papa!* A huge smile broke through the tears.

'What has happened?' Drumondir turned from father to daughter sensing a change but not understanding quite what it was.

'Papa,' Quenelda smiled. 'Papa can talk like a dragon in my head! He can talk to me now, too, not just through Stormcracker!' and as she ran up, the huge battledragon reached down to gently lift her up to her father. 'Oh, Papa! Papa! I'm not alone any more!'

'You were never alone, Goose,' her father smiled as his daughter flung herself about his neck. 'Armies will follow you.'

The wood-burning stove in Tangnost's quarters burned cherry red, *just like Dragonsdome*, Quenelda thought bitterly. For once, being here above the domestic roosts did not bring the peace and comfort it used to when Dragonsdome's esquires and roost hands gathered to hear stories in the evening. The Dragon Master himself was busy caring for the distressed dragons they had managed to round up; stabling, doctoring and feeding them, but everything was in desperately short supply.

Already there were riots and looting and half Dragonsdome's men-at-arms were deployed guarding the estate. What could be salvaged was being flown to Crannock Palace on the southern shores of the loch and stored in the vast tunnels beneath the Cauldron jousting amphitheatre, where the Winter Jousts had been held in happier times.

'Child,' Drumondir said gently, taking Quenelda's hand, mindful of the loss that was still raw, but knowing that lessons had to be learnt too. 'What did you learn today?' But Quenelda was in no mood for lessons. Her childhood home, the birthplace of the First Alliance between men and dragons lay in smouldering ruins!

'I hate him,' Quenelda balled her fists at her sides, before wiping away treacherous tears. 'How could he? Dragonsdome's gone!'

'Many have their dreams taken from them. It is only then that our true worth can be measured. Those who appear to have everything may have nothing they value; those who have nothing may have love that is priceless.'

'What do you mean?' Quenelda couldn't think straight,

let alone untangle puzzles. 'Who?'

'Your brother, for one.'

'Darcy? But he had everything!'

'Yes and no. I do not know him, but I believe from what you have told me he never wanted the responsibilities that fell upon his shoulders. He loved the glamour and romance of the Court did you not say? He is no soldier in a world where he must be one. Tangnost said he cannot fly well.....but he clearly was a good horseman, and could fight with a sword. He had everything *you* want, but did he have anything he wanted? Perhaps you had everything he wanted. I feel sorry for him; wherever he is, do you think he is truly happy tonight? Don't rush to condemn others. Life is not always as it seems.'

'Well I don't care!' Quenelda said rebelliously. 'I hate him. He destroyed my dragon and Dragonsdome! Nothing can excuse that.'

'Did I say it should, child? I am only pointing out that your path and his are similar in many ways. You want to fight with the SDS and are condemned; he wanted to stay at Court and was condemned. Who is right and who is wrong? Both of you seek to be different from the expectations laid on you at birth.'

Quenelda was silent a while, thinking. 'It's not the same,' she offered eventually. 'He hurts people deliberately. And...I - . ' '- have hurt people accidentally. Is one better than the other for those who have lost a loved one by your hand?' Grudgingly, Quenelda acknowledged the truth of it, and shook her head.

CHAPTER TWENTY-TWO

The HeartRock

The Imperial took off, leaving Drumondir and Quenelda behind; with the Black Isle in chaos, the Earl had sent his daughter back to the safety of Dragon Isle, under the care of the BoneCaster. In any event it was here that Drumondir believed the great Earth Wyrm of the Ice Clan sagas would reveal herself to guide the young Dragon Whisperer, and she was eager to explore the wonders of the HeartRock.

They had passed a steady stream of Imperials carrying emergency supplies and engineers to the stricken city. Tangnost had remained behind, organising repairs as best he could. The thick column of smoke which still shrouded the city, hiding its high towers and domes, could be seen beyond the Old Wall.

Hearing Quenelda's call, Two Gulps arrived. Almost tripping up over his huge feet, he bounded over one paddock wall and then straight through a second in his thoughtless haste to greet them. He was rested and had been well fed by admirers after the story of his flight from the Smoking Fort with Quenelda had spread. He enveloped Quenelda in a blaze of fire, forcing Drumondir to stand back hastily. Dragon Lords, esquires, academics, all stopped and stared. So the tales were true! Soldiers returning from the battlefield who had shared what they had seen had been scoffed at for telling stories. But the girl and dragon's reunion was witnessed by scores this time, and word rapidly spread through the island.

It is time...

Time...? Hugging her juvenile, Quenelda soaked up the warmth of his flame, drinking in his energy.

To spread your wings...can you not hear it?

Quenelda tilted her head, her eyes growing distant then widening in sudden recognition. 'I thought I dreamt it, it's like a song that slips away when I wake. It's the HeartRock... it's calling to me. It was faint but it's much stronger now.'

Drumondir nodded. She was not surprised.

'You hear it too?'

The BoneCaster nodded. 'Only faintly. I too have heard snatches in my sleep.'

*It is time...*Two Gulps repeated, *to shed your juvenile skin for harder scales, to spread your wings and fly...to grow...to learn...to lead...*

'It's time, child,' Drumondir echoed Two Gulp's unspoken conversation. 'Your inner dragon is waking from a long sleep. You were born to become a Dragon Whisperer, to inherit a great gift, great power. I believe that the HeartRock will reveal that inner soul to you and to what purpose you have inherited it.'

As they approached, Drumondir felt the HeartRock shiver with recognition. *It's been waiting for her* the BoneCaster marvelled. This time the carved stone wall vanished before Quenelda had even crossed the bridge that spanned the bottomless void below. By then both could clearly hear the sweet alluring dragonsong that beckoned Quenelda home.

But the Earl's daughter hesitated at the threshold, knowing that with her next step her world would change beyond imagining. And suddenly she was a young girl with only thirteen winters and was afraid of what was to come.

'Courage, child,' Drumondir encouraged her. 'This place is your sanctuary, it will not harm you, nor, I think, will it harm me or any under your protection. And I am here with you always, for I too have been waiting for you, as have BoneCasters before me.' She took Quenelda's hand firmly, her skin rough and calloused but dry. Her yellow eyes gleamed in the near darkness, reassuring, comforting. And so Quenelda stepped forwards.

BoneCaster and pupil now stood in a vast chamber, its depths lost in the darkness. The air thrummed like a harp string, its song louder now so that they simply stood there, ensnared by its beauty. The stars overhead gave out a soft light that fell upon six great carved dragons. *The six companions of Son of the Morning Star*, Drumondir thought with excitement. *Earth, Fire, Wind and Water,*

Stone and Wood. But they clearly were not the source of the song: the ancient dragonbone chair stood there as before, yellowed by age, its power a palpable aura.

Unexpectedly, it was slightly warm as Quenelda touched it with her fingers. She sat. Nothing happened. She pressed the scale on her left hand against the unyielding bone; a whisper from her dead battledragon, Two Gulps and You're Gone echoed softly in her head.

In this last dance of dragons
I grieve to say goodbye
For I will not be with you
When you spread your wings and fly...

A tear rolled down her cheek. With that thought the bones warmed and Quenelda felt a stirring of the slumbering life deep within and knew in the flash of a waking dream who lay beneath her.

'These are the bones of the first Dragon Whisperer!' she gasped out loud. 'Son of the Morning Star.'

Drumondir's eyes widened.

'He's still here, sleeping; I can only just sense him, curled within the HeartRock. He's calling to me...'

'Then listen to him.'

For several heartbeats nothing happened, and then Quenelda's fingertips tingled and the dome overhead took on a deeper hue. At her side, Drumondir could sense a change in the chamber, but it was not the dragon sentinels who moved this time, it was they themselves. As she sat, Quenelda felt the bones shift and close in about her and take on a different shape, stretching about her into a vast skeleton whose immense size should surely break the bounds of the chamber, only it too had vanished, and girl and BoneCaster were in the depths of the night sky.

Quenelda felt a sense of wonder and familiarity kindle within her as her sense of self was seared away, leaving only the inner hearts and soul of a dragon. Muscle and sinew sheathed the bones and scalding dragonfire raced through her blood as diamond bright scale clothed her. Energy, hot as the heart of the sun coursed through her, imbuing her with power beyond imagining. She was immense and infinitely old. She was a dragon, the Eldest, the Matriarch, and this was her story!

The air became chilly, frigid as the vacuum of space. Quenelda heard Drumondir gasp in pain, but the BoneCaster didn't let go of her hand. Then Quenelda was flying, Drumondir tiny on her back. This, the young Dragon Whisperer now knew, was where the age old Elders came from, sailing the boundless deeps of space, exploring the great darkness...searching...always searching for a new home for their children. The cold seared her scales and her heart yearned for a roost...for hers was long gone and her kindred were greatly diminished and scattered over the heavens.

Together, dragon and BoneCaster soared into that indigo sky amongst the stars which had stood watch since long before the One Earth was formed. The dragon Quenelda now was knew each star that burned in heaven's vault and the names of the planets that spun about them; they passed through gaseous clouds of unbelievable beauty that made the heart weep for their passing and new birthed planets of wondrous form and shape. With Drumondir on her back, Quenelda streaked across space chasing ice veiled comets for the joy of it.

And yet, between those bright stars that gave her strength lay the immense frigid dark of the abyss, darkness that sucked dying stars in so that their light disappeared forever from the night sky. Darkness that was boundless, timeless; and one by one the stars and their worlds were winking out as it devoured them. An ancient avaricious enemy with a new face; and Quenelda felt panic grip her, a memory of a WarLock's dark touch, the power of the maelstrom which had nearly bound her in its wild seductive song. Then Quenelda could feel the touch of Drumondir's hand in hers, and knew that part of her was anchored in the heart of Dragon Isle, and that gave her comfort for the battle that was yet to come.

Finally wearying of the search, she found a new birthed star. As boiling cauldrons of ash and dust spun about that star, so the Matriarch spun too weaving a new world about her. Her cooling skin became the Earth's crust, her spine became jagged mountain ranges, her breath the fiery heat of erupting volcanoes, her bone turned to stone and rock and wood, and rivers carried her blood into deep oceans where new life was spawned, infinitely small and in wondrous forms.

In turn she named each and every living thing that swam or crawled or flew on the One Earth, perceiving their potency and power; of oak and ash, of iron and copper, wood and stone, and the myriad creatures that were birthed, lived and died, returning to her once more. She knew dragonkind in their infinite variety and became each in turn and so came to understand their nature, powers and beauty. And she knew all the peoples of the One Earth through its countless ages until she was born again on a snowy dark night in a castle thirteen winters ago.

Quenelda found she was sitting on the Dragonbone Throne once more, she had not moved. And yet, and yet her world had utterly changed. The eyes she raised to Drumondir were no longer those of a child, they were sad, and infinitely older. And there was great power there now, ancient, elemental; Drumondir could see the aura blazing about her.

But it was the young girl who appealed to the BoneCaster. 'I don't want to be trapped by a legend, to be something I'm not. I don't want to lose everyone I love because of a legend.'

'Child,' Drumondir said softly. 'You will not lose those you love, you will bind them and the countless peoples and creatures of our One Earth together in your embrace.

CHAPTER TWENTY-THREE

The Great Fire

It was the tenth day and the wind had turned the flames back on themselves. Starved of fuel, what was already being called the Great Fire was finally over.

'Majesty, my Lords?'

The Captain of the Watch was shown in through the great hall of the palace where the Queen herself and her ladies-in-waiting were tending the wounded and burnt with their own hands. The injured lay in ragged rows moaning. Other homeless families were being fed soup and black bread, crowded into the dubious shelter of the inner bailey walls. And everyone, everything, was covered in a layer of dirty ash.

The Captain was filthy and reeked of smoke and magic and sweat, his eyes bloodshot and blinking in the chalky mask of his face. He hadn't slept in days; neither had his men nor his exhausted dragons.

'Sit,' the Queen's Constable commanded a footman to bring a chair. 'Please. You have news?'

The Captain nodded, tried to speak and coughed,

gratefully accepting a goblet of wine. 'There are scores, hundreds dead, mostly those trapped and unable to reach the safety of the harbours or the boulevards. Five warehouses are burnt down to the ground along with thirty six windmills, sixty stables and roosts, one bridge, thirty taverns, the west harbour and all the ships moored there. The tanners and merchant quarters are badly damaged. Thousands are without homes and are camped about the loch, but many of them too are dying of the cold and their injuries or starvation...'

Gharad Mowbray sat back and closed his eyes. The list went on and on. The transformation from order to chaos was terrifying in its swiftness. The Lord Protector had struck with a predetermined ruthlessness that was frightening; where would he strike next?

CHAPTER TWENTY-FOUR

Quester

The light was soft. Quester no longer knew if it were night or day. He had been here for ever, only disturbed by the hushed voices of the physicians. He thrashed and burned as fever took him, then shivered with cold. The unbearable pain, red hot with every breath, lanced through his body no matter how much poppy seed infusion they gave him.

'How is he?' The voice was anxious, familiar. Always there. 'Quester? Quester, can you hear me? Quester, fight! Don't die, please don't die!' Someone took his lifeless hand and wept. He could feel the warm tears trickling over his skin. But he couldn't move. His body was made of lead.

CHAPTER TWENTY-FIVE

Girl or Gnome

Magnus Fitzgerald, the Guardian of the Battle Academy, gazed out of his private observatory high atop the StarGazing Tower on Dragon Isle. Here the view of the surrounding Sorcerers Glen was unimpeded. Up here he and Jakart DeBessart and the Earl Rufus could think the unthinkable: that a warlock had been at the heart of their council for tens of years. That Hugo had forsaken his kindred in the pursuit of power and formed an unholy alliance with the hobgoblin swarms.

One time childhood friend of the former King, Magnus had arrived with the young Rufus DeWinter at the massacre of the Isle of Midges too late. Too late for the King, his son the Prince, and for the Earl Stoner DeWinter; who all died, along with their small escort, betrayed almost certainly by a very young Hugo Mandrake.

The Guardian's black academy armour beneath the multi-coloured robes of his academic office was functional rather than fancy; the woven gold chain formed of dragon links was the only other clue as to who he was. Magnus was not tall but strongly built and had a commanding air of authority about him. Lean and grave, like so many other families he had lost two of his six sons, one at the battle of the Westering Isles, and his second youngest son at the Battle of the Line.

For a blind and crippled man who had nearly died of the Black Death the Earl was looking remarkably well and unreasonably cheerful, unlike the bloodied and bruised SDS Commander, still shocked by his failure, and suffering three cracked ribs and a gash on his head that would leave him scarred for life.

'He escaped us, he escaped *me*!' Jakart berated himself. 'I can hardly believe he beat five BattleMages!'

'You had never fought chaotic magic. And Hugo does not have the formal training of Dragon Isle and that makes him unpredictable. We know he can unleash the maelstrom, but can he control it,' the Earl mused. 'And what does it cost him? If we push him might he lose control?'

'One thing is certain,' Jakart judged. 'With or without the hobgoblins he will attack while he thinks us weak and riven. It's just a question of when. Not enough trained dragons, men or brimstone. He'll throw everything he's got at us, and even without his hobgoblins, we will be hard pressed to hold the line.'

The Earl nodded. 'We need to immediately redeploy the FireStorm and the ShadowWraiths regiments from the east to the Wall and begin building new fortresses there to secure our frontier. The WinterKnights can reinforce the

StormBreakers in the Howling Glen, leaving the SeaReavers guarding our flank to the south. But that strips us of reserves.

We have to rebuild and quickly if we want to go on the offensive to secure brimstone for our dragons and deny Hugo the same before winter. We cannot afford three years' training before our Academy cadets become combat ready. Magnus, can your scholars teach them in a year?'

'Perhaps; if we rethink how we teach,' the Guardian was sombre. 'We cannot be shackled by tradition, for Hugo knows our strengths and our weaknesses. We need to train young minds which are not constrained by rigid theory or burdened by the history books.'

'I will speak to Tangnost. If anyone can train dragons so swiftly it is him, but bonding is fraught with danger as it is with Imperials and sabretooths, and we will need most dragon masters in the field. Perhaps it can be done if Quenelda helps him, but she is very young and still coming into her power. I hesitate to burden her further. I will talk to Drumondir also. Perhaps between the three it may be possible.'

'Rufus,' Magnus came to a decision. 'Your rescue points to our way forwards. Let us also open the ranks of the Dragon Lords to any who wish to serve, sorcerer or no, lord or commoner, gnome or girl.' He paused and shook his head in wonder. 'It still defies belief that Bark Oakley's son captured Galtekerion. His bravery is extraordinary,'

'I know,' the Earl agreed. 'Already he has surpassed every expectation I laid upon him. He is far more than an esquire to my daughter, he is her closest friend. And Gharad loves the boy dearly.'

'Mmmn...' Maximus nodded thoughtfully. 'It proves that bravery takes many forms and not all of us need to take up arms to make a difference.'

The Earl nodded. 'I can think of only one way to reward him. Let him become the first of his people to train as an Imperial navigator if that is his wish, and my daughter as the first girl to pilot an Imperial. Let them blaze a trail that others can follow.'

CHAPTER TWENTY-SIX

The Earth Wyrm

A cloaked royal Imperial with an escort of six had put down on the pads anchored about the StarLight Tower, in answer to an invitation by Drumondir. Only the Guardian, Jakart DeBessart and Tangnost were also invited, as the BoneCaster had warned them that what she was about to tell them should not be heard by any other ears.

'You say our daughter returned to the HeartRock today?' The Queen looked tired but her joy shone through and the Earl almost blazed with power and held her in the crook of his arm. It was time for secrets to be revealed.

Drumondir nodded. It had come as no surprise to discover Quenelda was the Queen's daughter, and so it should not have come as a surprise to learn that the young lovers had married in secret. Thrown together by mutual grief after the massacre on the Isle of Midges, the youthful Earl Rufus had protected the young Queen before her coronation a year later, ringing her in steel, driving the hobgoblin banners back by rallying a younger generation in service to the crown, most certainly thwarting the young Hugo Mandrake's ambitions.

'Majesty,' Drumondir bobbed her head. 'Guardian, Rufus. The HeartRock contains the memories, knowledge and power of dragonkind. A bone throne sits there, the bones of Son of the Morning Star, ringed by six sentinels carved of stone; I do not yet understand their purpose or meaning but they are clearly his six companions. When your daughter sat on the throne it revealed the story of dragonkind to us; they are infinitely old beyond our reckoning, and powerful beyond imagining. They were birthed amongst the stars, and the heavens belong to them.'

A shocked ring of faces greeted the BoneCaster.

'Dragons are not of the One Earth?' the Queen's hazel eyes were wide. 'They come from the stars?'

The BoneCaster nodded.

'Quenelda became the Eldest, the Matriarch, and took me on a journey through the stars beyond time and back until our sun was born, when she became the Earth Wyrm of Clan legend, the living One Earth and gave birth to her elemental sons and daughters, earth, wind, fire and water, ice and stone, the sources of all magic. The HeartRock is her living heart and the source of Dragon Isle's great power, and I believe it will nurture and protect Quenelda as a mother would, and any who are with her; a sanctuary where she can grow and learn what it is to be a Dragon Whisperer without peril to herself or others. What powers Quenelda will have at her command I do not yet know, but they are beyond our understanding. And...'

Drumondir hesitated. 'It appears that time itself does not pass within the HeartRock as it does in our world. Eons are mere heartbeats in its story, our life spans of no account. I think it will take time to discover its many secrets, and like any other child Quenelda will need time to learn and understand who she truly is and what she can do. And like any child of her age, she is vulnerable.'

'Then I task you with reporting her progress to us,' the Earl commanded. 'Also to share whatever you may discover within its sanctuary that will aid our daughter or our cause.'

'How do we protect her if she is to enrol in the Battle Academy?' the Queen asked. 'Surely now she is in great peril until she comes of age, until she is strong. What if the WarLock learns who she is? Will he not come for her?'

'She passed as one of Tangnost's esquires searching for you, my Lord Earl,' Drumondir argued. 'Named Quentin. No one saw through her disguise.'

'Save you,' the Earl pointed out.

Drumondir bobbed her head in acknowledgement. 'But I, and those who came before, have been waiting for her.'

'No others saw through her disguise,' my Lord,' Tangnost affirmed. 'She was ever the boy and the young lady has yet to emerge.'

'But she grows more like me every day,' the Queen objected.

'None will see that, sweetheart,' the Earl assured her. 'With her short hair, grubby hands and patched jacket, no one will see it. She will look like any of the thousand other cadets.'

'And there is little chance she will be wearing a dress anytime soon,' Tangnost smiled.

The Queen acknowledged the Dragon Master's point with an answering smile. 'No, I don't suppose there is.'

'But perhaps we could dye her hair black?' Drumondir suggested. 'No one will recognise her then, even if they are looking for her.'

CHAPTER TWENTY-SEVEN

Battle Academy

'Where are we going?' Root asked.

Quenelda shook her head. 'I don't know.' They had both been reluctant to leave Quester's side, had taken turns to watch over him, the other sleeping at the foot of the bed. Around them the hospital was slowly emptying as those with minor injuries left and others with fatal injuries died. But Quester had not yet regained consciousness, so pale and still, sometimes they thought he too had died.

'We have had to remove a leg,' the surgeon answered the pair's questions. 'It was shattered beyond repair. Without Drumondir he would have died from loss of blood. He may yet die I am afraid.'

'Go,' the BoneCaster gently shooed the tearful pair away. 'If the Queen summoned you to the Black Isle you must go. I will watch him for you, and yes,' she held up a hand to forestall their protest, 'I will send a courier if there is need. Now go!'

The royal footmen led Root and Quenelda through the upper corridors of the palace towards the royal chambers. They passed workmen still labouring to remove rubble and splintered timbers from a damaged corridor, the ceiling in places only held up by stout wooden stoops. Beyond, through gaps in the wall, powder snow blew in. Dust lay thickly everywhere, and here and there stains that looked like dried blood.

No one paid any attention to the youth with his servant, the Court had other things to debate. The departed Lord Protector for one, these ruined chambers, his parting legacy, for another. And then of course the return of the Earl, and rumours that it was his daughter and Shield Tangnost Bearhugger who had found him when no other had; flying his inured Imperial battledragon no less! But that was too farfetched, they shook their heads. Ridiculous! After all, the Earl's young daughter had not been seen in many moons, since it was rumoured once again, she and her dragon had been poisoned by the young Earl Darcy, who had mysteriously disappeared himself now, leaving his young wife behind! Some were even saying that the blind Earl Rufus could see through his dragon's eyes like Dragon Lords of old, and that his daughter could talk to the creatures! The world had turned topsy-turvy, and it was a time of ruin and wonder!

'My Lady, Master Root, this way,' the Queen's equerry greeted the pair and showed them into the presence chamber, itself damaged with one burnt wall: it was packed with nobles and soldiers and, unusually, the bright academic robes of the Battle Academy. This was where petitioners came, noble and base born, hoping to put their case for royal justice. With half the city in ashes there must have been no end to their pleas.

Quenelda searched for and found her father; he was deep in conversation with the SDS Commander and another man Quenelda had never seen before, with deep, intense hooded eyes. She could see a pure white aura, a *very* powerful battlemage, about him. He suddenly glanced up directly at her, his blue eyes capturing hers for a moment of penetrating scrutiny, and then he turned back to her father. Quenelda spotted Sir Gharad who gave her a beaming smile before disappearing into the inner chamber.

'Ah, Goose,' the Earl Rufus had guessed the reason for the dip in conversation. 'Come,' he beckoned them to the doorway as if he could still see, 'and you also, Root.' With his hand outstretched to the front the Earl led them into the inner presence chamber, where Queen Caitlin sat on a window seat tended by Armelia. The Queen's lady-in-waiting looked excited. The Earl went to stand by the Queen with barely a falter, placing a hand on her shoulder. As the Queen turned at her father's touch, Quenelda thought she looked radiant, pale but bright eyed and full of hope, and knew, on the cusp of growing into a young woman herself in that moment of sudden insight, that more than friendship and loyalty bound them.

The Queen's eyes widened with pleasure as Root bowed and Quenelda tried to curtsey, stifling a gasp of pain as her stitches stretched. She smiled warmly. 'You are most welcome, young Root and Quenelda. We have barely begun to hear about your many adventures, and yet it seems you succeeded where everyone else failed,' she reached up to take the Earl's hand. 'But what is clear, is that with the help of Bearhugger, you flew an Imperial into the frozen wastes of the north and survived a maelstrom to bring your father home. To bring the man who can unite and inspire us.'

'At the same time, young Root, you captured Galtekerion along with your injured friend; I have sent my royal physicians to tend him. These feats are worthy of the SDS.' Root flushed with pleasure as the Queen turned enquiringly to where the dark robed sorcerer stood. Feeling his gaze upon her once again, Quenelda raised her eyes to meet those of the unknown man who was considering her in frank appraisal. He nodded slightly as if he had come to a decision.

'This is Magnus Fitzgerald, Guardian of the Battle Academy.'

The Guardian! Quenelda's heart slammed. Rarely at Court, this battlemage's feats were famed in the Seven Kingdoms, both on the battlefield and as a scholar of great repute.

The Guardian's voice was deep and measured. 'Much has happened over the past year that no one would once have dreamt of; it is time to look to the future. In recognition of your journey, your bravery in bringing back the Earl, despite your youth, both of you have been accepted to study at the Battle Academy as Imperial pilot and navigator.'

With a cry of delight Quenelda ran to hug her father, and Sir Gharad opened his arms to embrace a dazed Root, to embrace a boy he realised, he looked upon as a son. Armelia stood awkwardly wanting to hug everyone and not knowing how: young ladies didn't hug. Even when one kissed one never actually kissed. One went 'mwah mwah'. She found to her pleasure that Quenelda and Root had enough hugs for the three of them.

'But both of us?' Root queried cautiously, eyes flicking anxiously from Sir Gharad to the Guardian. 'I thought only sorcerers could fly Imperials, could become...' He hardly dared say it. 'Dragon Lords? I thought gnomes could only be scouts, fly lesser dragons? That is the law. My people have no magic.'

'That is for the past,' the Guardian assured him. 'The SDS must change if we are to survive. We have to become one people again as we once were, who live and train and fight together, and you have both demonstrated your ability to do this, young though you both are. You come from different peoples; one noble born the other the son of a scout. One desiring to fly dragons when tradition allows only men to do so, the other proving in the best tradition of his people that you do not need to wield a sword in your hand to protect those you love.'

'This is a new beginning,' the Guardian promised Root. 'Our SpellMasters will fashion a new kind of armour and witchwood chair and you will be trained to use their sophisticated sorcery needed to navigate and defend your Imperial. 'Should you wish it, once your training is complete, you can become a Dragon Lord, a navigator on an Imperial Black. But if your desire is to follow in your father and people's footsteps as scout, then that wish shall be honoured also.'

Root grinned from ear to ear. He could barely believe it.

'But,' the Guardian warned, 'there are two conditions, neither of which will be easy for you to keep.'

The Earl nodded. 'Your part in the search for me, Goose, and you Root, and Quester should he live, and Galtekerion's capture must remain secret - for now. Given his place at the heart of the kingdom, Hugo has many allies, doubtless many spies. Galtekerion's disappearance will keep him puzzled, wasting precious time searching for answers.'

'Yes,' the Guardian added. 'Without him, we believe Hugo will find the hobgoblin banners difficult if not impossible to control, allowing us perhaps a year to rebuild the SDS and train a new generation.'

'And Quenelda,' the Earl knew how much his daughter would hate this. 'For now, you will continue to be Quentin, a younger son of lesser nobility. An esquire from Dragonsdome. Not the first girl to enter the Academy.'

'But I - '

'Quenelda,' the Queen said gently, taking her hand. 'It is not from shame we hide you, but to protect you. Rumours that you piloted Stormcracker, that you can talk to dragons, can survive their fiery kiss are already sweeping the Black Isle, and some will doubtless reach the ears of Hu-...the WarLock. He may try to kill or capture you, and we cannot allow that.'

'It will not be easy for either of you,' the Guardian promised. 'You will be younger than most and we are reducing three years of academic study and field training into one. That will be hard enough, perhaps beyond many. As a gnome and a common born esquire training to be Dragon Lords, you will both attract prejudice and fear. Do you still wish to join the Battle Academy?'

'Yes!' they both said.

CHAPTER TWENTY-EIGHT

The Hand of Friendship

Quenelda was packing what few processions she had from her journey north. Everything else was ashes in Dragonsdome. She was trying hard not to cry when Armelia found her.

'When do you leave?'

'Later today.'

Armelia nodded, trying to pluck up courage for the true purpose of her visit. She took a deep breath. 'When will you be back?'

'I don't know.'

'I know Dragonsdome has gone...perhaps you are thinking you might not want to come back here...I was thinking...I was wondering...um...if you...'

Quenelda noticed for the first time how pale and pinched Armelia was and somewhere along the way she had lost a lot of lace and ribbons too.

'If I?' Quenelda prompted gently, feeling a wash of sympathy.

'Ifyouwouldbemyfriend.' Armelia took a big gulp of

air. 'And come back here sometimes?'

'Yes,' Quenelda answered without thinking, and then found it to be true. They stared at each other.

Armelia rushed on. 'I thought, I thought you might take me out flying. Um, on your battledragon some time.'

'Two Gulps?' Quenelda looked amazed.

'B-b-but if you don't want to...' Armelia trailed off wretchedly.

'No, um, yes, it's just he's a bit overweight...not sure he could fly with two up yet... Or even one up!' Quenelda paused and fidgeted with her hair, wrapping it round a finger. 'Are you sure? No girl has ever wanted to be my friend before.'

'But I do!' And then Armelia took another risk and hugged Quenelda. They drew back and looked both amazed and horrified. The first tentative steps towards lasting friendship had been taken.

CHAPTER TWENTY-NINE

The Black Citadel

The weather had worsened. Although the wind had died the snow fell fat and feathery, burying the landscape. Darcy thought of Armelia far to the south. His anger towards his wife had cooled. He didn't want to be here, but what in truth, could he have expected of her? Like him she loved the courtly life of banquets and balls, parades and dragon racing. But now.... he pushed the thought aside because it hurt too much. But now they would build a new kingdom and then perhaps, he hoped, she would come to him?

He broke his fast with freshly baked bread, beer and cold chicken, and was standing by the fire when his father arrived dressed for travel.

'We're flying in this?' Darcy gestured at the window.

'Yes and no,' the WarLock shook his head. 'Come.'

Keeping his temper in check, angry at being treated like a child, Darcy donned his flying cloak and followed his father, sparing no thought for his onetime Dragon Master billeted out in the stables; Felix had not served him well.

Let his father find some menial use for him. At some point the crust had frozen overnight so that their footsteps crunched loudly. They passed across the covered wooden walkway that bridged the Keep to the heavily manned battlements, and then up to the great gate towers beyond, that jutted out over the gorge below.

Darcy was very confused now. Surely they weren't travelling without a large escort? What if the SDS caught up? Or they met patrols out of the Howling Glen?

Aren't we even taking a guard?

But he kept the thought to himself. Out through a hidden postern gate that opened into a ravine, they carefully negotiated the frost- rimed crags with care, one careless step would land them in the gorge far below. Darcy finally exhausted his patience. This was ridiculous!

'Aren't we flying?' He asked petulantly. 'Where on the One Earth are you taking me?'

'Here.'

'Here' was a scorched hollow scoured out of the mountainside. Strangely, the falling snow didn't lie on the charred earth which crunched beneath Darcy's boots. The WarLock King raised his arms. 'Do not be afraid.' *A command or reassurance?* Darcy was given no time to decide.

A wind rose out of nowhere and began to gently spiral about them. The ground vibrated. Loose stones and twigs whirled and spun, but it remained calm where they stood. A rip tore through the air. Darcy cried out in alarm as a dark gash appeared, jagged and rough edged. Like a living creature it came towards them open mouthed. With a cry of fear, Darcy tried to find his legs to run, but his father's hand gripped his shoulder hard as a rock and held him.

Then the world shook and the young man fell to his knees. The hillside disappeared. Light and dark spun then the world abruptly stopped spinning and they were spat out. The black hole behind them slammed shut with a thump that made his ears pop. As Darcy lifted his head to a very different world, the screaming wind hit the young man, knocking him from his feet. A flock of winter ravens disturbed by their unheralded arrival were screeching their displeasure, swirling round them.

'Eugh!' Disorientated, head spinning, on his hands and knees in deep snow, Darcy lost his breakfast. Cursing, afraid, the young man got to his feet on shaking legs, wiping his mouth with his glove he brushed the snow from his hands and knees. Squinting into the white brightness he looked about.

They were in the outer bailey of a ruined castle, overgrown and frost rimed. The rotting carcasses of dead dragons were heaped about, with ocean eagles and gulls too bloated to fly clustered about them. Darcy could taste the tang of salt on his lips. Moving cautiously he peered over a crumbling seawall. The high cliffs gave way to a deep ocean swell which crashed against the broken fingers of rocks far below.

'This?' Darcy's face twisted with disappointment as he turned a full circle to make sure he had missed nothing. 'This is what you promised? A broken castle on some god forsaken island?' He turned hands palm up. 'This is...it? *This* is our kingdom?'

'Wait,' the WarLock's eyes smouldered green.... Darcy felt a pang of unease. Danger and violence hung about his handsome, darkly charming father like a cloak.

'This is merely a cloak.' The WarLock King softly spoke an incantation. Tiny motes of green twinkled. There was a blurring of edges, a shiver as if the world shifted beneath Darcy's feet. In a few heartbeats the wreckage and ruin of centuries transformed itself. The gatehouse barbican of a vast citadel towered about them, its jagged heights reaching up into the snow laden sky. Towers and spires reached skyward, bridged by impossible arches and viaducts as the inner bailey took shape about them.

Fearsomely designed jagged dragon pads clustered about the scores of towers, hanging like cobs on invisible threads, and the heavy sky was alive with wheeling battledragons rising up until they were lost in the clouds. It was beautiful and strange, and very very frightening.

Darcy was stunned. 'How?' He stared open mouthed, quite stupefied. 'I've... never seen anything like this....' he husked. It was immense, as was surely the power that knit it together. Darcy could feel energy like a tingling on his skin as it thrummed throughout the island. Suddenly his loss and fear were forgotten as the possibilities of this place embraced him.

'Welcome to the Night Citadel, to the heart of our kingdom, my son. Just as Imperials cloak....so a seven layered nexus as powerful as that of Dragon Isle cloaks the island. It is triggered by any who are not marked by me, into as you saw an overgrown ruin on a wind blasted island. Here we are safe, hidden. The SDS will never find us.'

'But how?'

'Chaotic magic: dangerous, dark and powerful.'

Like you! Darcy thought with a shiver. 'Where are we? We're on an island? It's freezing!'

'Roarkinch.'

Darcy shook his head. 'Yes, no! I mean, where *is* Roarkinch?'

Leading his son up to the battlements, the WarLock pointed. 'The Ice Isles lie to our north, on a clear day you can see them. To the east...Cape Wrath. To the west... the Westering Isles and the hobgoblins.'

*And the hobgoblins...*Darcy had dozens of questions. *One at a time...*

'We travelled so far in such a short time? How? What was that... hole?'

'A bridge of sorts...a shortcut between one place and another.' *I need to renew my strength in the Abyss...it drains me to conjure them...*

'How...how many may travel this bridge? Can you ove an army?'

'No, not yet...'

'May I see the island? All of it?'

The WarLock nodded, pleased with his son's reaction. Alerted to their arrival, a bandy legged toad of a troll was descending from the gatehouse tower. He bowed, as much as his stomachs would allow.

'My King, welcome home. My Prince,' he bowed obsequiously to Darcy. 'I am yours to command.'

'Master Gnostfor, make sure my son's tower is prepared for him. Come,' the WarLock King smiled at Darcy. 'I will show you your new home.'

The armouries, barracks, great halls with arches that soared higher than the eye could see, the deep tunnel beneath the barbican gatehouse shaped like a dragon's maw, spiralling staircases that curved about towers; soon Darcy was exhausted, overwhelmed. And he had seen only a tiny part of the citadel and the island.

'Come,' the WarLock invited Darcy to a porting stone. 'From here, you can look down on our kingdom...'

The porting stone blurred and the next moment they were so high they were above the clouds, only the peaks of two volcanoes visible beneath a brilliant blue sky. Darcy reeled back from the battlement. Imperials wheeled about them, vast black shadows in the sunlight. *This must have taken half a lifetime to build...*

'How long have you...' Panicked, Darcy tried to think of the correct word...treason wasn't a good one.

'Been planning this?' His father was amused as if he had read Darcy's mind. 'Since I was younger than you.'

'Where-?' Before he rose to be the Grand Master's novice, no one knew where Hugo Mandrake had come from. 'Where did you come from? No one really knows anything about you.'

'My parents were fisherfolk from the Isle of Midges barely scraping a living. I had no intention of following my father's trade. I ran away at seven and one year later found myself homeless and alone in the Black Isle.

A seamstress took me in; she had lost her two sons when a ship foundered on the rocks. I took to theft to climb out of poverty, and where necessary, to murder. Soon I came to the attention of the Assassins Guild: they taught me how to kill, efficiently, silently, with a knife or a hand or a herb. Soon I became better than any of them. Removing those who opposed me, I became Master of the Assassins Guild but always I wanted to know more, to be challenged. I caught the eye of the Grand Master, Englethwit DeBruce. I became an apprentice in the Sorcerers Guild and mastered their magic easily; from apprentice at ten to Master at the age of nineteen. But manipulating the maelstrom, dark energy, black holes, tests your wits; the abyss will kill you if you make a single mistake!'

CHAPTER THIRTY

Thunder Rolling over the Mountains

'Tangnost!' The Earl had his back to the room and was gazing blindly out the training hall windows. The footsteps along the corridor slowed, and then continued, more softly. The Earl smiled.

'Rufus,' formalities were discarded when they met in private. 'How did you know it was me?'

From the sound of your steps, the smell of leather and saddle soap, the sweet smoke of pipeweed...the chink of your chain mail...the way you rub your blind eye socket...a thousand clues...

'I can not only hear Stormcracker's thoughts or draw upon his strength whilst he is near, now I can feel some of his power running through my veins. I may be blind, Tangnost, but I can see in some ways better than I ever did. I – I am developing my inner dragon awareness myself, it seems,' Quenelda's father mused. 'And I am growing stronger. Let me show you. Take up a stave and give me a training shield.'

Tangnost bent to select a light ash staff and balanced

it. Then he selected the largest of the small light training shields called a targe. Putting an arm through the loop the Earl clasped the leather handle with a fist.

'Come at me,' he invited Tangnost, raising the targe. 'Strike.'

Trusting the man he had fought with for so long, Tangnost raised the staff and struck – hard. The Earl caught the blow on the shield. Moving more swiftly, the dwarf then struck from the side and below. Again the blow was deflected. Swiftly spinning he brought the staff round in an arc, only for the Earl to nimbly side step.

'How?' The dwarf was awed. 'How can this be?'

'That cradle in the SeaDragon Citadel, it has renewed me. I am becoming part dragon, like my daughter.'

'You have scales on your brow and cheekbones and neck,' Tangnost told him, examining the Earl frankly, 'that are growing over the burns; the same on the back of your hands and wrists. It almost looks as if you are wearing a hauberk of overlapping scales; you are growing dragon armour!'

'I have to confess,' the Earl grinned lopsidedly at Tangnost. 'I am not ready to become a seadragon! I have asked Drumondir to find what she could in the Palace and Guild libraries about the first Dragon Lords. She tells me the oldest part of the library at Dragonsdome can be saved, ancient wards protected it.'

'Are you hungry?' Rufus asked his Dragon Master as servants came forwards to lay a table. 'Come, let's eat, and you can tell me if you think it possible to train cadets and dragons both to combat readiness in a single year instead of three.'

'Gladly,' Tangnost had been in the maternity roosts since before dawn and had not yet broken his fast. And so for three bells they discussed intensive field training and how many dragon masters could combine Academy training at this level as well as SDS operations; if there were enough juvenile ground and air attack dragons to train; the problems that commoners, trolls, gnomes and dwarves would encounter training with sorcerer lords to become Dragon Lords, and if the best of the Juveniles, as Academy cadets were known, could be ready for Operation Brimstone before winter stopped operations; and finally Quenelda.

'Tangnost, old friend, I leave her in your and Drumondir's capable hands for I plan to take to the field soon. I want you back in the Academy. With the Guardian's blessing I need you to train my daughter; instruct her in battlecraft to fight as one with her dragon and her comrades, teach her humility and how to earn the respect of others so she may lead them in battle. Drumondir will guide her in the HeartRock; together they can discover the nature of Dragon Whispering and its purpose.

But your true task must be hidden: we cannot burden her with our expectations and hopes. If we are to survive the hobgoblins when they finally come, it will only be because she can train and command our dragons. But she must come into her power in her own way and time. She will attend lectures and tutorials along with all the other cadets who will only know her as Quentin. Will you do this for me?'

A rare smile answered him. 'Willingly...always. You are taking to the field? What are you planning, Rufus?'

'I have been thinking that if we are to open the ranks of the SDS to all, so we should also rethink how the SDS fights. Fight chaos with chaos of a different kind,' the Earl clenched his fist. 'We need not fear the dark. I intend forming a stealth battlegroup that will take the fight to the WarLock and his minions: that can survive and fight far from DragonIsle for many moons. And I will create a Strategic Air Command on Stormcracker that mirrors the SeaDragon Tower. We will strike like lightning then disappear!'

'The dragons call you Thunder Rolling Over the Mountains. Perhaps you could name it the ThunderStorm Battlegroup? A Storm of battledragons.'

'I'll take the pick of this year's academy intake, cadets and dragons both,' Rufus agreed. 'Choose the brightest and the bravest; and those who think differently, and pair them with the best we have, like you, so that they can learn battlecraft from the elite. We will build it about Quenelda and Root; together you and I will create something new.'

CHAPTER THIRTY-ONE

Summons to War

Frowning, Darcy studied the lip of the long horn which sank into the rock bed of the sea cavern below the citadel. Here the smoothed flagstones that disappeared into the sea were beautiful, all the colours of coral and mother of pearl.

'What is it? I mean what is it for?'

'This is how I summon the hobgoblins and my razorbacks. Sound carries far under the water. It is a relic of the First Age. I think Dragon Lords once summoned their Sea Dragons here and in many other forgotten places.'

'How can you create new dragons like razorbacks?'

'The maelstrom has the power to... twist and bind creatures into new shape and form...I will have another dragon for the hobgoblins come spring: hammerheads. Blow,' he ordered one of his soldiers.

The huge troll, with a torso like a tree trunk, bent to the horn. Blood suffused his face before Darcy felt the vibration shiver through his boots and bones. Woooo...

the sound carried underwater. Wooooo...Darcy's heart hiccupped as he saw spines break the surface of the pool below him; sharp and black as a thorny thistle. Slowly the creature rose up, shedding seawater to reveal hobgoblins clustered like pale limpets between the spines. One bounded from the razorback's back to land scant strides from Darcy and his father. The young prince recoiled in disgust at the stench and the fishy mucus that spattered him.

The hobgoblin rose up and up to tower over him. At over six strides tall, Darcy was not used to anyone looking down on him. It wore bone armour festooned with kill fetishes; some looked like rotting tufts of human hair. It carried a long thin tube and a sheath of darts that were the spikes of a poisonous sea urchin. Blue tattoos covered its pale skin as it knelt before his father.

Rising, the hobgoblin fixed Darcy with fishy eyes and hissed. It took the young sorcerer a heart stopping moment to realise it must be speaking, as his father replied in the same guttural clicks and hisses, almost as if he were coughing to clear his throat. The hobgoblin's bulging eyes slid to Darcy and back again to the WarLock King, then it turned and knelt in front of Darcy.

'School your emotions!' his father warned. 'And never show fear. They are ravening creatures who desire hot blood more than anything. No, they will not dare harm you, and should you meet when I am not with you, your armour compels them to obedience.'

'Is this...is this Galtekerion?' Darcy asked. The creature certainly looked ghastly enough to be the feared

WarLord of the Thirteen Tribes.

'No,' but he is one of Galtekerion's Chosen. His guard,' he added, seeing Darcy's confusion. 'They are all warriors tested in battle, the greatest from amongst the tribes.'

As the hobgoblin remounted and the razorback turned to go, smoke puffed out of its maw, enveloping the troll who had blown the horn. With barely a shriek, he disappeared and a pile of bones clattered onto the rocks, and then sea dragon and hobgoblins were gone, leaving the sea wallowing in their wake. Darcy bit down on the bile that rose hotly in his throat as he looked at the remnants of the troll.

'I have summoned Galtekerion and his banners to assemble at the Isle of Midges in one moon's time,' the King informed his son. 'Then we will attack. Come, we have much to discuss.'

CHAPTER THIRTY-TWO

The Badger

Battle Academy: it was all Quenelda had ever dreamt of. But although she scoffed at Armelia's romantic dreams, Quenelda's own imaginings proved to be every bit as romantic and just as flimsy.

To begin with, she had died her hair as bidden by Drumondir and cut it even shorter, taking up the guise of Quentin again, the son of a humble roost master. That had been fun when searching for her father, but now it was frustrating; she had so longed for everyone to know that she, a girl, was going to be the first Dragon Lord! That she could outfly them and had piloted an Imperial. But she was not the only unhappy sorcerer lord whose expectations were being quashed.

Lesser sons knew that their path to glory had to be earned as esquires, that they could join many units including command of the elite BoneCrackers and SeaReavers... but the eldest sons of noble houses were trained from birth in the expectation that they would become Dragon Lords. Finding their way barred to lodging in the castle, the young men were outraged to find themselves assigned quarters in the lower barracks along with commoners and other races in the woods. Not only that, they had to eat together and learn how commoners fought!

Rebellion was fermenting by the time a broad shouldered dwarf missing half an arm strode across from the training grounds to where they had been ordered to gather by 1400 bells.

'My name is Sargeant Major Gimlet Badgerlock of the ShadowWraiths,' he growled as the snow coated their heads and lashes. 'But you will call me Sir! Am I clear?'

'Sir, Yes, Sir!'

'Louder!'

'Sir! Yes Sir!'

Brown eyes were unimpressed. Badgerlock had been expecting trouble and knew he had found it. The young Lords were defiantly silent. Such insubordination had to be quashed hard.

'Until you complete basic training in three moons hence, you belong to me. It doesn't matter who you were, how important you were, here you are all Juveniles. Here you are all equal. My task is to give you an appreciation of what it takes to become a commando or a marine. If you are to command the elite SeaReavers and the BoneCrackers you will first learn what it takes to become one.

'Why are we doing this?' a tall young sorcerer muttered mutinously. 'Who cares how others fight? They do what they're told. It comes down to sorcery; and gnomes, trolls and dwarves don't have any!'

A lanky, black-haired boy laughed. 'They won't last, Bracus,'

'Way to go, Ranulf!'

The pair clasped hands. 'Commoners shouldn't be here either,' Bracus hissed at Root in front of him. 'What do you know of magic?'

A lot more than you, I'll be bound, Root thought, but didn't say. Whoever this young lordling was, he and his friends were going to be trouble. But Badgerlock had also heard. The formidable dwarf came to stand in front of the cadet.

'You have something to say, cadet?'

'No! Sir, No!'

'No, sir,' Badgerlock repeated thoughtfully. 'Name cadet?'

'Lord Bracus Beaumont, Sir,' he added insolently.

At nearly seven strides tall Bracus Beaumont was as tall as a hobgoblin with broad shoulders to match. Red haired and freckled ....with three brothers and two uncles killed at the Westering Isles, at sixteen summers he was now the oldest in family and hot for revenge.

'Well, cadet,' Badgerlock smiled. 'There are no lords here, and before you can command anyone you have to learn how your men and dragons fight and how to fight together. There is no place here for individual heroics in this cadet AirWing. From here on in you eat together, sleep together, train together and fight together. If you have a problem with that, cadet, the boat for the Black Isle is moored down in the docks.'

'No! Sir, No!' Bracus fumed inwardly.

Badgerlock calmly held his rebellious eye until the cadet flushed and looked away.

'Form ranks, ten deep!' Badgerlock bellowed. 'One arm's length from the cadet on either side and the cadet to your front. Pace yourself...pace yourself...'

They shuffled into ragged lines. Quenelda, now Quentin, smothered a squeal as Bracus deliberately trampled on her heel. Biting down her temper, trying to act as a humble esquire would, Quentin ignored the provocation.

'Stand to attention! Let's take a look at you.' Badgerlock strode down the lines. 'Head up, he barked. 'Shoulders back. Feet together! Eyes front!'

'One pace forwards and right turn,' he roared, just to see how many knew their left from their right. It was a shambles. The commoners amongst them were treading on each other's toes and bumping each other, to the evident entertainment of Bracus and his friends.

'Abyss below!' Badgerlock shook his head in sorrow as he strode down the lines. 'My granny could do better!' He stopped in front of a young dwarf. 'How about facing me, son?' he said kindly.

It was only their first day. Only two moons to go...

CHAPTER THIRTY-THREE

We Speak No Treason

Sir Gharad stood wearily. The Queen's Council, save for the lately departed Lord Protector and those lords who had fled with him, was in session. The Kingdom's Earls, including Arundel, Lennox and Caithness were there, plus the Dukes of Glamis, Cawdor, Braemore and Orkney, along with the SDS Commander, the Chancellor and other Queen's ministers. So too Grand Master Spellskin, despite his broken jaw, accompanied by several other senior Guild Masters and Mistresses. With the fire finally extinguished they were attending to affairs of state; the treason and flight of the Lord Hugo Mandrake, former Lord Protector, and nearly King. Everyone was exhausted, and tempers were frayed to breaking, with arguments and blame being freely cast.

'As you all now know,' Sir Gharad was grim. 'The Earl Rufus returned from near death, airlifted out of the battlefield at the Smoking Fort. In the early watches of the following morning, before witnesses, the Lord Protector attempted to kill him. He failed, but so did we: evading capture, Hugo has fled into exile beyond the Wall, taking his son with him. And it is he, or on his orders, that Dragonsdome and the City were deliberately fired so that we would not pursue him.'

'But why?' the Earl of Lennox stood, a weak stoat of a man with an exaggerated limp that had allowed him to avoid military service despite his obligations to the Crown. He held extensive lands straddling the Wall in the east, and was close in council with the recently departed Lord Protector. 'Why would Hugo do such a thing? What has he to gain by killing the Earl? Or burning the city? I don't understand. He was to have wed the Queen and the kingdom would have been his – I mean theirs,' he quickly corrected himself. 'We all heard the thunder; many saw the lightning strike the palace and the city. Why is the Lord Protector being blamed?'

'Because, my Lord,' Sir Gharad repeated, his patience wearing thin, 'the Earl is the only survivor who witnessed Hugo's treachery at the Westering Isles; who witnessed the summoning of the maelstrom that destroyed the SDS. Rufus alone ~ *and Quenelda* ~ knew Hugo for what he truly is: a WarLock, and moreover one who commands the hobgoblin banners. Everything Hugo had gained when he thought the Earl dead and the SDS weakened was jeopardized by Rufus's return. Hugo has betrayed his own kind in his pursuit of power.'

'You seek to excuse your own failures with this talk of treason. Where is your proof?'

'Proof?' Jakart DeBessart shook his head in disgust. 'That was no thunderstorm you saw, that green lightning was the mark of the maelstrom! And is the fact that Hugo is not here not proof enough for you, man? It was as you say, his wedding day long since, yet he has fled. Why, unless he is guilty of what we say?'

'I-I'll give you proof!'

Grand Master Spellskin stood with great difficulty; helped to his feet by body servants, he lent heavily on his ornate staff of office. His head and jaw were bandaged, his beard scorched and his ears were still ringing, but he had been one of the lucky ones. The apothecaries had given him several goblets of poppy seed steeped in milk for the pain. But that was nothing to the cold rage in his heart that the Guild he revered, believed in, had been manipulated and bought with gold by the sorcerer at its very heart. For he had no doubts, having witnessed five battlemages being bested by one man, that the Lord Hugo Mandrake was a warlock. The Lord Protector had betrayed them all.

'W-why then,' Spellskin's voice trembled with anger. 'Why then, Your Grace, did he,' he spat the word, 'that WarLock try and kill the Earl? I – we,' he gestured to his fellow guildsmen with a shaking hand , 'bore witness to that, and six of our number are dead by his hand, and many soldiers that night past. You can see the damage for yourself!' he pointed at the cracked columns and walls. 'Is that not mayhem and murder enough for you?'

'Then how then did he escape your clutches?' the Duke laughed, a little too loudly. 'If, as you say, Commander,' he turned to Jakart DeBessart, 'you had him so neatly trapped by at least four battlemages other than yourself?' He raised his eyebrows in dramatic fashion and spread his hands. 'And yet,' he sneered, 'he is not here before us in chains?'

'He escaped because he is a WarLock and has the power of chaotic magic at his command. All such learning is forbidden; we did not, do not know what we are facing.' the SDS Commander repeated. Jakart DeBessart had been humbled and disturbed by his first encounter with chaotic magic, but now was no time to reveal that. 'He opened a black hole and vanished through it. We have never seen the like of it before. And we have not entirely failed. We unveiled him for who his is in time to stop him taking the throne. And he failed to kill the Earl.'

'This 'black hole' you speak of. What is it?'

'We do not know yet. Academics from the Faculties of Air and Battlemagic and the School of Astronomy are examining the chamber, their colleagues researching grimoires from the Mage Wars, but as you well know, all knowledge of the maelstrom was destroyed. But we think it is a rip in the fabric of creation that is conjured up and then disappears. Possibly he can cross great distances. This would explain how he could have been at the Westering Isles but then back here within a day. His mastery of it could explain many things.'

'Excuses! The SDS have failed time and again this last year since that battle.'

'And whose fault is that, Your Grace?' DeBessart's voice was soft with implied threat. 'This very council, urged by you, gave writ to the Lord Protector to raise an army of his own, against all the tenets of our law. It was you who urged grants of money and arms to the Army of the North. It was also you who gave him direct access to our brimstone mines which he now controls.'

'And it was you,' Spellskin joined the attack, 'w-who counselled the Guild – who counselled me that we give the WarLock the right to breed imperials. You said the day of the SDS was done! You who said they could no longer keep the Kingdoms safe! Your blind greed has imperilled the security of the Kingdoms.'

'But so he did keep the kingdom safe,' Lennox retorted, furious at being remonstrated by a…a merchant. 'He gave you back your fortress! He saved the Howling Glen and held the Wall against the hobgoblins.'

'He didn't keep us safe from the hobgoblins, you fool!' DeBessart finally lost patience, slamming his fist on the table, his aura becoming visible to everyone, making Lennox quail. 'He commanded them!'

'N-none the less,' Duke blustered, seeing his peril and changing his tack. 'Y-you are not fit guardians of the Kingdoms to let him slip through your hands. Now the hobgoblins will attack us. He will unleash his full force and we have nothing to stand against him.'

'It is true,' the SDS Commander conceded, 'that thanks to you we are under manned and under provisioned and our strategic advantage of stealth dragons has been squandered. We are weak, as Hugo intended; firing the city and our food supplies has weakened us further.'

'Then we are lost!' Spellskin said. 'He'll attack!'

'No, we are not!' A new voice answered. 'He will not unleash the hobgoblins,' the blind Earl, hand on Tangnost's shoulder joined the Council. 'He is in for a surprise, I suspect, when he returns to his northern holdfast which will keep him guessing for many moons, and will buy us precious time to regroup, recruit and train.'

'And w-why is that?' Lennox stared at the crippled man that was the missing Earl, who radiated authority and strength despite his appalling injuries.

'Fetch him in.'

Nodding, Tangnost left the hall.

'If proof is what you need of treachery, Lennox, then I have it. From the same battlefield I come from.'

CHAPTER THIRTY-FOUR

Galtekerion

There was the murmur of voices and then a short silence. A strange sucking, slapping sound could be heard, overlaid by the chink and rattle of metal. Beneath a casual glance, Sir Mowbray studied the puzzled frowns, the curiosity and outright confusion on the faces of the council as the noise approached.

Jakart DeBessart had chosen Marines, each troll nigh on eight strides tall, to guard him, but neither they nor the lack of armour or weapons did anything to diminish the threat their prisoner posed, nor his sheer raw power. Bound with wards, heavy manacles of sky iron about wrist and waist and ankle were chained together so the captive could only shuffle forwards and could not stand, but he fought his chains every step of the way. Suckers popped like seaweed as he moved huge webbed feet.

'Abyss below!' someone hissed, chair grating on flagstones as he stood.

Of those about the table, only the soldiers and those Guildsmen who had served as young men had ever seen the face of their mortal enemy. And what a sight the creature was.

Water pooled about him as Galtekerion raised lambent bulbous eyes to his captors and hissed, baring ragged rows of serrated teeth. A blast of rank fishy breath rolled over them, making many shrink back in horror and gag. Lunging towards the Council with suckers outstretched, the chains caught and pulled the creature back onto the floor on its back. Immediately, using his powerful thighs the hobgoblin sprang back up into a crouch ready to attack again. The point had been made.

The Earl nodded to Tangnost. 'Take him back to his prison.'

As the hobgoblin was dragged out, Duke Lennox picked himself up from where he had fallen backwards off his seat. 'S-so you have a h-hobgoblin? There are a m-million more.'

'My Lord,' the Earl Rufus said softly. 'This is no ordinary hobgoblin: this is Galtekerion.'

'By t-t-the One Earth!' Spellskin croaked, putting hand to mouth to cover his amazement.

'G-g-galtekerion? By all the Gods!' Lennox stuttered. 'H-h-how did you manage that?'

'Two courageous young men captured him: Bearhugger's esquires. One still fights for his life; the other is my daughter's esquire.'

'Esquires captured him? How?'

'That is a tale for another evening.'

'How do you know this is Galtekerion?' Lennox challenged.

The Earl Rufus shook his head. 'You have never fought the hobgoblins, my Lord, have you?' he said pointedly. 'Else you would know beyond doubt who it is. Clan tattoos, weaponry, his armour, kill fetishes, his standard. I am blind, but I know the face of my enemy. Do you?'

Lennox flushed red with fury. 'I cannot fight because I am cripple- '

'And your men?' Jakart said softly. 'Why can they not fight?'

'B-but how?' Lennox was trapped and in grave peril. A promising and highly lucrative alliance was imperilled by his patron's abrupt departure. He threw the dice one final time. 'How could the Lord Pro-, the WarLock, command hobgoblins? They are just mindless ravenous creatures.'

'Not quite, they may not understand why but they do understand what: they attacked the Old Wall as a diversion, whilst Galtekerion and his Chosen came after me, hoping to kill me before I could reach the sanctuary of Dragon Isle. They can be commanded or perhaps compelled to do his bidding.'

'So you see, my Lords,' the Earl looked about him with unsettling milky eyes. 'We are not ready for war, but neither is Hugo. With Galtekerion, the hobgoblins fight as one; without him they will fight for themselves or their tribes as they always have. It will take Hugo some time to realise his warlord is even missing, and then he will have to bring the tribes under control and choose a new leader...that may take him a year or longer. That is how long we have to regroup and train a new generation.'

CHAPTER THIRTY-FIVE

The Spell is Broken

Not surprisingly it happened in the HeartRock, that timeless world within a world. Together at every opportunity, Drumondir and Quenelda explored different places, times, peoples and dragons, combining that with teaching and testing Quenelda's new powers. Drumondir had first taught her how to weave a cloak, to hide herself should she ever need to from those who would hunt her. Already the young dragon whisperer was unthinkingly drawing bright elemental threads of magic together in sophisticated combinations and casting them in the blink of an eye without seeming to do anything. Quenelda was also learning military strategy and tactics by watching battles from long ago, and had already suggested to Tangnost a new way of launching dragons from the Old Wall without the need of slow dragon pads, as well as protecting those who fought there from dragon attacks themselves.

The two had been watching an ancient battle between sea eagle dragons and hobgoblins from a craggy bluff when suddenly a knot of ghostly hobgoblins charged at them, great flint swords raised. Drumondir found herself rooted to the spot...ghosts or not they were huge and the swords looked as real as their bloodcurdling cries!

Swiftly, unthinkingly, pushing Drumondir behind her, Quenelda flamed, a flute of withering dragon fire that engulfed their attackers. The hobgoblins vanished, which was excellent; but as Drumondir stepped backwards from the searing heat that did not harm her, she got an even bigger fright, although her long training meant the BoneCaster hid it well. One moment her pupil was a young girl and the next heartbeat Quenelda was clothed in glossy black scales from top to toe, still a girl, and yet also a dragon.

'And the most interesting part of it all,' Drumondir told Tangnost that evening, as they shared a pipe, now an established custom between the pair, 'was that Quenelda appeared completely unaware of her transformation!'

I did it! the young dragon informed the BoneCaster inside her head. *I did it! I flamed!*

'You have indeed,' Drumondir commented drily. 'Most impressive!' *So it truly begins. Will she shed her skin for scales forever or will she change back to a girl? What can she do as a dragon that she cannot do as a girl? How little we know!*

'Come; let us leave this battle and talk. How do you feel your studies are going?' Drumondir asked quietly as the battle faded from view and they were back in the central chamber of the HeartRock where beautifully carved chairs, a table and food awaited them. It had taken

Quenelda no time at all to realise that if she set her mind to something, or needed anything, it would appear.

As they moved to sit Quenelda's skin rippled and the young girl was back again before the tricky question of how she would sit with a tail could be explored; her smouldering eyes and the glowing yellow scale the only memory of what had happened.

Quenelda shivered stretching her limbs. 'It feels...far easier; instinctive, as if magic is at my fingertips now. And...because I am here, I'm not afraid of hurting anyone anymore... I know I can just do anything I want! No, I don't mean that, I know I have *so* much to learn, and so much yet to discover. It's just that inside...it must be your guidance...I feel I am growing, that I can finally use my power.'

'Mmnn...' Drumondir nodded, reaching for her pupil's hand. And so Quenelda listened open mouthed as the BoneCaster told her what had just happened.

'Close your mouth,' Drumondir said, gently tapping Quenelda's chin. 'You look like you are catching flies.' She sat quietly, letting the wide eyed girl take it all in.

'I was covered in scales?' Quenelda could still not believe it, holding a hand up and examining it. 'But how could I not notice?'

'Because,' Drumondir considered, 'I think your inner dragon spirit and you are one and the same, you are of OneKind, both dragon and man. And I think that inner spirit is growing stronger. Do you think you can change aspect again?'

Quenelda bit her lip doubtfully. 'I'm not sure. I don't

know what happened last time. Why can I suddenly do this? I've always been terrible, nothing ever worked before.'

The BoneCaster finally revealed her thoughts. 'I think that you have been spellbound from birth...to protect you from those who would do you harm before you come into your own power. And to prevent you from harming others,' Drumondir added. 'Else you would already be dead. You told me when you rescued your father at the Winter Jousts that you unleashed power that killed scores. And yet, the WarLock stood beside you and felt no threat. I - '

Sudden realisation hit Quenelda. 'Is that why I can never conjure spells? In case it revealed who I was? Everyone thinks I'm a dunce!'

Drumondir smiled. 'In part, yes; only in times of dire need would it answer your call. But I also believe you do not need props like wands and staffs or sorcery to cast your magic, they only confused your natural ability.'

The young girl was suddenly silent. 'What am I, Drumondir?' Quenelda asked at last. 'A dragon or a girl?' She was suddenly afraid. 'Everyone expects so much of me. What if I fail them, fail you and Tangnost and Papa?'

Drumondir drew on her pipe thoughtfully. 'Child you are changing, yes, but the changes are yours. The girl you are fashions the inner dragon, just as your inner dragon spirit guides the girl. Your lineage goes back hundreds of thousands of years, and yet you have not seen fourteen winters. Although you are a dragon whisperer you are also a girl at heart like any other; your father's daughter, heir to Dragonsdome, friend to Root and Quester, my pupil, and Tangnost's goddaughter.

We are all many things, we all wear many faces. You wear a second skin. Are you so very different? Does your gift really change how you think and feel in your hearts? Even were you not a whisperer, you would be asking these questions because you are becoming a young woman and leaving childhood behind. As are Root and Quester also growing up; it is a time of change for all of you.'

'As for failure, we all fail; all of us make mistakes and wish we had done something differently. Sometimes, if we are lucky, we have a chance to undo the damage, but often there is nothing to be done. If you have friends or a family who love you, they will help you through the difficult times such as these to give you guidance and love, and then failure doesn't seem so frightening. Learn from failure; that is how we all grow. Come now,' the BoneCaster tipped Quenelda's chin to look into her eyes and smiled. 'Let us build on what has happened today. Let's see if you can change aspect on command.'

CHAPTER THIRTY-SIX

High Treason

A pall of smoke still hung over the Black Isle, and the populace choked and coughed whilst the very young and old died as the freezing weather continued, with deep snowdrifts and the loch freezing over. Covered in chalky ash, hundreds of the homeless and destitute wandered the streets like ghosts, picking over the midden heaps. Barns were built to provide rough shelter, the Guild distributed food. The Apothecaries Guild and the Grave Yard Diggers tended the ill, the dying and the dead.

The cause of what was already being called the Great Fire was soon known. In Old Pentangle Square before the Guild Halls, and on the gates of the palace, a declaration was hammered up. For those many who could not read, royal heralds blew their trumpets. The Castle under-steward opened a scroll and cleared his throat.

'The Lord Hugo Mandrake, once Protector and Queen's Champion, who has fled into exile beyond the Old Wall, is hereby declared a WarLock and a traitor for the betrayal of the SDS to the hobgoblins at the Westering

Isles, and for the firing of the Black Isle. He is hereby forfeit of his titles, lands and life. He is to be brought to Dragon Isle for trial. A bounty of ten thousand gold crowns is placed upon his head.'

The mob surged forwards with a growl as word was passed from mouth to mouth. There were few in the City who would openly support Hugo Mandrake now, for fear of their lives.

CHAPTER THIRTY-SEVEN

Waxing and Wedding Dresses

Quenelda returned to the Black Isle and the palace for a few days to be with Armelia, at the Queen's suggestion. Darcy's wife was struggling with her husband's desertion, just as the Black Isle struggled to come to terms with the destruction and havoc wrecked by the WarLock King. Armelia, the Court and the populace needed something to take their minds from their misery, so the marriage of the Queen to the Earl had been announced, to take place at Beltane. The Guild, at their Grand Master's insistence, opened its treasure vaults to rebuild the city, providing skilled employment for its craftsmen and paid work for the dispossessed. Planning for the wedding should take everyone's mind off their misery.

'Em...' Armelia took a deep breath, anxious not to damage their new found friendship as they wandered about the royal studs. 'Em,' she dipped her toe in the pond. 'What are you wearing to the wedding?' she asked casually, as if it were of no account.

Quenelda shrugged equally casually. 'I hadn't thought about it...'

Armelia stared. There couldn't be another woman in the Kingdoms who hadn't thought about what to wear to the Royal wedding! 'Well,' she decided to go for it. 'Have you ever been, erm, shopping? Erm, to F&H?'

'No!' Quenelda looked horrified. 'Why would I go there?'

Armelia quailed and nearly gave up, but she gritted her teeth and plunged on. 'Well, to err, dress, to get a dress? Yes! For the wedding...'

'But I'm not a lady-in-waiting...I don't need a dress.'

'But you'll be the King's daughter! You're noble born and heir to Dragonsdome.'

Quenelda paused. 'I suppose I will be.'

Armelia shook her head in disbelief. 'Um, I'm going for my final fitting a week before the wedding, and I thought it might be fun for you to come too? To my dress fitting....and also I shall be spending time in the beauty parlour.'

'The beauty parlour!?' Quenelda wrinkled her nose. 'What happens there?'

'Um...painting fingernails, seaweed face packs... eyebrow plucking...leg waxing...'

'Leg waxing?' Quenelda had never heard of it.

'Well, you pour on warm wax and then get a strip and pull...it gets rid of hair...hairy legs.'

'But what does that matter? I always wear boots... and anyway,' Quenelda frowned. 'Hairy legs keep you warm in winter.'

Armelia swallowed a squeak of horror. 'But imagine... yes, well, imagine you wore a dress. You couldn't wear boots with a dress. You would want a pair of...well anything except boots.'

Quenelda nodded grudgingly.

'And if you were invited to dance...Everyone dances at weddings, you might crush the gentleman's toes or trip him up!'

'I don't know how to dance,' Quenelda pointed out with infuriating logic. 'I was never any good at it.'

Armelia took a deep breath and tried another tack. 'And they have maaarvellous hairdressers. Perhaps they might do something with your hair.'

'Why?' Quenelda was instantly defensive. 'What's wrong with my hair? Like what?'

'Well, anything really...perhaps run a comb through it?'

'But I wear a helmet. The minute I put one on it flattens it, and the wind tangles it. You'll see when I take you flying.'

Armelia took a last roll of the dice. 'You've grown this year...won't you need some new clothes?'

Quenelda nodded. It was true: her boots pinched a little and her breeches were too short....

'Well I suppose....' *It can't do any harm...if it makes Armelia happy...*

CHAPTER THIRTY-EIGHT

Basic Training – Boots on the Ground

Basic training began in earnest and it was neither glamorous nor fun, nor did it involve dragons in any shape, form or description. In fact it was exhausting and bruising right from day one, especially for the young pampered lords. They might be trained in the knightly arts and be able to fly thoroughbred dragons and wield a sword, but that had not prepared them for the gruelling training that BoneCrackers and the SeaReavers went through.

Throughout a cold spring, the Juveniles became fit and strong from running about the island, often carrying weights over obstacle courses and then in armour. There was snow and more snow, mud and more mud, drill and more drill, so that they learnt to move as one, think as one, fight as one. They learnt how to care for and mend all forms of mundane weapons and armour from rusting chain mail to war mallets. Root and Quentin and the younger cadets struggled even to lift the heavy chain mail hauberks and the tall curved marine shields causing mocking contempt from some of the young lords who had formed a cabal under Bracus's leadership. Quentin soon earned their enmity; the commoner appeared to have no idea of his proper place, and an astounding grasp of theoretical tactics and battlefield manoeuvres that surprised the cadet himself. Deliberately isolated, Root and Quentin soon took most of the commoners, dwarves and trolls under their wing.

'Form a line of linked shields....come on ladies; your grandma could break through the gaps in that!' Badgerlock lamented.

'Incoming, incoming, shields up...'

Missiles, from clods of earth to sticks and stones, arced skywards as the Juveniles struggled to form a defensive shield circle. The first rank dropped to their knees, the second interlinking as they stood and the third rank hefted shields as the volley of missiles rained down on them. There were muffled cries.

'Many darts and quarrels are poisoned...if you were just hit by a lump of mud you're dead,' Badgerlock warned them. 'Do it again!'

Basic flying training, too, began on the wooden dragon, a huge witchwood Imperial which could raise and lower its wings and sweep the length of the Endless Dragon Hall.

'It doesn't matter what some of you think you know about flying, none of you,' Badgerlock glanced at Quentin and Root, 'have flown an Imperial. When you are in the middle of a battle you will have to insert or extract your soldiers. You may be in the air, but they have boots on the ground. You must experience for yourself what it is like to mount and dismount in full armour and carrying injured comrades.'

'Sir!' A young troll raised his hand.

'Cadet?'

'What does i-insert and x-x...?'

There were guffaws up and down the lines from Bracus and his friends, Ranulf and Gwelhem, quickly silenced by Badgerlock's gimlet eyes. The sergeant major stopped in front of the arrogant young man. 'Explain, cadet, the terms insertion and extraction to those who have not had their own tutor since they were a toddler.'

Bracus's mouth set in an insolent sneer, his words dripped with contempt. 'Insert means 'drop off' and extract means 'lift off'.'

'Since you are so familiar with the terms, cadet, will you now demonstrate what they mean in action to the rest of your class? So that they may learn from your example? Combat take off.'

That wiped the smile from the young man's face.

The Juveniles gathered nervously half way down the long hall. Behind them, the Badger pressed an icon. Smoothly silently the wooden dragon's wings began to beat. 'In your own time, cadet.'

Bracus began to jog alongside the dragon, his long legs easily keeping pace.

As the wings came down, Bracus hesitated, waiting until they came down a third time before mounting. But he left it too late and the wing was already on the rise so he stumbled before tripping and toppling down the wing into the body of the dragon. Picking himself up, Bracus fell over again before managing to dismount, furious that he had been singled out to make a fool of himself.

'Would anyone care to comment on what went wrong?'

Root knew only too well, and sympathised with the young lord. He had never forgotten that day at Dragonsdome when he had just become Quenelda's esquire, watching other esquires fall and fail mounting an old harrier dragon, dreading the moment when he would be asked.

'He's not wearing flying boots,' Root offered to Bracus's fury.

'Correct, cadet! Has anyone else ignored my instructions to wear flying boots today?'

One or two hands went up, all young sorcerer lords who had not bothered to read the instructions posted outside Cloud Hall. 'Then go and fetch them. The rest of you do not attempt to mount unless you are certain you understand the rhythm. Who would like to show us how it's done?'

'Let's see you do any better!' Bracus shoved Root roughly forwards.

Here was an opportunity for mockery and derision, but to the disappointment of Bracus and his friends that did not include Root or Quentin, who appeared as if they had done it a dozen times.

'How can commoners know how to fly a dragon?' Bracus hissed in frustration, as he fell off a wing trying to repeat Quentin's light-footed feat.

CHAPTER THIRTY-NINE

Spread Your Wings and Fly

Root found Quenelda sitting alone in the mess hall, poking at her food. She looked tired. 'What's up?' He smiled. 'Has Drumondir been testing you too hard?'

Quenelda hesitated. *How will Root feel about me now that I'm changing?*

She's hiding something...she is afraid...of what? Root waited as he ate his meal; Quenelda would tell him when she was ready.

'Do you have time to go flying tonight?' She asked at last. *Let's see if I can fly outside the HeartRock now.*

'Yes!' Root was eager. 'Chasing the Stars is impatient to fly! I don't have enough time with her. It will make a change from training! And Bracus,' the gnome turned as the huge sorcerer lord entered the mess hall, bragging loudly as usual.

'Good,' Quenelda said, but she still looked worried. Root was even more confused when he was saddling up in the stables and she asked to ride pillion with him.

'I thought we were going flying?'

'We are!' she snapped. 'Let's go up to the top of the White Sorcerer, you remember above that waterfall where you first learnt to fly?'

A storm of wild dragons were gathered in huge numbers about the mountain tops as dusk settled darkly on the glen below, and they didn't take off when Chasing the Stars put down. *Tangnost told me this is how they gathered when I was born...*That gave Quenelda hope as she walked up to the spray-soaked ledge where the water burst horizontally out of the mountain. *Time to truly test the inner dragon soul...am I the person everyone thinks I am?*

She hesitated. This must have been what Root felt like the first time he sat here in the pilot's saddle of Chasing the Stars. Ready, but reluctant to take that next step or rather, as Drumondir had told her, 'to take that leap of faith into the void that sometimes needed to be taken in order to grow, to become something more.' Many hesitated at that threshold, Drumondir had warned her. *Well,* Quenelda thought, *I'm not going to be one of them!* She had been practising for days changing her aspect from girl to dragon and girl again, testing the limits of what she could do under Drumondir's watchful eye.

She lifted her head, gazing up at the diamond dust of the Dragon's Breath...those countless stars and planets were where dragonkind came from, where I came from, for their memories were now her memories. And so, with a deep breath, she leapt! Whatever a baffled Root was expecting as he sat astride Chasing the Stars, it certainly wasn't Quenelda falling off the rocky ledge into the emptiness of night.

'Quenelda!' Root screamed, stunned, almost leaping out of the saddle. 'Go, Girl! Go!' He urged Chasing the Stars over the precipice.

Quenelda was falling, and fast, the spirit of her dead battledragon calling to her from beyond the rainbow bridge. Sorcery stirred sluggishly in her veins. She fell, arms and legs outstretched; reaching for the wind, but her limbs felt like lead and would not respond. Below, the sharp crest of the Impassable Ridge raced to meet her. Closing her eyes, Quenelda surrendered her soul to Two Gulps and You're Gone.

In this last dance of dragons
I will fly with you no more,
We will never feel the wind
Beneath us when we soar.

'Quenelda! Quenelda!' Root was frantic as he plunged through the icy spray. The freezing water was soaking his flying leathers, pouring down his back, smashing off his helmet. Root couldn't see, couldn't hear, couldn't think! Chasing the Stars screamed her distress as the water hammered on her delicate wings and she began to fall. Banking out, knuckling his eyes Root scoured the unbroken snow below for a body, but it was so dark, and the snow was all shades of blue and moonlight. Sodden through, trembling with cold and fear, Root put Chasing the Stars down on a bluff. The wild dragons had formed a gyre, a spinning tunnel; the force of their wings threatening to suck Chasing the Stars in.

Suddenly Quenelda felt no fear. The air was her element, it always had been. Elder sorcery flared hotly inside her. The pulse of her twin hearts sang in her ears and a bright fierce joy suffused her veins. Elemental threads in half a hundred hues curled about her, the raw power of it filled her lungs as she felt a shiver across her skin and black scales covered her, a second living skin. She spread her nascent wings and soared upwards at the heart of the gyre.

'Quenelda! Quenelda!' The hoarse cry was frantic, cutting through the dance. With an effort Quenelda tore herself away and swooped down in search of her friend. Then abruptly Chasing the Stars shot past her. 'Where are you? Where are youuuu?'

Root! Root! I'm alright! Slow down!

Below her Chasing the Stars stalled; catching air in her wings the young mare swept up and onto a ledge shaking off the weight of ice that was forming on her wings. 'Quenelda?' Root shouted, not sure if he had heard anything. 'Where are you? Argh!' He yanked on the reins and threw up a hand to protect himself as a small dragon loomed out of the dark, landing beside them. It was a clumsy landing. The dragon nearly fell on its nose.

Root tried to back away, but Chasing the Stars

wouldn't budge, moving forwards instead to nuzzle inquisitively at the small dragon which flapped and fell over with an irritated squawk.

Stop it! Chasing the Stars! Stop it!

Stop it? That was Quenelda's voice! 'Quenelda?' Root peered over his dragon's head to where the small dragon struggled to fend off Chasing the Stars' enthusiastic lipping. No, it wasn't a small dragon as he had first thought; instead a figure scaled perfectly from tip to toe, with graceful frothy wings that swept down to the ground stood upright. Glossy black, save for the left claws and shoulder, and the odd scale here and there which were yellow gold...the colour of a sabretooth battledragon.

'Quenelda?!' Root thought he must be going mad.

Continuing to ignore him, the Quenelda-shaped dragon lifted a foreleg and examined the razor-sharp talons. Then it flicked its tail experimentally, making Chasing the Stars rise up in order to avoid being knocked off the ledge. The dragon, Root couldn't quite call it Quenelda, turned to consider its swishing tail, its head moving hypnotically from side to side as if about to pounce.

'Um???' Root ventured to distract the dragon. He felt a little silly. 'Um, can you talk?'

The head swung completely about and molten eyes considered him.

Of course I can talk! Quenelda said indignantly, her nose smoking.

Root looked over his shoulder. Where had that voice come from?

Me! Where do you think?

'But...but...' Root stuttered, 'your mouth isn't moving.' Which was just as well, as it was a rather larger mouth than he was accustomed to, with wicked looking teeth...he had better not annoy her when she was in this mood!

Isn't it? No...the dragon thoughtfully lipped back baring its teeth.

Am I...am I dragon whispering then?

Yes, I suppose so...you must hear me the same way I hear the dragons. What... Quenelda sounded suddenly uncertain. *What...what do I look like?*

You look like a... Root blinked. 'Girl.' Quenelda was back.

'How...? When did you learn to do that?' Root was awestruck. 'Can you change when you want?'

His friend didn't answer. 'You...' Quenelda put a hand to the scales on her brow which seemed to increase each time she changed aspect. 'Do you...still want to be my friend? I mean...I don't know who I am anymore, Root! What will people think of me?'

In seconds the young gnome had dismounted and wrapped his friend up in a wet hug. 'Don't be daft! You're still you, dragon or not! Scales, wings, it's part of who you are, and it doesn't matter what anyone else thinks!'

'Truly?'

'Truly.' He took her face gently in his hands, hinting at the young man he was on the cusp of becoming. 'Look at me! A gnome, a commoner, yet I'm training to be a Dragon Lord! The people we love, who love us, they're proud of us! We're changing things, Quenelda, to protect them.'

'This was the first time I tried outside the HeartRock,' Quenelda remounted Chasing the Stars behind her friend. 'To begin with it just happened. I didn't even notice.'

'You didn't notice you had wings and a tail?' Shaking his head in disbelief Root nudged Chasing the Stars forwards and they swept down to the loch, heading for Dragon Isle.

CHAPTER FORTY

You've Come Back to Us!

Quenelda was in the HeartRock and the Juveniles were practising in the Long Dragon Hall when word arrived.

'Oakley, step up,' Badgerlock said gruffly.

'Sir?'

'Your friend Quester has regained consciousness; go on, away with you! You are excused duties for the rest of the day.'

Root ran, forgetting about porting stones, forgetting everything in his haste. By the time he arrived at Quester's bed he couldn't speak, was shaking all over and was nearly sick. All he could do was take his friend's hand.

'You've come back to us,' Root smiled through tears of joy. 'Quester! You've come back!'

CHAPTER FORTY-ONE

The Dark Knights

The Beltane wedding was approaching which would bring a welcome break from training. But not for some Imperial crews; their training began in earnest. The elite aircrew of the Dark Knights were rarely seen these days; they were in the field hunting hobgoblins, but now they took to the skies to rehearse their display. Drop Dead was a favourite with the crowds, but Starburst was a close second.

Excused from training for the remainder of the day, Quentin and Root, along with hundreds of other Juveniles, crowded the paddocks, gantries and battlements on the north side of the island, searching the blue for specks or smoke trails.

'There they are!' someone cried pointing down the loch. The dark specks grew larger and larger closing at unbelievable speed. 'And there, too!' Quentin cried, pointing the other way. 'It's the tilting yard! They fly straight at each other as they do at the Winter Jousts, before swinging out to pass within two wing spans,' she

179

explained to Root.

The dragons were closing at speed now, smoke canisters blazing a colourful trail. There were cries and gasps of alarm and then sighs of relief as the two dragons rolled at the last moment, passing so close their wing tips almost touched, and leaving corkscrews of smoke in their wake. And then the thunderclap of their passing hit everyone, knocking some spectators to the ground, making others duck and put their hands over their ears.

There was a pause. A number of the Dark Knights were seen gathering on the northern headlands of the glen, but most of them had disappeared.

'Drop Dead,' someone whispered. 'It has to be!'

Heads craned skywards, eyes screwed up against the brilliance....

'No, Starburst! It's Starburst,' Quentin said.

Tiny specks in the azure blue grew larger and larger... and larger. There were some screams in the audience as younger cadets began to run. Others cowered down.

'Ha!' Bracus sneered.. 'They'll never be test pilots like the Dark Knights. Look at them running like rabbits!'

Root however stood there, Quentin by his side, gazing upwards. Upwards to where the razor talons sheathed in bright ceremonial colours grew larger and larger. Upwards towards the armoured underbellies, tails tucked beneath, dropping at immense speed. His heart started racing. Surely they were too close, too late to pull out?

And then their wings opened with a crack and tails came out, pointed inwards in perfect formation of a star, and the dragons' descent slowed. But still they were within a wing span of each other, forming a perfect outward ring, still falling...falling. Smoke canisters of gold and white exploded. The Imperials somersaulted so that their heads were facing outwards, and each broke away like the point of an exploding star, thunder rolling from their wings as they passed. Stardust slowly faded as it dropped down like golden rain.

Cheering broke out, and those that had fled returned, red faced, to join in the celebrations.

'I thought they weren't going to make it,' someone croaked hoarsely.

'I want to be one of the Dark Knights!' Quentin declared.

'I thought you might,' Root answered with a smile. 'I'm not sure that I do! I'd just be sick!'

CHAPTER FORTY-TWO

The Black Prince

A light offshore breeze was blowing the last snow clouds from the early morning sky, as grooms brought two pure black pedigree hippogriffs from the vast, dark, soaring roosts, along with helmets with dark visors.

'Snow blindness,' his father told Darcy, 'wear it or you risk your eyes.'

Mounting, the WarLock King and his son flew the length of the island. The volcano to the west was quiet, but a towering mushroom plume of grey smoke and ash billowed from the larger of the two to the south. It was a harsh primeval land of snow fields and lava plains, sulphurous pools and black volcanic sands, divided by glaciers achingly grinding their way to the sea. It was both a stark and wondrous land.

Bitter cold... Darcy thought. *Unforgiving... How can any one get used to this infernal cold?* And yet the Prince's Tower was luxuriously warm and the water that had flowed through a smooth channel into a basin in his room and into huge baths below was deliciously hot! Bathing was once a laborious affair. Now he stepped down into the huge mosaic tiled baths and soaked the aches and chill away. *How?*

Barrack upon barrack passed beneath. Frost dragon igloos were clustered everywhere. Training grounds... tilt yards...assault courses. Soldiers practising, drilling... there was an army here, training for war.

'It is like Dragon Isle! This *is* the size of a Kingdom,' Darcy acknowledged as they passed over a vast encampment of tents and a thousand fires. 'Is this the Army of the North?'

'No. The main army is marching south towards the Old Wall as we speak. These are our new recruits: paid, trained, and equipped by the Guild. Many men and dwarves have been lured to fight for gold and lands or blood feuds...fostered by my men.' He laughed. 'The fools! Poor deluded fools. The Guild's own dragons and gold will bring them down!'

'We are quite safe,' the WarLock assured Darcy as they put down on the lower slopes of the volcano, close to the vast sea wall that girdled the island. 'It's not erupted since the Second Age.'

'Does it have a name?'

'The hobgoblins call it the Kiss of Death. The Snowy Owl clan: Glacier Peak. There are other, older names.'

The hobgoblins? Darcy kept the shock from his face. *The hobgoblins have a name for a mountain?* They didn't even speak, did they? *Just mindless creatures...but how then does he command them?*

They took a porting stone down into the island, a blur of black that, to his frustration, made the young man's knees buckle again. After the freezing cold outside it was unexpectedly hot down in the depths and Darcy quickly shed his heavy cloak, giving it to a soldier who came swiftly to take it. Touching the walls, Darcy was puzzled when his fingers came away warm and wet.

'The volcano,' his father understood Darcy's confusion. 'There are lava passages everywhere beneath Roarkinch; we make sure our passageways are sealed from them, but we also make use of their heat.'

'The hot water in my tower?'

His father nodded. 'Just so. Hot water from the springs, hot floors...it might appear a barren island but if you know how to master the elements...'

'This is where most of the prisoners are held, save those in the brimstone and gold mines further south. None can escape the volcano and the sea. Fire or razorbacks, either way prisoners die if they try to run.'

Darcy followed his father through wide polished passageways that tunnelled through the island bedrock like a warren. He tried to remember the times in his childhood when his father, the man who he once thought of as his father, had taken him to Dragon Isle, but the memories had dimmed in a fog of resentment.

Armed soldiers were posted everywhere; trolls, dwarves, men, it was hard to know because of the fearsome masks they wore. *Why the masks?* Darcy wondered.

'Masks make our enemies afraid. They do not know who, or what, they are fighting. It adds to their fear.'

It adds to mine, but Darcy fervently hoped he kept that thought to himself. Then they came upon a great spiralling stair well that hung suspended in the air. Flames burning from fissures in the rock lit the way. Down they stepped and down past poorly lit caves where dozens and dozens of hammocks hung like slugs. Water buckets and ladles crowded the entrances. As they passed, Darcy heard moaning and crying.

'Slaves and prisoners taken in war,' he was told. 'Some work the foundries. Others await the kiss of the Abyss.'

They had reached the bottom of the great well. One of the caverns ahead was lit a lurid flickering red and clouds of smoke billowed up the passageway. It was oppressively hot. There was a heavy rhythmic pounding as if the island had a heartbeat. The warlock plucked a mask from many on the wall and handed it to his son. 'Put it on.'

Darcy obeyed not noticing his father didn't do the same.

As they rounded the corner Darcy thought that it must be a scene from the Abyss as he was assailed by a wall of heat that flayed his throat and stung his eyes. On the far side of the long sea cavern lava poured down a rock face and into the sea, raising smoking spitting spume fifty strides high. The lava flow had been funnelled into a system of roughhewn troughs and trenches that fired a dozen blazing foundries. Bellows and charcoal weren't needed here, but countless slaves were.

Galleons riding at anchor beside the docks beyond the cavern were off loading great leather buckets of red iron ore into wagons with rough wheels. These were pulled by gangs of slaves around the great cavern to where others tipped them into vast crucibles above the lava flow. Slaves, wrapped from head to toe in smoking salty wet rags to protect them from the heat, held long poles with hooks that snagged the crucibles over the lava pool, and then they were tipped so the molten metal ran along filling the moulds to become swords and spears and maces.

Thump... thump... thump... like an unholy heartbeat the rhythmic pounding of metal filled the air as shields and swords, helmets and breastplates and dragon armour were being cast and forged and cooled by troughs of seawater.

With swift sure steps the WarLock led Darcy towards a small group of smiths near an archway open to the sea breeze and daylight. The grizzled dwarf that stood there at the anvil, stripped to the waist save for a thick leather apron and mask, held tongs in one gauntleted hand that gripped a glowing length of metal, and a heavy mallet in the other that raised a fury of sparks.

The smith was huge, as broad as he was tall. Corded muscles glistened with sweat and the leather mask that protected him from the burning heat hid all but his eyes. His arms were decorated with clan tattoos of the Golden Eagle clan...and the crossed hammer and anvil tattoo on his upper arm marked him out as a master blacksmith. As the dwarf turned to plunge his handiwork into the water trough, raising billowing vapours, Darcy was startled to see that his back was crisscrossed with scars...many of them recent and unhealed. Then he noticed the heavy manacles about the master smith's ankles.

His eyes widened...*they're like dragon collars...bound with words of obedience and subservience...* He could feel the spell trying to dominate him and swayed on his feet.

The WarLock smiled mirthlessly. 'Yes, Faldir, the greatest smith in the Seven Kingdoms, missing these last three years after his longboat disappeared. He had to be... persuaded to work his craft...but when your family are being cared for here in the dungeons of Roarkinch...' He let the sentence hang. 'Tell my son how it is made,' he commanded. 'This blade is for him.'

'Truly?' Darcy was breathless with delight.

'Swords such as this are crafted from the purest steel...' Faldir explained. 'What the clans call diamond steel is entwined with sky metal. Diamond steel gives a razor sharp edge and the inner sky metal strength and resilience. The one is inlaid in the other and forged to make a single blade; thus you have a lethal killing edge fashioned about inner strength.'

'The SDS must miss their Master Smith must they not?' The WarLock smiled. 'For Faldir fashioned the blades of Dragon Lords as his father and grandfather before him.'

'Smith to the Dragon Lords?'

Faldir nodded.

'The armour,' the WarLock demanded. 'Is it complete?'

'Yes.' Laying down his tools, the dwarf moved away from the forges towards brightly lit lesser caverns, where goldsmiths and silversmiths were inlaying delicate traceries of precious metal. Beyond, a dozen wooden armour stands were clustered. Hanging on one was a full suit of armour. Darcy sucked in his breath. It was beautiful beyond words.

The suit of armour was black and yet not black. Black, perhaps, as a raven's wing might be in the sunlight...iridescent...alive with rippling colours that caught the light of the forges beyond. The dragon helmet, itself a marvel, was bound by a circlet of gold inlaid into witchwood.

'It's...fit for a King.' Darcy was envious of his father, had never seen anything he had wanted so much in his life. Not even the parade uniform of the Unicorn Household Guard matched this! It sang to him.

'No...Fit for a Prince...' Darcy's eyes widened as his father nodded. 'This is for you...'

'Crafted with magic as well as sky metal...Faldir still has the old words of Making that his forefathers used. Such lore has mostly been lost to the dwarves...so we are fortunate indeed to have him as our...guest.'

Already Darcy's fingers were tracing the inlaid gold and obsidian shards that spiked the helmet, the fluted dragon wings that swept back.

'It will protect you, my son. None can kill you wearing this armour....'

'May I try it on?' Darcy was eager as a child.

Eyes smouldering with hate as hot as his forge, Faldir nodded, motioning two of his apprentices forward.

Stripping Darcy down to his under-leggings they armoured him.

'It's so light!' Darcy was alight with fierce joy as dragon spurs were fitted. 'I truly feel like a Prince!'

Smiling, the WarLock knew he had chosen his gift well. Darcy's name would never be forgotten. 'Hereafter, my son, you shall be known as the Black Prince.'

CHAPTER FORTY-THREE

To Stop You from Hurting Yourself

Basic weapons training finally began and Quenelda departed for the HeartRock. Badgerlock drew Root aside to quietly tell the young gnome that he had to take part, but that his tuition would be purely defensive. At this the dwarf's eyes glinted and a smile twitched his stern lips, and Root knew that the gruff Sergeant Major appreciated who had captured Galtekerion. 'I'm watching your back, son,' he nodded. Root was further cheered when Tangnost joined them.

'Those who think they know how to fight, line up with Dragon Master Bearhugger. The rest of you stay with me.'

Bracus and all the young lords left with relief and open contempt for those left behind.

The Juveniles stepped forward in an eager line at the Quarter Master's for training armour and weaponry. Enthusiasm amongst the young sorcerer lords soon turned into open rebellion as they were issued with wooden practice swords.

'So!' Tangnost barked. 'Some of you are disappointed! Thought you'd be donning shining armour and magic swords, did you? Like the Dragon Lords?'

The Juveniles looked steadily at a point in the distance. Tangnost stopped in front of the tall broad shouldered youth who had openly complained.

'Name?'

'Bracus Beaumont.'

'Bracus Beaumont, *Sir*!'

'Bracus Beaumont, Sir!'

The young man's insolent tone made Tangnost bridle but he hid it well. 'Think you should already be a knight do you, Beaumont?'

'Sir, No, Sir!'

'No, Sir! And can you tell me why you have been issued wooden swords?'

'Sir, to stop me hurting anyone, Sir!'

'Wrong. To stop you hurting yourself, cadet. Let me show you why.'

Guffaws made Bracus flush with fury. Tangnost picked up a wooden practice sword and settled into a two-handed grip with his guard raised up.

'Pick up that claymore and try it for size.'

Bracus picked up the heavy weapon from the weapons rack, feeling its balance.

'See if you can beat me,' Tangnost invited.

Bracus smiled as he cut the air with his long claymore in a showy display. The dwarf was old, one eyed and limped. Bracus wasn't scared of Bearhugger's reputation. He may not be able to track through mud and muck, or sand down his armour, but he had been learning sword craft since he was knee high!

At his first attempt, Bracus slashed down from right to left, swinging hard, and felt the bone-jarring thump shiver up his arms and skull as his blade bit the floor. Tangnost side stepped up to place his wooden blade on the young man's throat. Angry, embarrassed, Bracus swung again more wildly. The weight pivoted him about in a circle of silver steel but Tangnost just danced out of range. As Bracus's arm was dragged down by the claymore's weight, the Dragon Master sidestepped smoothly and brought his sword down to rest against the young man's unprotected side.

'You're dead again, boy!'

Angered, without invitation, Bracus swung again as he rose, but Tangnost ducked and kicked out hard and the youth sprawled on the training floor. 'Never let anger use you,' Tangnost's one eye flashed. '*You* use anger! And you don't let your own weapon kill you! Never let its weight swing you round, leaving you exposed to your enemy's weapon!'

'You may be schooled in knightly combat, but those you will fight won't give a fig for chivalry. They fight dirty, and you will have to learn if you want to stay alive.'

Tangnost turned to his cadets. 'Something to think upon over the next week before I see you again. Now go! Make the most of your time on the Black Isle, it's the last you will be having for a very long time.'

CHAPTER FORTY-FOUR

Strike at their Heart

The WarLock King looked down from the heights of the Dark Citadel. The thaw had set in and his lords were gathering at Roarkinch for their orders. The tepid seas around the volcanic island were crammed with war galleons and long ships. Out on the sulphurous plain, the army was preparing to embark within the moon and scores of dragons were landing bell by bell. Down in the caverns and caves the drums were summoning the hobgoblins. Roarkinch was readying for war.

He turned back from the balcony to the men and women assembled around the table; Lords who owed their elevation and wealth to his patronage, war captains who held lands at his behest, mercenaries and his son; although the whereabouts of his Dragon Master, Knuckle Quarnack remained a mystery. He must have died on the night the Earl returned to the palace; no matter, there were plenty of other ruthless ambitious men to choose from. All here owed their loyalty to him and the hope that he would soon subdue the Seven Kingdoms, then wealth and lands would be theirs for the choosing. Loyalty always had a price.

'How are preparations for war?'

'My King...' The Duke of Kilntyre, a hard faced Stormspike Marcher lord from the far south answered first. 'I have four hundred ships nearing completion. We have press-ganged full fifty crews...cleaned out the fishing villages and coastal settlements...seized longboats. The SDS SeaReavers' fortress is seriously under-strength; at your command we will attack from the south.'

'Sir Garrick?'

The gaunt, one-armed Lord known as the Wolf of Baddenoch replied. 'We have over a hundred longships built and thirty six taken intact in raids, all anchored deep in Loch Snekkie, hidden from sight. We have cut down the oak forests for leagues about. Sixty are fully rigged but rope and sails had not arrived before the snow closed the passes.'

Finding the WarLock's unsettling gaze upon him a spindly weasel faced man stood, wringing his hands. The Master of the Cordage and Canvas Guild, long courted as an ally, had been bought long ago with gold and lands in the north. Pale faced and nervous, he looked to Darcy like he regretted the deal. Exile had yet to bring the hoped for comforts of his estate in the south.

'My Lord ....My Lord King, we have scores of children gathered from villages far and wide at work in the Rope Makers' Huts on the mainland, built near your dockyards. Sixty of your ice breaker galleons are now fully rigged in the deep inner lochs and we should be able to rig any ship that puts in now, if we are given the men?'

'And the sails?'

Mistress Martha Spinner of the Flax Spinners and Dyers Guild was one of the few woman to come north, she had been a guest who found suddenly she could not go home. But exile had its compensations. Dressed in fur lined robes she had the symbolic tools of her trade about her girdle, cast in silver; flax brake, rippler, scutching knife and hackle. 'The flax crop was damaged by the weather, Lord King. We have not enough flax to spin and so we are making sails of wool...'

And so it went on as Darcy fretted to be out with his friends. The detail of war did not interest him, the stockpiles of brimstone, sea currents and safe harbours...

'You have taken prisoners?'

'My Lord, many.'

'Bring them for the kiss of the Abyss, and then we will send them back to their loved ones.'

Darcy shivered. *Again that threat, the kiss of the Abyss?* He had not dared ask.

'The moment the hobgoblins swarm from the spawning pools we are going to attack, hit the SDS while they are still in disarray and distracted by the...wedding.' The WarLock King moved to the huge map carved on the table top.

'Half the hobgoblins have been summoned to Loch Kattaw, here at the head of the Brimstones, from where they will move east and south to strike the Howling Glen and the Old Wall. The Army of the North, currently overwintering here and here and here, will hit the Old Wall in support of the banners. You, my Lord Baddenoch attack the Howling Glen. The SDS must believe that these are our objectives.'

'Aren't they?' Darcy frowned.

'No! Galtekerion and his Chosen and the bulk of the tribal banners have been summoned to the Isle of Midges to await our fleet's arrival.

While they have emptied their roosts we strike at their heart. Two banners, three hundred Imperials, five thousand troops and tens of thousands of razorbacks bearing hobgoblins commanded by Galtekerion will strike at their heart and cut it out.'

Darcy frowned. 'Where then?'

The WarLock raised eyes that flared the green. He no longer needed to hide the mark of the maelstrom, the latticework that finely veined his pale skin, the smoke that flickered about his outline. Still darkly handsome he now also looked terrifying.

'Dragon Isle. For power lies there I am sure of it. They never let me set foot there. That island hides many secrets. We will unleash the maelstrom in the Sorcerers Glen, and destroy the heart of the SDS and the old Alliance. And Kilntyre, you hit the SeaReavers, make sure they cannot come to Dragon Isle's aid.'

CHAPTER FORTY-FIVE

Your Special Friend Is?

Granted a half-moon furlough to be with family and friends and to attend the Royal wedding before specialised training began, Quenelda and scores of others headed home to see the Black Isle for the first time since the Great Fire, leaving Root to spend time with Quester who was still seriously ill. From the Boulevard Circle down to the Gutters and the harbours beyond, the city was being rebuilt. Work gangs and scaffolding were everywhere, and a steady stream of carts and wagons loaded with timber, stone, thatching and tiles clogged the three causeways. Guild foresters, slaters, masons and thatchers had found work aplenty and a warm welcome from the citizens of the Black Isle who were eager to lend a hand. Like fresh shoots after a long winter, houses were rising again, as rickety and crowded as before. Some were five stories high so that refugees from the war could find a room of their own!

Predictably F&H's Exclusive Emporium was a hive of activity as the wealthy and noble flocked for last minute adjustments to their extravagant wedding robes and the latest 'must have' wedding accessories. F&H's numerous landing pads were all taken: the packed ones weighing anchor and floating up high and only coming down when summoned by their patrons. Once inside, a delectable range of wedding mementos were decking F&H's opulent halls. Wedding wands and staffs, crystal, plates, cushions and clocks emblazoned with the new royal coat of arms. Superlative designer hats were particularly popular. Plenty for everyone: there were even C&R chamber pots! And of course, all by royal appointment!

Circling carriages packed with anxious patrons were stacked, awaiting a dragon pad vacancy, when faint cries and shouts lifted everyone's heads skywards. The cause of their ire was weaving deftly in and out between them causing chaos. It was a lone dragon...a rather chubby looking juvenile which was flapping its wings desperately to keep airborne long enough to land on the vacant royal pad. The pad master signalled roost hands forwards. Outrageous that some scruff and his cloaked companion from the lower quarter thought he could land here!

The roost hands watched with interest as the young dragon attempted to land. Sweeping in and flapping its small wings frantically it overshot the pad and plunged downwards out of sight. Every one rushed to the rail to watch as it narrowly avoided crashing through the awnings below, before gathering enough momentum to fly through a narrow gap, collecting six rows of bunting on the way. The dragon flew a wide arc, gaining height before attempting to put down again. Somewhat clumsily, it tripped over its own huge feet and landed on its chin, drawing a shriek as its two passengers were unceremoniously dumped on the pad, one atop the other.

Already the footmen were closing in to eject the scruffy boy as he crawled out from beneath a dozen lacy petticoats, when it belatedly dawned on them that this dragon had a nasty assortment of large pointy teeth with matching talons. A narrow stream of plasma clarified the situation and helped them on their way over the edge of the pad with their kilts smoking, as a tousled young lady's head, bedecked with unravelled ribbons and smudged rouge, struggled to emerge from beneath the weight of her elaborate brocade dress. Unceremoniously yanked to her feet by the scruffy boy, the familiar face of the Armelia was at last recognised.

The Pad Master fixed her with a baleful stare. 'This ...boy is part of your entourage, Countess?'

Armelia nodded, carefully dusting herself down. 'Yes! Err, yes, sh-...he is...'

'Is that a battledragon...?'

'Yes. Please don't touch him; he bites,' Quenelda added wickedly.

Armelia wilted. It was only going to get worse. It did.

As the incongruous pair entered the hallowed ground of the Ladies Salon, a large perfumed lady floated up under full sail, outrage etched on her face, her double chin drawn back in disapproval. Samantha Spellgood took her responsibility of cosseting the wealthy from the uncomfortable realities of life very seriously indeed. 'G-ggentle- ' the word stuck in her throat. Whoever this tatty boy was, he was clearly not a gentleman! They totally ignored her and carried on! Hastening after them, she tried a different tack.

'Only ladies are allowed beyond this portal.'

This didn't have quite the effect she had hoped. The scruffy boy turned to stare at her whilst his companion looked flustered.

'Is there a problem?'

'No.' Quenelda offered haughtily. 'Not yet.' She knew she shouldn't have agreed to come to this awful place, so full of perfume and pretensions.

The exquisitely dressed young lady at the boy's side looked flustered. 'This...this...' Armelia waved her hands in the air as if she was about to conjure a rabbit out a hat.

'Why...Countess,' Samantha curtsied ...'Lady Armelia, what a deelight to see you again....and your special friend is?'

Armelia swallowed. Unsure of her friend's temper she drew herself up haughtily. 'This is...is the Lady Quenelda DeWinter.'

There was a loud silence as everyone gazed at the boots and patched jerkin in sheer disbelief. Then, seeing the desperate look on Armelia's face and realising that it was clearly not a jest, everyone within earshot curtsied. This young lady was the daughter of the Dragon Lord who was soon to be King! Samantha risked a discreet glance...certainly the look was haughty enough, and there! On her thumb, the fabled Dragonsdome ring! Now she thought about it, Samantha had heard many strange rumours…ridiculous of course….about this young… lady. Rising, Samantha rang a little bell to summon her team. She would need every one of them!

It was past the hour of the bad tempered stoat and Quenelda was feeling quite bad tempered herself. She tried not to roll her eyes. Why did they all twitter and flutter about her like a gaggle of headless chickens…and why did they insist upon talking in affected whispers?

'Perhaps Madam might like a manicure?' The girl looked at Quenelda's short broken fingernails, some of which were really rather grubby….

'Perhaps,' Armelia suggested meekly, 'perhaps you could give Lady Quenelda the full 'deluxe treatment?'

Well, thought Samantha Spellgood, *she certainly needs it!* She fixed a smile on her face. 'Madam will be threeled to know Foresights and Hindsight's have secured the services of Shortcut Stoneman? Stoneman is queet the best in the Seven Kingdoms!' *And he would need to be faced with this…through the hedge backwards style!*

Quenelda fixed Samantha with a baleful glare. 'Queeet the best what?'

Armelia hurriedly fanned herself to hide a smile. There were a few hastily smothered titters from the assistants.

The hair salon was right at the top of F&H, with views across the highest part of the city and the surrounding glen. Quenelda took a seat. There was the tinkling of little bells. Flamboyantly attired in F&H tartan and weighed down by a great deal of gold jewellery, Shortcut jingled into the salon. He was heavily armed with an assortment of scissors, combs and brushes of all sizes and shapes that would not look out of place in a torture chamber. Rising from the chair, Quenelda was stopped in her tracks by the dwarf's purple and blue hair, dressed in enamel and gold beads.

'Oh dearie, dearie, me,' the equally horror-struck dwarf stared at Quenelda, hand on heart as if he were about to pass away. 'Oh, Madam! Who was your last stylist? Disgrrrraceful!' He ran his fingers through Quenelda's tangled hair, ignoring her squeals of protest. 'Tut,' he blew out his cheeks. 'A beetroot and seaweed shampoo I think for those split ends and we must get rid of that dreadful black dye that doesn't suit Madam at all!' he fussed about her.... 'and perhaps horsetail, meadowfoam and millet seed to repair and protect...'

He waved an arm at his army of apprentices who scuttled to their weights and scales and pestles and mortars to do his bidding. 'And chamomile oil!!'

Quenelda finally managed to shut her mouth as she was whisked off to have her hair washed and treated. Scrubbed and dried, the Earl's daughter was plumped down in a padded seat in front of a mirror.

'I think something gamine for your Ladyship?'

'Um...playful,' Armelia interpreted in response to Quenelda's baffled stare. 'Boyish.'

'Oh,' Quenelda nodded. That was all right.

'I can chop it to create the look Madam suits!'

'That means making it look...ragged,' Armelia interpreted.

'But it already looks ragged!'

Shortcut looked pained. 'Yes, Madam! But by the time I am finished, everyone will know it for a designer ragged hair cut! It will be perfection!'

'Ow!!!'

Armelia winced. It didn't sound as if the eyebrow plucking was going very well, and she was sure leg waxing hadn't really merited a scream. Nervously, she had another sip of champagne and tried to relax.

Skin glowing pinkly, hair perfected, dressed in a baffling layer of pantaloons and corsets, Quenelda was trying on dresses.

'Try this one, Madam?' Madam's eyes crossed in horror.

'This suits madam's eyes...' Madam wrinkled her nose.

'Perhaps a little long for-' Madam shook her head.

Finally there were some muted murmurs and whispers and the dresses were removed. Armelia accepted another flute of champagne, and feeling a trifle dizzy she nibbled daintily at the tray of delectable petite fours. An endless line of seamstresses and assistants staggered in with boles of cloth...rich ambers, russet and gold, blue and soft white. The shoe maker followed a bell later. Several master jewellers were sent for. The Earl's daughter had finally discovered fashion!

As dark began to fall, even the young Countess's boundless enthusiasm for fashion was flagging, unlike

Quenelda who showed no sign of wanting to leave.

'May I come in?' Armelia asked tentatively.

'No!'

'Oh!' Deflated, Armelia returned to her couch, and finally fell asleep...

'Wake up!' Quenelda grinned like a cat that had not just got the cream but the entire milk bottle as well.

'What hour is it?'

'Nearly the hour of the very plump ptarmigan.'

'Goodness!' Armelia looked at her doubtfully. 'You seemed to be enjoying yourself in there?'

'Mmmn...' Quenelda agreed.

Armelia waited... and waited...

CHAPTER FORTY-SIX

My Dark Queen

Darcy and his father looked down at the tens of thousands of camp fires and galleon lanterns that lit Roarkinch and the surrounding seas like the night sky above.

'Dragon Isle? How, Father? Even your great fleet and the hobgoblin swarms could not take it.'

'Come, you have yet to meet my Dark Queen.'

Images of a beautiful woman dressed in black with emerald eyes flooded Darcy's memory; his mother who died in exile, banished by the Earl for betraying him. Was his mother still alive?

'No, my son,' his father said gently. 'Your mother died long ago, I could not save her. This is altogether a darker Queen I speak of; a creature of the maelstrom.'

Puzzled, Darcy followed his father through the extensive royal quarters onto a strange porting stone set about with symbols he had never seen before. They stepped off to the sound of the sea. A chain of massive sea caverns opened about them tinged with ethereal green...*the colour of the Abyss!* There was an awful stench...like the hobgoblins but worse – much, much worse if that were possible. The guards down here all wore masks.

'Your armour will protect you.'

Darcy nodded. 'What is it? What on the One Earth is down here?' He felt his hackles rise.

'Our razorback Queen: an ancient creature from the deeps given new form and purpose, part hobgoblin, she shares their appetite for hot blood. Those who do not obey are given to her, a morsel, a fleeting moment of fun. Like razorbacks and hobgoblins she can fight on land or sea. The SDS have no such creature to call upon. She will wreak havoc on Dragon Isle.'

'In the name of the Gods!' Darcy husked as a creature uncoiled from the greater darkness, phosphorescent green playing about her. Glistening spider eyes coldly considered him, as malevolence radiated out in waves from her segmented black carapaced body: a hideous mesh of insect and spider, sea dragon and razorback...a twisted ugly thing.

Darcy felt his legs turn to water, only his armour keeping him on his feet. He did not suffer an excess of imagination, and thank the gods! *But the power my father must have...* 'The abyss gives you the power to create, to control such a creature?'

'Yes,' the WarLock could hear the greed in his son's voice. Soon...soon Darcy would be ready to embrace the Abyss. 'Time to go a-hunting... Release her!'

'Lord King,' the jailor bowed. He would be delighted

to see the last of this fell creature. Countless guards had died down here, despite the masks. 'Release her!' he bellowed.

In another dimly lit cavern great chains hung down from vast metal winding gears.

'Up,' the guards' whips licked out. 'Up! Pull!' Stumbling to their feet, slaves took up the corroded chains, trying not to cry out as the jagged rust bit into open flesh wounds. For many heartbeats nothing happened. Then with a groan of protest the huge portcullis began to rise up from the seabed.

The dark Queen's head flicked round at the sound of freedom, marsh light played about her. Vast bulging eyes swung back and then the head struck forward making Darcy stumble backwards with a cry that choked in his throat. The WarLock hadn't moved. Even as the mucus dripped and pooled about him and the rows of massive teeth snapped together, Darcy's father turned to inky smoke and in the blurring blink of an eye was next to his shocked son.

'Oh no,' the WarLock smiled as he coalesced back into man shape. 'You can't harm me, my beauty. You have other prey to hunt.'

The Queen turned. A wall of water rose up as she plunged down, the spikes of her tail disappearing into the sea. It slammed against the sea wall, it's freezing frothy spume drenching Darcy.

CHAPTER FORTY-SEVEN

The Wedding

The Queen, attended by Armelia, swept into the Unicorn Hall of the palace. Caitlin was wearing a long hooded cloak of white, exquisitely stitched with gold unicorns and silver wolves. A brief glimpse of the dress below revealed silk of the same colour, but embroidered with antique blue seadragon pearls. Her pale honey hair was worn long and unadorned. Hidden by the hood until the Earl, by then King, would place the crown on her head, as she would crown him with her wedding gift: an exquisitely crafted dragon crown of black glass.

At Caitlin's side, Armelia's dress was softest pink with teardrop pearls. On the other side Sir Gharad stood in his ceremonial robes of royal blue, his hand on Root's shoulder. The youth was richly dressed in a doublet, leggings and soft boots, russet, amber and earth brown, the autumn colours of his people. His earrings were hoops of gold and a fine torque of twisted gold oak leaves hung about his neck. All gifted by the Constable.

'I-' Root had never seen anything so fine, so beautiful.

'No need to say anything,' the Constable had smiled shyly. 'You deserve so much more recognition for bringing the Earl back and capturing Galtekerion. For your bravery!'

The young gnome felt like a prince.

The royal trumpets blew a fanfare that echoed off the ancient hammerbeam roof. The early sun flooded through the high arched windows, throwing a kaleidoscope of colour across the flagged floor. Barely was the Queen seated on her throne than the clatter of hooves on flagstones was heard. Yet another tradition was being broken for the first time. Armelia smiled at Root. Only they, the Constable and the Earl Rufus, soon to be King, knew who would enter beneath that arch carved of spiralling unicorn horns; even so, Armelia had no idea how that person would be dressed. She felt her heart beat speed faster, trying to smother ghastly images of her friend in a dress, still with hairy legs!

Clip clop...clip clop...

The guests, nobles and courtiers strained their necks to see the beautiful twin-horned golden unicorn clattering beneath the Unicorn Arch, and whoever rode it. There was a soft murmur of admiration from the men and a gasp from many women. But who was she? The Earl's daughter, who vanished and reappeared only to vanish again, no one knew where or why? The Queen smiled. Armelia considered her friend...it was Quenelda, and yet not Quenelda; at least the not the Quenelda of old. Gone were the heavy buckled flying boots, the patched jerkin and breeches, the straw tangled hair. But it was the quality of Quenelda's clothes that had changed rather than the design, and she still rode like a man. Quenelda had created something new.

A dove-blue doublet slashed with soft gold over a cream shirt was gathered in by a beautifully tooled leather belt. Fawn breeches were tucked into matching blue boots that twinkled with sapphires. Her hair was wild, but in a stylish way that had probably cost Shortcut Stoneman and his hairdressers at F&H a sleepless night or two, and it twinkled and sparked with tiny diamonds which also hung from ears and throat and wrist. She was ....beautiful... Armelia realised...but wild as the heather on the mountains.

Golden Dawn proudly tossed her head. Her soft gold hide was dappled with cream that rippled as she moved, and her honey-pale mane and tail were netted in like Quenelda's, in diamonds. The unicorn stepped out slowly in an exquisite diagonal dance across the floor as the Courtiers and Lords parted for her then closed again behind. As Golden Dawn approached the throne Armelia was surprised to see her friend draw a sword, slim as a needle, and bring the hilt up to her chin in salute before sweeping it to point down. Quenelda had only ever carried a flying knife; Armelia glanced at her friend's right boot. There it was! Some things would never change!

'Majesty. I come to bring you to your betrothed.'

As Quenelda dismounted, the Queen stepped forwards to where her nobles lifted her off her feet and onto the unicorn. Led by Quenelda, they walked slowly outside to where the kingdoms waited for the wedding, and the crowing of a king.

'You may now exchange rings and vows,' the Constable's joy showed through his exhaustion. It had been a long ceremony; the procession through the city, and the banquet, had yet to come. Rufus took Caitlin's hand and slid the ring on her finger.

'I am your sun
And I am your moon
Your light in the dark
Your shade at noon

I am the stars
That girdle your brow
I am the past
The future the now

I am your sword
And I am your shield
To protect home and hearth
And never to yield.'

Caitlin placed the red gold ring on the thumb of Rufus's good hand.

'I am your voice
And I am your song
Always beside you

All the year long

I am the whisper of hope
in the warm spring air
I am the golden corn
When long days are fair

I dance with the leaves
when autumn's wind blows
I'm the warmth of a hearth
Through cold winter's snows.'

The Constable took their hands and raised them to show the rings to the assembled lords. 'You are now husband and wife.'

Rufus DeWinter knelt before his Queen and wife. Caitlin raised the black glass dragon crown.

'To the peoples of the north and south, the east and the west of the Seven Kingdoms, I crown you to rule by my side, King hereafter.'

Caitlin placed it on his head, then Rufus DeWinter stood to accept the fealty of all those gathered: a true Dragon Lord and King.

High above the bells pealed and in the City the crowds roared, eagerly awaiting the procession to come.

CHAPTER FORTY-EIGHT

The Knights of Chaos

'What do you think, Darcy?' Rupert DeGrime spread his gauntleted hands. Darcy grinned. Darcy's Devils now wore the finest black armour, identical to their prince save theirs was not crafted with spells or so richly inlaid with gold. Each bore the sigil of their house on their helms; Darcy's was an emerald green dragon instead of the wolves' paw of the DeWinters, now his sworn enemy.

The WarLock had given his son and his household guard juvenile Imperials, with forty seasoned men at arms each. Darcy had named his mount Dark Knight after the WarLock's mount Endless Knight. It had taken them longer to choose a new name for Darcy's Devils as the ranks of this once small group were being swelled by the noble sons of those Lords who had chosen to fight for the WarLock King. Then Rupert suggested the Knights of Chaos, and Darcy was delighted.

Imperials took some getting used to; their sheer size, their power and strength was unbelievable, but baleful dragon collars ensured their obedience, even though the young men who flew them had little training. None would admit it, but to begin with several of them were sick when they cloaked or decloaked. Each was anxious to show off his flying skills, to make a name for himself in their new kingdom.

'Come on!' Darcy smiled coldly. 'The Army of the North will be attacking the Old Wall. Let's have some fun while the SDS are busy and strike south. There are taxes to be collected, spoils to be taken, and prisoners for my father's mines and armies.'

With whoops of delight the young knights mounted their Imperials.

CHAPTER FORTY-NINE

Strategic Air Command

'When do you fly?'

'0200 bells,' the King reached out to take the Queen's hand and kiss it. 'I know, I know, sweeting, I have barely been back and am flying again but - '

'Hush,' Caitlin placed a finger lightly on his lips. 'I know what must be done, but I would not just wait again while others die in my name, while you nearly died...our daughter challenges tradition, I would too. Show me your battlegroup, your Strategic Air Command, your SAC, so I may understand better what you do and consider how I too might help.'

The Earl nodded.

The Battlegroup Hanger was readying for deployment north when the royal caparisoned Imperial put down, but the trumpet's silver notes brought its thousand odd deck and flight crew instantly to attention. There had been no warning and these notes had not been heard here since King Targus had flown to the Isle of Midges and his death so many years ago. The silence did not last. A muted cheer turned into a roar as fists were held on hearts for their King and his Queen.

'You will still fly Stormcracker?' Caitlin frowned as Stormcracker's great nose muzzled Rufus. 'I thought his wounds were too severe for him to remain operational?'

'Does that not also apply to me? And I am not being put out to pasture – not yet!'

The Queen smiled ruefully. 'That it does, my love.

'He is not operational, in the sense he will no longer fight battles any more than I, but together we will command battles. Ah, love,' Rufus reached out to brush a tear, 'don't weep. In many ways we are stronger you and I; we are together, our daughter grows under the watchful care of Bearhugger and Drumondir. Come, let me show you what we have done.'

Storm? Lift my lady to your back...

Your mate of long ago?

My mate...we are bonded now in the eyes of men also...

'Because he cannot cloak, we have bound Storm within the most complex nexus our academics and battlemages can devise to protect and hide us, for we have embedded magic of great power and sophistication into his armour and they conceal the wealth of our sorcery within.'

As the Queen walked forwards she could see the great spinal plates were alive with bright runes, symbols and complex cartouches, and beneath her feet runestones had been inset into the dragon's armour. Dozens of mages and dwarves were seated at their stations and six battlemages with their unique armour and coloured cloaks were seated in spinning witchwood chairs at the core of brilliant high magical displays along the centre.

'These are our primary flight displays including altitude indicator,' the King explained. 'Our air speed, heading vector and location...Apart from Strategic Air Command here on Stormcracker, we will carry our own surgeons and apothecaries....one Imperial is kitted out as a field hospital...another as a forge with armourers, scale smiths and dragon masters. Several carry only supplies, and we have five Search and Rescue Imperials.'

'Why, it is like the Sea Dragon Tower,' Caitlin was amazed. 'And combined, you mirror Dragon Isle.'

'You have it, sweetheart! We take the war to Hugo this way. Instead of having to return to Dragon Isle, we can stay in the field for many moons. We take Imperials, sabretooths, frosts, vampires, harriers spitting adders, chameleons...two crews for each Imperial, soldiers, archers, engineers, tunnel rats, scouts, battlemages...

We are stockpiling brimstone and supplies guarded by the Red Squirrel and other loyal clans ....the dragons can hunt or forage for their food. We take the war to him, sweetheart...if he strikes the Howling Glen we can be there within a day, less if we are close. We can strike at his castles, his supply lines. The Dragon Lords are rising again.'

CHAPTER FIFTY

High Cloud Hall

With the wedding over far too swiftly, the Juveniles returned to the Battle Academy. Up in High Cloud Hall, cadets were congregated about the posting board, looking to see if they had been accepted for the brigade of their choice and who their instructors were. There was a lot of cheering and fist punches going on as Root and Quentin arrived. Already back in comfortable scruffy clothes and dyed black hair, Quenelda – now Quentin again – was unrecognisable as the King's daughter from the royal wedding.

A gap-toothed son of a black smith grinned. 'I've been accepted to train as a navigator!'

'I've got the Light Lancers!' another said with relief. 'My family have been in the Light Lances for generations.'

'Vampires for me! The Dark Knights VI AirWing. We'll be night flying!'

'Pilot training for me,' Bracus boasted. 'I'm going to be a Dragon Lord.'

'Winter Knights 3rd Combat Brigade for me! Frost

dragons!'

'I'm the Sabretooth Junior Brigade,' a skinny boy piped up who introduced himself as Lachlan. 'I'm not noble born; my family are going to be so proud! I'll be the first.'

'Me too,' Root put in grinning at him. 'My father was a scout but I'm going to be a navigator! The first gnome to fly Imperials!'

'That will be the day,' Bracus sneered. 'Gnomes are only fit for scouting. And they don't fight; they leave the hard work to others.'

'A gnome as navigator? Whatever next?' Ranulf drawled. 'They'll be letting in cooks and servants!'

'Or women!' said Gwhelem.

'Ha!'

'How d-' Bristling with fury, Quentin began to turn on the arrogant youths.

'Let it go,' Root squeezed her arm hard.

Quenelda was also joining the III Sabretooth Junior Brigade to begin her and Two Gulps' formal training. For Root it meant he would be studying the theory and application of navigational arts in the Academy, and logging flying hours on windy witherglens before progressing to smaller attack dragons and finally Imperials. With moons of intensive training coming up it was unlikely they would see much of each other.

'Be safe,' Root said with a lopsided grin.

'Be strong,' Quenelda bit her lip. 'We'll be back together in no time at all!'

CHAPTER FIFTY-ONE

Where is He?

Darcy watched as three-score iron-shod longboats reefed their sails and weighed anchor off the Isle of Midges packed with warriors from the White Fox, the Grey Seal and a half dozen other clans answering his father's call to war. The WarLock King and his son were standing on the forecastle of the battle galleon, The Dark Dragon, a huge five master, surrounded by his battle fleet packed to the gunnels with twelve thousand soldiers, all hidden beneath a dense haar conjured effortlessly by the WarLock King. Far to the north, the Army of the North was poised to strike. About them the seas were alive with razorbacks and hobgoblins. Darcy couldn't understand his father's fury.

'But they have come,' Darcy frowned, 'haven't they?'

'No! These are only tens of thousands, many of whom spawned in the warm water caverns of Roarkinch and have yet to make their first kill. We need banners of proven warriors; hundreds of thousands if we are to take Dragon Isle! They are not enough! Neither Galtekerion nor any of his Chosen have answered my summons!'

'You said that he was to capture my – the King at the Smoking Fort. Perhaps he was killed?'

'No!' the WarLock King denied it, his outline rippling, making his son choke back his fear. 'I have spent decades planning towards this moment! Without them I cannot take Dragon Isle, I cannot strike while the SDS remain vulnerable. I know the limits of the Army of the North. Let them attack the Howling Glen and the Old Wall, they will be no use in an assault from the sea. I need Galtekerion. Something is wrong! Those I sent never returned. I must go to the Westering Isles.'

'What do we do?'

'We hit the Wall and the Howling Glen hard, Imperials in the vanguard and all the hobgoblins we have. Stretch the SDS before they have time to regroup and see if they break. They will not know that Galtekerion has disappeared, will believe this is just the vanguard and may flee. Without him to lead the banners I will compel them to my will. And you my son, harry and reave up and down the coast and the Wall. Take as many prisoners as you can and destroy what you cannot. Sow havoc and despair!'

'But they may yet come.'

'And it will be too late. Dragon Isle will have to wait, curse the hobgoblins!'

Where is Galtekerion?

CHAPTER FIFTY-TWO

The III Sabretooth Junior Brigade

It was a beautiful summer's day and a warm breeze was blowing. Those chosen for the III Junior Brigade gathered as ordered at the WestPort of the outer bailey wall. Most cadets were young sorcerer lords, but there were a half dozen commoners, dwarves, and one or two trolls.

'Bearhugger's practically a legend,' a tall boy named Fergus from the Isle of Midges explained, eager to show off his knowledge of the SDS. 'My father served with him!'

'He fought in over a hundred battles in the BoneCrackers! An-'

'He was the SDS Commander's Shield!'

'I heard he lost an eye to a hobgoblin cleaver!'

'And that he limps. He was wounded in the thigh!'

'He has over thirty wounds! More than any of the other dragon masters!'

'I heard forty!'

'He can talk to dragons! He was the first to treat an injured sabretooth!'

'No! No one can talk to dragons!'

'Dragon Whisperers can!' a short boy with ginger hair, named Dougal, asserted.

'Those are just legends,' Fergus scoffed. 'No such thing as Dragon Whisperers!'

'But he did fly north to the Ice Isles and come back with the Earl!' insisted Dougal. 'My dad is flight deck crew... to rescue the Commander from hobgoblins!'

'I heard say his daughter did, too!' Another put in. 'That she can fly imperials! Has a sabretooth battledragon of her own already! And she is barely thirteen summers old!'

'Oh you don't want to believe everything the peddlers sing,' Fergus said scathingly. 'As if a girl could fly!' they all laughed while Quentin bridled. 'Let alone pilot an Imperial or last up in the Frozen Wastes. Story peddlers just make up stories that sound good.'

Furious, Quenelda clamped her mouth shut, Drumondir's dire warnings about losing her temper ringing in her ears. As Root said, they had been warned. She'd show them! She and Two Gulps!

Tangnost stepped off the porting stone from the maternity roosts and made his way outside to where his class waited. Once again he was to be Quenelda's instructor and the dwarf would not have it any other way. From the moment of her birth his task was to protect the Princess Quenelda, and now that meant the challenge of training her and those with her in under a year, to be ready to deploy to take back the Brimstones, whilst the SDS held the line against the Army of the North. The WarLock would be struggling to bring the hobgoblins under control and worrying about who was attacking him north of the Old Wall...no one would imagine for a moment that the Juveniles would creep quietly in the back door as winter closed in to steal his brimstone. The Guardian and his academy faculties had a huge task on their hands!

Yes, the operation was low risk, the guards poorly trained and careless, but it would be a battle none the less. Normally after three years, trained cadets joined operational talons, airwings or brigades to continue their training until they became operational after the Dragathon.

Drumondir was tasked with training Quenelda as a Dragon Whisperer. Once she graduated as a Mage with a fully trained battledragon to rely on, and was deployed within the ThunderStorm Attack Battlegroup, Quenelda would be as safe as Dragon Isle could make her. Yes she was young, but many of those training with her were young, younger by years than those who had qualified before them. The world had changed.

'For those who don't know me,' the dwarf's voice carried effortlessly to those furthest away as they stood to attention in ranks. 'I am Dragon Master Tangnost Bearhugger, of the Cave Bear Clan. You will call me Dragon Master or Sir.'

'Sir! Yes, Sir!'

'I am going to push you to your limits. Training to fight with a sabretooth used to take a year, now I have you for three moons only. You are going to work harder than you ever have before.'

Tangnost led them through new leafed trees, deep into the woods. Here on the north side of Dragon Isle the island rose steeply with great jagged teeth of black soaring skywards in ragged formation called the Shards. Densely forested lower slopes gave way to paddocks and training courses and roosts which tunnelled deep into the scree skirts of the mountain. It was here that ground attack dragons: spitting adders, sabretooths and vipers were trained, along with harriers destined for Search and Rescue and chameleons of the Highland Scouts.

They passed by the Light Lancers stables where students were watching spitting adders of the Highlander 4th Battalion demonstrating manoeuvres by troopers about to be redeployed to the Wall after a tour of duty with the Household Cavalry. Lightly built and incredibly swift, spitting adders were rushing in to spit venom on stuffed dummies before veering off to the right and left leaving the smoking turnip heads shrivel up.

Moving on, they came to the vipers' paddocks where the heavier set dragons worked together in groups. Circling their enemy to cage them, the circle became tighter and tighter until finally the vipers swiftly charged, plunging their fangs left and right, jaws snaking out, and then they disappeared back into the trees, their mosaic of scales making them impossible to see in the dappled sunlight.

But the paddocks the cadets most wished to see were the Queen's Own Elf Light Archers, the legendary women warriors of the Sixth Kingdom. The stands about these paddocks were always crammed. Elves were feline in their grace, fine boned and amber eyed, and their woodleaf dragons unlike any other. Feathered, they changed hue with the seasons and were perfectly camouflaged in the great forests far to the east. In flight, they looked like darting birds on the wing. The elves wore bright lacquered, segmented wooden armour, all the colours of the rainbow, with small bows and quivers of arrows or light lances. They were rarely seen outside their own kingdom, save those who came each year to join the SDS.

Dragged away by Tangnost, the students arrived at the sabretooth paddocks which were disappointingly empty save for scores of turnip headed scarecrows, and took a seat on the stands.

'So,' Tangnost looked the eager and frightened faces over. 'What can you tell me about sabretooths?'

Hands went up.

'They're cave dragons!'

'Correct,' Tangnost nodded. 'What else?'

'They can flame!'

'They're coloured yellow through to flaming red,' someone offered.

'Mmn,' Tangnost nodded. And which end is yellow?

'The tail?' the boy named Fergus guessed, eyes squinted with the effort of remembering.

'No.' Dozens of hands then went up. 'Yes.' Tangnost smiled. 'You've guessed, the tail must be red. And anything more?'

'They're of stocky build, huge hind legs and have small

wings,' Quentin found her voice.

'They have huge incisors - all the better to eat hobgoblins with...' that caused a ripple of laughter.

'They can flame up to twenty strides,' Quentin couldn't resist showing off, causing an 'oohh' of amazement.

'And they have huge hind feet with six sharp talons to 'smash and mash' hobgoblins,' an older boy, Caradoc of Glamis, added.

Tangnost's mouth twitched. 'Smash and mash' was the unofficial rallying cry of the sabretooth brigades when clearing tunnels.

'Why are they so difficult to train?' the dwarf asked them. 'Or to treat for injuries?'

'Because they are highly strung, and as likely to kill those about them as a hobgoblin if they are not handled right,' heads turned towards Quentin. The black haired boy in brigandine and buckled boots seemed to know a lot for a commoner.

'Oooh...' The cadets turned to where a mounted sabretooth was coming out of the roosts on the other side of the paddock.

'Correct,' Tangnost stood to hold their attention. 'Sabretooths are unsurpassed predators when it comes to hunting hobgoblins underground. Their stocky build and powerful muscles are ideal for manoeuvring in confined passageways and tunnels. They are also formidable battledragons on the field. Like hobgoblins they can move swiftly in great leaps and bounds, one of the few ground dragons swift enough to outrun a hobgoblin.

They are trained to decapitate or disembowel with a

kick; and one snap of those jaws on a battlefield and a hobgoblin is dead meat. But they have weaknesses too. What are they?'

Quentin waited until Tangnost nodded. 'Because of their small stubby wings they cannot fly very far or very fast, and are often transported on battlegalleons or on the backs of Imperial Blacks. Their scales can stop an arrow, but not a cleaver or spear thrust so they have to wear heavy armour.'

There were a few blank faces. 'Sir, what does decapitate mean?' Dougal asked.

'Can someone tell us what decapitate means?'

'They can rrrrrrrrrrrrrippppppp off a hobgoblin's head!' Someone said to peals of laughter.

Tangnost pursed his lips in a thin line of disapproval. Bravado had no place in his lessons, but he let it go, for just this once. They would learn the hard way. There was nothing glamorous or fun about war: heroism yes, sacrifice, but not fun.

The fully armoured young mare who was ridden over to where they sat was in her prime, the result of generations of breeding. Beautiful, standing at the shoulder at twenty hands high, she was flawlessly coloured from gold through to her powerful red tail. She had the classic strong thighs and huge clawed hind feet, with smaller front legs. Her wings were long for a sabretooth and her eye was liquid gold. Smoke puffed from her nostrils. Fury of Sparks was beautiful, no doubt about it.

May the wind sing under your wings, Dancing with

*Dragons...*the mare acknowledged the young dragon whisperer.

And may the stars guide your path...Fury of Sparks... Quenelda replied, tears stinging her eyes; the mare would have been a perfect mate to her dead battledragon, Two Gulps and You're Gone. *When am I ever going to stop missing him?*

The sabretooth's harness, unlike parade harness and armour, was plain and functional, as was her spiked battle armour. She bore two up, the rider and an elven archer. Like their mount they were fully armoured in flexible segmented armour over boiled leather.

One of the young cadets foolishly stepped forwards only to be jerked back by Tangnost's iron grip. 'The first lesson you learn about sabretooths is respect,' he warned them all. 'Do not go anywhere near this battledragon or any other sabretooths unless you are certain their rider has seen you.' He nodded to the rider.

The trooper flicked a rein and spurred the mare forwards. With a huge leap Fury of Sparks landed on the first two scarecrows, turned to disembowel a further three, with a flap of her wings kicked backwards and forwards, spun while flaming and landed before a half dozen charred turnips landed it in the mud.

There was nervous laughter as several students fell off their benches in fright. The others cheered and clapped. Their training had begun in earnest.

CHAPTER FIFTY-THREE

A Call to Arms

Wwwooooooooooooooooooooooooooooooo

Beginning slowly, the sound vibrated throughout the coombs of Dragon Isle, building and building and building until the air itself shivered and thrummed like harp strings. And then it stopped.

Throughout the island it was as if everyone had been frozen in time where they stood, heads tilted, eyes wide with shock, mouths open. Never had the Call to Arms been sounded in living memory. Many had no idea what it meant.

And then the spell was broken.

'Scramble, scramble, scramble…this is not a drill, this is not a drill. This is a call to arms!'

Already the pilots and navigators of the Rapid Reaction Force, the RRF, were porting to where their five fully armoured Imperials were ready and waiting to go, to where fifteen hundred BoneCrackers were already streaming up their battledragon's wings strapping in, while seventy sabretooths and two-score scouting dragons were being urged up their tails by their riders.

'StormChaser, StormChaser,' the calm voice from Sea Dragon Tower came over the helmet and flight cavern coms. 'You are cleared for immediate take off. SAC will supply co-ordinates on the Old Wall.' And then the RRF were swooping down through the flight tunnels, bursting into the early morning sunshine, wings powering up. They had barely cleared Dragon Isle's perimeter, when their pilots gave their battledragons their head. The need was urgent. There was a series of thunderclaps, and then the Imperials were streaking north, gone in the blink of an eye.

'It's begun!' Quenelda burst into the map room. 'Come on!'

'What? What was that?' Root asked.

'A call to arms! The WarLock has attacked! The SDS are scrambling.'

'Where to?'

'The cliff tops,' Quenelda answered. 'We'll get the best view there.'

Out of breath, racing as fast as they could, Quenelda and Root joined the excited, jostling, shoving, swelling throng as cadets and academics in their bright robes poured into the corridors heading for balconies and gantries and towers.

'But I thought without the hobgoblins he wouldn't attack!' Root said breathlessly.

I know,' Quenelda looked worried. 'What if everyone was wrong?'

'Sixth Airborne requesting permission to take off...'

'Heading vector six by three five one.'

'Go! Go! Go! Mount up! Mount up!'

BoneCrackers, Marines, Lancers, Fusiliers, Dragoons, Highland Scouts and the vampire Black Watch were all swiftly donning their armour, grabbing shield and weapons and helmet they ran through the passageways to all eight operational flight hangers, buckling belts and boots as they ran.

Dragon Masters controlled the panic, anchoring ground crew in practised drills. 'Slow down, lad. Bring out the armour beginning with peytral...'

Muscled armourers swung winches over the armour pits as ostlers led their snorting mounts down... sabretooths, spitting adders, vampires queuing up ranks deep, eager for battle.

Dragon Lords were being armoured by esquires. Swords were scabbarded and battlestaffs sheathed in witchwood chairs.

Navigators keyed in vectors, rapidly checking co-ordinates from the Flight Tower, plotting flight paths to a hundred different targets on the Old Wall.

And far, far to the north came the voice of the King from SAC to the Thunderstorm Battlegroup, waiting, waiting to ambush the WarLock.

'Skirmisher units converge on the Howling Glen...assess disposition, composition and strength.'

'Delta wing, cloak and prepare to engage, attack pattern alpha.'

Cadets spilled from the training halls, lecture theatres, class rooms and paddocks, wide eyed, frightened, hearts thumping. Word was passed from mouth to mouth.

'The SDS have scrambled!'

'Which units?'

'All of them! Every dragon that can fly!'

'The ThunderStorm Battlegroup flew north two days ago! They'll already be there.'

'Where are they attacking?'

'The Old Wall!'

'The Howling Glen!'

As they reached the north gantries, the most amazing sight filled the air; streaming out of every flight hanger, joining together like a vast black thundercloud on a clear day, a storm of dragons were heading north, almost blocking out the sun. Squadron after squadron of Imperials bearing tens of thousands of troops and ground attack dragons, and escorted by airwings of vampires, harriers and frosts, were on their way to the battlefront.

The war had finally begun!

CHAPTER FIFTY-FOUR

Navigator Training

With relief, Root anticipated navigational studies and the chance to be free of Bracus. The young gnome was determined to excel, to prove that his peaceful people could become Dragon Lords, to prove those who thought only sorcerers should wield magic, wrong, who thought that anyone who did not wield a sword was cowardly. Expectations that a commoner would not even be able to read were swiftly dispelled as the scribes and cartographers were hugely impressed with Root's memory and skills.

He loved the endless peaceful hours with maps and cartography, poring over ancient sea and tidal charts, learning how to predict and measure wind and storms, all overseen by the aged Professor Overcloud, Dean of the Faculty of Air. Whilst searching for the missing Earl, Root had had moons to learn to read maps and hone his skills. Now he put that experience to good use. With his artist's eye for detail and a quick mind he swiftly stood out from the rest of his class.

Days were often swapped for chilly nights in the observatory, studying constellations and planets through great brass telescopes in the School of Stars because the SDS flew night operations. Root's Da had taught him the stars and constellations when he was knee high, and Root knew them all, but by different names to the SDS. Ursu the cave bear, the skye star that gleamed white and unmoving in the north, the fern...the oak...but there was one name that was the same across the Seven Kingdoms, a pale milky cluster of diamond dust stars called the Dragon's Breath in all seven tongues. No one knew why, but it was the most beautiful thing in the heavens. Root also had a natural affinity with the seasons and the phases of the moons, and again excelled under the expert tuition of Under Professor Twigsmith, one of the few gnomes who taught at the Battle Academy.

But these bookish studies were only a part of what was expected of him. Root was studying to become a Dragon Lord, and that meant, even if he did not lift a sword or staff, he had to understand warfare in theory and practice, and to deploy sophisticated defensive battle magic even if he could not conjure it. Beneath his bunk bed blankets, by shielded lantern light, Root studied past the witching hour every night, memorising runes, what each meant and how to combine them. With his classmates he then began to study battle runes and cartouches, learning how to identify and decipher their sophisticated construction and the power they commanded, not yet understanding how he could wield them without sorcery. But learn them he must before he could sit in the cherished witchwood chair of a Dragon Lord!

For all those cadets who could not fly, and those who thought they could, long days in the classrooms were sometimes exchanged for lessons in the roosts, or for a half moon in the Dragon Training Hall. Dragonsdome had one wooden dragon which was rare enough, and beyond the purse of many, but the SDS had dozens for each and every kind of breed, and again, unlike Dragonsdome, because these were witchwood and carved with runes they were imbued with a power of their own and able to mimic each dragon's unique characteristics as well as taking off, flying and landing, climbing and dropping. Root instinctively recognised the beauty and craft of his people in their carving and wondered if this would become his vanished people's legacy.

Midsummer came and went and elementary flying training, EFT, began. Navigators had to log thirty bells on windglen widdershanks before progressing on to small attack dragons: frost, vampires and highly trained harriers. Only then would they be allowed to sit on the cherished witchwood chair.

CHAPTER FIFTY-FIVE

Shattered Leg ~ Shattered Dreams

Whenever he could Root spent time with Quester. It was a particularly difficult time for his friend, knowing that Root and Quenelda had progressed to specialist training. Nearly eight moons after being badly wounded by Galtekerion, Quester was still bed bound and in great pain. Since his friend had regained consciousness Root had shared the ups and downs of basic training almost nightly before he went to bed, but he was no longer sure it was helping.

With every day that passed, Quester was being left further and further behind, his dreams of being a Dragon Lord shattered like his leg. Root's once cheery friend was becoming more and more miserable and morose, and increasingly silent and bitter, his crutches lying unused on the floor.

In response to Root's pleas, Drumondir joined them for an afternoon, bringing a pile of books and a carved chess set, teaching them both the rudiments of the game. Tangnost, too, dropped by to see how the esquire was feeling, but it didn't look good. The dwarf had lost family and friends on the battlefield, but many more afterwards who succumbed to their wounds and despair. Something had to be done. Tangnost shook his head. But what?

CHAPTER FIFTY-SIX

The Howling Glen

Thump! Thump!

Pop, pop, pop!

Explosions bracketed the air. There was a thunder of wings and a scream of outrage as an Imperial was hit by another, driving it down in a tangle of bodies and harness to the ground with a fearful thud, destroying the outer ramparts of the XIII StormBreakers fortress below and killing hundreds. Streaks of incoming battlemagic struck and struck again, but the SDS Imperials had cloaked and the heavy explosions bracketed thin air.

From the smoke-filled skies above the Howling Glen, a rainbow of dragonfire lit up the clouds. There was a concussion of thunder as spells detonated over the battlefield below, cast by SDS battlemages. A twisting vampire flamed as it went down, beset by two hostiles. Dragon Lords fought rebels: their Imperials' blue fire mingling with the brilliant starbursts and detonations of battlemagic might have been beautiful, were it not so deadly a dance. Reinforced by the IX WinterKnights from the far south, the XIII StormBreakers were holding.

Thump... thump... thump... The scorpions fired great bolts as crews ratcheted back the rope to fit another dart that tore shrieking through the massed ranks of foot soldiers, crowding through the gaps created by the downed Imperial. The bitter stench of battlemagic stung his eyes as the Storm Commander swept down through the sulphurous churning clouds, surveying the battlefield through his cloaked battledragon's eyes.

The Army of the North, including ten wings of Imperials, were coming at them from all angles...they had been well trained, but nowhere near as well as the SDS, and it showed. Tactically they were chaotic and undisciplined: several of their poorly trained Imperials had bolted; others had turned on their own crews when compelled with dragon collars to attack. Without the massed hobgoblin banners, the fortress was battling the WarLock's army to a standstill, neither side gaining advantage. There were hobgoblins, but they were fresh from the spawning pools and were dying in their thousands as the WarLock King threw them recklessly into the vanguard of his attack.

The Old Wall to the south was also holding. The Storm Commander had just despatched twenty Imperials supported by spitting adders and harriers to that battle, to attack the WarLock King's army from behind. Hugo may wield chaotic magic, but he was only one man and such virulence was cast at a price. Even with his black holes he could not be everywhere.

Swinging round for a low second pass, Stormcracker

flamed, clearing the ditches of hobgoblins on the western defences as they swept low. The King's vambrace lit up as he passed through the defensive nexus over the fortress and then he was out into clear air putting down on a crag.

My brothers and sisters are approaching swiftly... Stormcracker warned. *I can hear them...*

King Rufus frowned. They must be the WarLock's Imperials else his vambrace would have registered SDS dragons, and it was unlikely Hugo's runemasters would have broken new SDS codes. Where? They must be cloaked...

You cannot see them yet...but as your inner senses dragon grow, you will...

How many?

Twenty...they are young and untested...afraid...

Can they see us, sense us?

Yes, as I can see them...but not those who fly them...they come from where the sun sets....

'Strategic Air Command to all Red One, inbound... inbound,' the King strode along Stormcracker's back to where his battlemages controlled the battle. 'Twenty cloaked Imperials closing fast from the west. They cannot see us, we have the advantage. I will guide you: intercept and capture their Imperials.'

CHAPTER FIFTY-SEVEN

Command and Control

It was time for high battlemagic to begin. As part of their studies, those destined to be Dragon Lords spent time in the SeaDragon tower, the operational heart of Dragon Isle. Root had been here once before, but now he saw it through entirely new eyes.

It was a large and circular room with unhindered views of the glen above an encircling gantry and below the Sea Dragon observatory. Technicians were monitoring banks of complex runes, glyphs and displays inlaid into the stone tower wall or suspended in the air that ebbed and flowed, tracking hundreds of dragons, patrols and operations. The light was low, soft, blanketed almost in darkness, and constantly in the background were the soft muted sounds of air traffic control.

'Dragon Isle, Dragon Isle, this is Tango Patrol. Eta, a half bell, we have wounded on board.'

'Insurgency attack, vector north five...'

'Crash landing, crash landing, Smoking Stars is going down.'

'We have two sabretooths missing...'

The young sorcerer leant forwards, pressing an icon. 'Search and Rescue, Search and Rescue, scramble... scramble...scramble...'

'This is Seadragon Tower, emergency landing nets deployed, pads one and two, south flight cavern cleared for landing. Search and Rescue have been scrambled.'

After welcoming them, the Officer of the Watch, Major Stiles, moved to the centre of the CAC and onto what looked like an ordinary porting stone, one of a circle of eight except that it was inlaid with peculiar angular runes picked out in brilliant hues, none of which Root recognised from his studies. Instantly as the sorcerer stepped onto it he was cocooned by an opaque fluid array of globes, spheres, runes and colourful displays, spinning, changing hue.

'Come on, step in to the gyro.'

'Gyro?' Fergus asked.

'Named after a gyro of wild dragons,' Stiles explained. 'Few people ever see one in their lifetime.'

But I have... Root thought with wonder.

'But it's...too small,' Fergus trailed off as the hesitant cadets stepped in one by one and suddenly found the CAC had faded away and that the world within was huge. They gazed in open-mouthed awe.

'These stones allow us to see the overall scope of our operations right down to the last detail...' Stiles explained. 'Here you can see battlegroups, patrols, take offs and landings, search and rescue, reconnaissance and weather, allowing you to direct operations.' The Major reached out to pluck one dragon. Instantly its aspect grew and new information appeared.

'MoonWalker…an Imperial out of the Howling Glen, cloaked, bearing three six five eight.' He touched another rune. 'Pilot is Wing Commander Grimbold.'

'How much training do you need before you can serve in the CAC?' Root asked.

'Eight moons,' Stiles replied, 'and three winters before you can take command. It takes a long time to interpret incoming telemetry, and then to make the best decision.'

Stiles plucked several other symbols from the whole, widening them at a flick of the hand. The cadets stepped forwards to study the glyphs and cartouches, many of which they had not seen before. Some of the displays were baffling in their complexity.

'Are these the kind of displays we'll have on Imperials?' Bracus asked.

'Similar displays are inlaid into witchwood chairs and your vambrace carries weapons and sorcery particular to you, and of course your helmet is equipped with HUDs and night sights.'

'HUDs?'

'Heads up displays,' someone said quietly. They all turned round to look at Root, who flushed.

'From here,' the Major selected a rune. 'We track thousands of dragons with a range of three hundred to five hundred leagues from Dragon Isle in all directions.'

There was a group intake of breath.

'Three hundred leagues?'

'How can you do that?' Ranulph asked. The Major stepped across to a spherical map suspended in the air and drew it to him; drawing his thumb and forefinger apart, the map shrunk to that of the Highlands, and then again to the lowlands straddling the Old Wall.

'On all of our highest peaks,' where his finger pointed small red spheres appeared, 'there are powerful icons inset into the rock that can track anything airborne that passes over or through those glens. They allow navigators to plot their location, to track hobgoblin or warbands from beyond the Wall, allowing for a rapid response.

Likewise each of our dragons has a unique signature. Now we are fighting the WarLock, our Rune Masters are casting more sophisticated runes that he will not recognise, nor easily be able to break.'

'I'd like to train to be a Rune Master,' Lachlan said with awe. Being able to construct rune codes...'

'Is it true that without a rune to give us warning... that...that the WarLock's Imperials will ambush us and we'll never see them coming?'

'It is true that we cannot detect incoming cloaked imperials.'

There was a buzz of horror

'But neither can he. We do know that Imperials themselves appear to know when their kindred approach, so we are hoping that we can learn to recognise how.'

'Their body language,' Root said. Everyone looked at him.

'Dragons have language?' Caradoc asked.

'Of course!' Root looked equally astonished.

Major Stiles looked at Root keenly. 'Mmmn… Gnomes have an affinity with the land and its creatures… perhaps …that is something we should learn from…'

'What if you are tracking air wings or battle groups?' Root asked. 'There would be thousands of dragons all mixed up.'

'Good question,' the Major acknowledged, and put a finger to the transparent display which rippled like a pond, instantly reducing the hundreds of dots to a mere dozen. With the flick of a hand the grid map flared behind them.

'These are now airwings, squadrons or battlegroups,' he touched one and it broke apart into half a hundred, mostly in formation, with runes scrolling down the side of the display. 'That's a battlegroup with harrier escort.'

An icon pulsed into existence in front of them, causing a murmur of excitement. Stiles touched a few runes. 'Ground attack on a watch tower.' Let's see who steps forwards. 'Can anyone give us an eta to intercept from the nearest patrol or airwing?'

Root felt a thump of adrenaline. This was his chance. He might not have sat in a live witchwood chair, but unlike the rest of them, sat in one he had, and he had flown and navigated an Imperial in severe weather conditions using the instinctive skills of his people, to the Ice Isles and back. His eyes flicked to the different displays…co-ordinates there, wind speed; he recognised that combination rune…that was a stormfront racing up from the south. A battlegroup surely, the ThunderStorm mostly likely given its position just to the north of the Old

Wall...Root stepped forward into the hesitant silence.

There was a murmur of shock and outrage, what could a gnome understand of high magic? But the Major nodded, inviting the youth to stand at the centre of the gyre. Root's fingers floated lightly over the virtual map. Remembering the battle runes he had studied so hard, he swiftly made his selection, building a picture layer by layer and then with a flick of the wrist copied from the major refined his grid references. He dipped into the map which rippled, moving his target vector, a circle with a cross at its centre. A patrol there...they would be the closest....

'Here,' Root pressed a rune and honed in on the patrol he had selected. 'Midwinter patrol...eta...two and a half bells...'

The Major stepped forward to check. He nodded with respect, clearly impressed, and held out his hand to clasp Root's wrist, to the envy of the young gnome's classmates. 'If you ever want a posting to the CAC, young Oakley, you let me know!'

CHAPTER FIFTY-EIGHT

The Wrath of a WarLock

The sickle moons gave out little light as the rising wind chased the last of the clouds from the summer skies above the Westering Isles. It was the witching hour but it was still light this far north. Drums were beating but the Killing Caves were empty. The hot spawning pools lay neglected. The Isles and the seas were alive with warring hobgoblins. With Galtekerion and so many of his elite Chosen not returning, a bloody struggle was taking place and the slaughter was frenzied.

Wind suddenly rose, whipping the waves to froth though the sky remained clear. A spout began to form out at sea, spiralling up and up and growing and growing into a towering column. Waves of malevolence breaking on the shoreline heralded the WarLock King's arrival. Green lightning spiked, tendrils striking in all directions, vapourising scores of warriors. As the spout encountered the Killing Caves it suddenly died. The deep cold grew more intense. Rock pools froze. The sea cracked trapping many in the shallows. The drums of the Killing Caves stopped and a suffocating silence fell.

The oily darkness shifted. So did the hobgoblins, frantically scrabbling across the sand. Something was here, something ancient, and it was more frightening than they were. The shadow moved. Smoke coalesced into a vaguely man-like form...where the head should be, two orbs of green flared.

'Where is he?' The voice was as cold as the grave bringing the kiss of death to those it touched. 'Where is Galtekerion? Why did he not answer my summons?'

Only hissing answered him.

'Speak! Where is Galtekerion?'

An elder warrior of the Sarkrit tribe stood, the kill fetishes about him clinking, he rose and moved across the black sand to where the darker hole radiated terror, the only one brave enough to approach.

'None know, Dread Lord.' The creature kept his head bowed.

'None know? Who speaks now for the hobgoblins?'

Here and there a hobgoblin rose from the debris of the battle and made their way towards the WarLock to join the first. The shadow waited for them to come. 'Speak'

'We are all of the Chosssen that remain...none have ssseen our brothersss or Galtekerion ssssince the battle at the fort...they ussed dragon fire....sssssssssssss.....'

Since the battle! The darkness roiled forcing the hobgoblins back. He had not known! All those years to bind the tribes for nothing. Now when he needed to unleash them, the witless creatures were fighting, falling back into the senseless slaughter of each other, giving the

SDS precious time to regroup. *To grow strong! Curse them! Curse them!*

This was the second major setback to his plans, not easy for a man used to effortless success.....The WarLord must have died at the Smoking Fort, unrecognised amid the slaughter...for the SDS would surely have claimed his death. *They do not know...is there any way to use that?*

'Let the new Chosen stand forward for the thirteen tribes and I shall choose a WarLord from amongst you, the one who can command the many. Prove yourself in battle and we shall take the greatest prize of all: Dragon Isle.'

The darkness flowed out to sea and was then gone, leaving the coast line frozen.

CHAPTER FIFTY-NINE

A Right Pudding!

'Form a line!'

'Sir! yes Sir!' the Juvenile Sabretooths dashed to obey. Today the cadets would be paired with a juvenile through training and on to the battlefield, bonded for life. Finally they had been issued with training armour: studded boiled leather brigandine, breeches with knee protectors, heavy cavalry boots, gloves and a three quarter helm. They may not be knightly or glamorous but it meant they were one step closer to their dream.

All eyes were on the smoking roosts, clustered like mushrooms at the foot of the Shard. Ostlers who had nursed the juveniles from birth to when they shed their soft scales for those of an adult, were leading the nine moon old juvenile sabretooths out into the paddock, many of them already walking upright on their powerful hind legs. Quenelda deliberately stood at the far end. His ostler had been instructed to bring Two Gulps to her without knowing why.

As Quenelda bent to tighten a loose buckle, the 'oohs'

of excitement had suddenly turned into ripples of laughter. Turning to see the cause of such hilarity, the smile died on Quenelda's lips as she spied Two Gulps eating part of the fence despite his handler's furious attempts to stop him.

Two Gulps! She shouted. *Stop eating! Stop!*

Her sabretooth looked up, and, not being used to being shouted at, allowed himself be led on. But the laughter didn't abate. Quenelda realised with horror that it was not only her dragon's hind feet which were larger than any of the others, but his stomach was too, and his wings were tiny compared to those on either side! She was aware of the barely stifled laughter as he waddled forwards to her. Blood rushed to her face with angry embarrassment. She would show them what her dragon could do!

We will show them, Two Gulps corrected her for the first time.

Yes, Quenelda agreed. *We will show them! We have seen a battle!*

The line of ostlers leading the juveniles stopped opposite the esquires.

'Line up!' Tangnost barked. 'Step forwards two paces and allow the sabretooth in front of you to draw in your scent.'

'Bad luck, Quentin,' Lachlan nudged her. 'You've got a right pudding there!'

CHAPTER SIXTY

Dragon's Head Helmets

The combined class of navigator and pilot cadets were milling around outside the Display Range, eagerly awaiting their introduction to battle armour for the first time. Root looked for Quenelda and then remembered she didn't need either armour or helmet and wasn't there! Instead, his eyes found Bracus, hostile as ever, watching him whilst complaining that such high magic was beyond commoners!

A tall rangy sorcerer approached; his gown, worn over academy armour was the midnight blue of the Air Faculty, and his ornately inlaid staff declared him to be an ArchMage. Professor Dimplethwit was their tutor for Applied Aerial Weapons and Armour and had a brisk no nonsense attitude that instantly quelled Bracus.

'You will shortly be learning how to fly battledragons' Dimplethwit informed them. 'My job is to teach you how to survive aerial combat with an array of high battlemagic at your command. Please select your range and stand on the circular stone.'

Root chose a range as far away from Bracus as possible. On first inspection the Display Range was a large dark hall separated into high-walled long ranges; at one end, where they stood, a carved flagstone was inset into the floor next to a wooden tree with training armour, the other end stood empty and dark.

'Dragon helms and armour are individually crafted and spelled to fit you by a Forge Master Smith of which there are only a score in the entire kingdom and they are all here on Dragon Isle,' Dimplethwit informed them as he walked the length of the hall. 'And thus is imbued like witchwood with powerful magic, each piece seamlessly becoming part of the whole once it is put on. The weaponry and sorcery you are about to learn have been cast and conjured by battlemages and rune masters.

All helmets feature Target Acquisition Designation Systems (TADS), a helmet mounted display – HMD for short – giving you night vision sensors, a laser range finder and laser target designator and thermal imaging. In time pilots will progress to monocular eye pieces. This is the new vampire HMD VII model, recently modified for those who cannot conjure magic.'

'You may put your training helmets on.'

Along the length of the range, navigators and pilots like Root lifted the legendary Dragon's head helms.

It's much lighter than it looks, Root thought gratefully as the full-face helmet cushioned his head; the only visible part of his face was the eyes. Projected in front were scrolling data icons. As he moved his head, the dark hall took on a wholly different aspect; a bright three dimensional grid had appeared in front of his right eye giving him the contours of the hall and everyone in it.

'These helmets have integrated coms with Dragon Isle and with SAC who will direct operations beyond the Old Wall. You will be fighting for tactical air superiority; that means battling the WarLock King for control of air space so that you can provide close ground support for our armies and battlegroups. Meaning anyone? You've all read your theory. Oakley?'

'Insertion and extraction and fighting on the ground.'

'Correct. Over the next moon,' Dimplethwit promised, 'we are going to study command rune and icon recognition, targeting, night flying, helmet and vambrace integration, vector recognition, matrix grids and defensive manoeuvres.'

Dimplethwit kept his word. Exhausted by the relentless training, Root had no energy left to even visit Quester; endless theoretical and tactical exercises were combined with increasingly complex battlefield scenarios. And the SDS had kept their word. Root's helmet was unique, a prototype for those who could not conjure, imbued with power at the touch of an icon or a spoken word.

An icon on the young gnome's vambrace lit up. Immediately his helmet mounted display projected a dazzling array of information for him to assess; location and airspeed, altitude, target range, grid map reference and other information about his Imperial. He narrowed it down to incoming dragons, and then down to those with SDS runes. The others were presumed hostile.

Battlemagic flared brightly. *A pulse. Incoming bearing three five one, north, by six degrees north-east.* Root swiftly pressed a vambrace icon and this time the incoming fire dissipated over the surface of his defensive shield in a riot of sparks.

Almost immediately, incoming telemetry and messages revealed a search and attack patrol in difficulties northwest of the Wall. Root swiftly calculated their intercept time, feeding co-ordinates to his pilot.

'Black One, Black One to Alpha Brimstone patrol, this is Imperial Smoking Sunset, incoming... incoming... eta a quarter bell. Prepare for combat mount. We will drop in to secure perimeter.'

'Good work, Oakley,' Dimplethwit nodded. 'The high magic techs are working on those modifications you suggested.'

CHAPTER SIXTY-ONE

A Dark Cloud

It was like a small dark cloud racing the wind, only there was no wind, and the sky was crystal clear and sunny. The guard on the stockade tower squinted into the sun, hand ready on the bell. With the kingdoms at war, countless villages in the Deep Woods had been razed to the ground. Only the dead remained, the rest had disappeared; no one knew where they had gone or who had struck. Refugees flooded to the forts on the Old Wall seeking refuge behind its renewed walls and forts; more mouths for the Crown to feed, stretching already hard pressed supply lines.

Then the dark cloud disappeared. The lookout blinked then relaxed, gazing southwards nervously towards the Smoking Fort and the Old Wall on the horizon. It was the last thing he did before his tower was engulfed in searing purple dragonfire. The bell melted. The villagers' puny stockade was no defence against the most powerful dragons in the Seven Kingdoms. There were loud whoops and fireballs rained down, landing indiscriminately, tearing thatched stone crofts apart. Then a ring of Imperials put down and armed men with nets rounded up the dazed and weeping survivors. Swiftly roping them together, making sure no living were left behind to betray them, the Imperials cloaked, leaving the smoking ruins of the charcoal burners' village behind. Flying low to avoid SDS patrols, the Knights of Chaos headed north, leaving behind a pennant displaying a green dragon on black above crossed forks of lightning.

Major Cawdor, the young commander of the Smoking Fort, seeing the blue smoke rising, scrambled his command. The so called Knights of Chaos had struck again. The menfolk of fighting age lay slaughtered, the women and children, the old and the young taken. Why? Surveying the wreckage, Cawdor determined this wouldn't happen again; there was nothing chivalrous about attacking those who could not fight back. The King had promised five newly trained Imperials to patrol the heartlands; time to set a trap.

CHAPTER SIXTY-TWO

Stomp, Flame, Jump

The harvest moon was exhausting for the III Juvenile Sabretooth Brigade. The young battledragons negotiated higher and higher jumps and more difficult obstacles to develope their huge rear leg muscles. Soon they were big and strong enough to begin riding one up. Once their dragon was used to saddle and bridle, and their weight across the saddle, the class were allowed to mount, only to find their first lesson was then to learn how to fall without injuring themselves and a combat remount.

'You will fall,' Tangnost promised them. 'And so you must learn to do so without hurting yourselves. Kick your feet free of the stirrups, then curl up in a ball as you land to absorb the impact. Your armour will help protect you in the tunnels, but if you are trapped by the stirrup you could die. Then you will practice combat remount so that if you find yourself isolated from your talon or brigade, or your sabretooth is dead, you can be rescued under fire.'

As Two Gulps pounded over the paddock, Quentin kicked out of her stirrups and fell. Curling, rolling, she was on her feet calling to Two Gulps. As her dragon slowed she ran beside him, swiftly grasping the pommel and she was back up into the saddle. This was fun! Back in the training hall on a wooden sabretooth and then out in the paddocks, riders mastered how to use their dragon as a shield by slipping down either side of their mount with only one leg hooked about their special saddle pommels, denying hobgoblins a target, but then to swing up and strike swiftly, destroying targets. But not everyone found it easy and there was a steady stream of bruised and injured cadets heading for the hospital.

Gradually the juveniles began to move and fight as one talon, flushing out enemies hidden in woods or caves, encircling enemy soldiers, or protecting SDS ground troops isolated from their units. There was huge excitement as they were introduced to the Juvenile Light Lancers and Archers who would ride with them and protect them in battle once they began advanced operational training after graduation. Exhausted, saddle sore, black and blue despite their padded armour they fell into bed at night too tired to dream.

CHAPTER SIXTY-THREE

The Witchwood Chair

As their training neared completion, pilots and navigators destined to be Dragon Lords began one-to-one training with a Pilot Navigation Instructor, a PNI, on a flight simulator before graduating to Imperials.

'Sit, Sir,' the instructor asked kindly. 'But please don't touch anything.'

Root sat down in the training witchwood chair and put on the now familiar navigator's helmet and arm vambrace, which immediately linked in with his navigator displays. Unlike the chair in which he had flown during their adventures north with Quenelda, Quester and Tangnost, these runes were activated and alive the moment he sat.

'Belt in, Sir. If we corkscrew or drop dead you don't want left behind now do you?'

Root unconsciously reached for the parawings he was so familiar with, only for his instructor to remind him, 'The chair, Sir, is an ejector seat. You don't need to worry about dragonwings.'

'Ejector seat,' said Root weakly. 'Do we practise?'

'No, Sir. You are only allowed six ejections before you are grounded. The force is so great it shortens your spine. Ejector seats are your last option. So, Sir, please don't touch that icon unless you are very sure you need to.'

'Right, Sir, let's have pre-flight instrument check. Talk me through it, I'm your pilot, and then we'll take off.'

Two bells later they were half way through the flight. 'Now, Sir, there has been an attack on a brimstone convoy north-east of the Isle of Midges. Please plot your course.'

Root pressed an icon, and a map shimmered into existence. He pulled it towards him, dragging it to the left and down, then with a flick of a finger the detail leapt out. Checking the readouts for his current position he plugged in the co-ordinates and those of his destination. Several paths lit up. Taking a deep breath, Root checked his displays and punched in a solution.

'And headwind speed, Sir?'

Root closed his eyes. *What a careless rookie mistake!* He studied the weather displays to measure wind, and adjusted his bearing.

His instructor was unrelenting.

'Insurgents at grid north thirty two by west one hundred...scrambling all units....' Estimated time of arrival?'

Swiftly checking his position and wind speed, Root keyed in their co- ordinates...'Eta, half a bell at full flight...'

'This icon you have to identify what it is and fast.'

Root's fingers danced over runes inset into his chair. 'Incoming, incoming. An Imperial and fiveeee vampires.'

'Good,' the instructor nodded.

'Deploying cloak...'

Then the proximity alarm went off, the runes flashing warning red. Something was coming at them at great speed. Root's mind went blank. He froze.

'Sir, you at least have to shield yourself, or you will die.'

Feeling numb Root swiftly lent forwards. Too late! There was a percussion thump! thump! thump!.

'Sidewinder fireballs, Sir. Six strikes bracketing pilot and navigator. If you had not deployed shields you would be dead. If you cannot identify incoming hostile fire then always deploy your personal shielding.

'Let's try that again, Sir, shall we?'

Determined to excel, Root trained intensively over the next half moon, dawn till dusk. Flying at night took greater concentration but he swiftly mastered it.

'Patrol out of the ShadowWraiths,' Root swiftly reacted, concentration total. 'Five BoneCrackers, grid ref 69-20, isolated and under fire. Flight crew ready for combat drop...'

'A storm is coming. You need to get boots on the ground. What do you do?'

'Insurgence grid vector 291...'

With an excellent memory and instinctive feel for the witchwood, soon boy and chair were working in perfect harmony. 'You're ready to sit in the navigator's seat, Root,' Squadron Leader Wulfric told the delighted gnome at a post mission briefing. To Bracus's fury, Root was the second of the class to graduate to training on Imperials, assigned to Midnight Nightmare of the newly deployed FireStorm Regiment on the Wall.

CHAPTER SIXTY-FOUR

Crippled

'I can't!' Quester flung the crutch onto the floor and fell back on the bed. 'I can't! I'm crippled! It's no good, I'll never walk again. I'll never get to join the SDS now!'

And then to Quenelda and Drumondir's distress the youth began crying, great wrenching sobs that racked his thin body. Quenelda put her arm around him.

'No o-one visits anymore,' the words were muffled through his hands. 'Even R-root doesn't have the time now…everyone's training.'

Quenelda looked helplessly at the BoneCaster.

'Quester,' Drumondir said softly. 'I know it's difficult on crutches. I understand why you don't want to use them…you feel if you do, you are accepting what has happened, you are accepting you are a cripple. But if you refuse to try, if you fight against it, your dreams are somehow kept alive.' The BoneCaster took Quester's shaking hands. 'It is not so. With every step you are claiming your old life back again. You will never heal in your heart and head until you take that first step. No one knows what tomorrow may bring; there is always hope, and if you are weak chance may pass you by.'

If only he could just grow another leg. If only... Quenelda tensed...there was a memory just hanging out of reach...

CHAPTER SIXTY-FIVE

The Kiss of the Abyss

The Bottomless Firth below was calmer than usual as fifteen Imperials crossed from Cape Wrath to Roarkinch, their shadows flitting over the waves as they raced about the huge icebergs. The sky above was clear save for the now familiar mushroom of smoke from Glacier Peak.

Up ahead, surf broke frothily about the seemingly empty black sands of Roarkinch. The island was deserted save for winter ravens and the ruined castle to the north, slowly crumbling into the sea. Then the Knights of Chaos passed through the outer nexus and the spires and landing pads of the Night Citadel rose up above them, a sight that never failed to take Darcy's breath away. With whoops to announce their arrival, the Dark Knights dismounted from another successful seven days raiding just beyond the Old Wall.

'Darcy, are you coming?' Rupert called. Always when they returned the young knights headed for the hot baths in the Prince's Tower, before a banquet and celebration with the young ladies who were flocking to Court, their parents anxious to marry into the rising star of the WarLock King.

'In a moment!' Darcy watched as his captives were whipped towards the Dark Caves of the Night Citadel, feeling the sudden change in temperature that heralded the arrival of his father. The WarLock King coalesced in a flurry of inky smoke.

'Don't you have enough slaves for the mines? What use are children and elders? They won't last a moon.'

'They are not for the mines.'

'What then? They're weak: cottars and shepherds and children. What can you do with so many prisoners?'

'Make them into soldiers.'

'Sol- How?' Darcy frowned. 'What happens down there? What is the kiss of the abyss?' Finally he had asked, but dreaded the answer.

'As I have told you, it is death to approach the Abyss unprepared. Without defences the mere touch of the Abyss produces madness. It empties the mind, destroying free will, allowing me to mould them anew, to make them into creatures of chaos. They will be trained to utter obedience, to fight and to die for me. They will not tire or be afraid. It will weaken our enemies' resolve when they find they have been fighting their own kith and kin.'

'Great power always comes at a price. Your armour is born of the dark power between the stars, and already it protects you. But should you choose to wield the power of the Abyss, you must drink an elixir to prepare you as I had to.'

'What is this elixir?'

'Come.' He takes the first step freely...he has strength, he just has to find it...

Darcy had never set foot in Alchemists Tower. It hung improbably in the air above the WarLock Tower, and the only way in was a porting stone. The chamber he found himself in, with its smoking flasks and bubbling cauldrons, its bones and flesh and blood, was like a charnel house. Darcy shivered.

'This might make you a little...sick to begin with, so we begin with a small amount.'

The WarLock dipped into a great cauldron hanging suspended over a banked fire. 'Drink this.'

'What is it? Ah!' Darcy put the goblet down with an oath, spilling the dark liquid. The table wood smoked. 'It's freezing!'

His father did not answer. 'This elixir will give you strength beyond that of mere mortals. Do not fear, my son, you are not in peril. I do this to show you the heart of our power, our Kingdom. You may choose your own path if you wish. But every night you must drink. My cupbearer, Ignot, will bring the drink to you.'

With a trembling hand, Darcy lifted the goblet, doubt and disgust written on his face, but he threw the liquid down his throat.

The WarLock smiled. 'Now go and enjoy the masked ball and there is dragon racing tomorrow.'

CHAPTER SIXTY-SIX

Runt of the Litter

It had been an intense but calm morning of study in the classroom, studying sabretooth battlefield attack manoeuvres, when the cadets were invited to join Tangnost for his daily tour of operational battledragons, to discuss injuries with the surgeons and scale smiths, and to look over a recently born brood of sabretooths.

Visiting the maternity roosts deep within the island caused great excitement. It was the first time most of them had seen baby sabretooths, barely a moon old. It was steamy and hot and sulphurous, the darkness punctuated by small balls of fire as the fledglings rolled around and fought each other. There was a lot of squeaking and foot stomping.

Maternity Roost Master Tam Brandywine proudly told them all about ancient pedigree and breeding stock, and how Dragon Isle's sabretooths were the fiercest in the Seven Kingdoms. He answered questions about how often a breeding mare gave birth, how many were in a brood: how to care for them, and how long it took for them to fledge.

'They're so tiny, compared to ours!' Lachlan said.

'Aye, small enough to begin with,' Tam agreed. 'But not for long!'

'How can you tell they will make good battledragons?'

'Aye, good question,' Tam waded in to grab a struggling fledgling, which flamed all over his roost armour, frazzling his beard. Two others bit into his heavy boots and hung on, squeaking and growling. Firmly trapping his chosen sabretooth beneath one arm, where it squealed and wriggled, Tam lifted a hind leg.

'ere, ye see the bone here, the danklock bone? That big bone and they tendons and muscles here,' he ran a hand over the juvenile's flank, 'shows she's gonna have powerful strong legs. An' here,' he pulled the juvenile's stubby wing open for them to examine it. 'This here spindle bone? Already it's much thicker than other breeds and that means they can use their small wings to drive them forwards in the tunnels. Over short distances, with the help of these wings, they can leap as far and fast as hobgoblins above ground, but they're not too great in the air.'

'So how do you get sabretooths to the battlefield?' Lachlan asked.

Tangnost nodded his approval. 'On Imperials. Can anyone remember how many sabretooths an Imperial can carry?'

'Thirteen fully armoured sabretooths with a full payload of BoneCrackers,' Quentin answered when no one else did. 'Or fifty sabretooths on their own.'

'Correct,' Tangnost nodded. 'And how else?'

'On transports?' one of the boys answered.

'Correct. Guild battlegalleons are designed to transport a dozen sabretooths on each deck, with a dragon pad built high on the foredeck. We'll show you an armoured galleon so you can see for yourself,' Tangnost added. 'I hope none of you get too sea sick, since that is how you will be travelling sometimes.'

'See 're,' Tam continued with his lesson, lifting a foreleg as the fledgling flamed, driving the cadets backwards. 'Claw talon's beginning to grow already....and look at her teeth!'

'So do all juveniles become battledragons?'

'Nearly all. They're highly temperamental so unless some of that power is channelled into fighting they can be very dangerous to keep. But sometimes you get a runt...not much you can do with them...'er ladyship, the King's daughter, Lady Quenelda... she picked the runt of a litter.' He shook his head in sorrow. 'She can fly Imperials, any dragon they say, had the pick of her own battledragon, if rumours are true that the Earl Darcy had her own battledragon killed out of spite, but then she went and chose the runt of the litter. Too fat. Too lazy. Ate everything within reach...not that I'd say a word against her ladyship, what with 'er bringing back the Earl an' all, but clearly not a good judge of pedigree...'

Tam burbled on happily, not noticing that the entire class had swivelled to consider Quentin in a new light. They could hardly wait to get out of class.

'Are you...are you...?'

'You're the King's daughter!'

'But you're so scruffy! We thought you were a Roost Master's son!'

'You're not a boy?'

'You've flown Imperials?'

'Can you speak to dragons?'

Tangnost sighed, exasperated. Well, it was bound to happen sooner or later. It would have been hard to hide her forever, but they had not foreseen Tam and his runaway tongue!

CHAPTER SIXTY-SEVEN

Combat Flight Hanger

The reveille sounded, the silver notes finding their way into every dormitory. Unusually there was a flurry of activity.

'It's today!'

'Are you coming, Root...? Fergus hung upside down off the top bunk, hair framing his face like a beard.

'Mmmm?' Root was so tired he felt sick. Hearing from Quenelda how desperate his friend was, racked with guilt at neglecting Quester, Root was spending his precious few free hours of each day encouraging his friend to walk with crutches, but it meant going without sleep and he was exhausted.

'Inspection of the combat flight cavern today! Pilots and navigators!'

'Yes, of course,' Root replied brightly, as he leapt out of bed. 'I'm coming.' Once again he would have to pretend it was a first for him too. He was finding it increasingly difficult, especially since Quenelda's secret was out. Everyone was talking about the King's daughter;

the first girl in the SDS and the first of her class to fly a battledragon! Rumours that she had flown the King's Imperial to find her father were beginning to circulate again, but everyone had forgotten Quester and him. It was hard not to feel left out and he suddenly realised how Quester must be feeling. Would the SDS ever reveal that Galtekerion had been captured?

For the first time, the cadets passed below ground, leaving the Battle Academy behind. Great stone doors inset with vibrant blue runes brought them to a halt. There was a palm set into the stone at shoulder height, just like those on their witchwood seats. Tangnost placed his hand against it. The doors opened silently and closed behind them. Even Root had not been in these flawlessly smooth passageways but was immediately drawn to the runes set in the walls, that illuminated faintly as they passed.

'Root? Root? Keep up!' Tangnost smiled.

The cadets followed the dwarf to where an intersection of six great passages met, with a vast porting stone inset at its centre. Soldiers, deck crew, marines, BoneCrackers and a few Dragon Lords flowed about them, coming and going about their own business. The porting stone was unbelievably fast, and many of the boys who had never encountered one before buckled at the knees. When it stopped the cadets found themselves at a similar junction. Tangnost led them towards an archway, brightly lit from within.

'Awesome!'

What lay before them took their breath away. The

cadets found themselves on a metal gantry that ran about an immense cavern.

'Look!'

A patrol of six Imperials was taking off with a full payload of thirteen sabretooths and three-hundred Bonecrackers, escorted by harriers and vampires. Although Imperials were huge they were dwarfed by this cavern! A camouflage nexus outlined them in red as they left the cliffs of Dragon Isle.

A dwarf was in conversation with Tangnost, white haired, battle-scarred, with most of the fingers on his right hand missing. Tangnost turned back to them.   'Dragon Master Odin Whalebone will be your guide for the remainder of the afternoon. Pay attention.'

'Sir! Yes, Sir!'

'Follow me,' Odin commanded.   The class circled the gantry, stepping down two flights of steps and across a metal landing onto a dragon pad which began to drop. 'Now, look, but don't touch anything,' the Dragon Master warned.

'Pads are all different sizes? We've only one at our castle!'

'Yes, of course,' Odin nodded. 'How long are Imperials? Anyone?'

'A hundred and sixty strides from nose to tail,' Lachlan offered.

Odin nodded. 'And their wingspan?'

'One hundred and eighty five strides,' Quenelda answered.

'So,' the Dragon Master confirmed. 'You cannot have

an Imperial land on the same size pad as a harrier, can you?'

'Can we see where the pads are forged?' Caradoc asked, studying the intricate metalwork with fascination.

'Not today, but yes, you will visit the foundries. Now, some of you will be familiar with landing pads but this is no ordinary pad.' The dwarf let them walk about the pad first to examine the flight deck; the emergency nets and bright lights inset into the circumference.

'Control icons are inset into this instrumentation panel here and the gantry ledge above. Now, stand here, within this inner circle. Watch,' the Dragon Master pressed a rune. There was a click that shivered through the metal, and then they began to descend smoothly down, with a clang and clunk of gears.

As the docking pad crowded with cadets moved slowly beneath the flight deck, semi-circular doors overhead closed silently. Beneath was another world; a subterranean labyrinth of tunnels, roosts and armour pits, hot and sulphurous and noisy. The thump of hammer on anvil as armour was mended competed with the bellows of a nearby forge, and the shouts and calls of ostlers and armourers and the snorts of battledragons and jingle of harness.

Immediately to their left lay a deep, half circular pit, shaped like a slice of apple, Root thought, with a sloped entrance and exit. Chains hung from pulleys, some with heavy armour which also hung on nearby wooden tree frames. These were the sabretooth pits.

'Do they wear the same armour?' Ranulf asked.

'The same design, yes,' Odin nodded. 'But each bard of armour is forged for a particular dragon just as your armour will be made to fit you.'

They all turned at the sound of snorting and the scrape and spark of talons on stone. A sabretooth was being led through the stone-walled maze. Smoking Sulphur was a two year old stallion who was chaffing at the bridle, typically highly strung and eager to battle, lashing his powerful tail from side to side.

'Keep back,' an armourer warned them. 'That tail will break your bones.' Smoking Sulphur was led down and quietened with a nosebag of brimstone.

'Do they need to eat brimstone before battle?' Fergus asked.

'Yes,' Odin nodded. 'If they are to flame they need energy. They can fight without it, but eventually they would starve and die.'

Four armourers: three dwarves and a powerfully built man all in heavy boiled leather armour set swiftly to work.

'Which piece of armour is this?' Odin asked as one of the dwarves fitted armour that reached from the stallion's ears to her muzzle, with flanges protecting the eyes, and spikes along its nose.

'Shaffron,' a soft spoken troll from the far south offered, as the oiled leather straps were carefully secured under the colt's chin. One shake of the head and those muzzle spikes could catch an armourer, but they moved softly and swiftly, clearly practised.

The winch creaked as segmented plates that pivoted on loose rivets were lowered onto the dragon's crest with a matching one beneath to protect its neck. 'How much do you think this crinet weighs?'

'One scruple?' Athlestan, who was Grand Master Spellskin's grandson and came from a long line of merchants, hazarded a guess.

Odin shook his head. 'Ten! It's a half thumb thick. You are thinking of parade armour, nice and shiny but not much use when you have to break through a hobgoblin banner.'

The armourers hoisted the last piece. 'And this is?'

'The peytral,' Root answered as the final and heaviest piece of barding was lowered and fitted. Finally the bridle and saddle were swiftly strapped on. Smoking Sulphur was armoured and ready to go on patrol.

CHAPTER SIXTY-EIGHT

By Royal Appointment

Quenelda was having a decidedly bad influence: Armelia was no longer satisfied with life at court, and it was entirely her friend's fault. It was not that the banquets, the dancing and fashion were any less wonderful. It was just that the Queen's lady-in-waiting wanted to do something more. She knew that dwarf men and women both fought, on principle, and that amongst elves, warriors were mostly women. But she was not brave like Root and Quenelda, not in that way. The thought of battle petrified her, and her terrifying flight to F&H's on Two Gulps was best forgotten.

And so Armelia had decided to take matters into her own hands. Tentatively she raised her idea with Caitlin. The Queen had been both delighted and excited, for she too chaffed at the bonds of tradition. Things, she confided with Armelia, had not always been this way.

'Come, my dear.'

Exploring little used apartments in the oldest part of the castle they found paintings of previous kings and queens. And the further back they went, the more interesting it became.

'When I was a child I used to come here. I never understood why girls couldn't fight, and when my father and brother died on the Isle of Midges...' The Queen smiled. 'So, dearest Armelia, Quenelda is not so different after all.'

Armed with a letter of royal patronage, Armelia approached F&H's Ladies Salon with a few tentative sketches, and explained what she had in mind. Samantha Spellgood sat unmoving after Armelia finished.

'L-legs?' she finally managed, feeling faint. 'D-dragons? You intend to...to...?' She had known right from the beginning that the Lady Quenelda was going to be a bad influence.

Armelia nodded fervently and played her trump card. 'Of course,' she said casually, letting the letter of royal patent unroll with the royal seal attached. 'Her Majesty will patronise your establishment once the designer range has been completed. As you know, Her Majesty has a fine roost of pedigree racing dragons and may herself...' The Countess let the thought linger tantalisingly in their minds.

'Her Majesty...?' Samantha repeated. The sound of golden guineas finally broke through her stupor. 'By Royal Appointment' was worth its weight in gold.

'Oh, yes,' Armelia assured her. 'And the King...' she held out a purse. F&H entered into the spirit of things with gusto. The seamstresses set to work in great secrecy, doing their best to recreate Armelia's designs, which were a little vague on detail, while Armelia tried to remember all the thingies...bits of armour...padding, that Quenelda had pointed out... 'reinforced knee caps,' sounded positively painful.

Finally stage one of her plan was complete. This should surely persuade DragonIsle's gruff Dragon Master how serious she was!! It would most certainly get his attention, but would it win his approval? On reflection Armelia decided she needed some moral support and guidance, and so a message was sent to Dragon Isle. The second part of the plan involved Root.

The stage was set. Armelia took a deep breath; now for the hard part. Summoning her courage, head held high, attire carefully concealed beneath a long cloak and hood, minus her gaggle of companions and servants, Armelia headed for the Royal roosts of Crannock Castle. The Dragon Master had put down several bells earlier, having been summoned by the Queen on the pretext of a sickly mare, so Armelia knew where Tangnost would be.

Tangnost fretted, wondering what on the One Earth the Lady Armelia wished to see him about. He wasn't entirely comfortable with Court ladies. 'Are you certain it was not Drumondir that she asked after?' he pressed Root again, before the boy left.

'No,' Root shook his head, trying to keep his face strictly neutral, and determined to stick around. It would be worth it just to see Tangnost's face. He sneaked back into the roost and hid in one of the dragon stalls.

Armelia coughed. She had tiptoed so quietly no one had heard her, and shed her cloak. Tangnost looked up to see a vision in pink enter his roosts, and pink was most certainly not a colour that normally belonged there. Yes, very definitely pink, with hearts picked out in a darker shade, as were the pointy-toed boots which tinkled as she walked. A sparkly wand sheath was built into the right thigh to match the sparkly helmet. In fact there were a lot of sparkly bits.

Peering over one of the dragons, Root waited with bated breath. Hurriedly closing his mouth, Tangnost rushed to brush down a stool to hide his shock.

'Countess Armelia. Please, sit.'

Tangnost waited, trying to ignore the tassels and bells that tinkled as the Queen's lady-in-waiting made herself comfortable. Armelia stared at him; like a rabbit cornered by a weasel, she seemed frozen to the spot. Decidedly discombobulated, Tangnost drew on his pipe and coughed to cover his confusion. Root tried not to laugh.

Tangnost finally prompted his reluctant guest. 'Countess? You wanted to see me? Root did not say why?'

Armelia coughed. 'Um, yes,' she managed.

Tangnost raised his eyebrows in enquiry.

'What do you think? Of my, err, outfit?'

'It's very... pink,' Tangnost said, truthfully.

'I was hoping,' Armelia ventured, fanning away the clouds, 'you could teach me to...to... err... to err....'

'To err?' Tangnost found himself nodding in an effort to draw the words out.

'A dragon!' Armelia said triumphantly. There! She had said it, and couldn't take it back.

'To err a dragon?'

Armelia nodded manically, wondering if the Dragon Master was going soft in the head. 'Secretly,' she added, as if that clarified the situation.

'Secretly?'

'To fly,' Root hissed. 'To fly a dragon!'

'Fly!!!' Yes, to fly a dragon!'

'You want to learn to fly?' Tangnost was taken aback. Quenelda's friend was changing indeed.

'Um, yes. In time for the Graduation Ceremony. I thought it might surprise Quenelda?'

'But,' Tangnost said, feeling rapidly out of his depth in the world of pink leathers and pantaloons. 'Ladies don't fly.'

'I know one who does!' Armelia held his gaze. 'And so do you.'

The Dragon Master barked a laugh. 'That we do, Lady,' he nodded in amusement, respect tinging his words. 'That we do. Root? Come out from behind that dragon. Since you obviously know all about this, I task you with teaching Lady Armelia.'

Embarrassed, Root shuffled out of hiding. 'Me?'

'You! I can't think of anyone better, can you?' Tangnost smiled smugly. 'And Chasing the Stars is the perfect dragon, is she not, for a novice? You are doing so well with your studies that I will make sure you are allowed two afternoons off a quarter moon. And you have been saying Dragon Isle is not the place for your mare, so why not bring her here to stable?'

Armelia nodded enthusiastically. She loved Root's 'dear little dragon,' and 'dear little Root'; despite Court ladies saying the youth was 'just' a jumped up gnome, and a commoner to boot.

Armelia did not get up to leave.

'There is something else, my Lady?'

She asked him.

'Design what?' Tangnost coughed, smoke coming out of his nose.

'I need, err, advice how to do all the, err, armoured bits?'

'No!' Tangnost put his size twelve boot down hard. 'No!'

'No?' Armelia frowned. 'But how am I – how are we to design something for me to wear? With all those bits and pieces....armour...?'

Root glared at Tangnost. 'She,' the gnome coughed to cover his rudeness, 'the Countess needs someone who knows all about leather and armour; to keep her safe, and warm. I don't think,' he gestured at Armelia's outfit. 'Velvet would keep the wind and rain out...?'

Tangnost sighed with exasperation. 'As long as there are no...'

'Sequins?' Root helpfully supplied.

Armelia shook her head

'Lace?'

She nodded again.

'Bells?'

Armelia pouted.

'No bells?' Tangnost repeated.

'Oh, very well,' Armelia glowered. 'I promise!' He hadn't mentioned hearts! Or pink...

Tangnost Bearhugger was into fashion, and the exclusive F&H Dragon Master range of ladies flying leathers was born.

CHAPTER SIXTY-NINE

Ready, Steady, Go!

Summer passed in a blaze of blue skies and drowsy heat, bringing with it the conclusion of the Junior Sabretooth's individual training. The troop was out in the paddock, their mounts jumping and bumping, snorting flame.

'Let's see how much you have learned. Your juvenile must not only be able to fight but must learn discipline. War is violent,' Tangnost warned. 'We can teach you to wield a sword, to attack in formation, to lead; but what we cannot prepare you for is how loud war is. Sometimes the most unexpected thing, the thing that can freeze you on the battlefield, is the sound of war. The clash of swords, the cries of the injured, the rage of the dragons. So expect the unexpected.' He looked at the melee of eager faces. 'Now, get ready! Combat mount!'

Ostlers and grooms, cadets from other units, lined the route with anything that could be banged and clanged. Scores took to the wooden terraces to watch their charges and a number of scholars from the Tactical Ground Attack School in their colourful robes stopped by to watch.

The class donned their padded leather armour, strapping the buckles for back and breast plate, padded boiled leather elbow and knee protectors, and heavy boots. Quenelda pulled a half helm firmly down on her head and buckled it. She hated riding with a saddle but Tangnost insisted.

'You may be able to ride bareback, but there are few others, if any, who can. You are training to be part of a talon and a brigade. If you are injured and Two Gulps is the only mount available, he has to be ridden by anyone, so you both train and compete with bridle and saddle. In any event, battle harness allows you to carry all the equipment you will need to survive out in the field for weeks. So he must become used to standard issue harness and webbing.'

The juveniles lined up, snorting and nipping and kicking, barely held in check. Quenelda smiled confidently, this would be child's play. Others would have to learn the brutal reality of the battlefield but she and Two Gulps had already seen combat action. They weren't exactly fighting; in fact they were fleeing the battlefield just as swiftly as Two Gulps could manage! But they had probably trodden on a hobgoblin or two along the way, and two Gulps had certainly toasted one while saving her life. And now everyone knew who she was, she had something to prove, being the only girl!

The rowdy spectators gave it their all. Banging staves on shields, knocking pans together, howling, flapping their arms and cloaks they screamed and waved flags.

Tangnost brought down the flag.

In two strides, Quenelda vaulted up onto her young mount and they were away, a ragged line of juveniles, spurred on by their equally young riders, shoving, pushing, and gouging great clods of earth, their passing noise like thunder.

'Go, Two Gulps!'

'Thunderfoot forwards!'

'Phoenix Flame, go go! Go!'

Egged on with whoops and knees and spurs, cheered on by their ostlers, grooms and smiths in the wooden stands, the young battledragons picked up their taloned feet.

Thud... Thud... Thud... Thud...

Within strides, some of the more powerfully built juveniles were pulling away.

Two Gulps!! Quenelda urged him forwards, before she was conscious of a sideways wiggle. Beneath her boots, Two Gulps' tummy was swinging from side to side like a pendulum, which was slowing his forward pace. Already they were among the stragglers! Quenelda cursed in dwarfish in a very unladylike way as clods and stones kicked back from those in front peppered her, pinging off her helmet. Spitting dirt, she urged her mount forwards.

Faster and faster the dragons picked up their pace around their first circuit of the paddocks, then as the leaders began to pull away the field began to spread out. Bright cloaks were flapped and clods of earth thrown. Several had found bells.

Thud... Thud... Thud... thud...

Two Gulps was slowly gaining. A sabretooth next to them caught a talon and crashed into the stands in a flurry of splinters and screaming spectators. Quenelda was aware of another rider tumbling from the saddle to her right when his sabretooth bounded over a log. Another one down!

Two Gulps began to get into his stride. A series of huge boulders loomed up ahead and the juveniles split left and right, only Two Gulps sprang, great thigh muscles bunching, talons grooving the rock, one hop, two, a huge third and they were airborne, wings out for balance and then down again with a thud, and almost up with the leaders!!

The tunnel mouth was visible through the trees, a dark smudge in the craggy skirts of the mountain. The six sabretooths ahead of Two Gulps and Quenelda converged, each vying to be the first to enter. The passage was narrow to begin with and they couldn't let another get ahead! Two collided with a fearful thump, one tumbling head over heels unseating its rider and slamming into the rock face. The second held its balance, skidded and spun and then was through into the tunnels.

Thump... thump... thump... thump... The sound was amplified by the narrow walls. The sabretooths were darting left and right, ducking under stalactites, leaping over boulders. Together, stirrup to stirrup they pushed and shoved, scale to scale, head butting, Dropping down into an old watercourse, Two Gulps caught the leaders.

Suddenly, soldiers appeared to their left, thumping on shields, and the sabretooth neck and neck with them veered away, while Two Gulps smoked, a curl of flame steaming in the frigid air and forcing the soldiers back. Up ahead, two sabretooths collided and went down in a tangle of claws and harness. Round a bend and Two Gulps and Quenelda burst out into daylight. Buoyed up by shouts of encouragement, it looked like half the Battle Academy were there to see them win, Quenelda slackened the reins and gave Two Gulps his head.

Up ahead the finish beckoned.

Two Gulps! Quenelda was ecstatic as the sabretooth's great loping stride ate up the distance, effortlessly flowing over tussocks and hillocks of the home circuit! We're going to win!

Suddenly Two Gulps' head snapped around, and his talons scored great grooves in the dirt. Caught out, Quenelda soared overhead, the impact slamming her into the ground. She curled up tightly as the following dragons tried to avoid standing on her, rolling to the side. She looked up as the field flowed past. Two Gulps was nose down in a pile of brimstone and thistles.

CHAPTER SEVENTY

Witchwood Song

'We fly in dual witchwood training chairs, where I can override your instructions if needs be.'

Ascending to the waiting Imperial on the pad, Root felt wobbly with nerves, but they were forgotten as he discovered his navigator's chair between instructor and pilot.

"This is my actual chair?' Root ran fingers over the beautifully carved and polished witchwood. 'For me?' He had only seen work like this in the Elder's Burrow in his warren, an old chair handed down the generations carved from his family tree.

His instructor nodded. 'Yes, it has been carved to fit you. You can visit the Wood Hall; Master Carpenter Rowan said you may wish to. Now, let's see it imprint on you. Place your hand there,' he indicated a hand carved into the left arm of the chair. Nothing happened! Root's heart began to beat faster...he forgot to breathe.

'Patience...let it reach out to you, let the wood decide.'

Then Root's hand began to tingle like pins and needles.

Soft motes of white and green twinkled and winked and Root heard the whisper of wind through the trees. The wood about him sprang to life. The warmth of it embraced the youth; like roots questing in the loamy earth he felt its strength cocooning him, nurturing him, wrapping him in song. The deep grained seat took on the hue of honey shot through with gold.

'It's so beautiful!'

A powerful reaction... the instructor nodded thoughtfully. 'Its power is now at your command and the chair will answer only to you. Now, Sir,' he pointed to the icons of all sizes and colours that ebbed and flowed through the grain of the wood, 'these icons and glyphs have been cast for you by the Guardian himself. Now, to work. I am going to set you a series of challenges. Let's see if you are as good as your instructors say you are, young Root.'

'Take off,' he told his pilot, and the Imperial lifted into the night.

'Lift off, lift off,' the Seadragon Tower crackled in Root's helmet. 'Good hunting.' Root's first operational patrol!

'He's a natural,' Root's trainer was reporting back to the Guardian. 'The boy has an affinity with the witchwood which I did not expect to find in one not sorcerer born.' He was still amazed. 'I have never seen such a powerful aura before in a novice.'

'His people live as one with the land,' Drumondir suggested. 'Perhaps gnomes can draw upon the Old Magic that used to reside in all living things? From stone and wood and water...'

'He found his way to the drop zone and extracted twelve sabretooths and a platoon of BoneCrackers. He's ready to go on combined battle exercises.'

CHAPTER SEVENTY-ONE

Defiance

'Or what?' the town elder was an SDS veteran. Built like a bull, he had never backed down from a fight. Only Imperials had always been on the same side – until now.

'Do you think your puny town walls can save you from us?' Darcy's voice was soft, menacing. 'Submit to my father.'

'Never. Our loyalty lies with Dragon Isle.'

'Submit to the WarLock King... or die.'

The veteran considered the invitation. 'We choose Dragon Isle.'

Darcy grinned at his companions. Rupert whooped and spurred his Imperial forward to crush the town walls. That was when the air warped and six SDS Imperials materialised and battlemagic arced across the clearing. Rupert was engulfed by a pulse that killed a dozen of his men.

With an oath Darcy yanked the reins of his Imperial. 'Cloak!' Tormenting and killing the defenceless was one thing, fighting Dragon Lords another. 'Ugh!' he grunted as a pulse took him in the chest just as he cloaked, shattering his pilot's chair. A net fell on Euan, Quester's eldest brother, snatching him from his saddle. Cloaked, the rest fell back in disarray and fled north.

CHAPTER SEVENTY-TWO

This Is Not about You

'Two Gulps!' Quenelda was furious, furious at him for letting her down. Furious that so many in the stands were laughing at her battledragon face down in the brimstone and her futile attempts to pull him away. 'The King's daughter,' she could hear them, 'I told you girls can't ride dragons!' Furious at Tangnost for doing this to her! After all they had done together! So furious she didn't know what to do.

Why? Why are you angry? The food is here to eat. Why are you so angry?

She couldn't find the words...

But you said this is not battle...you are not in danger...

Tangnost finally found her throwing tack across the saddle room in fury.

'Out!' he barked at cadets and roost hands. They ran. 'Stop! Stop that now!' Tangnost's voice was soft; she should have heeded that warning but she didn't, hurling a bucket of soapy water across the tack room.

'What? Why are you angry?'

'Why? Why do you think! That was unfair! Putting food down for him! You knew he'd take it!'

'What? You think this is about you? About Two Gulps? Have you learnt nothing these past five moons? This is not about you or Two Gulps, or any one of us! It's about our very future and all you can do is think about yourself!'

Aghast, Quenelda stared at him open mouthed. Tangnost had hardly ever raised his voice.

'Discipline is what makes us different from the hobgoblins. It's the only thing that stops their banners overwhelming us. We cannot afford one break in our shield wall or they are through. Two Gulps is a weak link. If he does that on a battlefield, you are dead,' Tangnst said grimly. 'You are both dead. You are part of a talon now, and in time part of a brigade and a regiment, which in turn is part of the SDS. There is no room for you on Dragon Isle. We are fighting for our very survival!'

'It wasn't fair!' Quenelda was in tears now. She had so wanted to win, to show off Two Gulps, that he was stronger, better, faster! To end the mockery! To prove a girl could do just as well as any boy!

'Why is it unfair? You talk like a child! You can talk to dragons, is that not unfair? You can think like a dragon, is that not unfair? It's always about you. What you can do. How special you are. You have a battledragon when no one else does. Is that not unfair?

Root is unstintingly loyal to you, but how do you think he feels when you take all the glory, but it he who captured Galtekerion! He who might have died along with Quester and your father, because of your indiscipline, because of your dragon's indiscipline. He is being bullied, and can't strike back, can't tell anyone what happened. He doesn't because he is disciplined, he puts the SDS before himself.

'Think on it, Quenelda! You had better learn that lesson; and so had Two Gulps. Or he is failed. And you too.'

CHAPTER SEVENTY-THREE

Beginner's Lesson

Root gently led his mare out the royal stables at Crannock. It was a glorious late summer's afternoon and the views of the loch were spectacular. A light cooling breeze blew from the west.

'She is really gentle and perfect for learning how to fly. Honestly,' Root assured Armelia. 'I was petrified. I was scared of heights and I got airsick too. We'll just walk about to begin with until you feel comfortable in the saddle, then you can ride pillion with me and we'll do a low flight above the paddocks.'

'You were afraid? Of Chasing the Stars?' Armelia pulled a face. No one could be as scared as she was.

'Yes! Truly! I fainted,' he looked at her ruefully, a tinge of embarrassment colouring his cheeks. 'She's a windyglen withershanks; very gentle. I'm going to teach you how to say hello to a dragon.'

Armelia looked doubtful.

'Blow gently on her muzzle, here, like this.' Chasing the Stars nuzzled the youth as he rested his head against her long nose. 'Come on, she won't bite!' he joked. 'She's a vegetarian like me! Go on, be brave!'

Armelia lowered her head, pursed her lips and puffed feebly like she was kissing someone at Court. Chasing the Stars replied with a great deal more enthusiasm. Jerking her head back Armelia was surprised. 'She smells of hay and honey!'

Root grinned. 'That will be these,' he held out a handful of large tablets. 'Honey tablets; thistle, honey, oats and dried cranberries. All the dragons love them,' he spilt them into her hand. 'Hold your hand out flat. No, fingers flat, or she might bite you accidently. There, Lady, that wasn't so hard was it?' he encouraged Armelia, as the mare's hot tongue licked her hand for crumbs.

'Armelia.'

'Lady Armelia,' Root bowed his head, acknowledging his over familiarity.

'Root,' Armelia took his hands gently. 'Just Armelia will do.'

'But you're a lady and I'm just a commoner.'

'You're not 'just' anything, Root. I was born to an ancient noble family with no money and married into one of the greatest Earldoms in the Kingdoms...' For a moment she looked as if she would cry. 'You were born the son of the Earl's scout. Why should that make me any better than you? We can't choose our parents...we can't choose our birth right.'

'My parents... they measure a person's worth by their wealth, and yet they inherited theirs and spent it all. You've taught me that it's who you are that matters, the real meaning of friendship. Now,' she took a deep breath. 'Show me how to fly!'

Root nodded, and then smiled. 'As you say, L-Armelia.' He turned to his dragon. 'Down, Chasing the Stars, down. Dragons respond to commands and to hand signals,' he explained as his dragon sank to the grass where she contentedly began grazing on clover.

'This is the saddle. You sit here, and these are the stirrups which can be adjusted. This strap that goes about her tummy is called the girth. And I've chosen a sheep skin to pad the saddle so that...erm...so that it em, well it can be sore to begin with. Your um...' Root racked his brains for the word young ladies used. Rump didn't sound quite so right when applied to Armelia.

'D-d-errrr...' he tried to remember the word Armelia would understand.

'Rump,' Armelia offered helpfully. She was becoming quite robust...quite forward thinking.

Root nodded gratefully. 'Rump, yes. If you are not used to riding or flying it can be quite sore until you develop your flying muscles. So you may be a little stiff tomorrow.'

'How do I... steer her?'

'With the bridle. This is the rein which you hold onto and they are attached to a 'bit' here in her mouth. Open,' he asked his dragon, who obliged, revealing a lot of clover-studded stubby teeth. 'If you pull gently to the right or left she turns that way. Right, mount up as I showed you. No! No! Not that leg or you'll end up...facing backwards...' Root smiled, helping Armelia dismount. 'Let's try again.'

'Giddy up,' Armelia said hopefully as she settled in the saddle. Someone had told her that was what you said, but they must have been wrong because Chasing the Stars continued to graze. 'Isn't that what you are supposed to say?'

'Weeellll....' Root said, wrinkling his nose. 'There's a little bit more to it than that. Let me show you.'

So in one of the corner paddocks, Root gave Armelia her first lesson, only realising when he stood back and saw them together that Armelia had colour coordinated her leathers to match the dragon; F&H must have worked night and day to produce that flying suit for her so quickly. How sweet! Root smiled, touched by how much Armelia cared for Chasing the Stars; magenta helmet down to the same shade of blue boots as Chasing the Star's tail! He suspected, were he to look, that Armelia's nail varnish would match the mare's talons. He felt at peace for the first time since Tangnost suggested his mare stay here at the castle. She'll be safe here with Armelia, and loved to bits.

'I think,' Root smiled, 'you are ready for your first flight!'

CHAPTER SEVENTY-FOUR

Death on a Hot Afternoon

Darcy spurred his imperial towards the safety of Borzall castle, in a fury at being thwarted. His ensorcerelled armour was smoking, having taken a direct hit, and yet, although he was sore and bruised and his ears were ringing, he was unhurt; unlike one of his friends, and where was Euan? As they put down in the outer bailey, Darcy ran down his dragon's wing and swiftly mounted his friend's Imperial which had put down without a pilot.

'Rupert? Rupert?'

Already the men-at-arms were pulling their young lord from the wreckage of his pilot's chair to lay him down on the Imperial's back.

'Gods!' Darcy looked at the buckled armour, the clotted black blood and pale broken ribs and was nearly sick. With shaking hands he removed Rupert's helmet. His friend was moon pale and a froth of blood bubbled from his mouth, spattering his face like freckles.

'Physicians!' he shouted as two men at arms took off on thistle dragons up into the castle. 'Get Archibald.

Now!'

'It doesn't look good, Darcy,' Simon warned.

'Hang on, Rupert...the physic is coming!' Darcy took his friend's hand and screamed when the arm came away flopping out of the twisted armour.

The physician took one look and shook his head.

'Save him!' Darcy swore at the man, threatened and cajoled in turn.

The man knelt. Only the whites of the eyes were visible as he lifted Rupert's lids. Shaking his head he put fingers against the young man's throat.

'There is no heartbeat. He's a dead man, my Prince, there is nothing to be done for him.'

'But he's stopped bleeding!'

'That's because he has bled out and his heart has stopped. It's too late, no one can save him.'

CHAPTER SEVENTY-FIVE

Many Gulps Too Many

We are to be parted?

Yes. Quenelda swallowed, real fear gripping her. *One Eye says that if we were at war, and you stopped to eat, I may die, or others may die...And you have to eat less because you are too heavy to fly in battle, too slow to carry me from battle...*

The young dragon considered her words.

But we are one...One Kind...you are part dragon...

Quenelda rested her head against Two Gulps' cool scales and felt a tear track down her face.

You still grieve for my sire?

My lifelong I will grieve for him...he was part of me; my hearts were his...he is waiting for me across the rainbow bridge...

And now your hearts are mine?

And now are yours...Two Gulps, I could not bear to lose you, too...

The sabretooth turned to nuzzle her, his tongue tasting the salty tears. In distress and confusion he flamed. On surrounding paddocks everyone turned to stare at the whirlwind of golden fire that engulfed the Earl's daughter and her sabretooth. There were cries of shock and screams from cadets; ostlers came running, shouting for a Dragon Master or Roost Mistress. But their cries turned to amazement as the flames and smoke died back and Quenelda stood untouched, the wings of her battledragon about her, the great head resting against hers. Word passed from mouth to mouth...

'Child,' somehow Drumondir had found Quenelda, curled up in Dragonsdome's roosts with a dejected Two Gulps. 'What is wrong?'

'Tangnost doesn't love me! He made a fool of me, in front of everyone!'

'No child, he did not. You did that all by yourself.'

'What!' Quenelda went stiff.

'You wanted to win?'

'Of course!'

'Why? To show that you were better than the rest, had been in a battle?'

Quenelda let out a deep breath in reluctant consent. 'They laughed at me! All the boys...some of them are saying they knew a girl couldn't fly a battledragon!'

'How many times has Tangnost warned you that your dragon's love of food is a danger? Not just to you but to others. At my clan home he ate a good part of our winter stock of seal and fish; my people may have starved. Th-'

'He saved me at the Smoking Fort!' Quenelda was still looking for excuses for Two Gulps, for herself.

'But child, it was his greed that put you and others at risk, was it not? He was feeding in the brimstone pits?'

'What do you mean others?'

'Your father delayed taking off to wait for you. By the time Stormcracker finally got airborne,' Drumondir was coming to grips with SDS terminology, 'Galtekerion and his Chosen had killed nearly everyone on board and were closing on your father. Only Quester and Root stood in his way.'

Quenelda was finally silent, eyes wide with shock. 'You mean, it was because of me...' she said in a small voice. 'And Two Gulps, that Quester has been crippled?'

'Yes, and you were fortunate. All three might have died.' Drumondir was relentless but reality had to be driven home. 'Don't be so hasty to accord blame for your failures on others. Think about what Tangnost asks of you, and why you have not taken his warnings to heart.'

'Child,' Drumondir opened her arms inviting a hug. 'Tangnost loves you as one of his own children and you know it is so. From the moment you were born he has been at your side, protecting you and guiding you, but this was one lesson that you had yet to take seriously. He does this because he loves you, he is teaching you to protect yourself and others. You are blinded by your love for this dragon of yours.'

'But I don't want to lose him...like I lost Two Gulps!' Quenelda was openly sobbing.

Drumondir thought of Tangnost's anquish and anger and regret. ...fell weather for foul deeds... 'Tell me,' she said simply.

'It was...misty...grey,' it was the first time she had ever talked about it. 'He-he called to me; he was afraid for the first time in his life...I had to race to reach him before his hearts stopped...I could feel them slowing beat by beat...I begged him not to go, not to leave me be-behind...but he flew without me...'

'Ah, child, he might have died alone on the battlefield; instead he was cradled in your arms when he crossed the rainbow bridge. None of us could ask for more. And part of him is with you always...he gave you his heart, it beats side by side with yours...' Drumondir held Quenelda while the girl wept her heart out.

'The price of love is inevitably loss,' the Bonecaster said gently after a time. 'Death and renewal are a part of life, as are the passing of the seasons. All who die return to the One Earth, to the Great Earth Wyrm where they nurture new life. You lost Two Gulps and You're Gone but you gained his fledgling, Two Gulps Too Many, who has stolen your heart also. But by spoiling him, you risk losing him...he will die, or you will die and others will die, because you love him too much to teach him discipline. Tangnost wants Two Gulps and you to lead your talon, to help him train other juveniles, people and dragons both, because the need is urgent. How can you, if you cannot control your own dragon?'

CHAPTER SEVENTY-SIX

Battlegames: Survival of the Fittest

'As you know this is the first year in living memory that the hobgoblins have not come with the spring thaw. But,' Tangnost looked over the combined AirWing Juvenile cadets. 'Dragon now fights dragon and we are taking heavy losses. Dragons are going down beyond the Old Wall in enemy territory and few of their crew, if any, return. We are training another twenty five imperial and thirty harrier crews to join Search and Rescue, but that takes time. You've learnt war craft, now you must learn field craft if you are to survive.'

There were some murmurs of disquiet. All of a sudden the reality of fighting their kindred was reaching out to touch the young cadets. Root thought, with compassion, of Quester who did not know yet of his family's decision to fight for the WarLock King. If his friend ever fought again, it might be against his own family!

'You are going on a survival training exercise with the 2nd troop, 3rd battalion of the Junior Mountain Rangers. They will be tracking you down, that's what they have trained to do this year, to find and recover downed aircrews. But for this exercise they are your enemy. Once airborne, you will be given your mission parameters and target co-ordinates.

Bracus, you're team leader. Root, you're scout. Your joint objective is for your team to reach the lift zone without being captured or killed, and along the way to learn the basics of survival that might just keep you alive. Take off is 2000 bells, west lower pads. Full battlegame gear and kit, including night sights and training staffs. Understood?'

'Sir! Yes, Sir!'

Root shrugged into his battlegame body armour, over his scouting gear from the Ice Isles, and checked his kit bag one final time: hammock and bedding roll, water bottle, standard military food rations, a flint stone and knife sheathed on his thigh, his medicine bag recently replenished in webbing pouches. Why, oh why, had Tangnost picked Bracus as team leader? If only his friend Quester could share this adventure. If only Quenelda were coming. But Drumondir had made clear that any time she was not training with Two Gulps or her Junior Brigade were to be spent in the HeartRock. Root quashed the momentary self-pity. Putting on the half helm with night sights he headed for the dragon pads.

Tangnost was waiting. 'You have all the necessary skills to achieve this objective, but you will have to work together. Now, mount up and show us what you can learn!'

'Sir! Yes! Sir!' the cadets ran for the waiting Imperial. Quickly buckling in, they were eager to prove themselves, laughing loudly to cover their fear. This was their first live battlegame where all their training came together. Full dark was falling and dense cloud meant there would be no moonlight or stars to help them as the Imperial took off, making it impossible to judge direction or speed.

By the time a green light flared, no one had any idea where they were.

'Tag up' a gruff trooper said, as a flare was dropped to mark the landing site. Cleats were hooked into the d-rings on spinal plates and fifty eight recruits swung out, playing out their ropes through gloved hands, legs held free to drop as fast as possible; they abseiled down the Imperial's flanks before swiftly sliding down to the ground. Unbuckling immediately, they deployed into a defensive star perimeter, staffs and swords unsheathed. Root crouched at their centre already scanning the drop zone. The Imperial's backwash died.

They were on their own.

CHAPTER SEVENTY-SEVEN

Yum

Further...? With a lot of huffing and puffing Two Gulps landed on a cliff top. Quenelda had finally taken Tangnost and Drumondir's dire warnings to heart. Every day at dusk, she took Two Gulps out flying. To begin with, the chubby sabretooth had struggled to fly even half a league downhill. But day by day he got stronger, became leaner. Quenelda was very strict, sticking to the diet that Tangnost had prescribed, and not allowing Two Gulps to snack on seagulls, sheep, or a sleeping bear they disturbed. Now the increased weight was due to his strengthening muscles and growing wings.

Further...? you could hear the exhaustion in Two Gulps' thoughts.

Yes, a little further...

But I am tired...

I'm not...

But you're not flying...

Even as a protest formed in her mind, Quenelda reminded herself that she could fly now, should fly now to gather her own strength. After all, she didn't normally go around flapping her arms to get about, those muscles were rather feeble, and a tail took some getting used to. In the gathering dusk on this empty stretch of coast no one should spot her.

Then we shall fly together! With a thought her aspect changed into that of a black scaled girl and with a flick of a tail, the two dragons headed westward. One bell later they put down on a rocky headland to the south of the Sorcerers Glen for a rest.

Food? Two Gulps asked hopefully. He hadn't eaten since he left the roost. Quenelda had only managed a bowl of broth earlier in the day.

Yes, Quenelda had brought a small bag of honey tablets. *I'm hungry too.* She shivered as she shed her scales back to her flying leathers, and unslung the satchel from around her shoulders.

Yum! She dipped in, placing a handful on the rocks for Two Gulps, but when the next handful came out she ate them herself voraciously.

Yum! What? She looked up some time later to find Two Gulps staring at her miserably, tail and ears drooping. *What?* she happily brushed the last crumbs from her mouth and dusted herself down.

You've eaten all the honey tablets!

CHAPTER SEVENTY-EIGHT

Take Off and Crash Landings

Tangnost looked over the eager young faces of III Junior Sabretooth Brigade. Will they be ready to attack the Brimstones in barely a moon? The night before, Dragon Masters, Deans of Faculty, Heads of Schools and the Guardian had met to discuss how the cadets were responding to intensive training. The number of injured was high and some were struggling to keep up or had failed and left, but, undeniably a core of cadets were thriving and they would take part in Operation Brimstone, while the SDS struck north towards the Lord Protector's strongholds of Borzall and Beddenoch Castles. No one would expect Juveniles to become operational so quickly, least of all the WarLock. Imperials and their pilots and navigators took four years of training; sabretooths could only be handled by experienced Dragon Masters – unless you had a dragon whisperer. Only Quenelda now knew why they were training so hard, how much they needed her skill with dragons if they were to survive the coming winter.

'Over the next moon you will begin advanced training.' He glanced at Quenelda, much depended on the key role she would play and if she had taken his lessons to heart. There were whoops and cheers. 'You will then be embedded in a combat unit so you can begin battlegames, culminating in the greatest battle game of all: the Dragathon next spring.

You will practise how to mount and dismount Imperials swiftly during combat, to identify bugle calls, learn how to fight in your dragon's world of caves and caverns, and begin flying training. All of which you need for Operation Brimstone. Are you ready?'

'Sir! Yes, Sir!'

'Until now we have been developing your sabretooth's strengths, but as you have guessed from recent training with dragon wings and wing strengthening exercises, we are now going to work on the sabretooth's one serious weakness: flying.

In the wild, sabretooths will avoid flying unless it's a matter of survival and even then they are poor, but in the SDS there are times you will need them to fly. We are going on exercises in Glen Etive at the end of the week, so you have five days to perfect combat mount and dismount.'

Phoenix Firestorm piloted by Guy DeBessart was waiting in the training pads around the skirts of the Shard.

'I volunteered,' he grinned at Quenelda who returned his welcome. 'I want to be a part of whatever you do, Lady. To pilot your talon once we're combat operational.'

'Quenelda is going to show you how to introduce yourself and your battledragon to your Imperial Phoenix Firestorm,' Tangnost instructed them, so that you begin to bond. An exercise which normally takes five painstaking moons... 'So that you and he will learn to recognise each other in the heat of battle. Then we begin combat mount and dismount which limits the time you arc on the ground in a battle, thereby increasing your chance of surviving in combat.'

Phoenix Firestorm, may the wind ride under your wings...

Dancing with Dragons may the stars light your path...

Now I understand why we greet each other so...long ago we came from the stars...Another piece of the puzzle fell into place. Phoenix Firestorm... these dragons will become your bond brothers and sisters in battle...will you welcome them and those who fly with them?

Within a bell, people were gathering to watch, talking excitedly. Within two, the paddock was surrounded as the Imperial bent its head to nuzzle cadet and sabretooth one by one, blowing warmly over them before lifting both onto its back. To give the cadets credit, only seven of them screamed.

Well, Tangnost smiled. *No one, not even the Dragon Lords, has ever seen this before...if she can train all our young dragons.....*

High above, the Guardian knocked out his pipe and nodded at Jakart DeBessart. There was no stopping it now; rumours of a dragon whisperer would spread like dragonfire; the legend was coming to life.

CHAPTER SEVENTY-NINE

Happy Camping

Root surveyed their landing site, wondering why the trainers had dropped them here. They were in a deep basin bounded by rocks and traversed by a swollen stream fed by a pounding waterfall higher up. Despite the fact it was summer, his breath clouded the air, which meant they were high up. Thick shrubs and mountain myrtleberry dotted the ground and the dell was edged by stands of small spindly rowan and gorse. There was little by way of cover and the ground was soft and spongy. Hmmm…Root quickly realised why this drop zone, but no one else had. *It's too tempting! And too dangerous!*

'Right,' Bracus said throwing his pack to the ground. 'This will do, it's nice and soft. We can move out at first light.'

'I think,' Root said quietly, only for him. 'That's this is not a good place to camp.'

'Oh?' Bracus drawled loudly. 'And why is that, little newt?'

'Because snowmelt means the river is already high, and

if it rises another stride, it will flood this bowl.'

'It's summer!'

'Exactly. A thaw is on, and it's going to rain.'

'It's going to rain...' Bracus mimicked...'there's been no rain for moons...'

'Because,' Root kept his temper in check. 'The mountains catch the clouds and dump all the rain here. Didn't you pay any attention in Cloud Studies? And hobgoblins come with the dark and the rain.'

'Hobgoblins here?' Bracus scoffed. 'This far behind the Wall?'

'Who says we're behind the Wall?'

That shocked them. No one had even considered that.

'Do you think we're beyond the wall?' One of the few young trolls looked frightened.

'No,' Root said, 'we'd be too vulnerable. But camping next to mountain streams is dangerous. Hobgoblins can ride the rapids. We should -'

'Well,' Bracus swaggered and drew his staff with a flourish. 'There isn't anything can touch us. We are seriously bad!' A tendril of light arced from the tip of his M8 training staff, and a gorse bush burst into flames.

'Now you've given our position away! To the Mountain Rangers, the hobgoblins, or the WarLock!' Root shook his head in disgust. 'Lighting a bush isn't going to save us if we're attacked.'

'And what do you know about magic?' Bracus challenged. 'Or fighting hobgoblins? You missed all the weapons and sorcery classes. Newt!' He spun his staff in a blaze of fire that lit up the bowl to appreciative howls from his friends.

'More than you!' Root muttered as he turned away disgusted. 'Although that wouldn't be hard.'

'What? What did you say?'

Shrugging his shoulders, Root moved away from the soft ground onto some boulders, searching for and finding a spot with a slight overhang, giving him a clear field of view. From when Root was barely knee high, he and other youngsters of his warren were taught by their Elders and Grandfolk how to be at one with the land; how to forage with the passing of the seasons, taking no more than they needed, how to cover their tracks so the hobgoblins could not find them. The young lordlings may know about battlemagic, but Root knew the land.

The young gnome left to explore beyond the dell as Bracus's AirWing troop pegged out their tents, although a number of them just curled up in their bed rolls. They didn't even post guards! Returning a bell later with a sack of foraged roots, berries and mushrooms, Root set about hacking down a thicket of alder deftly weaving saplings together to form a bower. Ripping up grass and heather he thatched it thickly then took it back and lodged it beneath the overhang with some boulders, making it look like a natural rocky outcrop. Unrolling his bed roll, the young gnome wriggled in and ate a few bannocks.

Thunder rolled on the other side of the mountains. Root smiled. Within two bells the river began to rise. Then the rain hammered down. There were curses and shouts as his troop were roused from sleep. Grabbing their sodden bedrolls and packs the cadets careened into each other in their haste to find shelter.

'There is dense woodland just over this rise,' Root suggested. 'It will be a lot drier.'

'I don-' Bracus began. But his troop was already following Root up the lip of the dell, rushing to avoid the freezing water bubbling about their feet. Here, tall interwoven pines wove a roof above their heads, and a dense carpet of needles carpeted the forest floor. It was dry and warm.

'This will do,' Bracus said, throwing down his sodden pack.

Kneeling, inspecting the ground, Root was really worried. 'It's not safe. This is a game track....look,' he pointed to the trampled ground. 'Giant elk - '

'So? You're not scared of an elk are you?'

'Soooo...if it's a well-used game trail the predators won't be far behind.'

'I give the orders,' Bracus spat. 'You're just a scout. Do what I order you to,' he repeated, not realising it made him look more like a bully than a leader. He turned to the others. 'We camp here. Sentries - '

'Then at least we should string up hammocks in the trees,' Root persisted.

'Trees? We're not gnomes! We don't live up trees.'

'What kind of predators?' Elfiin, a young navigator who studied with Root asked quietly, as the scout examined the track.

'Sabretooth lions, cave bears...direwolves...' Root pointed. 'This is a cave bear's paw. Look! Here and here!'

Ranulf, the tall lanky pilot cadet who was a close friend of Bracus, joined them, peering at the ground in the poor light. He shook his head. 'I can't see anything!'

'Me neither!' Elfiin agreed.

Root traced the outline of a print again with a twig. 'Look, here's the pad, and these are the claw tips...' he fingered the deep dips, and then spread his hand. 'They're a finger length apart...means it's an adult, a big one. Passed this way in the last couple of days.'

'But that's huge! That's one paw?'

'How do you know?' Ranulf asked.

'Scat,' Root pointed to a pile of droppings. 'Barely dry, and look at this tree.' He pointed upwards to where gashed bark was oozing pine resin. 'Marking its territory!'

'But that's nearly twenty strides high!'

'Rrrrright ...' Ranulf nodded and cleared his throat to cover his discomfort. He had no desire to meet a direwolf or a cave bear. 'I think I'll follow your example.' So, ignoring Bracus's taunts, the three climbed a tree and Root showed them how to build a bower for their hammocks.

The night passed. Root snapped awake.

It's quiet. Too quiet... the young gnome thought as he peered down from his perch. Through his night sights the scout saw the ghostly forms of a giant elk herd move into the clearing below, grazing quietly, their splayed hooves making little noise as they picked their way amongst the tents.

Then one of them raised her head. Ears flicked back,

the doe snorted a warning. The rest of the herd slowed, the adults males turning and lowering their antlers. Then Root saw them, shadows flowing through the woods.

'Get up, get into the trees!' the young scout shouted a warning as he tumbled down his tree. And then the direwolves were upon them and the elk stampeded. There were screams and growls and cries of pain and confusion, which rapidly became fear as the pack of direwolves trampled through the makeshift camp, snapping at those who stumbled out of tents into their path.

Grabbing a log from the fire, Root frantically waved it from side to side, trying to make the wolves go about the camp, but they were immense beasts and in the thrill of the hunt.

'Arrggghh!' Bracus fell, as a huge direwolf leapt over him as he crawled out of his tent, his staff tumbling away into the embers of the fire as huge jaws snapped shut barely a hand span from his face. The thunder of flight and growling faded and a shaky silence fell, punctuated by groans.

As dawn broke in a glory of gold that lit the peaks of the mountains high above, Bracus's troop surveyed the wreckage of their camp. Tents were torn and poles snapped. Equipment was trampled and scattered and four cadets were injured: Ranulf had a deep gash that was already turning red and swollen, two cadets had broken ribs, and a fourth, a pilot named Gwelhelm, a broken leg. Root carefully examined the wounds, including a small gash on Bracus's head.

'Ranulf needs airlifted out.'

'No!' Bracus protested hotly. 'If we fire a red flare for extraction we've lost the game. It's not a dangerous injury is it? You can walk can't you, ?' the tall young man blustered. 'It's barely a scratch.' They couldn't admit defeat this early, not with his first command!

'Yes! Yes, just a scratch,' Ranulf gritted his teeth and smiled manfully.

'Just patch them up, can't you?'

Root ministered to the wounded as best he could, setting the broken leg in splints of alder, and bandaging the broken ribs. He ground up murtleweed from the boggy dell into a paste for gashes, to combat infection. 'That's the best I can do,' he told Bracus. 'I'm not sure they can last until this exercise is over.'

As the sun rose, Root folded the map and shed his battlegame body armour and shrugged into his webbing, then bent to cut grasses and bracken and pull clumps of soft moss from the trees, before covering his face and neck in mud.

'What are you doing?' Bracus demanded as Root poked small conifer branches beneath his boot laces and through his belt.

'I'm going scouting to see where the Rangers are, and to study the lie of the land between us and our objective. Ranulf and Gwelhelm need to get to a proper surgeon,' Root added pointedly.

'You look like a scarecrow!' Bracus mocked, but by now no one else was laughing.

'How do you know all this?' Ranulf asked with respect.

'My people...' Root faltered. Where were his people? All gone...vanished.... 'my father taug-'

'Your people don't fight, though, do they?' Bracus said contemptuously, cutting him off. 'They hide in their bolt holes and leave it to others to protect them. They-'

'That's not true,' Root retorted angrily. 'My Pa saved the Howling Glen!'

'Ha!'

'My Pa died! He was the Earl's, the King's scout! He was the best in the SDS!'

'Oakley?' Ranulf said, pushing Bracus aside roughly. 'It was your father who saved the Howling Glen?'

'Yes. He died warning them of the hobgoblins under the mountains.'

'He saved my brother's life,' Ranulf addressed everyone, 'although Ned died at the Westering Isles, along with everyone else. My father said yours was a hero.'

Bracus bit his lips, finally shamed. 'I didn't know.'

'No,' Root said bitterly, turning away. 'There's a lot you don't know.'

From their position high above, SDS instructors watched and listened through their enhanced night sights.

CHAPTER EIGHTY

Dragon Whispers

The WarLock King brooded over the news that had reached him from one of his lords on the Wall, secretly loyal to him. It merely confirmed what he had already heard from his spies on the Black Isle, but this time his liegeman had seen Rufus for himself when the King had put down at the Smoking Fort to inspect the two new fortresses the SDS were building.

Rufus can clearly see through his battledragon's eyes, but how? He was blind, I saw it.

Searching through precious manuscripts and ancient texts on the Dragon Lords of the First Age, looted from both the Sorcerers Guild and Dragonsdome, he discovered such magic was attributed to the first Dragon Lords who truly bonded with their dragons and who fought the hobgoblin scourge beneath the sea. The WarLock looked again at the ancient histories on the table...the colours were faded but the picture remained clear...a SeaDragon Lord, scaled, fighting as one with his seadragon, imbued with the same powers as his dragon; a man with webbing between his fingers, and gills on his neck. He had always thought them fanciful tales, but now...now he was not so certain.

Was Rufus becoming part seadragon? How? They were long extinct. Is that how he survived the Black Death? How could that have happened? Rufus should be dead, yet he had risen. I must find out how...I must...

Unbearable that Rufus should discover what he had failed to find.

Hugo Mandrake looked at his own hands, finely veined with green, as was his body. The maelstrom was slowly claiming him, but he need not expend energy hiding it any more. Its mark made men afraid, and fear was a powerful weapon. Sometimes when chaotic magic filled him, it took time to take back his human form. Instead, his being became fluid in the pit above the Abyss, a dark formless shadow of immense power. How much longer could his body survive its corrosive energy? He had found several references from the Mage Wars, descriptions of WarLocks taking another's body, shrugging off their own decayed flesh. The idea appealed to him. There were powerful secrets to be unlocked – if only he could find the fabled Dragonsdome Chronicles.

CHAPTER EIGHTY-ONE

Crash Landings

Five days of intensive training, and a line of sabretooths on the parade ground stood at the ready, watching Firestorm Phoenix landing. Barely were the great wings lowered than the bugle call summoned them. Short... long...short...In three ranks of ten on either side, the cadets spurred forwards.

'Go, go, go!' Tangnost urged them up both wings.

*Calm...there is nothing to fear...*Quenelda whispered. *You are bond brothers and sisters now with your two legs...trust them...they also cannot fly well...you are their shield and they are your sword...*

Scarcely had the last sabretooth scrambled onto Phoenix Firestorm's back when the Imperial began to charge, massive wings sweeping up and down, up and up, powerful strides and then there was a gut churning dip and they were flying over the loch, before beginning to climb steeply.

'Get your mounts tethered.....buckle up. Too slow,' Tangnost warned them. 'You cannot afford one single sabretooth stampeding on board. Do it again!'

The training was relentless.

Long... long... long...short... the bugle cried. Half the brigade went one way, the rest, the opposite. Up they charged and down they charged.... ragged... tripping... bumping....sprawling, falling...but instead of beating everyone, Quenelda was everywhere, helping all her classmates so that often she was last in an exercise instead of first. A confident, tightly disciplined and talented talon of junior sabretooths soon began to emerge, built around the young dragon whisperer.

Tangnost decided to test Quenelda and her fledgling brigade and begin advanced combat training; particularly in the light of huge sabretooth casualties when a fully loaded Imperial went down. Other dragons could at least try to escape, but the sabretooths were dying because they would not fly.

'There are going to be times when your Imperial can't land or can't do a combat lading, perhaps because of cliffs or steep gorges. Or a time when your Imperial may be injured and you have to bail out. That is when ground attack dragons do a tail drop, or you use your dragon wings and leave your dragon to get itself down.'

So began a week of dragon wing training and drops from the jump tower.

Smack!

'Oooff '

'Arrggghhhhhhhhhhhhhhhh!!'

No wonder casualties are so high, Tangnost thought, as he watched a sabretooth belly-flop, summersaulting its young pilot face down in the sand pits. Like fledglings too early from their nest, the stubby-winged sabretooths were all over the place, and their young pilots fared no better with their own dragon wings. Drumondir was kept busy bandaging sprains and bumps. Searching ancient memories Quenelda found she instinctively knew the answer to one problem; she needed to visit the wing armourers first and then put the result to the test in the HeartRock, or rather Root could put it to the test!

'Mount up,' Tangnost ordered. 'Let's see if we do any better in the field!'

Time to see if she could also solve the second problem: like Root, sabretooths were scared of heights, and with their stubby wings they tired easily. Put together and they would not willingly jump from their Imperial. Guy brought Phoenix Firestorm about over the flat valley floor of Glen Etive and glided down to five hundred strides.

'Saddle up,' Tangnost ordered.

Not surprisingly, the first two balked at jumping off the tail, and panic swept down the line as the sabretooths refused to budge. Tangnost watched intently. He wasn't disappointed.

Two Gulps... Quenelda nudged her young battledragon forwards.

Dancing with Dragons?

We must show them how to fly; not to be afraid...

As we did at the battle?

At the battle when we swooped down over the cliff and you saved my life...

Together?

*Together...*Together they pounded along the Imperial's back, gaining speed, and leapt. And plunged down...down like they had at the Smoking Fort, as they had at F&H's...down and down...and then two Gulps' powerful, stubby wings caught the air and his muscles bunched and his wings swept down over the heather and he climbed upwards to cheers. Seeing 'the pudding' doing a victory roll, the cadets were queuing up to go next.

Quenelda dismounted and talked quietly to each of her talon and their dragons. *The sky is nothing to fear... we will show you how...the sky gives you a freedom the caves cannot...* The sabretooths quietened. Guy swung round for another pass.

Three bells later and Tangnost's mouth pursed thoughtfully as they took off to head home. Quenelda had got them all down, which was little short of miraculous. Several had got stuck in trees and two in a gorse bush. Five had landed in a lochan. Drumondir was being kept busy pulling out thorns and doctoring nettle stings. But Quenelda could train juvenile dragons and cadets faster than any Dragon Master had! These were raw recruits, what could she do with veterans? Well, these Juveniles were ready for Operation Brimstone!

There were sudden screams. One of the juveniles had decided to join Quenelda, who was flying on their flank, but the Imperial was not high enough and the sabretooth was struggling to get air in its wings.

'Your dragonwings! Your dragonwings!' Tangnost

shouted. Fergus pulled his cord and fell away from his dragon but, caught by the massive downdraft, he went into a crazy spin and was tumbling head over heels towards the rock slabs below. Tangnost searched the sky for Quenelda: there she was, but Two Gulps would not be in time. No one was sure what happened next.

Out of nowhere, a small dragon clad in black scales dived as gracefully and swiftly as a swallow, catching Fergus it swooped up to Phoenix Firestorm and put Fergus down, before flexing its wings.

What? Quenelda asked, as everyone stared at her.

CHAPTER EIGHTY-TWO

Attack at Dawn

'He should be back by now, it's nearly dark fall.'

Bracus's troop were stiff and hungry, having long since eaten the food Root had foraged. The injured were cold and Gwelhelm semiconscious. Even Bracus looked anxious, the reality of life in the wild beginning to sink home. He had no idea what to do any more if Root didn't return, except fire a flare for extraction. But then he would never be selected for the Dragathon, the first in countless generations of Beaumonts to fail.

'He's back!' Elfiin called.

Suddenly the young gnome was amongst them although none of the sentries had seen him pass. Root retrieved the waxed map from his rucksack and spread it out. He broke a flare. 'I've found them... they were spread out searching for us here because this pass is the natural route to take to our target extraction co-ordinates here. They are expecting us to take the easiest, most direct route to safety; they'll think the AirWing haven't a clue on the ground.'

The navigator cadets in the group were also studying the map but the young sorcerer lords were struggling, although they would never admit it. Bracus went on the offensive.

'And they didn't see you?'

Root ignored the comment. 'So, we are here,' he pointed, 'and the slopes of the mountains are here to our back. They were taking up position on this spur on high ground to the south. Lots of boulders, so a naturally defensive position with a clear view all round. But they've been lazy; they haven't bothered to cover their rear and there is no rampart or ditch.'

'If we had dragons we could just hit them from the air!' Bracus complained. 'What is the point of this exercise? We belong in the air, not crawling around down here!'

'You're not just fighting hobgoblins anymore, Bracus...' Ranulf snapped, his patience worn thin by his pain. 'We're fighting each other...they have dragons, too.... aerial combat. Dragons are going to come down. We *have* to learn how to survive out here.'

Bracus's petrified, Root thought with sudden insight. *He's frightened of being alone out here in the same way I was frightened of dragons to begin with...*

'I'm not sure our wounded can make our objective,' Root looked at Ranulf who was shivering. 'But there is a way we could take the Mountain Rangers and win the game quickly.' Root suggested quietly to Bracus.

'What? We're just going walk up and ask them to surrender a fortified position?' Bracus laughed.

'Tangnost always said attack is the first line of

defence. They expect to track us down easily. Let's turn the tables on them. We move out now under cover of dark and come on them just before dawn,' Root looked up to gauge their reaction.

'How far?'

To Bracus's fury, the cadets were grouped about the gnome, listening earnestly.

'If we circle around...' Root thought, 'three leagues, mostly uphill, then two across the moors.'

'Five leagues? Crawling through a bog?'

Root nodded curtly. Would Bracus never be satisfied? 'We must leave now if we are to hit them before day break.'

'You scouted that far and back again today?' Ranulf asked.

Root nodded. Moving to kneel beside Gwelhelm, he felt the boy's forehead. 'He's got a fever. It's going to be very hard going on the moorland. I think we should leave our injured in one of the caves I scouted out at the edge of the glen, with some guards. No noise,' Root warned. 'No complaining. Understood?'

They all nodded, except Bracus.

The twilight sky turned from lavender to blue and then darker blue. Stars twinkled. The endless Midge Infested Moor stretched out in front of them. The injured had been left in a cave under the care of six cadets.

'We need to camouflage ourselves,' Root suggested. 'Junior Rangers or not, they've been training all year to track and find downed flight crew. This will help confuse them.'

'How?' Brachus asked.

'Do what I've done.'

And so the pilot and navigator cadets daubed each other with mud, mosses and bracken. The youths were beginning to enjoy themselves for the first time, anticipating a victory despite their earlier disasters. They disguised each other until Root was satisfied. Even standing now, their outlines were so broken up it would be hard to spot them, let alone in the dim light of early dawn. 'It's going to be a cold wet trudge,' Root warned them. 'Let's move out.'

Dawn was barely a thin pencil on the horizon by the time they closed on the Rangers' position. The cadets had slogged through the sucking bog for bells it seemed, before they gained the respite of a large boulder ledge which overlooked their enemy's camp.

'First we take out their guards and replace them. I need a couple of volunteers to work their way around to the north of the camp and create a distraction there.' Root chose three of the largest, including Bracus, from the hands that went up. 'A flare will be your signal. Slash the guy ropes and hit them as they come out of their tents and they will run into the bog; and us. Agreed?' he looked around at the nodding heads. The cadets were checking their webbing for flash bangs and drawing their battle staffs, shorter than full staffs and only able to stun.

'And how are you going to fight?' Bracus asked pointedly, trying to re-establish himself as leader.

'Cooking pots,' Root grinned infuriatingly. 'Can be

very effective!'

Root crept forwards on his elbows. The grass he had stuffed into his clothing padded him from the cold to begin with, but as water seeped through he began to shiver. He flicked down his night sights to survey the marching camp.

The young gnome shook his head in disbelief. If this were not a battlegame, the hobgoblins could hear and smell them leagues away. The rangers had killed and roasted a deer. Their over-confidence would be their downfall. *No one attacks at night! Except the hobgoblins... Except us! Well they told us they want us to think differently...*

The instructors watched with interest from their concealed observation positions.

Root lay unmoving as the watch changed on the crown of the hill. To begin with, the new sentries were alert but soon began talking softly amongst themselves. One lit a pipe; another went to get some food. *Careless.*

And yet Root sensed there was something, someone watchful out there apart from him. Slowly, carefully he inspected the dark night about them, at one point staring straight at three instructors, before turning his attention back to his objective.

Checking that he had not missed anything with his HUD on thermal, Root turned. He indicated the position of three sentries with his fingers, then circled to signal to those nearest to take them out. The dozing sentries fell; they were 'dead' and out of the exercise.

Root fired a flare.

Bracus and his companions charged, slashing tent guy ropes as they ran.

Bang! Bang! Pop! Pop!

It was bedlam; a total rout. Lances of white battlegame magic crisscrossed the camp as the AirWing cadets took out the Rangers as they scrambled to get out of their collapsed tents into the early morning. Most didn't even have their battlegame armour on so didn't light up when they were hit by crisscrossed training staff hits, but they knew they had lost.

The AirWing cadets took only two registered hits on their battlegame armour. They were cheering and slapping each other and Root on the back with delight, when it looked as if the moor had suddenly come alive. SDS Highland Scouts rose up from rocks and trees and bogs about the camp. Within moments an Imperial materialised on the moor behind them.

The senior instructor nodded. 'Well done, Root. Tell your troop to mount up, you're going home.'

CHAPTER EIGHTY-THREE

Going Underground

Tangnost's practised eye looked over his pale-faced recruits, seeing the worry and fear on some faces. Late mellow autumn had the lower slopes ablaze with bracken, and the midges were a torment as the cadets gathered with their mounts in Glen Inversnekkie.

'It is time for you to enter your dragon's realm. I know you have been through the tunnel on Dragon Isle but that is neither deep nor long, you can see the daylight from one end to another. Much of the Heavy Brigade's work is clearing tunnels and caves, hunting out hobgoblins and forcing them above ground where our troops and battledragons are waiting. Now is the right time to find out if you can cope, or if you need to rethink which unit you want to serve in.' There will be some of you who will find it unbearable when the walls close in and you have difficulty breathing.

'There is no dishonour in changing your mind. Your training will stand you in good stead to apply for other ground attack units. Now, follow Quenelda and me and get your first sight of the caves which is where the best of you will be competing in the Dragathon next year.'

'The draga- dragathon?' a young troll queried, as he followed the Dragon Master along a path bound about with dense woods.

'It's the greatest endurance race in the Kingdoms, and takes place in the Sorcerers and surrounding glens!' Quenelda told him. 'At the end of SDS training in early spring, the regiments all compete for the highest prize of all and the best of the current year's cadets take part! Winning is the highest regimental honour ever!'

'The Dungeons,' Tangnost gestured as they found themselves in a sloping cavern, 'consists of a thousand linked caves with canyons, gorges, underground rivulets and deep cliffs. This is the world of the sabretooth. Mount up,' Tangnost mounted behind Quenelda. 'We have a long way to go. Strap your helmet on, I don't want anyone knocking themselves out, and make sure you all have flares, you don't want to get lost underground without them.'

'This is the Battlefield Cavern...' Tangnost's deep voice echoed, as they walked slowly through this subterranean world.

'It's beautiful!' Quenelda said, as they gazed at the shimmering stream of water which fell through the funnel high above into a startlingly blue pool. Here it was vast, but elsewhere as they picked their way over rubble and an old watercourse, the walls crept in and the roof sloped down; some of the cadets began to feel panicked. One fainted and Fergus was struggling to breathe.

'Take a deep breath,' Tangnost encouraged the young man, 'slowly now. We'll begin the climb out when you are ready, before it gets dark, that's enough for one day.'

CHAPTER EIGHTY-FOUR

The Abyss

Darcy handed the empty goblet back to his father's cup bearer. Every night he was brought the dark smoking liquid to drink. It was so cold it burned, and yet Darcy felt it filling him with a new strength, a new courage. Until they stood on that same porting stone as before and he found himself deep below the citadel; that was where his courage deserted him.

The young man was afraid, so afraid he could barely breathe, barely walk, as these rough hewn tunnels forever led down and down, and a strange whisper hung in the air. The suffocating darkness closed all around and it became bitterly cold. Ice sheathed everything and Darcy's head ached with every indrawn breath. His torch wobbled and wavered in his hand, but his father in front did not seem to need its insignificant light or comfort. And then the tunnel walls were gone, taking the last vestiges of security with them.

They appeared to be in a vast dark place that felt as if it had no boundaries, as infinite as the night sky. Its sucking power was immense beyond imagining, crushing, pressing in on Darcy's chest. It was utterly still; the only sound, the young man's ragged breathing and his teeth chattering uncontrollably. He clamped his jaw, which only served to make his head nod manically. Fear squeezed Darcy's heart. He turned gratefully as his father's strong hand momentarily settled on his shoulder and the darkness settled like a cloak. Darcy's torch snuffed out.

The young man had the sense of something ancient stirring into wakefulness; a clot of greater darkness, within the black that flowed about them. It felt like a living thing as its cold bloodless attention fixed upon him. Terrifying images flicked through Darcy's head.

'W-w-what is this p-place?' Darcy ground his teeth in the effort to speak. But his father was gone....

His father *was* this ancient darkness.

Darcy fled.

CHAPTER EIGHTY-FIVE

Thunderstorm Battlegroup

The cloaked Thunderstorm Battlegroup put down behind the Old Wall beside the newly completed IV FireStorm's Fortress, as dark fell. Five-hundred-and-eighty-eight Imperials, seven hundred air and ground attack dragons, and tens of thousands of crews and troops were getting some much-needed rest and hot food after nine weary moons along the battlefront, before returning to Dragon Isle for the winter. They had beseiged and taken one of the WarLock's castles, intercepted gold and brimstone shipments and harried his supply lines and ships. Hugo must be wondering how he was being attacked so far from the Old Wall, let alone Dragon Isle! Doubt must surely be gnawing at him.

Withdrawing the Thunderstorm Battlegroup would still leave the XX ShadowWraiths and IV FireStorm regiments to protect the Wall, from their newly built fortresses. The WarLock's vaunted Army of the north was bogged down in snow and mud and retreating.

To the north, in the Howling Glen, the StormBreakers, reinforced by the IX WinterKnights from the far south, had fared better, pushing their attackers out of the glen and across the moors, back half a hundred leagues, but then they had to withdraw for winter back into their fortress.

But ...they were all exhausted; soldiers and dragons pushed to their limit and beyond, and he had no reserves left. Too many had died, or were badly injured, and they could not train replacements quickly enough... unless... unless the messages from Tangnost truly held out hope that his daughter was coming into her power. And brimstone... brimstone was critically low. If they did not secure supplies many battledragons would not live out the winter. They had battled each other to an exhausted standstill and both armies were withdrawing to lick their wounds.

Operation Brimstone would not only strike back at the WarLock King, securing desperately needed brimstone supplies, it would also give the best of the Juveniles a taste of battle under the watchful eyes of veterans too old still to wield a sword. Time to reveal the whereabouts of Galtekerion, a hammer blow to the WarLock; it would surely distract him whilst the sons and daughters of those who had died at the Westering Isles struck back.

CHAPTER EIGHTY-SIX

Know Your Enemy

Pilot and navigator cadets were gathered together in the Training Hall. What was happening?

'Although you have been taught how to fight the hobgoblins,' Tangnost cast his eye over the sea of eager faces, 'few of you have even seen one. They are bigger, stronger and faster, with better senses than we have, and even without weapons they are dangerous. They have more teeth than you, three rows. Th-'

'Just big frogs, slimy and soft with a few teeth,' someone caused a muted ripple of laughter.

'Big frogs?' Tangnost smiled grimly. 'You think you could best a hobgoblin?'

There were nods and grins of bravado.

'How many of you have seen a hobgoblin....? Come on. Don't be shy. How many of you have seen a hobgoblin?'

There was a lot of awkward shuffling...Only two hands were raised: Root's and Quenelda's. Root found Bracus's eyes on him. For once they were thoughtful rather than hostile.

'And how many of you lost a brother or sister, a father or mother or an uncle at the Westering Isles? Or at the battle of the Line?'

Almost all hands went up. 'And they served in the Night Stalkers? The Mountain Rangers? The First Born? The Boar's Head Brigade? The Tunnel Rats? Countless others... Over three regiments and nine thousand dragons died. Do you truly believe they were defeated by frogs?'

'Chaotic magic,' someone said. 'We were beaten by the Warlock.'

'It wasn't just the maelstrom that beat the SDS at the Westering Isles. Our tactics were betrayed. And... make no mistake; the Warlock's hobgoblins are formidable warriors. Do not underrate them; under the control of the Warlock the banners not only fought as one, but executed an understanding of our regimental tactics.'

'How many hobgoblins to a banner?'

'One hundred thousand.'

'Correct! And how many to a Regiment?'

'Six thousand, Sir! And auxiliaries...and three thousand battledragons.'

Tangnost nodded. 'At full strength the SDS fields six regiments and one battlegroup of six thousand men, up to three thousand auxiliaries, and three thousand dragons each; a total of forty two thousand men, twenty one thousand auxiliaries and twenty one thousand dragons against millions. And you think you have nothing to learn, we have nothing to fear? An entire regiment disappeared, its fortress raised to the ground, lost in the snows. No one knows what happened to the NightStalkers, but you can be sure the hobgobins overran them.'

There was a sobering silence, a collective shiver of horror.

'Then why have there been no attacks by the hobgoblins, only skirmishes, Sir? Now, when we are vulnerable?'

Many had wondered when the hammer blow would come: yet summer had turned to autumn to early winter and still they did not come, and because of that, the Old Wall and the Howling Glen had held.

'Intelligence suggests that the tribes have reverted to fighting amongst themselves. They are being torn apart by treachery and rivalry. It is buying us precious time to regroup.'

'But why, sir? What has happened to Galtekerion? Why don't they attack?'

Tangnost nodded. It was past time to reveal the SDS's closest kept secret. 'I'll show you why.'

CHAPTER EIGHTY-SEVEN

Sharp-Toothed Frogs

Tangnost led the excited cadets through the Lower Training Hall, through familiar corridors that passed the dormitories, the mess hall, the armoury, the battle games hall and then beyond where they had never been before. This was the ancient heart of the castle...where the walls were thick and redolent with magic. Here, the foundation of the First Alliance with the dragons was forged by Son of the Morning Star and his six companions. This was their ancient home.

'Where are we going?'

'Wait and see, boy.'

The wide saddle-backed steps corkscrewed down and down. Shields, their coats of arms unrecognisable and faded, hung on the walls and ancient tattered banners overhead. Wood wainscoting was exquisitely carved into a living tapestry of the seven kingdoms as they spiralled down. Then the steps opened on to a wide passageway so vast it could only be an Imperial coomb. The very air thrummed with magic like a faint song. Now they could feel rather than hear a subterranean river pounding its course down through Dragon Isle from Citadel Peak far above. Unaware, the cadets passed through four ancient wards before they came to a stone door. It was inlaid with runes that glowed gold and red as they approached. A complex cartouche was inlaid at hand height.

'High battlemagic, inlaid with wards!' someone breathed as a beam of light passed over them. None of the students had seen something so sophisticated and Root instinctively bent forwards to study them. Tangnost punched in a sequence and the heavy stone door opened.

Inside it was nearly dark, but as they stepped through the threshold after the dwarf, and their eyes adjusted, the young men could make out a ring of battleroosts set about a deep dark pit. The air was hot and humid, and stank of brimstone, catching their throats. A sabretooth flamed, lighting up the cavern before it died again to darkness.

'Roost masks,' Tangnost gestured to where they hung on pegs. 'It's toxic in here if you stay too long.'

Flame from the roost pipes licked out over a spherical object in the centre of the chamber that hung suspended in nothingness. It was fed by the water course they had heard. It was almost impossible to hear each other without shouting. Crowding about the lip of the chasm the youths stared wide-eyed at the churning pool that shimmered with a bluish light. The water swirled and bubbled and they began to turn to Tangnost to ask what they were here to see, when there was the faintest of shadows passing so swiftly it was gone in the blink of an eye.

'What was that?'

'What? I never saw anything!'

'There! There! That shadow. There it is again!'

Galtekerion. Root knew it instantly and his heart began to race. He had wondered where the WarLord was held captive. He wasn't told and had never asked. Memories of that night at the Smoking Fort, the chaos, the screams, the wall of dragonfire, thinking he had lost Quenelda, Quester being cut down, all flashed through his mind. And overlaying it all - the unearthly battle cries of the hobgoblins and the huge War Lord coming up behind the blind Earl. And in that one heartbeat it might all have been for nothing. He flexed his left hand, remembering the frying pan...

Thunk!

The sudden collision, followed by cries of alarm, broke into his reverie as something slammed into the nexus, raising a flurry of blue sparks and making the cadets scramble back in fright, and then the shadow was gone again into the depths, leaving the briefest of impressions of serrated teeth, suckers, and luminous eyes.

'Abyss below!' someone swore a soldier's oath as the cadets exchanged horrified glances, and a few laughed nervously at their class mates' fright.

'*That's* a hobgoblin?' someone asked throatily.

'Aye, that it is,' Tangnost nodded. 'Some hobgoblins stand nearly eight strides tall. They can leap distances of fifteen strides. Their suckers allow them to climb just about anything, though they aren't too good with ice.... hate the stuff. They have three rows of teeth, so if one breaks another takes it place. Until the WarLock enslaved them, they hibernated overwinter, allowing us time to rest. Now, with dark sorcery he kept them fighting through the snows of last year: they died in their tens, hundreds of thousands, but more keep coming.'

There was a collective shiver of horror.

'So,' the dwarf looked them over. 'Do you still think they are just frogs?'

'No, sir, No!' The cadets fervently shook their heads.

'It's huge,' someone whispered.

'Sir,' one of the younger boys asked. 'I didn't know we took prisoners....'

'We don't – normally,' Tangnost's voice was calm, reassuring and belied his words. 'They are ravening and lethal, killing at any opportunity. But this hobgoblin is special.'

The group held their breath. *Special? Surely not...?*

'Galtekerion,' Tangnost confirmed their suspicions.

'Is that why they haven't attacked us, Sir?'

'Almost certainly, yes. The WarLock has no warlord to keep the thirteen tribes together. They've fallen on each other as we hoped.'

'But, Sir, Dragon Master,' it was Bracus who asked the question on every lip. 'Sir, how was he captured? We've been taught that he was always guarded by his Chosen. And why has no one heard such good news?'

They crowded round Tangnost, eyes alight; this was the stuff of legends. 'Which regiment had the honour, Sir? Was it the Rangers? Or the FirstBorn?'

'Was it a battlespell or in hand to hand combat?'

'You want to know how he was taken?' Tangnost was drawing out the moment. Eager debate broke out...such information was classified! They could only guess.

Time for a lesson in humility...

'As you know, Root's people do not permit the taking of life. Some of you think that only those with swords or sorcery can fight, that those who shun the taking of life are cowards and worthy only of contempt. There are many who think only those who wield magic should rule, should be Dragon Lords, including the WarLock. But bravery takes many guises.' Tangnost paused, to let them consider his words.

'It was Root who captured Galtekerion at the battle of the Smoking Fort. And it was Root, and his friend Quester, who saved the King from certain death, by facing Galtekerion and his Chosen.'

There was a breathless moment as wide-eyed cadets searched for the young gnome. But Tangnost wasn't finished yet.

'And this young man captured Galtekerion with the humblest and most mundane of weapons...' the dwarf paused, knowing he had their rapt attention. 'A frying pan!'

Bracus stood, dumfounded.

Already they had surrounded Root, banging him on the back...grinning stupidly...reaching out just to touch him....

'A frying pan! Way to go, Root!'

'Root what happened?'

'Why did you never say you fought at the battle?'

'How did you do it?'

'It's true then, all those stories about you and Quenelda?'

'Why were you on the battlefield?'

The young sorcerer lords, dwarves and trolls were all talking at once, vying for Root's attention. In moments the young gnome was hoisted up on their shoulders and carried forward to cheers; leaving a few standing in disbelief and doubting themselves for the first time.

The SDS Dragon Master nodded. *A lesson in humility well learnt.*

CHAPTER EIGHTY-EIGHT

A Frenzy of Celebration

Word rapidly spread throughout the Academy that not only had Root been the navigator on the Imperial which had found the Earl, but that he had captured the War Lord Galtekerion. And Root made sure that everyone knew how his brave friend, Quester, had protected the blind Earl, nearly at the cost of his own life. The healers found the hospital wing overwhelmed with visitors for Quester, bringing the recovering youth small gifts and begging to hear how he came by his injuries.

Overnight it changed the mood of Dragon Isle. The Warlock's hobgoblin banners hadn't been unleashed, because they were out of control, reverting to attacking each other! Suddenly all the rumours made sense!

At the same time, the news that the hobgoblin WarLord was captured and his Chosen were dead was posted on the Black Isle, outside the Guild and the Palace, and the city went into a frenzy of celebration.

CHAPTER EIGHTY-NINE

Dearest Wee Dragon

Armelia was in the royal paddocks at Crannock Castle near the Cauldron, determined that she would be able to fly Chasing the Stars to the Graduation on Dragon Isle, come what may, for both Quenelda and Root. Already attention had been lavished on the young mare, as Armelia attempted to stop Chasing the Stars pining for the young gnome. The mare was stabled with the Queen's personal mounts in the finest of stalls, thick with hay and thistles, her scales polished to a sheen, and fed as many chocolate mushrooms as could be foraged by stable boys. In return the young mare worked her magic. Soon Armelia was spending part of every day with her. The unconditional love Chasing the Stars gave the young girl, the evident joy in the way she nickered and muzzled Armelia, blowing sweet warm breath as she searched for honey tablets, melted Armelia's heart. Dragons never questioned Armelia, never criticised her, never let her down, never got angry, never talked behind her back; Armelia was growing to understand Root and Quenelda more with each and every passing day.

Now, in Root's absence, one of the Queen's finest trainers was teaching Armelia how to fly, and Armelia's 'dearest wee dragon' had become the focus of much attention. On a bright late summer's afternoon, the Queen with her Master of the Dragons, and attended by a half dozen grooms, appeared at Armelia's side on her racing mare Moonstruck, in flying leathers.

There was a predictable stampede, at a ladylike pace of course, to the ornate doors of F&H, and the Ladies Salon was flooded with patrons all seeking to choose from Armelia's newly named Moonstruck Ladies Leathers range, in honour of the Queen, or Tangnost's Dragon Master collection, both of course By Royal Appointment. There was not, however, a stampede to the royal roosts to ride dragons. One took the latest fashion only so far!

If Quenelda could, Armelia decided fiercely, she could. It would be a huge surprise for Quenelda to discover her friend was to fly to the Graduation and, Tangnost had promised, if she could to identify her dragon breeds, be a Steward at the Dragathon! Quenelda was going to be so surprised!! And after that who knew? There was no doubt a war for their survival was coming. She trembled a little at the thought, but perhaps…just perhaps …where Quenelda led, surely other girls could follow?

CHAPTER NINETY

Whooo! I Can fly!

'I wondered if you'd have time to come to the HeartRock?' Quenelda asked mischievously, knowing full well what the answer would be. Root had been dying to explore this new world with her, and everyone had been given four days off training.

The young gnome's eyes lit up. 'Yes! You know I'd love to!'

'And I wondered if you'd like to try something out for me...'

Root was surprised. 'In the HeartRock? What?'

'Dragon wings.'

'Oh!' Remembering the series of disasters that befell his outings with dragon wings while learning to be Quenelda's esquire, Root drooped. 'I ended up in the loch and stuck up a tree!'

'I know. But you won't this time – I promise. I've redesigned them, copying my wings when I fly. People are dying because dragon wings are difficult to control, especially in bad weather. One of my talon was nearly killed.'

Root had heard, everyone had heard by now, how Quenelda saved the life of Fergus, who was telling anyone who would listen about his dramatic rescue by a beautiful black dragon.

'Of course I'll help. But how can I test them in the HeartRock? The young boy was puzzled. 'Don't we have to be outside in the training grounds?'

'Wait and see,' Quenelda grinned. 'Come on! Training paddocks first!'

For Root it was an afternoon of wonders. For Quenelda it was time for renewed friendship. As he entered the HeartRock for the first time, Root was half excited, half petrified. The glossy, star-speckled darkness that lightened to reveal an amazing throne, vast, yellowed and polished bone, guarded by six black dragons, facing outwards like sentinels, took his breath away. Quenelda let her friend take his time to explore this new and hidden world, knowing how intrigued he was by the strange runes inset in the floor, noticing how he cocked his head to one side as if hearing a faint whisper.

'You can hear the song too?' *But, of course*, she frowned, suddenly finding memories that were not her own. He would, for Root's people lived as one with the land, in harmony with its song and its seasons. Perhaps Root could help her unravel the mysteries of the HeartRock too?

'Here you are,' Quenelda lifted her new design of dragon wings. 'They are a little heavier, but not much!

That's part of the problem; if you're wearing heavy armour then the old wings are too weak and can't catch enough air. These are more like proper wings.'

Root examined the design, the way the wing was attached at wrist and belt, the wing far larger than the usual design. He shrugged into them, buckling up with trembling hands, feeling as he did when he flew Chasing the Stars for the first time. But this would be his first independent flight – without his beloved mare! He had been practising take-off and landing in the training paddocks for several bells, until he was black and blue and Quenelda was satisfied. He tightened the last buckle. 'Now what?' He looked around the imposing chamber. 'How do I learn here?'

With a thought, the HeartRock disappeared and they were standing on a low hillock, broken by boulders and gorse. It was autumn, the hills a blaze of russet ferns, red berries on the scattered stands of rowan trees. The ground was thick and spongy with moss; the wind soft and warm. And there, grazing in the bogs, a memory of mammoths, feeding and nurturing their young!

Root stared awestruck. He turned a full circle to gaze at the snow-capped mountains behind and the glint of sea beyond, then bent down to rub the grass and heather between thumb and finger. 'We're still in the HeartRock? It feels so real!'

'It is real,' Quenelda reassured him. 'Just a long time ago.'

Root experimentally opened his wings. Feeling the sudden tug of the wind encouraging him forward, he resisted bringing his arms down.

'Relax. Remember, even though it looks like you're high in the sky you're not. You're a few strides from the ground.'

'Mnnn,' Root wasn't convinced, but still, he obediently spread his wings...and was whisked gently upwards on the draft of warm air.

'Wooa!' he wobbled from side to side, 'I'm g-going to fall! I'm go-argh!' He went face down in the spongy moss.

'No, you're not,' Quenelda helped him to his feet and removed a bit of moss from his nose. She took his hand firmly. 'Trust me.' She lifted off and Root rose with her. They glided down over the floor of the valley above the mammoths who raised their heads and trumpeted a warning. They floated above a bubbling burn and drifted over boulder strewn moors. Gradually Root stopped wobbling and began to enjoy himself. Without even noticing, the youth let go of Quenelda's hand. It was thrilling, it was exciting... unimaginable.

'I'm flying!' He said, soaring upwards. Heartbeats later he swung to the left, drifting on a gust of wind. 'I can fly!' he whooped, 'look - '

'R - '

Quenelda's warning was too late. Not looking where he was going, Root had got tangled in an aged stand of rowan trees. A branch cracked beneath his weight and he was falling. Only he did not suffer the shock of a fall onto the boulders below. Immediately the landscape disappeared and Root was sitting on the floor in a tangle of wings.

'Oh, Root!' Quenelda darted to help him. But her friend was smiling.

'That was awesome!' he said. 'Can we try again?'

CHAPTER NINETY-ONE

Operation Brimstone

The Guardian and the King sat in the Special Ops Room in Dragon Isle along with a half dozen Dragon Masters, three Academy Deans and several flying officer instructors. Two Professors, from the Schools of Military Studies and Stealth Warfare respectively, made up the numbers. In the King's absence from the battlefield, Jakart DeBessert and his Strike Commanders were at the Wall, inspecting the modified fortifications suggested by Quenelda before blizzards made flying impossible. The SDS had survived the year, but only just.

In the darkened room a bright display hung above the centre of the great oval table. Gold described the mountains of the northern Brimstones, pale blue the Old Wall, and white the forts along its length.

'So,' the King summed up. 'We are agreed. Attack the largest high grade mine and Brimstone Cove where Hugo's galleons are anchored. We airlift over two hundred seasoned soldiers and miners from the Wildcat Clan under the leadership of Malachite Thornaxe to replace the slaves. They suffered a brutal attack in our Cairnmore mine and are eager for revenge. Then we pick off the smaller mines one by one over winter.'

'Agreed. We,' The Guardian nodded to his Professors and instructors 'have selected a combined Juvenile AirWing of Imperials, frosts and a half talon of sabretooths; this will give dragons and cadets combat experience alongside seasoned veterans. With the element of surprise and poorly armed guards there should be little risk.'

The King nodded. 'But we need better reconnaissance before we go in. We have no idea exactly where the mines are located. If Root's people are in there, as we suspect, we need him in the vanguard of the main attack to talk to them. Is he ready?'

Professor Dimplethwit nodded. 'The boy has demonstrated a natural ability with high magic, and was the second on his class to graduate to the witchwood chair which bonded powerfully with him. He quickly mastered the runes and icons cast for him and even suggested modifications to his helm and vambrace. I wasn't sure, but confess I am impressed.'

'Root has also shown exceptional skill as scout and navigator,' Squadron Leader Wulfric reported, 'and following battlegame field exercises, we believe he is also ready for command.'

The King nodded. 'I owe him this chance in the name of his father, and he has earned it in his own right many times. And my daughter? Despite our efforts to hide her, many rumours have reached the Wall of dragon whispering.'

'She has grown up, as has Two Gulps,' Tangnost reported. 'More importantly she has begun to use her gift to help others, to lead by example. Many now have seen her survive dragon fire, command Imperials with a word, and train sabretooths. Without her knowing, I put her to the test and she did not let me down; her entire juvenile talon successfully executed a flight drop under her guidance.'

As expected, there was a stunned silence.

'Drumondir said she has also been working with Root in the HeartRock with a new design of dragon wings. And...as you know from my despatches, my Lord King, she can now change aspect at will; she rescued one of her team mates from his foolishness. She is both dragon and girl; they are one and the same.'

'She becomes a dragon already?'

'No, she...is still a girl but scaled like a dragon with wings and a tail.'

The Guardian nodded. 'I myself watched her quiet an Imperial and bond him with his sabretooths in an afternoon! A fledgling Dragon Whisper is emerging; there is hope for us yet.'

'I am envious,' the King admitted. 'My daughter is taking wing without me; I have missed so much this year.'

'You need to spend time with her, Rufus,' the Guardian suggested. 'She needs her father. You also have a young bride who needs you. Give over command of this operation to me. I will take four Imperials from the Faculty Guard, they are the best trained we have, along with five of our battlemages. It may be some time since they tasted combat, but they are the best.'

The King nodded. 'Take five scouts from the 4th Battalion the Highland Scouts and two dozen skirmishers from the 34th Frost Squadron. They stood down from combat a moon ago and should be rested. Sabretooths, Tangnost?'

'I think four veteran talons from the 7th Armoured Sabretooth Brigade supported by the Wildcat Clan will be more than enough.'

'Agreed,' the King said, 'now to the detail.'

And so the SDS laid their plans.

CHAPTER NINETY-TWO

Behind Enemy Lines

Guy DeBessart was given overall command of the reconnaissance exercise, along with Tangnost as his Shield, so that he could learn from the best. As the eldest son, Guy had learnt warfare at his father's side since he was knee high, but Jakart was keen for the one-handed young man to get operational experience before he became combat ready.

'We are calling for volunteers for reconnaissance beyond the Wall as a prelude to striking back against the WarLock. This is not an exercise. The mines of the North Brimstones lie within the Warlock's control. As you know, supplies have been dwindling, many mines lying close to Dragon Isle were stripped long ago, and those that remain have to delve deeper and deeper, with all the dangers that go with mining the deeps.'

'We intend taking the Brimstones back to supply us, and to deny the Warlock. Intelligence suggests that slaves,' Guy's eyes found Root's with gentle compassion. 'Possibly our own captured troops, as well as villages and burrows raided, work the mines. We intend to free them.'

There was a muted growl of approval as cadets and veterans sat forward to hear more. A three-dimensional map materialised, to hang in front of the tiered horseshoe of benches of the Briefing Room.

'This is a dangerous mission: a sortie behind enemy lines.' Guy glanced at Tangnost for reassurance. 'Scouts will cross the wall unseen and survive without aid, living off the land. You have to be invisible; else the WarLock will guess our intent. We will strike just before snow finally closes the passes and Brimstone Cove freezes over.

Following the Warlock's yearlong assault on the Howling Glen and the Old Wall, we need to strike back. A victory will lift morale in the Kingdoms; will prove to one and all that the SDS are still a force to be reckoned with: that we can and will strike back, now we know the true face of our enemy. We need the ore and the victory both, and,' he added grimly, 'we need to free the slaves. But first, we need better intelligence.'

'We want a two man team,' Tangnost took over. 'Scout and shield.'

A dozen stood.

'Oakley,' Guy nodded. The youth was growing up into a young man who had already made his extraordinary mark in the war. 'It's yours. Choose your shield.'

A number of hands went up, but Bracus swiftly stood. There was a murmur of surprise. Bracus had hopes of being chosen as a Dragon Lord with the new batttlestrike group.

'I'll be your Shield Mate, I'll guard your back, Root.'

Bracus leant forwards and held out his hand. 'Brother.'

Root took it gladly in a warrior's clasp. 'You will be the first sorcerer to be a scout!'

Bracus grinned. 'Then I will be in the best of company for you are the first scout to become a Dragon Lord. It will be an honour.'

Tangnost nodded. Many lessons had been learnt this year.

CHAPTER NINETY-THREE

Family Trees

'My Lord?' Root stepped into the Queen's Constable's chambers. 'You wished to see me?'

Sir Gharad looked up from the table. It was late and he looked tired, dressed informally in dark bedding robes. 'Come,' the old man beckoned the youth forwards to where a scroll lay weighted beneath a branch of candles. 'Sit by an old man.'

Root took a stool back to the warm fire that had burnt down to embers in the grate.

'Rufus tells me you leave at dawn to scout out mines in the Brimstones?'

Root nodded.

'It will be very dangerous. It is brave of you to volunteer.'

'They're all that are left of my people. I have no family.'

Sir Gharad nodded distractedly. 'I know, boy, I know. That is why I asked you to come. See here, this is my family tree. I know it is not the true living tree of your people, that your warren was carved into the branches of a great oak, branching out with every generation. But here, I can trace my lineage back thousands of years...'

Root bent over the ancient parchment, fascinated as ever by anything new. He traced his fingers up the lines working it out. To where the ink was faded and cracked.

'See how each generation was added, the devices of those who married into our house marked by their coat of arms. And this, as you know, is my coat of arms: the mountain hare slashed with the royal unicorn.

As you can see, I am the last of my family to bear the ancient title Earl of Dunsinain. My brother and his son were killed at the Isle of Midges and my wife and I had no children. She died of fever when still young, and I have not remarried.

'I-' Sir Gharad looked hesitant. 'I know you have suffered great loss; your family all taken by hobgoblins. Your father dying at the Howling Glen,' he took Root's hands in his bony dry hands. 'I know what it is like to have no family, to be alone in a room full of people.'

Root nodded mutely, not sure what was coming.

'I would not have you go beyond the Wall without knowing you were loved, that you had something, someone to come back to. I wish to take you into my household, as my son.'

'A-as your son?'

'Only if you wish it,' Sir Gharad mistook the youth's sudden pallor, the evident shock. 'To give you my protection, to share all I have with you. I-I cannot take the place of your father, but I can offer you the protection of my name and a place in my heart and my home.'

Tears pricked Root's eyes, but he smiled whole-heartedly. 'Oh, yes!' And then he moved forwards into his father's loving embrace.

CHAPTER NINETY-FOUR

Beyond the Wall

It was a dark stormy night. Root and Bracus were on their way to the Brimstones, flying at ten thousand strides on a cloaked Imperial, well above hostile patrols. They were getting a final briefing from Tangnost and checking their equipment. Bracus had learnt well and was dressed like Root as a scout, in a ragged mix of dark and light materials over winter issue combat kit...both wore webbing hidden beneath their cloaks. Bracus was armed with an AK0 staff, light and powerful, plus sword, detonators, flash bangs and throwing stars. Root was armed with his charcoal and parchment; Bracus would cover his back.

'You have three-quarters of a moon, then get back to your pick up zone,' the dwarf repeated. 'Root, here are the backup co-ordinates should you be unable to make the first. If you get into trouble fire off your flare. An Imperial will be on constant patrol. Be careful.' He paused. 'I am proud of you both. Come home safely.'

CHAPTER NINETY-FIVE

He's Gone!

'He's gone? But he never said goodbye!' Quenelda was distraught. 'We were supposed to visit Quester today.'

'Hush,' Drumondir looked at Tangnost, who had brought the unwelcome news barely a bell after returning from the Wall. 'I - '

There was an approaching thunder of feet and a crash as Two Gulps barrelled through the door to comfort her. It had been shut. Ducking to avoid the splinters Tangnost bit back a smile in spite of himself. The young sabretooth was getting bigger day by day, and in all the right places. But he was almost too big now to be following Quenelda around indoors, like a puppy. He must weigh in at about five thousand sruples at least!

'Quenelda,' Tangnost took her in his arms as Two Gulps offered slobbery kisses. 'Root didn't have the chance. We lifted off late last night from Dragon Isle on a cloaked Imperial. No one outside the briefing knows, save you. We are going to be attacking the Brimstones to take the mines back. We need to know where the entrances are to the mines, the slave huts, the galleries and tunnels.'

'But why him...there are other scouts with battle experience. Wouldn't the Tunnel Rats have been better? Wh-'

'You know the answer, lass. Many scouts have been killed this past two years, the rest are deployed. And we believe those are his people are in there. If what you say you saw at Roarkinch is true, then it will be the same in the Brimstones. He volunteered.'

Quenelda's shoulders slumped. 'How long is he gone for? We've hardly seen each other this year.'

Tangnost shook his head. 'A three-quarter moon, and if they fail to make contact, another quarter. He's not on his own, Bracus volunteered to be his Shield.'

'Bracus?' Quenelda was stunned.

Tangnost nodded. 'There was no shortage of volunteers. He has won many friends.'

'But what if he never comes back?'

'He will. He said that he knew you and Two Gulps would come for him if he got into trouble. Will Two Gulps be combat ready? Will your talon?'

'Yes,' she said fiercely, balling her fists. 'Yes! We've been training every day, combat dismount...throwing out a perimeter...I want to be there for him.' She looked up at Tangnost. 'For you. For Papa!'

'I knew you would. III Junior Brigade are now on three weeks of battlegames with the Heavy Brigade: cave training, drop dead, combat mounting and dismounting and talon tactics. You have three weeks, along with the rest of the brigade, to earn a place on this deployment.'

'We're going to free his people?'

'Yes.'

'Two Gulps and I, the entire talon will be ready! We'll make you proud! I promise.'

'I know you will,' Tangnost replied gently, wiping a tear from her chin. 'And you will meet an old friend. Malachite and the Wildcat Clan are deploying with us. They will take over the mine once the slaves are freed.'

CHAPTER NINETY-SIX

The Root of an Idea

With Root away, Quenelda began to visit Quester as often as she could. She had visited the esquire many times, but for the first time she truly saw him and was horrified. Not just by the pain etched on his face, but the bitterness that masked Root's once cheery friend.

'Where's Root?' Quester tried not to sound petulant, for he had many visitors now, including several Dragon Lords and even the Guardian. 'He's not come by for days?'

Quenelda hesitated on the edge of a lie then decided to tell the truth. 'He's flown north on a mission,' she said gently.

'A mission?' Envy and misery weighed down Quester's words. He had come so far and could go no further. Root was his friend, but that did little to quell the jealously that boiled up inside him.

Guilt flooded Quenelda. She had been thinking only of herself since she was accepted into the Battle Academy... her problems... Two Gulps. She had done nothing for the youth who had saved her father's life and paid a high price for it. How could she help? And then she felt a familiar awareness suffuse her. All her senses became keener as her inner dragon settled about her like an invisible mantle.

Quester looked at her with confusion and awe. Root had described it; else he might have been afraid of the sudden stillness, of her glowing eyes growing distant as if she looked out on another world.

There *was* a way to help Quester; Quenelda's inner dragon knew it...if only she could remember. But every time she tried to capture the thought it slipped away like a dream.

'Witchwood!' She said suddenly, smiling.

'Witchwood?' Quester echoed. 'What about it?'

Quenelda shook her head. It made no sense. 'I must go,' she reached out to touch his hand. 'I'll be back tomorrow.'

CHAPTER NINETY-SEVEN

Cave Bears

Bracus and Root lay in the heather, warmed by the early winter sun on their backs. They had crossed the Wall a week ago one misty evening and moved north-west, scouting as they went. Root had swiftly found a cave deep within the dark cover of the Caledonian forest to use as a base – where even by day, light failed to penetrate these snow-shrouded woods.

'Keep your head down and your helmet on,' Root warned Bracus. 'The roof of the cave is very low in parts.'

'Am I going to fit through?'

'Oh, yes,' Root replied cheerfully. 'It opens up further inside; it used to be the den of a cave bear.'

'What!?' Bracus stuttered, remembering their field exercise and Root's dire warnings. 'A cave bear, Argh!' Standing up in horror, he cracked his head against the low ceiling and sat down hard on the dirt packed floor. 'But they're huge! Didn't you say they can kill a sabretooth!'

'That is why there will be plenty of room for you!

There is no one home,' Root reassured his tall shield mate. 'It's too early for them to hibernate. Don't worry!'

'Don't worry,' Bracus muttered ruefully trying to rub his head through his helmet, 'just a twenty stride bad tempered bear comes home at night and wonders who is sleeping in his bed!'

The spongy needles of the forest floor swiftly gave way to hard rock and packed dirt. Old bones crunched beneath their feet. After several bends the cave opened out, so that even Bracus could stand. Root struck his flint and knife and coaxed a flame from the dry bark slithers he flaked earlier, gradually building the fire up with dead wood, before lighting a roughly made pine resin torch he had shown Bracus how to make out in the woods. He lodged it on the floor between boulders so that they could see better. 'This is perfect,' he confirmed, pointing to narrow cracks high above in the ceiling. 'That will conceal our smoke.'

Root scooped up a handful of cold sweet water and drank deeply. 'See there! A constant supply of fresh water.' But Bracus was looking at the cave bear claw marks high on the sides of the rock, and the large bones of its many victims. He picked one up weighing it in his hands; it was thick and heavy.

'Elk,' Root told him. 'Bears are like you, they eat meat or berries...whatever they can find.'

Bracus fervently hoped he would not cross tracks with a bear.

Root unhooked the foraging sack from his belt; he had been collecting as they moved. 'Chocolate mushrooms,' he smiled happily, showing Bracus. 'Make sure you never confuse them with the death cap toadstool. They look very similar, but the frills are different.'

Bracus nodded doubtfully. 'I would never trust myself.'

'Chasing the Stars loves these, and so will you.' Root tipped out the bag to sort their meal out. 'These are wood acorns, pine cones and walnuts; wild garlic, some onions. Toast berries and brambles…a feast fit for Kings! Here,' he handed the larger cones to Bracus. Open these and get the nuts. I'll get some rocks on the fire.'

Bracus's tummy rumbled as he smelt the enticing aroma of the stew Root had made. He had never eaten mushroom stew before, but it was strong and gamey and delicious, so chewy it was almost like meat.

CHAPTER NINETY-EIGHT

Wands and Weaponry

Phoenix Firestorm and ten other Imperials levelled out at six thousand strides above the glen and headed north. The sky had grown darker and the dense milky stars of the Dragon's Breath were clearly visible. The fully armoured sabretooths moved restlessly, sensing they were far from the comfort of tunnels and caves, and the youngsters of the III Juvenile Brigade weren't much happier. Donning high sky gear was exciting; the quality of their fleeced armoured leathers better than many had ever worn. They also wore full-face helmets for the first time; with visors that could be opened once back on the ground. Sitting on dragon wings, they were trying to be brave, but the air was thin and brittle and it was so high! Had they been able to look, instead of being buckled against the inner side of the spinal plates, they would have seen the Seven Kingdoms laid out like a map far below and the Ice Isle and the Westering Isles to the west. Then the Imperial folded its wings and dropped like a stone down a well.

At first it was totally silent; sound didn't travel well so high. But soon screaming filled the air. Whether it was the wind or the juveniles it was hard to tell, but it was a tooth rattling ride. Already Tangnost and the dragon masters on their respective Imperials had unhooked their tethers and were striding down the lines of white knuckled Juveniles, some of whom were trying to empty their helmets.

'Prepare to unbuckle,' Tangnost barked. 'Sling your shields over your backs. Check your dragon's harness and mount up; prepare for a full-scale combat landing exercise. Quenelda, you take the lead.'

CHAPTER NINETY-NINE

The Witchwood Grove

'I have never seen its like,' Drumondir's voice was full of wonder as she pressed hands to the rough sweet smelling bark. 'There are tales in the sagas of trees that touch the sky, but I never thought to see one.' She and Quenelda stood in the HeartRock, dwarfed by the immense witchwood forest. Strange creatures called and slithered in the lush undergrowth.

'The whole land was once covered in trees,' Quenelda said wistfully, snaring a memory that was not her own. 'Every animal and stone, every plant, had a power of its own and its place in the web of life was understood and honoured, its gifts used wisely. But its peoples lost their way long ago; they no longer harvest only what they need, they no longer think of their children. They burn and plunder, leaving nothing but a wilderness behind. The ancestral groves are long gone. Only witchwood reveals its power.' She reached out to also touch the rough bark. 'When freshly harvested, it can still put down roots, can still grow.'

With a sudden intake of breath, Drumondir realised what Quenelda intended, why she had been invited into this ancient woodland. 'You can knit witchwood and flesh?'

'My memories tell me, yes. Long ago it could heal, could knit sinew and flesh and bone. I can heal dragons; I think we should try, else Quester may never recover.'

Quester was feather light in Tangnost's arms as the Dragon Master carried him across the bridge to the HeartRock and into the DragonBone chamber. Drumondir bore the witchwood leg. Jakart DeBessart had readily agreed to Quenelda's request to release Master Carpenter Rowan from his duties. For a quarter moon the gnome had worked on nothing else, barely eating, barely sleeping; the result was a thing of beauty that matched Quester's right leg perfectly.

Barely had they crossed the threshold than the small group found themselves in the witchwood forest, a place of immense calm and power. Birds sang, animals called. Sun dappled the forest floor. Quester was wide eyed with wonder as Quenelda told Tangnost to lay the esquire on roots at the foot of a tree. 'Sleep,' she commanded as the roots grew and cradled the young man.

Drumondir unwound the stump of Quester's left thigh where the flesh was pink and puckered. Quenelda placed the wooden leg against it. They all held their breath as the young Dragon Whisperer laid a hand on the sleeping youth. She closed her eyes. The hue of the wood deepened and then tendrils quested out like roots searching for water. All about the injured thigh, they sank into Quester's skin and disappeared, and bone and flesh and wood knitted together.

The BoneCaster reached out in amazement. The wood had become soft and warm to the touch like flesh.

'Let him sleep,' Quenelda smiled. 'Now all he needs to do is to learn to walk again.'

CHAPTER ONE-HUNDRED

Reconnaissance

Over the following half moon, Root plotted all the mines whilst Bracus guarded his back and learnt how to live off the land, turning his hand to foraging and camouflage. At dark fall, the pair returned to their cave and ate a hot supper whilst the temperature outside dropped like a stone and winter arrived in a flurry of snow. But as dark fell on the tenth day of their mission, the pair left the safety of their cave for good, and set out for the final time through densely forested gorges for the largest and most northern mine of all.

The Frost Moons were rising like newly minted gold coins, casting strong light on the snow. Bracus felt the cold seeping permanently into his bones and his respect for SDS mountain scouts increased. For the first time, the young sorcerer lord became truly aware of how isolated and skilful their task was. Gnomes may not fight, but theirs was a dangerous and difficult task worthy of great honour, and many like Root's father died. Bracus wiggled his toes in his heavy boots and flexed his numb fingers, trying to get some feeling back so that he could wield sword and staff should he need to. Soon he was shivering.

'Drink this,' Root passed him a small hip flask 'I've been saving this for the first frosts.'

'What is it?'

'Dwarf cider. Tangnost gave it to me.'

Bracus took a gulp and almost choked as the fiery liquid coursed down his throat. He blew out his cheeks in appreciation as a warm glow suffused his aching body. Root grinned in the darkness, before taking a slug himself, feeling the golden warmth of apple and spices trickle down to his toes.

Over the past couple of days they had scouted the skirts of the Troll Fells Ridge for the main entrances to a vast subterranean network of galleries, tunnels and shafts that burrowed deep into the heart rock of the Brimstones. Moving mostly by night, they had discovered the entrance and at least a half dozen shafts which might be used to escape. Over a three-day close reconnaissance, the pair had counted some hundred odd guards and slave drivers.

The heavy snow at this height made their task harder because it betrayed them. But Root had carved pads to fit on their snow shoes making them look like bear tracks. As they followed heavily used game trails about the lower wooded skirts of the Brimstones, Bracus learnt to identify many wild animals from predator to prey.

Soft as shadows, the pair followed the slave gangs that laboured night and day to haul the heavy ore to the galleons at anchor in Brimstone Cove. There, on a rough-hewn jetty great stockpiles of ore were loaded on iron shod ice galleons for shipping to Roarkinch and the studs of the Black Citadel. Great sledges were being made by slave gangs, mostly dwarves, felling trees and working the wood for hauling brimstone to the WarLock's castles north of the Old Wall.

The captives were impossible to count as one ragged figure looked like another. All along the trail, bodies frozen in grotesque shapes lay beneath the snow, and worse, one night they had heard a groan as they passed. Despite the danger, Root had cradled the dying gnome until the last breath left his body, whispering memories of sunshine and mellow autumn that made Bracus weep.

They had to be careful of patrols out to catch game at night; caught once between a foraging party and an ore caravan, they simply fell down in the snow - no one noticed two more bodies on the trail. Every day, resting up high in the tree tops beneath their bowers, Root added to the rolled leather map, carefully scribing every piece of information which might help free his people. The moons waxed full and began to wane. It was time to go home.

'That's it! If we leave now we'll make it to the lift co-ordinates. I admit I'll be glad to get back in the air. I never...' Bracus shook his head. 'I never understood what scouts go through for us, Root...'

'I'm not coming,' Root said quietly

'*What?*'

'I have to go in,' Root had long since decided. 'I need to know the layout of the galleries and shafts, if we are to get any of my people out alive once the attack has started.'

'No!' Bracus protested hoarsely. 'Root, you can't go

in there. It's too heavily guarded. I can't protect you!'

'They're my people, Bracus!' Root swallowed. 'They're all that's left of my people.'

'But they'll spot you. Th-'

'No, they won't,' the young gnome said gently. 'The guards will see what they expect to see. I can tear strips to bind my hands and disguise my boots.'

'No, Root! I ca-'

'They are only stopping prisoners escaping!' Root argued. 'They won't expect anyone to be breaking in.... who'd infiltrate a slave mine?'

'But the chains!' Bracus cast about for another reason. 'They're all shackled.'

But Root had thought about that too. He pointed to the moonlit tail through the woods, the uneven shapes and mounds that boarded it. 'There are plenty of chains and shackles,' he said bitterly.

'I'll come with you,' Bracus declared.

'No! Bracus you can't. You're too big; you'd stand out! Take this,' he handed his shield mate the rolled map.

As dusk fell, the pair prepared Root, removing anything that might attract attention, binding his good boots with torn strips from Bracus's cloak to hide them. The only things Root kept were the rest of their dried fruit and oatcakes, concealed beneath his shirt. 'Be safe, Root.' Bracus echoed the SDS farewell before battle in honour of his Shield Mate. 'I will never forgive myself if you are killed. The Lady Quenelda wouldn't forgive me either, and I don't want to make her mad. So stay safe!'

Root made his move towards the back of the slave

huts. The guard would change soon and the night shift roused. Asking forgiveness from the ancestral spirit world, he crawled through the frozen bodies and broke a rigid arm, and then again, the loud cracks masked by the bellow of the dale dragons returning from an ore shipment. The manacles were too big for the young girl he took them from, she was all skin and bone, but tight for him, taking the skin from Root's hand. Numb with horror and cold, he never even noticed. Instead he wrapped the chains about his shoulders and squirmed forwards.

It was easy. The hut was poorly made and rotting beneath the weight of snow. Root softly pulled the planking aside, careful not to dislodge the long icicles that bearded the roof, and crawled through the gap. Inside, figures huddled under sacking on rickety bunks in threes and fours, their breath frosting in the cold. No one stirred as he curled up next to them and, shivering with cold and fear, Root tried to sleep. It was his fourteenth naming day.

CHAPTER ONE-HUNDRED-AND-ONE

Put Your Best Foot Forward

'Try again,' Drumondir encouraged the youth. Quester was still painfully thin and pallid, but now the cheerful, determined young man they knew was re-emerging. Quenelda's whispering had worked; the bond between boy and witchwood had taken. Taking a deep breath, Quester stood, trying to find his balance with a leg again. Hesitantly, he stepped forwards, Drumondir by his side. Another step...then another...

'I can't believe it,' Quester looked down on his wooden leg and bent his knee and twiddled his toes.

You're not the only one! Drumondir thought. The healer in her was consumed with curiosity but she kept it in check; the important thing was to get Quester back on his feet. She had prepared a strength giving brew for him to drink every day.

'There!' Drumondir nodded, as they stood on the balcony bathed in early winter sunshine. 'You can walk! It will get easier day by day, I promise.'

Quester nodded. 'Do you think... do you think I can

manage to fly to...' he hesitated, and Drumondir sensed a world of disappointment underlying his next few words, despite the brave face he put on. 'To see Root and Quenelda graduate?'

The BoneCaster encouraged him with a smile. 'I think you are a very determined and brave young man, Quester. You will be there with your friends.' Quester's body was undoubtedly healing, but as yet, his heart and mind were not.

Chapter One-Hundred-and-Two

Legends Come to Life

Finally the WarLock knew, and his anger was terrifying. News had reached him at Borzall Castle, forty leagues north of the Howling Glen, that the hobgoblin WarLord was held prisoner in Dragon Isle: all those moons waiting, searching, delaying his attack! Tongues of green flickered about him as he vented his fury and the courier who had struggled through a blizzard for six days to deliver the news fled for his life.

And the same absurd despatch said it was some runt of a gnome and the Earl's...the King's daughter who had not only rescued Rufus on his injured battledragon, but captured Galtekerion too! It didn't make sense; the same wretched daughter who had been training on Dragon Isle disguised as a boy, apparently...it appeared there was little the girl could not do despite the fact she had only thirteen or fourteen summers. *She could survive dragon fire. She could enter a place called the HeartRock,* he had yet to discover its meaning. *She could command Imperials, train sabretooths... She could fly without dragon wings...*

she was a dragon! Absurd!

Unless...unless...all the rumours were not so absurd after all...could it be possible she was a Dragon Whisperer? No...surely just legends...but then Rufus was becoming like a Dragon Lord of old and no one knew how...and how did they escape the maelstrom he conjured? No one should have survived that.

Galtekerion's loss was yet another major failure in a year of setbacks: he had failed to take the Howling Glen, nor breach the Old Wall. The WinterKnights from the Stormspike Mountains far to the south had matched his frost dragons move for move, driving him out of the Howling Glen and beyond, even retaking Dunsinain Castle. His supply lines were being attacked far to the north of the Old Wall let alone from Dragon Isle. How? And inexplicably, some of his Imperials were simply vanishing...

We must capture her. It's time to find out who or what the girl was. A task for Darcy when they attacked the Sorcerers Glen and Dragon Isle, a task his son would relish.

He turned at the sound of Darcy's footsteps and gave him the despatch.

'So...' the WarLock King said   'Your sister has once again emerged as a Dragon Whisperer...'

Darcy laughed, throwing the paper in the hearth. 'A Dragon Whisperer! Not this fairy tale again! She's still a child!   She never even earned a wand! Everyone says she is hopeless at magic.'

'Certainly, these are only whispers, but her name is

heard from many lips and strange things happen when she is around. And legends can be wielded like weapons,' the WarLock King brooded. 'A tool to rouse the rabble from their stupor. True or false, if they believe they have a Dragon Whisperer in their midst, that is worth ten armies in the field. I think it is time to remove her from this game, and find who or what she is. You never heard anything about who her mother was?'

Darcy shrugged. 'Everyone said it was some low born woman he could not marry, but he took the child as a ward. That is common enough.'

'But what,' the WarLock closed his eyes in sudden realisation, 'if her mother were the Queen?' His outline smoked and eddied.

Darcy shrugged. 'Yes, it's possible, but what would it matter? She's the daughter of a King anyway since my fa- since the Earl married the Queen.'

'It makes all the difference! Dragon Whisperers are said to be of royal blood...an unbroken line since Son of the Morning Star. What a fool I've been! '

'You're taking these...rumours seriously?' Darcy was astounded.

'When we attack the Sorcerers Glen in the spring you are to capture her and bring her to Roarkinch,' his father's eyes glinted coldly. 'Then we'll discover the truth.'

CHAPTER ONE-HUNDRED-AND-THREE

Into the Abyss

Clang! Clang! The mine bell was tolling, echoed in the deeps by others, summoning the night shift up. Barely asleep, Root fell off the end of the pallet just as the door was kicked open, threatening to bring down the entire hut. 'Up, up, you scum,' the troll cursed as two strides of snow crowned him. 'There's work to be done,' he shrugged the snow off his broad shoulders. 'Last transport till the spring an' the Wolverine wants a full load by sundown. And you don't want to make the Wolverine unhappy or it will be the Pit for you! Move!'

Root had thought it freezing outside, but as the bitter cold mouth of the mine swallowed them in its frigid dripping maw, the young gnome's heart sank to his boots. Already the cold iron was biting into Root's ankle bones, although he wore warmer garments beneath his rags than any about him. His folk were gentle and generous, quick to offer friendship and trust. They loved the warmth of late summer, moving south with the seasons to avoid the cold.

Now, starved and freezing, his people moved like the living dead; filthy, scarred by the whip, wearing feeble layers of ragged clothes against the cold, eyes weeping and clogged, lungs and mouths choked with brimstone dust. How Root longed to reach out to offer words of comfort and hope. But he couldn't, he could not risk betraying the coming operation.

In a side cavern, a kitchen of sorts with rough wooden benches was set up, large cauldrons hung over meagre fires. The thin gruel slopped into the filthy wooden bowls was barely warm, oats and water. Twisted dried strips of meat heaped on the table went untouched by the gnomes; dragon gristle, from those that died each week from exhaustion, starvation and injury; dragon meat for a people who ate no fowl or flesh. They were dying in their droves, dragons and gnomes both.

As they descended, the chill grew deeper and the air thicker and darker. The noise of pickaxe and hammer blow on rock in the third gallery was like hail, chains rattled and wagons screeched on the icy rails; a never ending, jarring cacophony of noise. At a large junction of many tunnels, the night shift halted and were split up into work details. Root's went down three more levels.

Here, in perpetual darkness barely penetrated by shuttered lamps, the heavy ore was lifted into small leather buckets, handed from hand to hand in a living chain, up and slowly up to where the shaft opened out enough to fill large, wheeled metal cauldrons. From there chain gangs hauled it up another two levels through tunnels to where the cavern opened out; finally it was harnessed to a team of six dale dragons, the lead two dragons harnessed to the pulling teams; slaves with special spiked shoes to help them grip the icy slick surface.

A deep rumble travelled through the mine. Root's chain gang froze, huddling in towards each other for comfort.

'What was that?' Root whispered, through the scarf that muffled his face. 'What's wrong?'

No one replied and he thought for a moment they were deaf from the endless noise. A grey haired gnome gave him a queer look as guards ran past in their spiked boots. 'Cave in. More deaths... Just been caught, lad?'

Root's heart hit his chest. 'Yes,' he whispered, head down.

'No prisoners save dwarves been brought in for half a moon, boy. Keep your mouth shut and do what I do. Here take my cloak; yours ain't got no brimstone dust. I'll take yours. What's your name?'

'Root.'

'Well Root, I'll look out for you, boy. Name's Squirrel. There now,' he settled the ragged cloak about the boy's shoulders. 'You look more like us. Now, keep your head down.'

'Watch out,' someone hissed. 'The Wolverine's coming.' The slaves bunched closer together.

'Who?'

'Gang Master,' his new found friend answered. 'A killer. Don't want to attract his attention, boy.'

'What is it?' A man wrapped behind layers of furs arrived. 'What is wrong this time?'

'Cave in...'

'So? We got plenty more where they came from.' The Wolverine gestured carelessly to where the chain gang cowered nearby. He took his mine mask off to reveal an angry pinched face.

Felix! Root was horror struck. *Felix DeLancey...* Darcy's so called dragon master who fled with the young Earl. No one had heard of him since. Root pulled up the rag over his face. He mustn't be recognised.

The guard nervously licked his lips. 'It was on deep seam eleven. Dwarves. The *last* of our dwarves.'

'What?!' Felix was furious. 'You had them all in one shaft?' He raised a gloved hand to strike.

'But that seam was the richest yet!' the guard protested. 'The upper shafts are cleaned out. We need more dwarves to open new seams. And a dozen died last week trying to escape up the flume!'

'The Warlock King doesn't like to be kept waiting!' the Gang Master threatened. 'Nor the Black Prince! Send down gangs to see if you can dig out any of the ore bins or you'll pay for your stupidity!'

How about the miners? Root wanted to shout at Felix. *They might be still alive.* Then he felt a grip on his arm, heard Squirrel's whispered warning. 'Don't do nothing foolish, boy. Relax.'

'Right,' the nearest guard aggressively cracked his whip as he and the other guards crowded forwards. 'Down you go, you scum, down to level ten...'

Despite the lash, there were groans of fear and desperation as some attempted futilely to flee. Cave-ins and explosions were frequent in the lower shafts, where tunnels were cramped and pit props were few and far between, where they could barely breathe for the choking dust, barely enough air for shuttered lamps.

'Move!' The guards' whips snaked out. 'Or it's the Pit for you!'

That threat got them moving as rapidly as the shackles allowed. Root cried out as his feet slid away from him on the ice bringing down those nearest to him. The impact stunned him, rattling his head. He lay there.

'Up!' The lash whipped again. With cries of despair the fallen struggled to their feet.

The Pit! Root shivered, the hairs on the back of his neck rose like hackles. Whatever it was, it must be truly horrible if it were worse than this hell.

CHAPTER ONE-HUNDRED-AND-FOUR

Extraction

A whisper of air betrayed the large harrier hovering above the clearing.

'Target acquired.' The pilot put down softly while the others held back, night sights scanning the area, altert to patrols.

'We were told there were two of you.'

'Root's not coming,' Bracus replied. He would bring down a storm of dragons and end this nightmare for Root's people. 'I swear, brother,' he whispered, I'll be back.'

'Mount up.'

And then they were gone.

CHAPTER ONE-HUNDRED-AND-FIVE

The Good and The Bad

'How is he?'

'He is growing stronger,' the King's surgeon answered. 'He can walk now. Clumsy perhaps, but...he believes he will never fight again, that his dream of becoming a Dragon Lord has passed beyond his reach whilst his friends are close to graduating. I was afraid he would simply fade, until we learnt he saved your life by fighting Galtekerion. He has never wanted for company since, from cadets to Dragon Lords and they have been giving him gifts, even a young dragon or two I believe.'

The King sighed. 'I fear he has paid the highest price of all for our silence. We wanted to keep Hugo guessing where his warlord was. The strategy worked; for the hobgoblins have not come and we have held the line but-'

The surgeon put a hand on the King's shoulder. 'He will understand, Rufus, if you explain.'

The King sat down. 'How do you feel? They said you are beginning to walk with your new witchwood leg?'

Quester swallowed. 'I thought...' tears welled in his eyes. 'I thought you'd forgotten me. That everyone had forgotten me.'

The King nodded. 'Forgive me. You were unconscious still, when I left, but I should have sent word.' He beckoned an esquire forwards, bearing a sword. It was notched in several places.

'This is the blade that saved my life in your hands; it's yours, in recognition of your bravery. It will be reforged. You must build your strength so that you may be knighted after the Graduation Ceremony. You will then serve with me in the ThunderStorm Battlegroup and take the place of my son at my side. And who knows, in time, you may become strong enough to be a Dragon Lord.

'My King, I don't have the wo-'

The King smiled. 'I am crippled and blind. Yet I can fight and fly. I believe you will also be able to, in time.'

Quester sank back onto the bed in a daze. The King did not make to move.

'I have some news about your family, why they have not come.' he said gently. 'I fear it is not good.'

'They're not...?' Quester's joy turned to dread at the King's words. 'They're not dead, are they?'

'No,' the King sighed. 'But your brother Euan has been wounded.'

'Wounded?' Quester's eyes lit up. 'Is he here? Can I see him?'

'Son, there is no easy way to say this.' The King tried to soften the blow by resting a hand on Quester's shoulder. 'Your family fight for the WarLock King. Your brother was raiding villages and settlements taking prisoners for the mines.' The King closed his ruined eyes. 'With my...under the command of Darcy. Euan was one of the Knights of Chaos.'

'No!' Quester denied it. He had heard the horrendous tails of slaughter and mayhem from many of his visitors.

'Your brother is held in the prisons below. He does not want to see you. I am sorry.'

CHAPTER ONE-HUNDRED-AND-SIX

Scrambled

It was going to be a beautiful night, the deep indigo sky was studded with cold stars, and the moons would soon rise. Frost crackled off the wings of Phoenix Firestorm as the cloaked Imperial flew to meet up with the Guardian's legendary Faculty Guard on the Impossible Peaks of the southern Brimstones. The dark world ten thousand strides below passed in a blur, but far ahead they could see green flashes of light on the horizon. The WarLock had flung his exhausted depleted army at the Wall in a futile fury of rage. The SDS had known! They had known all along! But Jakart DeBessart had cast them back, and was now harrying the retreating army north towards Borzall castle, away from the Brimstones.

They were flying faster than the speed of sound in the thin air, at the very limit of the Imperials' endurance and well above any hostile patrols they might encounter.

Unlike the rest of her talon, who were tightly strapped in, Quenelda was pacing up and down, fiddling with her armour, tightening buckles. She and Two Gulps and twelve others, including Caradoc and Fergus, had been selected to join Operation Brimstone; their task was to locate and protect slaves and escort them out, while Malachite and his people fought the guards. They had been due to fly the next day; instead they had been scrambled for immediate take off with an escort of five Imperials, to head north with all speed to join up with the battlegroup. It had been a confusing and panicked time, the first time the cadets had scrambled for real, but Tangnost had anchored them in the drill they had practised again and again. The Imperials had climbed steeply, not the sheer vertical climb if they had been carrying troops, only because of the sabretooths, but it scared the Juveniles to bits and soon they would be dropping down. Quenelda found she was shaking. Dragon memories were forgotten, and it was only a young girl who faced her first battle.

'Calm, child,' Drumondir had found her; she too had been summoned north. 'Drink this, it will soothe and warm you. Soon you will be with your friend again.'

'I'm just...'

'I know, child, it is natural to be afraid. It is only a fool who is not.'

'I have memories of many battles...'

'But this is *your* first...'

Quenelda nodded. 'I hope I've, I hope I've trained them well enough.'

'The Guardian would not have agreed if he did not believe in you. This is your chance to repay his faith.'

Drumondir had come to care for the injured and sick who would be brought out of the mines. A lifetime in the frozen north meant she knew all there was to know about snow sickness and frostbite, but she was also a BoneCaster Mage skilled at medicine of all kinds. The Juveniles had taken to calling her Grandmother, a mark of respect and affection, and were comforted by her presence.

The necklace of lights far below picked out the Old Wall to the east, braziers strung along its length and bright clusters where the forts were, until it was lost in the dusk. They were putting down soon to collect the Wildcat Clan.

Soon... Quenelda thought. *Soon we'll be meeting up with Root...*

Two Gulps nuzzled her impatiently. *Soon we go into the caves...*

Suddenly their descent slowed and they began to pick up speed and height, the dragon climbing as steeply as she dared with sabretooths.

Quenelda ran up to where Tangnost was talking urgently to Guy. The dwarf straightened up.

'What?' Quenelda frowned. 'What's happened? Why aren't we stopping? How about the Wildcats?'

'I don't know, lass, but we've been ordered forward with all speed. The Clan are already there waiting for us.'

CHAPTER ONE-HUNDRED-AND-SEVEN

The Death Knell

Despite his training over the last ten moons, nothing had prepared the young gnome for the hardship at the mine face, deep down in the bowels of the Brimstones. As the night wore on, Root could feel his legs turn to rubber with exhaustion and hunger, and his arms grow heavy as lead. The relentless strike of the pick against the stone jarred up his arms into his skull, so that his head was aching, yet he dislodged only shards and chips. Despite the scarf tied about his face, the fine dust was choking and soon he was hacking and coughing: the death knell they called it. Those slaves who had been in the mines the longest were gasping open mouthed for air like stranded fish and would soon be dead.

A cauldron of lukewarm water, and crumbled blackened oatcakes, was all they were given for nourishment. If it had not been for the Badger's relentless basic training, Root would barely be able to lift the loaded shovel. The heavy manacles, which hadn't been removed, were rubbing his wrists raw and bruised his ankles with every movement.

'Here, lad,' Squirrel waited till the guards were talking, and then emptied half his ore into Root's bucket. 'Need more than that if you don't want to attract the guard's attention.'

It was impossible to know what time of day it was down in this endless night, and Root, with a sudden flash of insight, understood how the Earl Rufus's battledragon, Stormcracker Thundercloud, must have suffered in captivity in another mine, because he was a creature of the air! At the memory of that broken, dying dragon sudden panic tightened the youth's chest, so that he fell to the floor. What if he never saw daylight again? What if he were trapped down here? Never to see Chasing the Stars, Quenelda, Tangnost, or his father Sir Gharad, ever again? Tears ran tracks through his dusty face, and he regretted his impulse: he had only wanted to save his people.

'Hush, boy,' Squirrel held him. 'It gets 'em all the first time, like this. But you get used to it.'

In the freezing depths of a brimstone mine, overwhelmed by fear, held in the arms of a stranger, Root wept his heart out.

CHAPTER ONE-HUNDRED-AND-EIGHT

Out of the Frying Pan and into the Fire

Exhausted, mind numb, Root heard the clang of a bell. Head down, shaking from head to toe, Root stumbled upwards with the rest. The young gnome had almost made it to the mouth of the mine when a figure in front of him collapsed.

'Warmth....' The young woman begged, her teeth chattering. 'A t-t-turn by the fire I beg o-o-of you!' Those around her hesitated, then lowered their heads and tramped on, their spirits and bodies already broken. Turning, Root bent to lift her. The pleading eyes held his as he cradled her awkwardly in his arms, trying to warm her.

'Please,' he whispered in their own tongue... 'please hold on. Don't give up...' he rocked her gently... 'It's not for much longer...truly. Hold on just a little longer.'

A whip lashed out catching his cheek. Blood trickled down Root's face. A guard in black leather and thick furs stood over them in fury, coiling the whip for a second strike. 'Get back to the lines, boy!'

'But she's dying!'

'Then ain't nothing you can do! Move!'

'No! She needs warmth!'

'Leave him a' Squirrel buckled under a vicious blow to the head.

Shuddering under the lash, Root held her till she died and the tiny bloom of breath in the frigid air faded. They had to drag him away.

He was thrown in the Pit.

CHAPTER ONE-HUNDRED-AND-NINE

We're Going In

The cloaked Imperials of the Faculty Guard had put down on the Unforgiving Crags, great slabs of limestone that jutted out in the lee of the White Giant Mountain in the Brimstones.

'Come with me,' Tangnost told Quenelda quietly as she was already saddling with the other Juveniles. 'Leave Two Gulps, you won't need him yet. We're going in sooner than expected at dark fall. Search and rescue; three two man teams on harriers.'

'What?' Quenelda went cold; this was why they had scrambled. 'W-what's happened?' She shivered, knowing the answer already. 'Who's missing?' Not Root!?

'I'm sorry, lass,' Tangnost's voice was gentle, as if that could cushion the blow. 'Root went into the mine and he hasn't come out.'

Quenelda's hearts sank to her boots. 'What? Why? Why did he do that?' Tears pricked her eyes, she couldn't breathe.

'Because he's afraid slaves will be killed in the attack.

He wanted to know the layout of the mine so those who went in the first wave knew where the guards were, knew where his people were, and would be able to protect them.'

Bracus arrived on Phoenix Firestorm, imposing even in his scouting gear for the drop. 'Lady...Quenelda,' he swallowed. 'I- scouts went into the slave huts to retrieve him after the shift changed, but he wasn't there! I'm sorry, Lady! He insisted and I – I would never have let him go if I had thought he wouldn't come out. We waited all day for him to come out, and then we started searching.' Bracus was in tears.

Quenelda shook her head trying to find her voice. 'I know you love him...he can be stubborn...' she smiled weakly at the towering young man who had chosen this mission, finally seeing a friend.

'Bearhugger?' A frost dragon had put down behind them. The pilot had a hurried conference and Quenelda felt time itself was stopping with her heart, as Tangnost raised his ashen face to hers and Root's friend.

'They've picked up faint thermal images in some kind of pit. We think it's him. You're going in to get him out. Now!'

CHAPTER ONE-HUNDRED-AND-TEN

The Pit

Weak winter sunshine had given way to the cold deep bluc of twilight. The first stars were twinkling when the snow suddenly sifted and swirled, although there was no wind. Six harriers took off from a cloaked Imperial. A guard on his way to the latrines keeled over, a throwing star lodged in his throat.

To a watching horn-beam owl, it was as if the frozen land had come alive. Frost glittered, shadows flitted. Moonlight caught the curve of a talon as a perimeter was thrown by frost dragons. Three figures dismounted their harriers and ran forwards to where a deep well was sunk in the bedrock. There were bodies there, flesh hard as rock, frozen in grotesque shapes as they scrabbled to get out, hands raised, fingers clawing for an elusive nook or cranny. For a hand given in friendship.

'Root?' Quenelda whispered peering over the rim into the darkness below, her dragon eyes struggling to identify her friend. There was no reply.

'Root?' Tears pricked her eyes. 'Oh Tangnost! What

if h-'

'He's alive,' Bracus's tone on the coms brooked no argument, 'or I'd have gone in earlier, orders or not. He's still registering on my HUD thermal readout.'

'Here,' Tangnost coiled the rope about his waist, and dug his spiked boots in as Bracus, sick with anxiety, stood guard, battlestaff raised. 'I can easily take your weight. Get him out of there! Before he dies!'

CHAPTER ONE-HUNDRED-AND-ELEVEN

Report

'I-i-it's..'

'Take your time, Root,' Drumondir cautioned. 'Drink slowly!'

The boy looks like death, Tangnost thought, as they sat, gathered on Scholar's Wrath, the Guardian's Imperial. Without Drumondir, Root would certainly be dead, and the Guardian had promised the Queen's Constable he would bring the boy safely home. Unconscious and lifeless as he was gently lifted out of the pit, they had nearly lost the young scout until the Ice Bear BoneCaster, long skilled in saving lives nearly stolen by the cold, dripped a hot brew of a dried leaf tea through his frozen lips, and brought him shivering and shaking back to life. A bath of hot water, specially prepared by Two Gulps, treatment for his wounds on wrists and ankles, and some hot food, had completed Root's recovery, but had done nothing to change the haunted look in his eyes. He was rocking backwards and forwards like a child, Quenelda anxiously fussing by his side, at a loss what to do. Bracus prowled up and down anxiously outside, sent out because the huge youth was getting in everyone's way.

'Now,' the Guardian commanded. 'Tell your friend Malachite and my Faculty commanders what you saw.'

Gratefully swallowing a second bowl of soup, dressed warmly, Root reported back, describing what he had seen. The Wildcat clansmen who were to follow the Faculty knights in, listened intently whilst battlemages overlaid plans into their virtual displays.

Seated on a camping chair, Tangnost nodded with approval at the changes he saw. The youth was not allowing his emotions to warp his judgement. His report was calm and he thought carefully before answering Malachite's questions. Yet a fire burned in his too bright eyes that spoke of the horrors Root had seen. Only when he described that they were trying to feed his starving people with dragon meat from those that died in the mine every moon, did the youth finally choke, as Quenelda sobbed in horror with him.

'The Slave Master,' Root suddenly remembered as they were leaving. 'It's Felix,' Root looked at Tangnost who would know. 'Felix DeLancy! I'm sure of it. They call him the Wolverine, but I'm sure it's him. They said he invented the Pit.'

'Darcy's Dragon Master,' Tangnost clarified for the Guardian. 'He always was an ugly one, a bully. Seems like he has finally found a task that suits him.'

CHAPTER ONE-HUNDRED-AND-TWELVE

Mission Briefing

The Juveniles' briefing was coming to a close on Phoenix Firestorm. Quenelda's reunion with Malachite Thornaxe had been both a joyous and sorrowful one.

'Lady,' the dwarf bowed his head. 'We are yours to command. We have heard many tales since we last saw you.' He turned to Root. 'And news of your capture of Galtekerion also. We will free your people tonight.'

Tangnost nodded, he had liked Malachite from the moment they met. '34 Frost Squadron and the 4th Battalion the Highland Scouts have already been deployed to secure an outer perimeter and the mountain chimneys and exits you marked, Root. The 7th Armoured Sabretooth Brigade, supported by Malachite's BoneCracker veterans, will drop just before you do, and they will take out the mine guards. If, as Root said, they are likely to be clustered at certain locations in the mine, then it should be all over by the time you enter.'

'Two Imperials with Drumondir, healers and surgeons will be waiting outside the mine to fly freed slaves straight to Dragon Isle.'

'Quenelda, please talk to the dragons, guide them in the mines. Keep them calm. Like you all, this is their first live operation too, and sabretooths are notorious for becoming over-excited. I don't want any of them bolting out of control in there.'

'And I will help with their healing,' Quenelda added.

'Do *not* engage the enemy,' Tangnost looked sternly over the Juveniles chosen to be part of this exercise. 'Do not engage. You have yet to play battle games and are not fully trained. Am I clearly understood? Leave the fighting to the Faculty knights and Malachite and his veterans. I will be watching and guiding your progress from Scholar's Wrath. The School of Applied Warfare have been working hard on developing coms, though we may lose contact if you go into the deeper levels. If you find you cannot cope with the dark, withdraw immediately.'

'Sir! Yes, Sir!'

'Dismiss!'

Quenelda was waiting for Root with Two Gulps. Root blinked.

He's as big as Chasing the Stars!' The fledgling had finally lost his juvenile plumpness and gained rippling muscles. Two Gulps craned his neck forward in greeting, but his hot tongue licked out, looking for those honey tablets he was still so fond of.

'Quenelda, he looks amazing! You've been training?'

Quenelda smiled. 'Yes, we've been flying together…'

'Flying…together?' Root queried.

His friend gave a sideways grin. 'Side by side.

I'm...not used to flying...my arms get really sore.' Root nodded weakly, he could only imagine.

There was a moment's hesitation. 'Be safe,' Quenelda said, suddenly fighting back tears. *He was so brave, going into that mine on his own; he might have died in that pit...* 'Don't go in till I'm there this time, Root, till we're both there to protect you. Promise? Promise me, Root!' she said fiercely.

Root nodded. 'Come swiftly.'

They hugged.

'Oakley...' the frost pilot's voice crackled in his helmet coms. 'We are good to go.' A command, couched in polite language.

'I must go. They are dropping us off in a clearing in the woods and I have to work my way back to the mine.' And then Root disappeared around the sabretooths to where Bracus was impatiently waiting for him.

CHAPTER ONE-HUNDRED-AND-THIRTEEN

No One Knows We Are Here

Exhausted lines of slaves shuffled through the slush towards their rickety huts, passing those entering the mine for the night shift. Guards shouted, whips cracked, laden wagons squealed and slithered on the icy rails as they were hauled outside and harnessed up. Dale dragons bugled pitifully, pressed beyond endurance, and squealed as they were prodded forwards with spiked poles from their sheds. And coughs, everywhere the rasping coughs of the dying as their lungs filled up with brimstone dust. But this time, lying unseen in the snow, sometimes scant strides from the huts, lay a ring of Mountain Scouts – and Root.

The young gnome watched through the night lens of his scouting helmet, impatient, afraid. How many of his people had survived their brutal captivity? How many more might die tonight? He felt sick with tension.

Given the navigator's chair on Scholar's Wrath, high above on the mountain peak, Tangnost watched the grainy green view from fourteen Juvenile helmet cams and listened to the heavy breathing, it wasn't just coming from the sabretooths. 'Calm now; calm down your mounts. You won't see any action...just focus on your task of rescuing the slaves and ignore everything else.' He didn't tell them that the thermal signatures of the prisoners in the huts were alarmingly low, fading rapidly. Soon many would be beyond help. That would be one more distraction.

A convoy of laden wagons was being prepared to haul through the deep woods to the lochside and the waiting ships, to feed the insatiable needs of the WarLock's growing army of battledragons. Felix DeLancy, one time esquire and dragon master, now reviled as the Wolverine, shivered as he readied the escort. The ore from today's and tonight's shifts were the final shipment before the tracks became impassable.

Failure meant he would join those slaving in the mine, as had happened to his luckless predecessor. The Warlock did not tolerate failure and his son, the Black Prince, was just as unforgiving. Languishing as a lowly esquire in the stables of Stirling castle, Felix had sent a desperate plea, begging to serve the young Prince Darcy again. His wish had been granted, with curt orders to take charge of this mine and to deliver impossible amounts of ore to the WarLock's castles north of the Wall, and to Roarkinch. Furious at such a menial task, Felix had vented his spleen on the prisoners. Driving them and the guards hard night and day, ruthless to the core, he had soon earned the nickname the Wolverine – a killer.

But unexpectedly, the mine had its compensations: gold, silver and precious stones, rings and bracelets and fine furs. Felix was amassing a fortune, looted from his captives. When the time came he would disappear – a wealthy man.

But despite the invention of the Pit to spur the slave gangs to greater efforts, Felix was worried. Slaves were dying in their droves from the cold and exhaustion and gnomes refused to eat dragon meat, would rather die than eat dragons. Gnomes were soft and weak, Felix spat in the snow as he returned to the mine to inspect the discovery of a new ore seam for himself. What he really needed were dwarves or trolls, strong hard workers; but of course much more dangerous. Gnomes didn't believe in fighting, and that made his job much easier.

Thousands of strides above the disappearing Slave Master, Quenelda shifted restlessly on Two Gulps along with the other thirteen fully armoured sabretooths on Phoenix Firestorm. The night was freezing, but whether it was cold or fear that made her shiver she couldn't say. The last time she and Two Gulps had been caught up in a battle, there had been no time to think. This was different. Although they had trained all year for this, her stomach was in knots; she felt nauseous and was glad she hadn't eaten. Behind her Fergus was copiously sick, next second, half a dozen were heaving up their suppers. Tangnost shook his head in sorrow – he had warned them. Hopefully most of them got their helmets off in time.

Malachite and his veterans calmly prepared for their first combat drop in decades, and eagerly fingered their axes and war mallets, hot for revenge for their enslaved comrades and families below.

In the slave huts, a mother lay dying.

'H-here....' Heather, her eldest daughter, held out her bowl of thin gruel, barely warmed porridge. 'Eat mine. I'm n-not hungry.' The young woman shivered from the inside out beneath her rags.

Wren lay back on her bunk. 'I am d-d-dying,' she husked. 'Hush, child....I-I have lingered too long here.' A spasm of shivering took her. 'But you must survive, you are the last of our family; the last of our warren. Else our people will pass from memory, remembered only by the trees and hills. Fight to live every day as I have taught you. Take my clothes. I won't need them. Survive, child, survive. They *will* find us.'

But who are they? Heather thought with despair. *It has been eight winters since we were taken. We are forgotten. No one knows we are here.*

'Mother?' the young woman cradled her mother's head to her chest, rocking back and forward. 'Mother?'

But Wren had flown.

CHAPTER ONE-HUNDRED-AND-FOURTEEN

Strike Back

As the witching hour approached, the first wing of cloaked Imperials from the Faculty Guard took off from the mountain peaks. The wind sobbed round the crags of the Plunging Gorge as forty white-clad Mountain Rangers abseiled down in groups of six, targeting the clefts and chimneys Root had marked on his map. None would escape from this mine to tell others what had happened. What the WarLock King could do, the SDS could do also.

A second and third Imperial, accompanied by two Air Wings of frosts, put down in the shallows of the sea loch, Brimstone Cove, cracking the thick ice like caramel.

'What the-?' A sleepy guard on the forecastle of a galleon stood staring as the Imperials materialised and dismounting figures in white and black flitted between the galleons at anchor till an arrow took him in the chest. A second reached for the watch bell when the breath of a frost dragon froze his arm and side. The sailor crumpled, shattering in shards that skittered across the frozen deck.

Guards reached for their weapons only to find them frozen in their sheaths. 'Sword stuck?' A marine grinned, before smashing his war mallet down. The rest were dealt with as they tumbled from their hammocks. The WarLock's merchant galleons were taken without a fight. The battle to retake the Brimstones had begun!

Softly, wriggling slowly forwards on their elbows, Root and the other scouts passed through the outer perimeter of mine guards, taking up position close to the guard huts hidden in the dense woods, waiting for the word. The guards were talking loudly about their fire pits, playing dice, smoking pipes, never looking outwards. Some would be going back to overwinter with their families soon and their minds were now on the winter festivities to come.

'Strike Back is a go, Strike Back is a go.'
Armour piercing quarrels sped through the woods from the Queen's Own Elf Light Archers. Perimeter guards crumpled, pinned to the trees they slept against. Leaping forwards through the heavy snow, Root and six other scouts struck flares in the snow about the guard huts, painting them in fiery red, before rolling swiftly away back into dappled shadow.
Root toggled his helmet. 'Flares deployed.'
'Affirmative; targets marked, targets marked.' The navigator on the lead Imperial stallion, Leave in Smoking Ruins, keyed in co-ordinates for his pilot.
'Weapons hot! Weapons hot!' The pilot warned.
'Incoming... Incoming...'

Boom… boom… boom… boom… boom…

Fire lit up the quarry as the guard huts were taken out in a series of brilliant explosions that bracketed the edge of the clearing. Sparks and snow spun and swirled. Tall pine trees cracked and broke as landing Imperials rapidly deployed sixty sabretooths from the 7th Armoured Heavy Brigade. Behind them, Malachite and his veteran Bone Crackers spilled off their wings and into the mine, axes and swords raised, howling their clan battle cry.

The night was a confusion of flame and darting shadows. Guards rushing outside to see what was happening died as they were struck by pulses and lances of battlemagic from the Faculty Knights on Imperials ringing the entrance, but it would be mundane weapons of steel and iron that would win the day in a volatile brimstone mine. Others standing bewildered in the main gallery were mown down beneath the first talon of sabretooths. The few that survived were finished off by the Wildcats who fanned out into the mine on the heels of fleeing guards. Slaves screamed as some of them hauling up wagons were hit by shards of ice and several were knocked to the ground and dragged by their chains as the sabretooths passed.

Despite their two moons' training, it was a chaos of Juveniles that tumbled from Phoenix Firestorm into the battlefield.

'Root! Root! Saddle up!' the young gnome heard Quenelda screaming behind him, as Two Gulps skidded down Phoenix Firestorm's wings in a flurry of snow. 'Saddle up!'

Blessing the hours of training on the wooden dragon, Root vaulted up behind her with practised ease as Two Gulps passed by.

'Hang on tight!' Quenelda cried a warning, but barely had the words come out than they were off, leaping forwards in a huge bound, both nearly jerked out of their saddles.

'Ouff!' Root grunted as the back of Quenelda's helmet caught his chin guard with a crack. Standing in her stirrups, Quenelda was riding half out of the saddle, urging Two Gulps forwards with knees and heels, reins held loosely, still only a young girl, dragon whisperer forgotten, eager to free Root's people.

Along the newly opened upper shaft ten, it sounded at first as if the brimstone mine had exploded. Felix froze. Fires in mines were very very dangerous; they had to get out quickly. Crack... crack... pop... He frowned. That sounded like fireworks. Crack...pop...the screams were coming from the entrance! Thump...that was an Imperial putting down; once heard, you never forgot that sound. Thump! Thump! Thump! Thump!

'That's the SDS!' Felix hissed. 'They've found us!'
'Juveniles to the slave huts!' Tangnost's calm voice came over the coms as he sat watching telemetry and helmet cam feedback from SAC. 'Guards confirmed down. Get the slaves up into the field hospitals ready for evac to Dragon Isle.'

Four Juveniles peeled off to protect the slave huts, the youngsters trying to calm and reassure the prisoners cowering inside as their dragons kept watch outside.

'We're the SDS,' Fergus smiled, breathing heavily with excitement and fear. 'We're here to free you. Come,' the youngsters beckoned gently. 'Come, we'll fly you to Dragon Isle.' A young girl with a tear-stained face looked up in a daze, as more youngsters came forwards with cloaks, flasks of dwarf cider and sticks of spun sugar, to usher them out onto the wings of mighty Imperials to freedom; trolls, dwarves and young sorcerers. *How could this be?*

It was like riding white water rapids, Root thought, as he gripped the saddle with his thighs as the sabretooth dodged round blazing broken trees and huts and raced across the clearing in an explosion of branches and melting snow. An arrow thudded into the saddle and a second skated off Two Gulps' scales. Six Juveniles followed, with three-score Wildcats as escort. There was a scream as a sabretooth went down, but there was no stopping.

'You're with me!' Felix snapped at his bodyguards as the rolling thunder of sabretooths died away. *He had to get to his quarters...his escape route. How?* There were more explosions and the sound of battle closing fast. This was a new shaft and hidden. 'Listen,' Felix looked at the chain gang cowering near the ore face. 'This is what we are going to do.'

'Get to the sides and stay still! The dragons will not hurt you.' Root cried in his own tongue till he was hoarse. 'Run to the sides - ' he ducked as an arrow zipped past him to shatter on the side of the shaft. 'We're here to rescue you! The SDS are here! The Wildcat dwarves and medics will care for you.'

The chained slaves in upper shaft ten stood no chance as seven of their number were cut down in cold blood by Felix's bodyguards. With the rattle of talons on ice, the shouts and screams and flash bangs, no one would hear.

'Quiet or you're next,' Felix promised as he and his men stripped the bodies of ragged cloaks and bloodied tunics, hiding their armour and weapons, removing helmets and smearing their faces and hands with blood and brimstone dust. Then they took hold of the chains and bunched their captives between them.

'Not a sound,' the Wolverine warned, lifting a blade to Squirrel's back. 'If you want to stay alive!'

Already Malachite's men and Juveniles, tasked with getting slaves out, were forming protective shield walls about chain gangs on the upper levels, cutting away the traces from the ore wagons and gently guiding them about the bodies towards the waiting dragons and healers already at work outside the slave huts.

More and more slaves were emerging like ghosts into the early dawn, bewildered and scared even of the eager youngsters and smiling faces.

'Fergus, Ban,' Tangnost directed his young riders. 'Get

as many more as you can onto Star Fury. They are readying to take off for Dragon Isle.'

Malachite was escorting slaves out when there was a sudden rumble that rolled through the rock near the entrance.

'That's a cave in,' he said. 'Not an explosion. Come on, lads!' Next second dust and debris blew out through a small shaft to their left. There were screams.

'There's been a cave in,' someone shouted. 'Help! Help!' as a group of slaves staggered out into the dust choked gallery, faces masks of dust and blood.

'There's another group back there...the roof's collapsed,' Felix called. 'Save our friends!'

It was indeed a cave in. The wooden stoops that held the ceiling up were snapped and a great slab had fallen in. The tunnel was thick with dust but you could see a smashed leg sticking out, and a broken pickaxe.

'Can you hear us?' Malachite shouted. It would be hard work to make the tunnel safe and reach those trapped. Only there was no one to answer them.

Some freed captives were struggling to understand they were being rescued, as Root and Quenelda led Two Gulps towards them.

'You're safe,' Root repeated as he lifted a weeping figure, man, woman, child, he couldn't tell beneath the bundled rags.

'S-s-safe? Truly?' someone sobbed.

'Safe,' Root said softly, handing out oat bannocks which were wolfed down. 'The SDS are freeing all the mines. You'll be flown back to Dragon Isle. The healers are waiting for you outside with warm cloaks and hot food.'

Several collapsed weeping. Others cried out in joy, reaching out to touch the young gnome in SDS scouting gear, the great flame battledragon he rode.

*Two Gulps, you are going to carry them out ...they are too weak...*Quenelda helped the sick up into her saddle. 'He will not harm you he is here to rescue you.'

'Have any of you seen Squirrel?' Root asked again and again as his people emerged. Where was his friend? And where was Felix?

CHAPTER ONE-HUNDRED-AND-FIFTEEN

The Hunt's Afoot

Light bled into the world. Five Imperials of the Faculty Guard were perched on ridges and outcrops about the mine in a show of force. It had been a total rout, with the SDS and Wildcat Clan suffering only minor injuries.

A third Imperial airwing took off for Dragon Isle, bearing survivors from the mine and a few injured BoneCrackers. Drumondir and other healers were treating those injured during the rescue before they were airlifted to Dragon Isle. As she gently peeled away their rags, the BoneCaster was horrified to discover the slaves were all elbows and knees and bones, their parchment thin skin covered in raw sores.

Out beside Phoenix Firestorm, one of the young sabretooths flamed, causing medics and soldiers to scatter. 'I-it's alright-t,' Fergus gritted his teeth and tried to smile, as he brought her under control. The arrow had pinned him to the saddle through his thigh. His young mount was skittish and fired up, muzzle foam flecked, she had taken two arrows herself that had found chinks in her boiled leather armour.

'Quenelda,' Tangnost called, as Two Gulps was about to re-enter the mine to help Root find his friend. 'Quieten Red Dawn down so we can get Fergus treated, and then get her mounted up. Her wounds are not serious; she can be treated on Dragon Isle.

Red Dawn...your bond brother is injured... we need to help him...then I will tend you before you fly home together to the roosts of Dragon Isle...

'Hold his hand,' the healer barked at Caradoc who was dismounting. 'I'm going to pull the shaft out so we can move you.'

Turning, Fergus grinned manfully at his approaching friend. 'Don't worry about me...I aarrrrrggghhhhhhh!!!'

The medic smiled sweetly. 'There, that wasn't so bad was it, Sir?' He held up the arrow. Fergus fainted.

'Stretcher bearers!'

'Sir?' The Wildcat veterans had found something as Root was making his way back into the mine to see if he could find Squirrel. It was a narrow passage hidden behind a natural cleft in the rock so easy to miss, but beyond, it was stone flagged, clean, with niches cut for lanterns which had burnt down but were still warm. There were bodies up ahead in the flickering torchlight. Root checked them all and shook his head. None was his friend.

'There's a door, the troop leader shouted from beyond as she raised her war mallet. 'Metal shod. It's bolted from the inside.'

Felix!

'Break it down.'

They lifted their war mallets. Even so the studded oak door held out stubbornly until they could put a hand through to lift the heavy bars on the other side, and to push the bodies piled against it gently out the way.

It was a cave, but oh, how different to all the others; here it was bright and dry. Soft light globes hung in the air and the walls were covered with tapestries and floored with rugs, a fire burnt in the great hearth, all the comforts of home. A table with a plate of venison and a goblet still full of ruby wine. It led off to other caverns, a bed chamber, another filled with jars and bags of food, smoked hams and venison; Felix's looted larder. He grew fat while prisoners starved.

The youth moved in a daze to where a score of wooden chests lay spilled open, the sign of a hurried departure. They were filled with gold torques, bracelets and rings; enamel and silver the work of dwarves smiths, and beautiful soft spun cloaks - the work of his own people. How many, how many had died in this hell hole stripped of all they owned?

'Find him!' The fury built in Root. 'Find Felix DeLancey!' He ordered. 'We'll bring him back to Dragon Isle in chains, to face justice!' The dwarves fanned out through the mine, murder on their minds.

Eight hundred strides above, a group of guards clambered out through a chimney into the freezing dawn. Powder snow was swirling. Trees cracked and groaned.

'Made it,' a guard swore hoarsely. 'Those cursed Dragon Lords won't find us up here. '

'Wrong,' the Guardian's voice said.

There was the sound of sucking air and then purple fire lit the mountainside.

Then Root saw it. The cloak he had given Squirrel in exchange for one covered in brimstone dust. He had not spied it amongst the spilled loot. He looked more carefully. There had been a struggle. There must be a hidden door. He ripped the tapestry down. There it was, cunningly concealed; the handiwork of dwarves. Root's heart sank, such doors were notoriously hard to open.

Root pounded on the door, but it would not give. Leaning his head on the cool stone in exhaustion it smoothly swivelled and he stumbled through. Leaving it open for others to follow, Root stepped into the tunnel and stopped to let his eyes adjust and to listen. He heard a muffled cry, abruptly cut off. He began running.

Ouff! Root tripped over a body and lay winded. Blood was still hotly pooling, he couldn't be far behind. The guards were lashing and whipping in frenzy, pulling the chain gang behind them using them as shields or bargaining chips. Those who could not keep up lay discarded by the wayside, and here and there lay spilt booty, a cup or necklace or sword. The passage forked up ahead but it was clear which one Felix had chosen by the trail of bodies.

'No!'

Root recognised that voice. *Squirrel!*

'Why kill us? You are fleeing, we will only slow you. Let us li-'

There were screams as the guards turned to kill those remaining, so they were not able to tell what happened here.

'Nnooo!' Frantically Root began to run. 'Nooooooo!' He crunched over a silver goblet, a scatter of coins.

Dressed in stolen captive's cloaks, the only way to tell the guards from their prisoners in the flickering light of a single torch were the raised swords and the bulging bags of treasure they clung to.

'Felix!'

The head turned automatically. Root smiled coldly... so he was right.

Raising his torch and seeing a single scout, Felix smiled and pulled the nearest slave to him, placing a knife on Squirrel's throat. 'Let us go or we'll kill them all.'

The slaves were moaning with fear.

'Let them go!' Root commanded. 'You can't escape: the mine is surrounded. Enough of my people have died.'

'Enough of *your* people?'

'*My* people, Felix DeLancy.'

The Slave Master froze. No one knew his real name. 'Who are you?'

Root took off his helmet and stepped into the light.

Felix laughed. 'You! The runt of the litter.'

'I'm an SDS Dragon Lord now.' *Nearly an SDS Dragon Lord!*

'Ha, ha!' Felix laughed, his guards with him. 'You? That will be the day! You're a nobody.'

'He *is* a Dragon Lord,' a deep voice said. 'As am I. Touch him or your prisoners and you will die.' There was a calm certainty, an underlying threat that made them all pause.

Root turned towards the voice that was both familiar and frightening. Quenelda had found them but Two Gulps could not fit along the narrow corridor. They could hear him tearing frantically at the stone. Soft blossoms of light lit the cavern as he flamed, silhouetting the slim figure standing above. Quenelda stepped into the flickering light. She carried no weapons, not even a wand.

'What? A boy? Without even any fuzz on your cheeks? What are you going to do all by yourself? There is a network of tunnels down here. You'll never find us.'

'I'm no boy.'

Felix's eyes narrowed. He laughed. 'You! Lady high and mighty. Not so mighty now are you? Dragonsdome gone. That dragon of yours gone.'

'I have another.' Quenelda's voice had gone entirely now, another more ancient and powerful had taken its place as she moved down close to Root. Felix didn't notice.

'He won't fit through. I thought of that.'

'That won't save you.'

'No?

'I don't need my dragon.'

'Why is that, little girl?' Felix smirked as his guards raised their swords and bows.

The air shivered...Felix's torch snuffed out. It was difficult to see in the dark but there was a glint of scale and the scrape of talon sparking on stone.   Two molten eyes opened; eyes that could see easily in the dark.

Felix screamed; just the once.

'I would like to offer myself in service to you, to care for you wherever you may go...'

'But I'm no Lord!' Root protested, as the pair stepped out into the dawn.

'But you are, my Lord,' Squirrel said earnestly. 'You freed our people from the mines. You could have died in the Pit for that girl. And you're a Dragon Lord. I'm your sworn man, if you'll take me? My Lord, I have nowhere else to go.'

Root shrugged helplessly, taking his helmet off and running a hand through unruly hair.

Squirrel grinned.   'Here, my Lord, let me carry that.'

CHAPTER ONE-HUNDRED-AND-SIXTEEN

Ding Dong Merrily on High

Ding dong! ding dong! Ding dong!

It was two days later and bells all over the Black Isle were peeling out in celebration. The SDS had hit back at the WarLock! The Brimstones had been retaken! Gentle gnomes, cottars, farmers and fisher folk and hundreds of captured soldiers had been freed from slaving in the mines! The watch towers on Dragon Isle and the Black Isle were blazing in celebration! Families of missing soldiers flocked to the north harbour, desperate that their own missing loved ones might return home.

Academy Imperials and air attack dragons were returning all day long to Dragon Isle, welcomed home by clusters of brilliantly coloured hot air balloons and crowded boats out on the loch, waving and cheering their soldiers. Many bore the dangerously ill and dying slaves from the mines to the Academy Hospice and the surgeons and apothecaries of the School of Healing. Shackles struck off and wrapped in warm, military winter cloaks, those strong enough sailed by battlegalleon or dwarf longboats east to the crowded harbours of the Black Isle, where the newly rebuilt city had thrown open its great hammered oak gates to the refugees. Dazed gnomes, half-starved and stumbling down the gangplanks onto the wharves, were invited in by citizens opening their hearts and homes to strangers who had suffered unimaginably for years. Numb with grief, having accepted soup and bread, Heather walked through the crowds as if in a dream. If only her mother had survived one more day, she would be safe with the healers of Dragon Isle. But she had died, her body thrown out like rubbish into the snow by the guards, and Heather could not find it later on.

As the sun set and the moons rose, the lanterns strung from turret to gable end cast mellow caves of marigold light and warmth, and braziers sprang up about the city walls and in the streets, steaming in the frigid air. In a dream, Heather followed the growing crowds streaming towards the Pentangle Square in front of the Guild, a riot of noise and celebration. Young sorcerer lords, dwarves, gnomes and trolls who had helped free the Brimstones were walking through the city with broad grins, accepting the heartfelt thanks, small gifts and good wishes showered upon them.

Jugglers were throwing coloured balls and flaming brands. There were stalls of sausages, crystalised slugs, beaver burgers, enticing aromas of roast chestnuts and toffee apples, fresh baked bannocks of oat and cranberry. The Guild warehouses had rolled out barrels of oat beer and bottles of oak and bramble wine. Dwarf cider, warmed and spiced with cinnamon flavoured the air.

Heather stared at the stalls, her mouth watering. Noticing the skinny, pale young woman with haunted eyes, the matron called her over.

'Here, take your fill. Sweet chestnuts, cranberry scones... ripe apples...'

'I -' Heather was shaking now from hunger and exhaustion. 'I have nothing with which to pay you.'

'Tis free, young miss. Here, sit you down. The harvest was good, the Guilds are sharing with all who are needy... and beds too... all are opening up their homes and shops, there are pallets of straw aplenty beside a good fire.'

It was too much. Weakly sinking to the stool, Heather wept.

'There, there, chickadee,' the matron soothed her. 'You're here now, you're safe. You can come back to my rooms. Got five young 'uns, always room for one more. Here, take your fill, there now, that's better, ain't it?'

There was a powerful draught of wind overhead and the crowds surged forwards to where Imperials flying the banners of the Crown and the DeWinters were putting down on Guild landing pads, young dwarves and trolls and dragon lords coming fresh from the battle to celebrate their victory! Cheering, the crowds moved forwards to greet them, reaching out to touch them, to shout their thanks. These youngsters yet to graduate were the future of the Seven Kingdoms, the future hope for everyone.

Heather blinked as she saw the strangest of sights: a young man, no, a young woman in flying leathers with wild fair hair and strange amber eyes that almost glowed, walking and laughing with a shorter youth, richly dressed, flanked by a huge young sorcerer lord in black armour and an achingly thin young man who limped heavily, but had laughter in his eyes. She started: there was a large battledragon at their heels, just like the ones who had rescued her people! Red gold scales and copper burnished talons glinting in the light of hundreds of torches who...who had just clamped its mouth firmly about a dozen string of sausages from a stall in passing and was sucking them in so swiftly they were gone in the blink of an eye!!

She was not the only one staring, as the crowd moved back from the dragon who was sniffing them over. There was a wail as the dragon's tongue snaked out to steal a child's beaver burger.

'That's Quenelda DeWinter!' The matron said to Heather, wide eyed. 'Her brother poisoned her dragon and they both died. But then she came back to life and found her father in the frozen north, still alive after the great battle, and flew him home. That is one of her battle dragons...she can talk to them!'

'They say she can fly,' another voice added. 'Without wings!'

'Quenelda!' A voice called out... 'DeWinter... DeWinter...' and the elfin-faced girl turned towards the crowd and smiled, torchlight glinting off tiny scales on her brow and cheek.

'Lord Root!' others in the crowd called out, throwing rosemary and flowers. 'He captured Galtekerion!' shouted a man behind Heather.

Root! The name hit the young woman like a hammer blow, memories of her youngest brother killed when hobgoblins attacked their burrow. *But what an odd name for a sorcerer lord!* Heather looked again at the group who had stopped at the matron's stall, right in front of her. *But...but surely not?* The smaller of the two lords was a gnome...skin the colour of light bronze in the firelight, dark eyed and dark haired, threaded with beads, gear all the colours of autumn, and he bore a noble's coat of arms on his sleeve; a leaping hare and an oak tree. An oak tree...Oakley...

'R...' her throat caught. 'Root?'

The young man's head turned towards the sound, dark eyes passing over her, scanning the crowd in the flickering candlelight.

'Root! It's me...Heather...' she opened her arms in a helpless gesture. *Was this a dream, also?*

Root stared at the gaunt young woman in rags, wrapped in a cloak... with a cry he bounded round the stall to her, wrapping her up, laughing and crying.

CHAPTER ONE-HUNDRED-AND-SEVENTEEN

Graduation Ceremony

'Do I look alright?' Root swung his arms around, feeling trapped inside his armoured shell, wondering if this was what beetles felt like and that was why they were so deliberate and blundering. It was not as heavy as he feared, if anything it was surprisingly light, lighter than battlegame armour, but to a free spirit such as Root he felt imprisoned in the black metal.

'Have I done it correctly?' Squirrel stood back anxiously. He had been practicing with the esquires, but there were so many bits he might have put some on the wrong way up or even back to front! And because Root was not a sorcerer he couldn't wear traditional Dragon Lord armour that meshed seamlessly like a second skin; his was held together with mundane buckles and ties. Dozens of them!

'What happens if I want to scratch?' Root held up the segmented gauntlet and opened his fingers and closed them experimentally.

'Scratch!' Squirrel shook his head, horrified. 'Knights

don't scratch!'

Sighing Root clanked from the Armour Room through to the Lower Knight's Hall to join Quenelda and Bracus and other Dragon Lords-to-be. Squirrel's adulation was a little hard to deal with sometimes!

Why it's beautiful, Armelia thought in wonder, as the royal entourage wove through scores of brilliantly coloured hot air balloons anchored around Dragon Isle for the Graduation Ceremony. It was all so *thrilling* to be flying Chasing the Stars, caparisoned in royal barding, escorted by the shining helms and ceremonial armour of the Queen's Household Airborne Guard! How amazed Quenelda would be to see her friend flying a dragon all by herself, and in racing leathers to boot! And Tangnost had agreed that she could become a steward for the yearly Beltane Dragathon to celebrate the greatest regimental battlegame ever. There was so much to look forward to!

The island was larger even than Armelia had imagined from Root's description, its massive sheer cliffs giving way to a patchwork of forest and paddocks and training courses, flanked to the west by soaring jagged peaks of the Shard and a waterfall shrouded in mist. And carved out of those soaring peaks was the most amazing castle she had ever seen.

Up and up and up, the twisting spires of the fortress rose, black walled, blue tiled, beautiful, unearthly, reaching for the sky and knit together with sorcery that defied gravity, whilst the slabs and shards of jagged black outcroppings cradled the towers like ragged crowns.

Tethered about them were hundreds of military armoured dragon pads unlike any Armelia had seen before, hanging like predatory gigantic spiders about the spires and turrets, rising and falling on unseen threads. And unlike the royal palaces on the Black Isle or Crannock Castle on the south cliffs of the loch, Armelia realised this vast sweeping castle was clearly built with dragons in mind: massive wide battlements curled up and up, and impossible arches leapt from tower to tower, providing perches now crowded with Imperials of the III FirstBorn Regiment.

Quenelda and Root, flanked by Bracus, stood to attention, eyes front, along with all those destined to be Dragon Lords, in armour that had been crafted individually for them by Dragon Isle's master smiths. By the sound of the cheers, the Queen had arrived. Quenelda closed her eyes: this was a dream come true. She had been waiting all her life for this moment! In six months they would be fully fledged, operational Dragon Lords. Between now and then would be more training within their chosen regiments, culminating in the Dragathon, the greatest endurance race in the Seven Kingdoms. She could hardly wait.

The Guardian's pad the royal party put down on was of carved stone and the size of a plaza, flanked by the Crucible – a great horseshoe amphitheatre built into the lower flanks of the Academy on one side – and by the parade ground on the other, where the massed ranks of the III FirstBorn Regiment were drawn up. High above, every window and balcony of the Academy was crowded with academics and their apprentices and acolytes waving. The Regiment came to attention as grooms ran to assist Armelia dismount and take care of Chasing the Stars, whilst the royal footmen helped the Queen down from the coach's steps and onto the red carpet, where a soldier in unadorned dragon armour waited. A murmur swept around the Crucible and loud cheers rang from the stands about the parade ground. Unlike the Countess DeWinter, the Queen was actually wearing a dress, but she was also wearing a breastplate and a half helm and wore a slender sword at her hip! Armelia smiled, pleased with the reaction.

'My dearest friend,' Caitlin had said. 'We shall both give them something to think about. If you are to ride a dragon in leathers, then I shall wear armour, as my ancestors once did. Together with Quenelda, we shall throw away all those traditions that bind us, and become free spirits, able to choose how we live our lives, able to fight for those who are precious to us.'

'Majesty,' the Guardian bowed over the Queen's hand. A strong rugged face, a stern glance that flicked to Armelia, a fleeting smile in the fierce blue eyes that did not reach the mouth as he took in the Countess's flying outfit, and then the man stood upright, his multi-hued scholar's cloak splashing colour against his black armour, as he led them down the wide, curving saddle-backed steps, worn by time and tradition, to the Crucible, and to the three thrones set at their centre where the King awaited them.

Here too, the nobility of the Seven Kingdoms were seated in ancient stone tiers honeycombed into the stone, with their coats of arms on their stalls, including Armelia's family, the DeBurghs. Below them, the Faculty Guard and the Academy's foremost scholars and military strategists in their ceremonial finery and fantastical hats were seated. The entire lower portion of the amphitheatre was occupied by Dragon Lords, Regimental Strike Commanders, and other high ranking SDS officers, dwarf Clan Chieftains including Malachite and troll Thanes, and one young woman named Bracken, to represent her vanished people.

Battle standards and regimental flags fluttered as the King came down the steps dressed in black armour of an ancient design, the armour of his distant ancestors, discovered in the SeaDragon Citadel. Caitlin looked at her husband with joy. *How much stronger he is...standing tall once again...*she glanced to the side where a massive Imperial was lying, great golden eyes watching. Even if Stormcracker could not fit in the royal palaces, her husband's uncanny power meant for the most part that his crippled young knight, Quester, rarely had to lead him. A few scales on neck and arms were a small price to pay for this Dragon Lord, this true Dragon Lord, to be himself once again. As ever, she wondered at the growing power of their daughter and when it would be safe to reveal her identity to the Kingdoms.

'Not yet,' Rufus had cautioned. 'Let her come into her full power before revealing her as heir to the throne. The moment Hugo learns she is our daughter, he will know the rumours of her dragon whispering to be true, at least he will fear so.'

'And she would be in mortal danger,' Tangnost nodded agreement. 'If she ever left the sanctuary of Dragon Isle.'

'Drumondir?' they turned to the BoneCaster, tasked with their daughter's tuition. 'With every day, her awareness grows, but she still needs to be taught as any other child would on how to use her gift with wisdom. The HeartRock has much still to teach her.'

'But she grows more like me,' Caitlin had protested softy.

'Sweetheart,' the King had smiled. 'None can see it yet. With her short hair, her boy's clothes...perhaps if she wore dresses...but we need have no fear on that account!'

They had all smiled at that.

As the Queen took the throne beside her husband, a young knight stepped down to guide Armelia to a lesser seat, close to Caitlin's throne. Guy DeBessart was a very handsome young man, Armelia thought, as she took his armoured arm, before reminding herself she was married! She had actually begun to forget about Darcy for periods of time, it seemed so very long ago since they last saw each other, and so much had happened since. She felt self-conscious in her royal blue and saffron flying leathers, and was aware of many amazed and scandalised eyes upon her. Well, if Quenelda and the Queen could do it, so could she. Things were going to change, and for the better!

Root searched the honeycombed Crucible for his father and sister among the noble balconies but there were so many shields and flags he couldn't spot them. Sir Gharad had welcomed Heather from the moment they met, when Root's adoptive father had opened his arms to the skeletal, ragged creature that was his son's sister.

She had been given chambers of her own next to Root's, had the luxury of a hot bath in the copper tub in front of a roaring fire and new, soft warm clothes before Sir Gharad's own physicians and apothecaries had tended to her. Over the following weeks, Root and his father had listened in utter horror to Heather talking about how their warren and countless others had been attacked by troops working with the hobgoblins. How they had suffered a terrible sea journey to a northern island to slave in the foundries and gold mines there. Within moons, all the old and young had died, unable to survive the biting cold and arduous work. Only the strongest had lived on in slavery year after year, before being flown on the back of a cloaked Imperial to the Brimstones, where only Root's mother and oldest sister had survived, the last of their warren, forgotten by the world. Until now.

Brother and sister wept together as Heather spoke of their mother, and how she had never given up hope that they would be remembered, only to die on the very eve her youngest son and the SDS had liberated their people.

Quenelda, standing in the front rank of Dragon Lords-to-be, had been searching for her friend amongst the flurry of ladies-in-waiting who accompanied the Queen, and was bitterly disappointed. She could see Drumondir and Tangnost, both seated about the thrones, but not Armelia. She thought with her new interest in dragons and flying, Armelia would be here to applaud her friend's achievement, and found herself considerably upset.

A royal fanfare rang out...the silver notes thrown out by the Crucible as each graduate in turn was called to pledge their oath of allegiance to the throne, and to receive the coveted Dragon Lord's helmet and SDS wings. As Bracus rose to his considerable height and she was next in line, Quenelda suddenly realised that the youth whom she had mistaken for one of the Queen's esquires in royal livery was in fact Armelia!! Armelia in racing leathers...with short hair, with legs...and not a single pink heart or ribbon in sight!

'Mouth,' Root hissed out the side of his own.

'What?'

'Close it! *She did it for you,*' Root whispered, as Quenelda's name was announced. '*She can fly now, too!*' Staring at him, Quenelda almost tripped over her armoured toes.

As Root approached the three thrones to kneel, Heather shook her head as if to shed the cobwebs of a dream. Barely a moon ago, her people were bound in slavery and death. Now her brother would become an Imperial Dragon Lord and had the protection and name of the kindest and most generous of knights, and had captured the hobgoblin WarLord...with a frying pan! Her little brother, Root! A warm hand was laid over hers. Sir Gharad smiled shyly. 'We'll free the rest of your people, my dear.'

Root did not receive a battlestaff and wings as he offered his oath of fealty. In its stead, the King turned blind eyes to the young household knight at his shoulder and nodded. Quester grinned at Root who grinned wholeheartedly back, overjoyed to see his friend himself once again.

'Although you bear no weapon,' the King said, his voice ringing out across the plaza, 'you have defended the Kingdoms by capturing Galtekerion and saving my life. And so you are declared a Royal Shield and we give you a coat of arms to reflect your deeds.'

Limping, only his friends knew what the effort cost him, Quester brought the shield forwards with pride. It bore a quartered design, and the Constable, King and Queen, Heather, Quester, Armelia, Drumondir and Tangnost had all had a hand in its design. The triple-headed dragon of the SDS was quartered diagonally with the Queen's golden unicorn, and the leaping hare of the Mowbrays with an oak tree, this last for his family name. Root had half expected to see a frying pan, given how much admiring teasing he had been subject to!

Root's lip trembled with pride as Squirrel rushed forwards to accept the shield and strap it to his Lord's right arm. Forgetting her fear, her nerves, Heather stood weeping, shouted her brother's name to the groundswell of cheers from the assembled ranks of the SDS and their families beyond.

'Root! Root! Root!'

There were some hostile eyes but no one was watching for them. Root had earned his moment of glory. There was the slow beat of swords against shields from the massed ranks of the III FirstBorn that grew and grew. Thump... thump... thump...thump... the heartbeat of DragonIsle boomed out across the loch.

Squashing an unwelcome pang of jealousy, remembering both Drumondir and Tangnost's words of warning, Quenelda joined in. *Root deserves this moment and more! Without him, without his friendship and bravery, none of this would have happened...*

The youth turned, opening his arms wide, generously inviting Quester and Quenelda, Armelia and Bracus to join him. *Without their friendship, none of this would be happening!*

The five of them stood side by side. Behind them the King and Queen, the Guardian, Sir Gharad and Drumondir and Tangnost, stood to salute the new generation.

Root....The first gnome to become a Dragon Lord, Heather thought. *My brother!'*

Quenelda...the first girl Dragon Lord, the Queen smiled. *My daughter...*

Bracus...the first Dragon Lord to be a scout, Root grinned. *My friend...*

*Quester...the first crippled esquire to be knighted...*the King thought...*a brave young man, he shall take the place of my son...*

*Armelia...the first lady at Court to learn to fly...*Quenelda raised their clasped hands...*my friend...*

They are the future, the Guardian nodded, satisfied. *The SDS will survive. The WarLock will not have foreseen that we can change.* He glanced at his old friend, now King. *Hugo thought to break us by his treachery, to kill Rufus and his battledragon, and yet both have become stronger somehow, a true DragonLord bonded to his dragon. We are all stronger now, we are all OneKind.*

CHAPTER ONE-HUNDRED-AND-EIGHTEEN

On Wings of Vengeance

The dragon horn on the cliffs rang out, slowly at first, the sound built so that it thrummed through the air, bringing down snow from the academy turrets and steep gabled roofs. Slowly silence fell across the Crucible and the parade ground and the stands beyond. The Guardian stood and moved forwards to the triple-headed dragon lectern.

'Today you graduate to join our ranks. Whatever regiment, brigade or talon you serve with, you will be in the vanguard of our fight against the Warlock King and his hobgoblin banners.'

He looked over to the packed stands of family and friends, many commoners, who could not have dreamt of this moment a year before.

'You and your families come from far flung corners of the Seven Kingdoms, allies together against the hobgoblin scourge and the treachery of the WarLock King. Now the Seven Kingdoms fight as one: no one is a stranger any more: you are our friends and kindred, our brothers and sisters in arms, and our city and Glen are open to all who need sanctuary.

'The WarLock will use our different ways of life, our fears and our past divisions against us. He will try to set brother against brother, family against family, clan against clan, for that is where his power lies, in fear and deceit. We are different in many ways, but that is not something to be feared, rather to be celebrated.

'Make no mistake: the Maelstrom is rising and never have we been betrayed by our own kith and kin. But the love that binds us to each other in the SDS is an unbreakable bond. Now, any of you with ability may become a Dragon Lord, even if you wield no magic, for there are many powers on this One Earth and in the heavens that are beyond our ken.

'And now we will take the fight to him.'

The Guardian paused, his eyes passing over the massed ranks of graduates and dragons below him. His powerful voice rang out from the Crucible.

'In the name of all those who died at the Westering Isle and the Battle of the Line, in the name of those whom the WarLock has enslaved, we are the SDS, and we are coming for you...On Wings of Vengeance!'

'On Wings of Vengeance!' Thirty thousand throats roared the SDS battle cry.

'On Wings of Vengeance!'